Pure Blood

"*Pure Blood* pounds along hard on the heels of *Night Life*, and is every bit as much fun as the first in the series. With a gutsy, likable protagonist and a well-made fantasy world, *Pure Blood* is real enough to make you think twice about locking your doors at night. A swiftly paced plot, a growing cast of solid supporting characters, and a lead character you can actually care about—Kittredge is a winner."

—Jim Butcher

"With enough supernatural death and romance to keep readers glued to the pages…Jump in with both feet and hang on tight because *Pure Blood* is an emotion-filled ride."   —*Darque Reviews*

"The pacing is rapid and the peril imminent…This is a series and an author that are definitely going places!"

—*Romantic Times BOOKreviews*

"The unexpected plot twists and high-octane action of *Pure Blood* kept me turning the pages until the wee hours of the morning."   —*Romance Junkies*

Night Life

"Dark and cutting-edge."

—*Romantic Times BOOKreviews*
MORE…

Caitlin Kittredge

St. Martin's Paperbacks

This is a work of fiction. All of the characters, organizations, and events portrayed in this novel are either products of the author's imagination or are used fictitiously.

STREET MAGIC

Copyright © 2009 by Caitlin Kittredge.
Excerpt from *Demon Bound* copyright © 2009 by Caitlin Kittredge.

For information address St. Martin's Press, 175 Fifth Avenue, New York, NY 10010.

ISBN: 0-312-94361-X
EAN: 978-0-312-94361-5

Printed in the United States of America

St. Martin's Paperbacks edition / June 2009

St. Martin's Paperbacks are published by St. Martin's Press, 175 Fifth Avenue, New York, NY 10010.

10 9 8 7 6 5 4 3 2

For my dad, Jim Van Fleet
1948–1994

Acknowledgments

Street Magic is a labor of love, and the book would never have come into being without the assistance, support, and occasional arse-kicking from a great many people.

Rachel Vater, my amazing agent, deserves credit for taking that initial draft and making it into a Real Book. Rose Hilliard, my esteemed editor, gave Pete, Jack, and Black London a home and took them to a new level with her enthusiasm and deft editorial hand.

Richelle Mead, owner of a sofa on which a large portion of the first draft was written and fellow *Vampire Justice* superfan, ensured with her encouragement that I would write the hardest and simultaneously most fun novel of my career to date.

Stacia Kane read an early draft and got every single one of my punk rock references, thus proving that she has both excellent taste in music and a slightly twisted imagination. I couldn't ask for a better crit partner and I'm thrilled this was the book that brought us together.

Cherie Priest and Kat Richardson gave me cover quotes and encouragement, and along with all of Team Seattle, gave me drinks, dinner, and dance-offs during the marathon revision process. Jim Butcher also gave me a lovely cover quote while trapped with me in a small car in Seattle traffic, and

did so with grace and aplomb. Jim, I promise never to do that again.

Karen Mahoney showed me London and conspired to make me sound English.

Liz Bourke translated the Irish flawlessly and didn't think it was strange that I was asking for exorcism spells and curse words.

Sara McDonald has seen every iteration of Pete and Jack since the beginning, and has been a tireless cheerleader.

Chris McGrath, for the gorgeous cover and Adam Auerbach for stellar design.

Mom and Hal, my number-one fans.

And finally, the bands who made the music that is the lifeblood of Black London: the Clash, the Sex Pistols, the Anti-Nowhere League, Nick Cave, Concrete Blonde, the Pogues, Generation X, the Supersuckers, and many more.

Rock on.

PART 1

London

Animate London, with smarting eyes and irritated lungs, was blinking, wheezing, and choking; inanimate London was a sooty spectre, divided in purpose between being visible and invisible, and so being wholly neither.

—Charles Dickens

Chapter 1

Michaelmas daisies bloomed around Pete Caldecott's feet the day she met Jack Winter, just as they had twelve years ago on the day he died.

That day, the unassuming tomb in a back corner of Highgate Cemetery was overrun with the small purple flowers. Jack crushed them under his boots as he levered the mausoleum door open.

Fear had stirred in Pete's stomach as the tomb breathed out bitter-smelling air. "Jack, I don't know about all this."

He flashed a smile. "Afraid, luv? Don't be. I'm here, after all."

Biting her lip, Pete put one foot over the threshold of the tomb, then the other. A wind whispered out from the shadowed depths and ruffled her school skirt around her knees. She backed out of the doorway immediately. "We shouldn't be here, Jack."

He sighed, pushing a hand through his bleached crop of hair. It stood out in wild spikes, gleaming in the low light. His hair was the first thing Pete had seen of Jack in Fiver's club three months ago, molten under the stage lights as he gripped his microphone like a dying man and screamed.

"Don't be a ninny, Pete. Nothing in here is going to bite

you. Not yet, anyway." The devil-grin appeared on his face again. Jack held out his hand to her. "Come into my parlor."

Pete grasped his hand, felt where the ridges of his fingers were callused from playing guitar, and used the warm shiver it sent through her to propel herself into the tomb. The stone structure was bigger than it appeared from the outside and her hard-soled shoes rang on the stone when she planted her stride firmly. She hugged herself to ward off the chill.

"I'm not a ninny."

Jack laughed and tossed the green canvas satchel he'd brought into a corner. "Sorry. Must have been thinking of your sister."

Pete punched him in the shoulder. "That's your girlfriend you're slagging off. You're wicked."

Jack caught her hand again and folded it into his, eyes darkening when Pete didn't pull away. "You don't know the half of it."

Pete met his stare, listening to them both breathe for a moment before she disengaged her hand. "Thought you said we were here to do some magic, Jack."

Jack cleared his throat and moved away from her. "So I did." He pulled a piece of chalk from his pocket and began drawing a crooked circle on the flags, one that quickly grew lines and squiggles radiating toward the center. "And we will, luv. Just got to set up some preparations to ensure everything stays nice and nonthreatening for your first time."

The way he said it could have made any of Pete's classmates at Our Lady of Penitence blush. "Jack, why'd you bring me?" she asked abruptly. "This pagan demon-worshipper crap is MG's thing, not mine. I shouldn't even be alone with you. You're far too old."

"I'm twenty-six," Jack protested. He finished the circle, which had grown into something that resembled a cage, giving Pete the sense of flat, cold iron. Jack took two fat candles, black and white, from his satchel. "You act like I've got one foot in the sodding grave, you do."

And I'm sixteen, Pete had whispered to herself. *And if MG ever found out the two of us have been alone—if Da ever found out . . .*

"I asked you to come along because I need you," Jack said, sitting back on his heels. His serious tone pulled Pete back from imagining what if MG witnessed the scene. Her sister could throw a fit akin to a nuclear explosion. And Da—he'd send Pete to a convent, or a tower, or wherever angry fathers sent recalcitrant daughters in fairy tales.

Pete blinked. "Why on earth would you *need* me?"

Jack brushed the chalk dust off his hands and stood, patting the pockets of his battered black jeans. "Let's see— you're sensible, cool in crisis, rather adorable. What bloke wouldn't want you about?"

"Shut your gob," Pete muttered. "What'd MG say, she heard you talking like that?"

"MG," said Jack. "MG knows what I'm about. She wouldn't say a bloody thing, because she won't ask and I won't tell her." He searched his studded jacket next, without fruition. "Bloody fucking hell. You got a light?"

Pete dug in her school bag and found her Silk Cut and disposable lighter, hidden inside a tampon box. MG might treat Pete indifferently at best, but she did teach her a few good tricks.

"Cheers," Jack said when she tossed it to him, lighting the candles and placing them at the head and foot of the circle. The longer Pete looked at it, the more her eyes hurt and her head rang, so she looked away, at the bar of light that was the door back to the world.

"Almost there . . ." Jack muttered. He pulled his flick-knife from a hidden pocket—or maybe it just appeared, in the dim light Pete couldn't be sure—and pricked his finger, squeezing three precise droplets over the chalk.

Pete had watched Jack work magic before, simple street tricks like disappearing cards, the queen of spades slipping between his thin fingers, or small conjurations like a cigarette that came from the packet already lit.

But here, in the tomb, Pete remembered thinking, it was different. It was real *magic*. Silly, of course, that, through and through. She was the daughter of a police inspector, and the Caldecott family—less MG—didn't put stock in that sort of thing. But Jack . . . Jack *made* you believe, with his very existing. He crackled the air around him like a changeling among men. People looked into his eyes and believed, because you could see a devil dancing in the bright flame of his soul.

Jack Winter *was* magic.

"Ready?" Jack asked from the head of the circle. Pete felt something wild and electric settle around them, like a phantom storm brushing her face with rain.

"What should I do?" Pete asked. Jack beckoned to her and hissed when she almost scuffed over some of the markings.

"Mind the edge, luv. Wouldn't want you lopped off at the knees."

"Bloody hell, really?" Pete asked, eyeing the circle circumspectly. She wasn't her sister, nattering on about "the energy," but she knew, in a way that was deep and brooked no logical argument, that she had stepped into something otherworldly when she came to this place with Jack. He radiated a power she could taste on her tongue.

"The circle won't *hurt* you," Jack admitted, stroking the darker stubble at his jaw. "But don't disturb the sigils. You don't want what'll be inside on the outside. Trust me." He took Pete's hand as she got close and raised the flick-knife. Pete jerked, but he was too quick, scoring a neat crosscut on her palm.

"Ow!" Pete said in irritation. All of the questions she should have asked raced to mind in a sick sensation of falling and the excitement of a moment ago washed away on a red tide of fear.

She hadn't asked why they'd come here, sneaked past the admissions booth at the cemetery gates and broken into this tomb, hadn't pressed Jack on purpose, because then she'd get scared, and Jack was never scared. Not when a pack of skinheads made trouble in Fiver's. Not of Da, DI Caldecott himself, who had chased off every one of MG's previous deadbeat boyfriends. Jack just extended a hand and a smile and people would throw themselves off Tower Bridge to stand next to him, to reap a little of the danger that seemed to permeate everything he touched.

As the chalk soaked up her blood, the sigils fading to red like a blushing cheek, Pete knew she didn't want to pull back. Questions be damned. Jack wanted—*needed*—her here, and she was here.

"You all right, luv?" Jack said, pressing a tattered handkerchief over her cut and closing her fist around it.

"I'm fine. I'm ready," Pete said. She wouldn't think about what might crawl out of a tomb under Jack's deft hands, nor about how mad her believing that Jack had power was in the first place. She'd just know that he picked her, Pete Caldecott, who never had friends or friends who were boys, and bollocks to a boyfriend—if she had one of those, she'd go buy a lotto ticket. Jack Winter, magician and singer for the Poor Dead Bastards, needed Pete with him in this old dark place.

Jack guided Pete to the black candle at the foot of the circle, and she made sure to stand ramrod straight so he'd know she wasn't scared, not a bit, wasn't thinking this was a bit dodgy and odd. Not Pete.

"Now you hold on to me," Jack said, lacing their fingers

together in a blood-smeared lattice across the markings on the floor. "And whatever happens, you keep holding on— all right?"

"What might happen that'd make me let go?" Pete's stomach churned into overdrive.

Standing at his spot by the white candle, Jack flashed her the devil-grin one more time. "That's what we're going to find out."

He started to speak Irish, long passages, rhythmic. It sounded like it should be solemn, intoned by robed priests over a stone altar, but Jack half slurred through the stanzas as though he were reciting lyrics to one of his songs and had a few pints in him while he did it.

For a moment, nothing happened. Pete looked at Jack through her lashes, half feeling pity because he seemed so set on something odd or spooky taking place.

And then something did.

Pete felt the *pull*, the separation of things that were comfortable and real from the dark place behind her eyes. Something was swirling up, through the layers of the veil between Pete and Jack and what lay beyond, and she could almost see it, a welter of black smoke growing in the center of the circle as Jack raised his voice, chanting rhythmically now that the fruits of his spell were visible. The chalk lines clung like bone fingers, holding the smoke-shape in place.

Jack's eyes flamed blue as the spell snapped into place, and the fire traveled over the planes of his cheeks and his arms and hands and blossomed all around him as Pete gasped, and the thing in the circle grew more and more solid.

The shape was human, a wicker man of smoke. The chalk lines did not hold it for more than a moment, and it fixated on Pete, eyeless but staring through her all the same. And then it was moving, in a straight and inexorable line, right for her. The primitive cold in her gut told Pete something was horribly wrong.

"Jack?" Her voice was high and unrecognizable to her own ears. The wicker man had a face now, and hints of silver in its eye sockets, and hands with impossibly long fingers that reached out, *clawed* at her. Whispers crowded Pete's brain, and a pressure fell on her skull so unbearable that she screamed, loudly.

And Jack, where was Jack? He stood watching the smoke with a measured eye, as if Pete were the mouse and he were the python enthusiast.

"Jack," she said again, summoning every steady nerve in her body to speak. "What is it?"

He bent to one knee and quickly chalked a symbol on the floor. *"Bínasctha,"* he breathed.

The wicker man stumbled, like a drunk or a man who just had a heavy load thrown on him. But he walked still, one foot straight in front of the other.

"Ah, tits," hissed Jack. He rechalked the symbol, and still the wicker man walked.

"Jack." She said it loudly, echoingly so, the first fissures of real panic opening in her gut.

"Shut it, will you!" he demanded. Pete saw from his expression that he was finally catching on to what she knew—never mind how; it had fallen into her head when that terrible pressure had eased, like waking up and suddenly knowing the answer to last night's math homework. She just knew, as if she'd experienced this ritual a thousand times before, that Jack's magic was awry and now the smoke man was awake and walking the world.

"Is that all you can say?" she cried. "Jack, do something!"

He tried. Pete would always say that, when she had to talk about the day, even though her memories of the whole event were thin and unreliable by choice. He tried. And when Jack tried to keep the wicker man from her, all that he got for his efforts was screaming, and blackness, and blood.

Chapter 2

The sign on the building, half off its hinges, optimistically proclaimed HOTEL. Underneath, in smaller gold script that had faded, "Grand Montresor."

The tiny purple asters grew all around the crumbling concrete steps, forcing their way out of the cracks in a great spray of example for nature versus man.

Pete stepped over them, careful to avoid crushing any blossoms, and pushed her way into bleach-scented gloom. The Montresor, like the whole of the block around it, had seen better days and couldn't remember exactly when they were. It stood out like a dark pock on the face of Blooms-bury, and Pete wondered why information always had to be garnered in the filthiest, most shadowy places of her city.

A clerk straight out of *The Vampyre* ruffled his *Hello!* magazine in annoyance when Pete came to reception. "Yeah?"

"Could you tell me about the person staying in room twenty-six?" Pete said, trying to sound bright and official. It took more than a forced smile and a chipper tone to garner a reaction from the clerk, for he just grunted.

Pete unfolded the note Oliver Heath, her desk mate at the Metropolitan Police, had handed her. "Grand Montresor, Bloomsbury by King's Cross. Room 26 @ 3 P.M." "Said he had information on the Killigan child-snatching." Ollie had shrugged, the gesture expansive as his Midlands drawl, when she'd questioned him. "Said that the lead inspector were to come alone, and not be late."

Bridget Killigan. Six years old. Disappeared from her primary-school playground when her father was late fetching her. In normal cases Pete advised the parents to be hopeful, that children were usually found, that nothing would happen to their family. Because in normal cases, the child was snatched by a parent in a custody case or an older schoolmate as a prank, or simply said *Bugger this* and ran off on their own, only to be confounded by the tube system and get stranded in Brixton. Strangers took children in folktales, not Pete Caldecott's London.

Even so, when the Killigan case came to Pete, she got that sink in her chest that always heralded an unsolvable crime. Bridget had no divorced parents, no creepy uncles. The girl had been taken by a figment with no ties to the world Pete could discover, and she *knew,* in the leaden and otherworldly way she just knew some things, that the only way they'd find Bridget Killigan would be dead.

The clerk was giving her the eye, so Pete showed her warrant card. "Does the lift work?" she asked.

The clerk snorted. "What d'you think, Inspector?"

Pete sighed resignedly and mounted the stairs. She'd been meaning to get more time at the gym, hadn't she? One didn't become a twenty-eight-year-old detective inspector without spending every waking moment plastered to a case. At least, one didn't if one didn't want to endure the whispers about DI Caldecott the elder and how he'd *worked* for his position, he had, wasn't right how some young slip just waltzed right in . . .

Room 26 matched all the other doors in the hallway, robin's egg blue, like a door in a dirty London sky. Pete lifted her hand to knock and then dropped it. She'd tried to ignore that *knowing*, of course. You couldn't *know* things you hadn't deduced with fact. The feelings of tight pressure behind her eyes, the whispers of the future echoing down the time stream to her ears—those things were stress, or low blood sugar.

Not real. Had never *been* real. Maybe she'd had a good hunch a time or two, was all. She was good at her job. Nothing spooky about it.

Pete lifted her hand again and knocked this time, firmly and thrice. "C'min," someone mumbled from behind the door. "'S open."

"Not very smart in this city," Pete replied, knowing the best she could hope for on the other side of the door was a shifty-eyed informant who had heard some fifth-hand story about Bridget Killigan and needed a few quid.

She turned the knob and stepped in, keeping her chin up on the off chance that it was a shifty-eyed axe murderer, instead. "I'm DI Caldecott. You wanted to speak about Bridget Killigan?"

He was slouched on the sill, a lit cigarette dangling from his lower lip. The sun was low over King's Cross and it lit up the man's platinum-dyed hair, a halo over a dirty hollow-cheeked face.

"Yes," said Jack Winter, exhaling smoke through his nose. "I did."

He'd been bloody and still the last time Pete saw him. Eyes staring at the ceiling of another's tomb. Pete could only stare for a moment, and her heart fluttered as the two images of Jack overlaid one another, spattering blood droplets and pain across the living incarnation's face. He'd been so still.

Younger, too. Bigger. A body gained from nights sleeping on a floor and fights outside the club after his sets. That was gone now. Jack was all sharp corners and creases. He flicked his ash on the sill and unfolded his long arms and legs, gesturing Pete to the bed.

"Sit, if you like."

Pete couldn't have, not if God himself commanded it. She was rooted surely as an old oak.

Bloody and still. Dead.

"You . . ." The word came out on a shiver. "You."

"Yeah, I'm surprised a bit meself," Jack said, dragging on his cigarette like he was underwater and it was oxygen. "I mean, I rang asking for the inspector on the Killigan case and they give me your name. Almost said fuck it, then. You don't deserve the success."

Pete finally managed to blink, to set the world right side up again and march ahead despite the thousand screaming questions ringing inside her skull. Jack Winter was alive. Right. On with it.

"What do you mean by that?"

He threw down the butt of his cigarette and stamped on it with a jackbooted foot. "You know bloody well what I mean, you fickle bitch."

"I don't—" Pete started, but he cut her off, grabbing up an old leather jacket from the bed and shrugging it onto shoulders that showed their bones.

"Bridget Killigan will be found tomorrow at the entrance to Highgate Cemetery," Jack cut her off. "I'd prefer five hundred pounds cash reward, but since you're a copper I know your heartfelt thanks will have to do."

He went around Pete for the door, stamping his feet in a jerky stride like he was cold. Pete decided that her mind might be standing agape, but the rest of her didn't need to be. She caught him by the wrist. "Wait! Jack, how do you know that? Please."

Please tell me why you've been alive all along and never breathed a word to me. Please tell me how you survived that day.

He sneered. "Let go of me."

Pete held on, and he wriggled in her grasp. "I just want to have a word, Jack—after twelve years, don't you?"

"No," he said. "I told you what I needed to tell you, and now I'm off to the pub. *Leggo,* you bloody fascist!"

He ripped his arm away and the sleeve of the jacket jerked back, revealing a miniature tube system of veins and punctures on his forearm. Numbness stole over Pete as she stared, until Jack glared and pushed his sleeve down again.

"How long?" she asked.

Jack shoved a cigarette between his lips and touched it with the tip of his finger. An ember sprang to life. "Like you bloody care."

With a slam of the broken door, he vanished.

Pete dialed MG at her commune in Sussex on her mobile when she left the Grand Montresor and hung up. She dialed her desk at Scotland Yard. Ollie picked up, but Pete rang off with him as well.

What the bloody hell would she say? *"By the way, that bloke who dropped dead in front of me when I was sixteen? Saw him today. Yeah. Gives his love."*

Ollie was ill equipped to offer advice, unless it was regarding Leeds United football or cheap minibreak destinations. MG already had enough reasons to think Pete was a raving nutter. After the graveyard, after Pete had started talking again a few weeks later, MG had screamed and slapped her and demanded to know what had happened to her boyfriend.

I wish I knew, I really do, Pete had said, but it wasn't good enough. MG had never really trusted her again. She had been the one to introduce Pete to Jack, taken her to hear the Poor Dead Bastards play, so in MG's mind, where the universe rotated around MG, it was MG's fault that Jack was dead, and Pete's fault that she didn't throw herself on the same sword. Picking up and getting on with things was Da's way, and MG wouldn't hear of it.

Pete leaned her head against the steering wheel of her

Mini, and tried unsuccessfully to reconcile the wasted middle-aged man in room 26 with the memory she'd carried for a dozen years. She hadn't brought Jack to mind often. It was painful to think of even the first time she'd seen Jack, at Fiver's, torn up and bloody even though his set had just started. That image stayed with her, Jack screaming and bleeding and irrefutably alive.

In the dreams that came in the twelve intervening years, the two pictures of Jack—alive and inanimate—blended, and Pete often found herself standing alone in the pit at Fiver's, being sung to by a dead man.

Pete's mobile rang and she jerked, dropping it between the driver's seat and the shift console. She swore as it continued to chirp and finally dug it out from the crevice. "DI Caldecott."

"Where are you?"

Pete held the phone away and checked the caller ID screen. TERRY (WORK) blinked in red letters. She took a breath and shoved everything that had happened inside the Montresor into the tidy bin she kept at the back of her mind for information too awful or real to process.

"I was working and I turned off my mobile. I do have a job still, Terry."

Terry drew in a breath. "You were supposed to be at the estate agent's to sign the sale papers at four."

Pete turned the key in the Mini's ignition and the faulty dash clock flickered to life. Three forty-five. "Terry, there's no way I can make it in traffic," Pete said. "We're going to have to put it off until tomorrow."

"Pete." Terry sighed. "Just because we're no longer together doesn't mean you can dispose of our communal property at your leisure. I want the flat sold by summer. I'm going on holiday to Spain and I don't want to deal with it."

"God forbid I should intrude on your precious holiday," Pete muttered. "Because it's all about you, Terry. Isn't it?"

"Pete," he said. "We bought the flat together, and we're no longer together, and I am going to get my money and wash my hands of it. That's all there is."

Pete had nearly forgotten the patronizing tone Terry pulled out, the one that made her feel like a first-year recruit every time, but it came back to her in a rush. "Terry, I'm working," she snapped. "I don't have time for you."

"That was always your whole problem," said Terry. After a moment a bleep told Pete she'd been disconnected.

"And a fine afternoon to you, too," Pete muttered, tossing the mobile into the back seat. Terry had a job that began and ended at the same time every day. He never got blood on his shoes.

He never saw people return from the dead.

Pete gripped the Mini's wheel for a long thirty seconds before she felt steady enough to drive. She tried to blot Jack's face out and replace it with Bridget Killigan's, because the little girl was who she should be dwelling on. Not Mr. Risen from the Bloody Dead.

Bridget Killigan will be found tomorrow at the entrance to Highgate Cemetery.

"Bollocks," Pete said firmly, and pulled away from the curb.

Chapter 3

DI Ollie Heath was leaving for the day when Pete slumped at her desk in the warrenlike Homicide and Serious Crime division, and he stopped and folded his coat over his ample stomach. "You look a fright, Caldecott."

"Ta muchly," Pete muttered.

"Is it that tosser you were to marry?" Ollie asked. "I'm sure I could work up a traffic warrant or two if he's giving you trouble."

"It's not Terry," said Pete. "Just . . . someone I knew, a long while back."

"Unpleasant reunion?" Ollie said.

Jack's eyes, a blue like the coldest part of a glacier, wide and staring, his skin and his platinum hair dappled in blood. Pete pushed, hard, against the flood of grief and other, darker thoughts that Jack's face stirred up. Thoughts that she'd put away for good, denied as hallucinations and dreams covering the ugly, bloodstained truth. "No. Just old, bad memories."

Ollie patted her awkwardly on the shoulder a few times. Pete felt herself go stiff as a mannequin, and Ollie quickly drew back, his pudgy hand disappearing into his pocket. "Don't work too late, Caldecott. Can't find Bridget Killigan if you're dead from exhaustion."

"Right. 'Night, Ollie."

Ollie left without any further thought, home to his tidy flat and his cat and his telly. Pete wanted to follow him, but her flat would be cold. Too many ghosts were around her tonight for any sort of rest. Jack, MG, Terry, Da. Da would have known what to do. He would have known whether to trust Jack, if that man in the hotel *was* Jack. In the sharp glow of the Major Investigation Room and her computer screen, Pete found it easier to believe she'd dreamed it entirely.

"Why did you come back to me?" she muttered, putting her hands on her desk and her face on her hands. Because she *knew* it was Jack. Pete had known things only a few times before—that storms were blowing, and that when the oncologist took the first X-rays of Connor's lungs that he was going to die. She tried to push her intuition back at every turn, because admitting the rightness of the thing would open the door to the very path Jack's reappearance was leading her inexorably down. To that day, the thing in the center of the stone tomb . . .

"Stop it," Pete murmured, and only Jack's phantom voice answered her back.

Bridget Killigan will be found tomorrow at the entrance to Highgate Cemetery.

Pete sat up, rubbed her eyes, tried to fill out paperwork and ignore the heavy weight of certainty against her mind. Connor would have laughed at her, even at the end when he was strapped to an oxygen tank twenty-four hours a day.

"Bugger this," Pete muttered. She got her things and strode down the corridor to the rear exit, where the night air was still sharp and cold, real winter in the rain and the scent of the turning trees. Leaving the Mini in the lot, she walked for a time, going over all of the reasons why she shouldn't believe a word that came out of Jack Winter's mouth. He was dead, for a first. Untrustworthy even when alive, for a second.

But when she shut her eyes, his face would not leave her, nor what he'd said.

"I don't have anything else," Pete sighed into the air when she'd walked as far as she could before falling into the Thames. And if she wasted a few hours chasing Jack's dragons, she hadn't lost. Bridget Killigan had been missing for three days and it was as if the girl had become vapor. "I don't have anything else," Pete repeated, and at the late hour it made a bit of sense.

Chapter 4

At six A.M. silver bathed the street and cooled Pete's skin to the temperature of the air. The brick wall of the East Cemetery at her back prodded, keeping her from nodding off as she watched the plain black iron gates, locked up with a modern chain and padlock that jarred any sense of mystery right out of the scene.

Ridiculous was more like it. She was too bloody sensible to be here, with four hours of sleep behind her, waiting for a promise made by the shade of Jack Winter.

Bridget Killigan will be found tomorrow at the entrance to Highgate Cemetery.

Pete stuck a Parliament in her mouth and lit it with an inhale of regret. Hadn't she promised everyone who mattered that she'd quit? A dozen times over, at least.

But it was a hard morning, an autumn morning, and it was cold. Her jacket was too thin and she was rattled and everywhere she looked she saw bloody Bridget Killigan, six years old, grinning out from a school photo.

The smoke rubbed her throat and Pete exhaled. She couldn't erase Bridget from the backs of her eyes any more than she could erase Jack. She couldn't stop seeing her face, feeling the seconds run through her fingers as days passed.

Crying. Bridget was crying. Pete snapped her head up,

the Parliament falling to the pavement. She stepped on it as she moved into the street, listening over the ever-present whisper of traffic, the slamming of doors from the block of flats nearby, a dog howling. She refused to believe she was so far gone that she was hearing phantom sobs.

Crying, issuing from under a low-hanging tree with glossy leaves near the barriers that closed off Highgate Cemetery and divided the land of the living from the land of the dead. Senseless and wordless and filled with pain, it rose and wavered and mingled with Pete's own wordless exclamation.

She shoved branches aside and saw Bridget Killigan hunched on the ivy with her knees pulled to her chin, sobbing softly but shedding no tears. She refused to look at Pete when Pete gathered her into her arms, and from what Pete saw never looked at anything with her white and staring eyes, ever again.

"Shock," said Ollie when Bridget and her crying parents had been loaded into an ambulance and sent streaming away into thick morning traffic. "Poor bit's obviously had a time of it."

Pete lit the fifth Parliament of the day.

"That's not shock, Ollie," she said. "I've seen shock."

Ollie shook out his tidy notebook with the blue cover, turning a new page because Bridget Killigan was found and there was no reason to open to her anymore. "Then what is it?"

White eyes. Tearless and staring into forever. Pete took a long drag on the cigarette. "That? That was bloody haunted."

Ollie shook his head, a forelock of ashen hair falling into his eyes. "Whatever it was, Caldecott, you'd better pull a marvelous story out of your arse as to how you found the kid. I know you're good but what you did here, that ain't good—that's witchcraft."

Pete blinked. "What'd you say, Ollie?"

"Witchcraft," said Ollie. "Ruddy magic, you going to the

exact spot and finding the Killigan brat, even if she is too damaged to make heads or tails of what happened for us."

Pete chewed on her lip and kept silent. If only Ollie Heath knew how eerily prophetic he could be at times. He was busy fussing with his collar now, putting himself in order, resetting the gears to begin a new set of problems and intricacies that new cases would bring. "Say," he said after a moment, "how'd that tip come out? The dodgy one I took over the phone?"

"Oh, that," said Pete, stabbing her Parliament against the brick wall next to her and watching the smoke curl up from the dead ash. "That was nothing."

Chapter 5

In all her time, Pete would never know why she trusted Jack Winter. Why she'd put her faith in him time and time again, as a child and now, and why she willingly followed where he led. She'd had no earthly reason to go to Highgate, to think for one minute that his words were anything but the sputtering of junkie circuitry.

But she'd gone. On nothing more than a feeling and a flutter in that dark cage where she'd locked up everything when Jack had died. Pete knew what Connor would have to say about that, and it was nothing that would put a spring in her step.

The MIT room in New Scotland Yard, no longer housed in the halls of visiting monarchy but a chapel for the warriors who trod the tangled veins and arteries of London, was dark. Pete's desk lamp created an oasis, but it didn't reach far.

She was searching for Jack Winter, not in her dreams as she had so many times, stumbling over headstones and blackened brush, but with cold key clicks, seeing what the Metropolitan Police had to offer on twelve years that she'd willfully missed.

The screen turned out drugs. Arrests. Minor vagrancies and trespasses that earned Jack stints in rehabilitation. Outpatient. Inpatient. Involuntary. Jail.

His life had not been kind, and it twisted Pete up like only Connor dying had before. But Jack had died, too, once, and Pete wasn't yet sure if it was relief or fear she felt at seeing him breathing. Jack certainly hadn't been thrilled to meet her again, for whatever secreted reasons Jack held.

Pete pushed back from her desk and looked at the glowing numerals of the wall clock. It was after midnight, and she felt it in the weight of her body. She shut off her light and walked out in the dark. In the morning, she would find Jack and make him tell her how he'd done the magic of finding Bridget, and why. Why now.

And why her.

Weevil Bill tried to run when he saw Pete coming, but she grabbed him by the sleeve of his silk windcheater and he tripped, crashing into the phone box bolted to the corner where Weevil Bill spent the vast portion of his life.

"I didn't do nuffink!" Weevil Bill squeaked. He was Pete's height, run to fat, and his breath smelled like a night of cheap pints and disappointment.

"I never said you did," said Pete. "But blurting it out like that makes you seem awfully guilty."

Weevil Bill slumped. "Wot you want?" he muttered. "I got places to be, y'know. I'm a legitimate businessman."

"Dealing hash to university students is a step up for you, certainly," Pete agreed. Weevil Bill started to slide down and sideways to make his escape and Pete helped him along, sending him to the pavement on his stomach.

"My friend in the Organised Crime Command out of EK tells me that you still deal the odd bit of smack, Bill."

"No . . . no, I'm out of that ever since the bloody Chinese moved in . . . they carve your organs out if you cross them."

"Bad luck that you got picked up with three grams last week then, isn't it?" Pete said. "You tell me what I want to know, I'll take you in and let you cool off in a cell until the

Chinese are more amenable. You fuck me about, and I'll leave your arse sprawled on the corner."

Weevil Bill dropped his forehead to the pavement and moaned. In this bleak corner of the city, none of the passing cars slowed down to see what the fuss was, and the scant pedestrian traffic gave Pete a wide berth. She lifted Weevil Bill's chin with the toe of her shoe. "I'm looking for a bloke named Jack Winter—about three and a half meters tall, platinum hair, fucking junkie. Anyone of that description score with you lately?"

"Mebbe they did," Weevil Bill muttered. "But you put the bracelets on before I tell you."

"Some other morning I'd be cooperative," said Pete, feeling the crawl of exhaustion along her spine. "I'm not an unreasonable woman, after all."

She hadn't slept when she'd been in bed, and when her eyes finally drifted closed the images of smoke on dark stone and Jack's eyes, his old smile and his new needle marks, made her prefer a pot of strong tea and late-night telly. "But that morning—it's not this morning," Pete told Bill. "Let's have it."

"Winter don't score from me much, but he runs with the blokes who use the galleries in Southwark, 'round where it ain't been torn down and built up so's only God himself could afford it," Weevil Bill said. "And that's all I know, as my witness."

Pete hauled Weevil Bill to his feet, handcuffing him with suitable ceremony and attaching the free end to a lamppost. "Oi!" Weevil Bill shouted. "What about my arrest?"

"Don't fret," said Pete, flipping open her mobile. "Mark. Yeah. Pete Caldecott here. Listen, I got a bust for you . . . he's handcuffed to a post up near the Camden Lock. You can't miss him."

The DS sputtered a laugh. "I'll hurry then."

"Oh, don't bother," Pete said, smiling at Weevil Bill.

"He's got nothing but time." She rung off with Mark and asked Weevil Bill, "Satisfied?"

Weevil Bill let out a miserable little sound, which Pete took as acquiescence. She got back into the Mini and gunned the engine.

The corner, the post, and Weevil Bill rapidly became a speck in her rearview mirror as she drove through the City and pointed the Mini across Blackfriars Bridge, toward the docks of Southwark.

Chapter 6

The smell of the Thames, rotted and salty, permeated everything in the street when Pete exited the Mini, and something darker than the damp chill in the air slithered against the underside of her mind.

She pushed it away. Nothing here except a disintegrating row of flats that exuded silent hopelessness.

A boy in a cheap leather jacket dozed on the stoop at the far end of the block, spotting for police and rival dealers and giving the place away as a shooting gallery. Pete kicked his foot once, twice. He snorted and shifted in his sleep, but nothing more. She was insubstantial as a fever dream.

A token agent's notice on the front of the building was covered with spray-painted obscenities, and faded enough that Pete thought even Susan, Terry's hopelessly cheery estate agent, would throw her hands up in despair. The door, half off its hinges from some long-ago bust, grinned at Pete with a gargoyle knocker as she pushed it open, feeling sticky dampness from the decayed wood and stippled paint. "Hello."

Shredded shades were pulled over the windows, and in the blue-gray ghost light Pete barely avoided overturned furniture, Margaret Thatcher vintage, and a surfeit of filthy

mattresses and crumpled blankets, like bodies under turned
earth.

Pete took her penlight from her pocket and flashed it
into the corners of the room, illuminating a gaunt sleeping
face. Not Jack's.

A kitchen filled with more dripping rust and cock-
roaches than any one room had a right to contain sped Pete
up a set of rickety stairs and into a narrow hallway with
bedrooms to each side. The first still held vestiges of wallpaper and an iron bed, like something one would find in an
orphanage of Dickensian origin. A mother, who couldn't
have been more than the age Pete was when she first met
with Jack, looked up with wide black eyes. Her skinny
baby let out a wail.

"Sorry," Pete muttered. "Just looking for . . . I'm looking for a friend."

The mother watched her silently, not breathing. "Jack
Winter," Pete said desperately. "He's not here, is he?" He
hadn't been at the last half-dozen squats she'd visited. No
reason to think he'd turn up here. He'd vanish as surely as
he had after . . . well. Pete didn't think about that.

"He's next door," the mother whispered. The baby
grasped at the air around her face, cries weakening, and she
dropped her head to soothe it without taking her eyes off
Pete.

"Ah," said Pete. "Thank you." She stepped backward
into the hall and went into the next room with a low thrumming in her blood, excitement and fear she had no right to
feel because you didn't trust the ramblings of addicts and
crazy people, Connor Caldecott's first rule in his long list.

The front bedroom looked out onto the street and the
Thames, a view that would have been worth something
once, just like the house and the men sleeping or murmur-
ing on the floor.

Pete shone her light on each face in turn. They were

mostly white, all thin and bones, stubble and dirt, and sometimes blood or vomit caking. Eyes glared at her dully in the
thin beam of light.

Until she hit on the platinum shock topping Jack's drawn
face. He threw an arm over his eyes and swore. "Who's that?"

Pete swallowed. She couldn't speak. It was the hotel room
all over again, and she was dumb from the sight of him. Jack
groaned and sat up. "You've got a hell of a lot of nerve, whoever you are. Got a mind to put my fist in your teeth, cunt."

"It's me," Pete managed finally.

Jack squinted for a moment, and then flopped back on
his mattress with a sigh. "And just what do you want?"

The wavering blade of the penlight illuminated the dull
flash of a disposable needle at his hand. "We found Bridget
Killigan."

"Of course you did," said Jack. "I said it, didn't I?"

Pete crouched and touched his shoulder. Jack jerked
away from her and then hissed, rubbing his arms as a
shiver racked him. "Get out of here," he said.

"How did you do it?" Pete said. "How did you know
where to find her? Jack, I'm not leaving without an answer."

Jack sat up and rooted through a plastic Sainsbury's tote.
Disposable sharps, a battered shaving case containing a
shooting kit, and empty bags coated with crystalline dust
slid through his fingers as he shook.

Pete clamped her hands around his wrists. "Jack. Answer
me."

His face was wreathed in droplets of sweat and she
fought the urge to brush them away.

"Leave me alone, Pete," he rasped. "I don't want to see
you again. Not ever." He pulled loose, picked up an empty
twist of plastic and held it to the light. "Shit." His slow-burn
gaze shot back to Pete. "You're still here? I said get the
bloody hell out!"

There was a time, Pete knew, that those words from him

would have devastated her. Words from Jack were like the tears of angels. Wounding words stabbed directly to the heart of her.

But this was the real and painful present, not a memory of the fragile girl who'd loved Jack the moment she saw him sing. "No," Pete said, jerking the bag out of Jack's hands. "No, Jack, we're going to have a word."

He snatched for it. "Give that back," he warned.

"You want this?" Pete told him, holding his sharps and drugs just out of reach. "Then you talk with me."

Jack swiped at her once more and then sat down hard, glaring. "Fuckin' hell. When did you become a raging bitch?"

Pete straightened and crumpled the bag between her fists. "I don't know, Jack, but I think it was right around the time I watched you die."

Jack threw an arm back across his face. "Did you come here merely to grasp at my balls, or was there something you wanted?"

"Tell me how you knew about Bridget Killigan," said Pete. "Right now, I'm trying to believe you had nothing to do with snatching and blinding the poor girl, but it's becoming very hard, Jack."

Jack grunted and Pete thumped him on the arm with her closed fist. "Tell me."

He opened his eyes and met hers, and Pete was swept away again as quickly as she'd been at sixteen. *Damn you, Jack Winter.* She bit her lower lip to keep her face expressionless.

"It's a simple thing, luv," said Jack. "Magic."

And God, she wanted to believe him. *Would* have, before. Even pale and scraped as his face was now, he was still Jack. And he was still feeding her lies because he thought her stupid.

"You're a bastard," she whispered, jerking her hand

away. Didn't matter that she wanted him not to be taking the piss, to be telling what he at least thought was the truth.

"Takes one to know one," said Jack shortly, rolling over on his side and facing away. Pete cocked her arm and flung the plastic bag. It burst, scattering the contents across the filmy floor.

"Oi!" Jack shouted, scrambling after the needles as they clattered away.

"The person who blinded that little girl is going to get away with it because you're a git. Go to hell," Pete hissed.

Jack stood, crossing the space between them, his expression going hard quickly as a flick-knife appears. "Look around you, Pete," he grated, gripping her arm. "We're *in* hell."

A human-sized lump on the mattress next to Jack's stirred. "Shaddup. 'M trying to sleep."

Pete bored into Jack, hoping her gaze scorched him. "Let go of me."

His mouth twisted. "Did that a dozen years ago." He left her and went back to his mattress.

Pete backed out of the room and half fell down the shadowed stairs to the front door, sucking in cold, clean outside air as she leaned against the Mini. She didn't know why Jack was angry, but it didn't matter, did it? He was still the same charlatan, still using smoke and tricks up his sleeves to avoid the realities of the world. Pete dug her knuckles into her eyes until her tears retreated.

I will not think of him. I will not gift him my tears. I will not let Jack Winter touch me.

Chapter 7

Scotland Yard flowed around Pete, shuffling papers and ringing phones, inspectors each wrapped in a cocoon of worry and mystery, weighted by their unsolved cases.

Pete sat at the double desk she shared with Ollie, hands pressed over her eyes. They felt of sandpaper, as if tiny grains made up the inside of her eyeballs.

Fuck, she wanted a cigarette.

"DCI Newell wants to see you." Ollie touched her shoulder, and Pete jerked. Every time she got close to Jack she came away jumpy and displaced.

She wanted to believe him, that was the problem. He'd let the word roll so indolently out. *Magic.*

The hiss of *knowing* pressed on Pete's mind, begging her to admit that it was as likely an explanation as any, but she wouldn't allow herself to think of it. Connor's voice, his strong hands gripping her shoulders. *You listen and you listen good, girl. There ain't no such thing as what you say Winter did.*

There ain't no such thing as magic.

"Thanks, Ollie." Pete sighed.

"You look like shite, still," said Ollie bluntly, settling his comfortable bulk into his chair and rattling a used copy of the *Times.*

"Love you, too, Ollie." Pete shoved her chair back. Chief Inspector Newell would have all manner of questions about the Killigan case, and Pete deflected them the only way she knew how—she came into Newell's office on the offensive.

"No, I don't know how she got there or who took her. She hasn't spoken. For God's sake, Nigel, she's been blinded."

Nigel Newell blinked twice at Pete. "Thank you for that succinct update, DI Caldecott. However, I called you in on another matter."

Pete drew in a breath, wishing desperately it was the end of a Parliament. Sod it, before this morning she'd been meaning to *quit*. Jack had raked all her old vices to front and center.

"Sorry, sir. What is it you wanted to see me on?"

"The Superintendent has deemed it appropriate to dedicate a small auxiliary parking structure to Inspector Caldecott, senior. Your father," said Newell as if she might have forgotten. He gave the impression of examining Pete over his glasses, even though his nose was bare. "They would like you to write a brief statement to be engraved on the plaque that will bear his name, if that isn't too taxing."

Bloody foolishness. Connor coughed at her from that hospital bed, so diminished but still full of fight. *Tell him to sod his parking structure—did my job and never asked for anything more.*

"Of course, sir," she said aloud, willing Newell, *Don't ask about Bridget Killigan.*

"Very well," said Newell. "You're dismissed."

Relief, and a fag waiting outside.

"And Inspector?" said Newell. Pete's feet ground to a halt against her will.

"Sir?"

"Don't think that I won't be asking for a full accounting

of the Killigan matter when the girl is released from the hospital."

Damn you, Jack. "Of course, sir." Pete tipped her head in deference and escaped into the wider office.

"Someone sent you papers by courier," said Ollie, with a nod toward the flat tan package on Pete's desk. The return label was the crest of Terry's architectural firm. Pete ripped the package with a letter opener, being more vicious than she strictly had to be.

Tight orderly lines of black type marched across the columns and Pete swore in a whisper before she punched up an outside line and called Terry at work.

"Mr. Hanover."

"This is *not* the price we agreed on, you wanker," Pete gritted into the mouthpiece. Ollie raised his eyebrows at that, and strategically went to refill his tea mug with hot water.

On the other end of the line, Terry sighed. "The estate agent priced it for a quick sale, Pete, just like you wanted. You told me yourself you didn't want to waste any time haggling over the flat—just get it sold."

"Yes." Pete turned her back on the MIT room at large and stared at the National Health advisories pinned to the wall behind her desk. "Yes, I do want it sold, sold at the price we gave the estate agent."

"The market's gone downhill since then. Martha said—"

"Who the bloody hell is Martha?"

She could picture Terry's sour pout when he answered. "My new estate agent. Miss Tabram."

"She's Susan's assistant, the one who had her knees stuck in your ears when I came over to sign the credit check forms last week?"

"We're seeing each other." Terry sounded far too re-laxed for Pete to do anything except get into her car, drive to his firm, and shove his drafting pencil into his ear canal. She couldn't, so she snapped, "Raise the price up, Terry. I'm not going to waste my time with your fucking about," and slammed the receiver down with a crack like bones snapping.

"Now I really do need that fag," she said to Ollie when he sat down again. "He ordered my food on our first date and he hasn't stopped shoving his bloody opinions down my throat since."

A clerk came through the maze of desks and touched Pete on the shoulder. "Sorry to bother you, Inspector . . . four persons to see you waiting in the visitor's room."

Pete wrapped her fist longingly around the crumpled pack of Parliaments in her pocket.

"Not the ruddy press, is it?" said Ollie suspiciously. "PR office has been ringing off the hook with tosspots wanting an interview with you, Pete."

"It's not the press," said the clerk. "It's . . . well . . ." Her tan brow crinkled nervously. "They wouldn't exactly say, Inspector . . . only that it was very urgent."

"All right, all right." Pete sighed. "I'll be out in a moment. Tell them to keep their knickers on that long."

Ollie found Pete half an hour later, in her customary spot near the parking shed for the armed response vehicles.

"What happened, Caldecott?"

Rain peppered the puddle at Pete's feet, and she threw her cigarette into it, where it floated on the oil-stained water like a tiny corpse. "Two more."

Ollie sagged a bit, and rubbed his forehead. "Bugger it. When?"

"This afternoon," said Pete. "After school. Two children, friends, live near each other. They didn't come home, and the parents thought they'd run away."

"I'll tell Newell," said Ollie, making a move for the door.

"I did it," said Pete. "Patrols are searching the neighborhood. I'm following momentarily." Even to her ears, she sounded flat and uninterested, as if a boring program were on BBC 4 but she couldn't be bothered to change the channel.

She could lie and say it was Jack's fault, for jerking her about rather than telling the truth, but it was hers. Two more children. An agonizing five days, if she was lucky, before they showed up in the same fashion as Bridget Killigan. Pete didn't even bother to tell herself that these were just suspicions, not fact. She was too tired to deny that she was certain.

"I'll fetch my car, head over there as well," said Ollie.

"Heath, wait," said Pete. Ollie paused. "Would you . . . would you mind going on ahead and taking point on the case, just for today?"

Ollie's lips pursed. "You've been eerie ever since we found the Killigan child, Caldecott. You need a bit of rest. If that's what you're asking for, take it. With my blessing."

"Not a rest," said Pete. She felt mad, as if she were standing on a cliff with paper wings strapped to her back. But the simple fact, the only *fact* in this at all, was that Jack had been right. Never mind *how*, he'd found Bridget. He would find the two new missing.

Pete didn't allow herself the glaring thought that her faith in Jack was as misplaced as it had ever been. Or the new wrinkle, that he hated her for something she couldn't fathom.

"Not a rest," Pete repeated to Ollie. "There's something that I have to do. It may take me thirty-six hours or so, Ollie . . . cover my arse with Newell until then?"

Ollie Heath, God bless him, just nodded. "Of course, Pete."

He went to look for the missing children, and Pete went hunting for Jack, not knowing if she was going to hit him or embrace him when they met, just that she needed to find him, and so she would.

Chapter 8

She'd never intended to rescue him, of course. Of all the strung-out lost boys in London, Jack was the least in need of that.

Pete knew she'd been spending too much time around Southwark when the shifty bloke on the steps of Jack's squat waved to her.

And she waved back. "Jack in?"

"Nah," said the kid, sniffling and shivering even inside his parka. "He moved on last night. Prolly over near Borough High Street in the close. There's a few beds."

It was twilight, witchy and shadowed along the narrow street. The night citizens were beginning to stir, but there was enough daylight left to allow her safe passage to Jack's latest shooting gallery.

He was nodding against the wall in the front room, burning cigarette dangling between his lips and a crackling copy of *London Calling* on the turntable. Pete pushed the needle off track with a squeal and Jack cracked one eye.

"Hasn't anyone told you it's rude to burst into other people's houses?"

"I need to talk to you," Pete said. She crossed her arms and made sure to appear stern and unyielding. Jack was in the throes of a hit, and damn it all, he'd listen to her one way or another.

"I recall we've played this scene before," said Jack. "Only this time you haven't got my stash to threaten me with. So what are you going to do, DI Caldecott—beat me about the head with a great bloody stick?"

"Don't think it hasn't crossed my mind," Pete assured him. Jack exhaled a cloud of blue, the nubby cigarette falling to the floor. He didn't appear to notice, tapping his dirty fingertips to the time of "Clampdown." A stray line of blood painted the path between the clustered punctures on his forearm, and Pete stooped to press the napkin she'd received with her breakfast buttie against the spot. The faint smell of eggs and ham rose between them, blending the tobacco and the sour undertone of the squat into something almost home.

"Someone who didn't know would almost think you cared," Jack muttered, but he didn't pull his arm away.

"I care," Pete said. "I care about Diana Leroy and Patrick Dumbershall."

Jack yawned languidly. "Who, now?"

"You know bloody well who they are," Pete said, slipping one end of the metal links from her belt around Jack's wrist. He jerked as soon as the handcuffs clicked closed and Pete's wrist bruised with a sharp jab.

"You slag!" Jack spat when he realized what Pete had done. "If you're still trying to get into me knickers, there's better ways."

"Your knickers don't concern me in the least," Pete said crisply.

"Please, Pete," Jack said with a pathetic jangle of the cuffs. "Don't do this to me. I can't do another stretch. Prison's bloody murder for me." He was like the roving harlequin at a carnival, trying on masks until he found one that the audience favored, one to draw them into his web of seduction and illusion.

And in that other time, with the other Jack, it would have worked. Pete knew she'd be helpless, she'd go stand in his circle and feel his black magic flow through them both.

But now all she saw was Jack grinning at her as the smoke man came, and she felt the screaming vibrations inside her own head as her mind struggled to contain something that no one was meant to endure. And his pathetic attempts to con her weren't helping.

"Get up," she snarled, hauling Jack to his feet. He was light, far beneath healthy, like a starving vampire or a re-animated sack of bones. Pete turned her head determinedly so Jack wouldn't see the pity on her face. Pity was something neither of them wanted. "You're coming along to the Yard and we're going to talk about the two more missing children."

Jack dug in his heels. "I can't leave me things, some cunt'll nick them."

Pete stopped, making Jack stumble closer to her by their connected arms. "I am going to get some bloody answers out of you, Jack Winter, and I prefer to do it in the comparative clean and comfort of a place that is not a druggie squat, so you are *going* out that door and I don't give a fuck whether it pleases you or not."

Jack blinked. Pete had never known she had the ability to leave him at a loss, and it was rather powerful. Well, nights upon rainy nights of dealing with drunken soccer hooligans who decided just because she was small and slight that she was easily intimidated would put steel into any woman's backbone.

"I get some clean clothes, yeah?" Jack said as Pete forcibly led him out the door and down the mossy steps to the Mini. "And a drink. God, I'd murder a pint."

"You get to sit down in the car and shut your gob," said

Pete, thrusting Jack into the passenger side of the Mini. She clipped her end of the cuffs to the door bar and got in.

By the time they cleared the wharves and drove over the bridge back into the City, Jack was nodding again, in the dream place between the heroin and the barren expanse of needing it. Pete slapped his shoulder with her free hand. "Keep awake. This isn't a minicab."

"Mmph," said Jack. "Bloody hell, you're violent. Got some sort of repressed urge you're takin' out on me?"

"My urges are none of your sodding business," Pete snapped, then pressed her lips together. He still had that current, that disconcerting air that made her blurt out things that should have stayed a secret.

Jack smirked. "So you say, luv."

"Why don't you make this easy on yourself and tell me what you know about the missing kids," Pete suggested as she turned onto a thoroughfare crowded with taxis and the late rush hour.

"I know fuck-all," said Jack promptly. "May I please be let go now, Inspector? I'll be ever so good and won't cause a fuss again."

Pete gripped the wheel. She wanted to throw her two hands around Jack's neck, but the Mini's steering wheel would have to do. "You told me exactly where to find Bridget Killigan and when, and you expect me to believe that you know nothing about two other children abducted by the same bloody person in the same bloody way?"

"I do, and I don't." Jack nodded. "Let me out of the fucking car, Pete. I'll crash us into an abutment if that's what it takes."

Pete crossed two lanes of traffic and screeched into the bus dropoff zone, laying on the Mini's brakes in a way the manufacturer never intended. "Sod you, you bastard!" she yelled. "You think just because you're some poor wounded addict I'm supposed to believe your line of innocent bullshit?"

"What I *think*," Jack yelled back, "is that you've turned from a sweet girl into a harpy from hell, and that I bloody hate the sight of you and if you don't unlock these bloody handcuffs right now, I'll hurt you, Pete. I swear to whatever gods you pray to."

It flamed up in his eyes first, the bluer light of witchfire. Pete gasped as it spilled from his fingers, his lips—pure raw magic seeping out and forming a tangible golem of Jack's rage. Of his magic.

Pete wanted more than anything to turn her eyes and pretend that she was just tired, or just crazy, or just . . . But the weight of *knowing* laid itself upon her, *knowing* in the pit of her stomach, the thing that wouldn't go away no matter how many years spanned between Jack holding her hands as the flames wreathed them and Jack glaring at her now, melting her skin with his stare to reach the truth underneath. And she could ignore it, but she'd never stop the *knowing,* stop seeing things she shouldn't know for truth or fiction, or be able to deny what the witchfire wreathing Jack meant.

It spilled off him in waves now as he jerked against the cuffs, touching the spiked tips of his hair and gathering at the corners of his mouth, racing over the dials in the Mini's dash. Where it kissed Pete's rigid body, it stung.

A shudder passed through her, like she'd just been doused with ice water. Jack's breathing was the loudest thing inside the car, ragged and enraged. Everything was bathed in blue.

"Bloody hell," Pete whispered. "You weren't lying."

"Magic," Jack agreed with a hiss, his lips parting. The witchfire retreated and coiled about his head like a blazing ice crown, angry and chained.

Pete swallowed as a lorry whooshed by her window, horn blaring. "I know you can tell me what happened to those children." She didn't add, *And now I have to believe that what happened to you really* happened, *and God, Jack, you just made every nightmare I've had for twelve years real again.* Her stomach and her vision both lurched but she kept herself steady, from the outside anyway. The outside mattered.

"Very probable," Jack agreed, settling back into his seat. The witchfire abated until there was only the slightest glow to his eyes.

"Then tell me," Pete said. She heard a begging tone creep in, and hated herself for it.

Jack eyed her for a moment and Pete tried unsuccessfully not to feel naked. The drugs had muted Jack's vitality but they did nothing for his gaze, which burned hotter than she'd ever remembered, fired with rock-bottom desperation.

"I *might* tell you," he considered. "But I've got a couple of conditions if I should decide to divulge my specific arcane knowledge."

"Name them," said Pete instantly. She'd clear whatever-it-was with Chief Inspector Newell later—right now Diana and Patrick's timetable was winding inexorably down.

"Condition one: I get a shower, clean clothes, a place to stay—and not some dodgy hostel you shove witnesses into either, a *real* place," Jack said. "Whether or not I decide to tell you anything, you take me there right now."

He'd never tell her anything useful, of course. Pete wasn't stupid and she could see from the way Jack talked and held himself that he was hating her for something, that her need for what he had was getting him off.

But she *wasn't* stupid, so she said, "Done."

"Condition two," said Jack. "If I tell you something, Pete, no matter how bloody outlandish it sounds to your cotton-packed copper ears—you listen. And you believe me."

How she'd wanted to do that, every second they'd spent together. Couldn't, because admitting the truth of the matter with Jack would have driven anyone reasonable mad. Believing him would be admitting that everything in the world wasn't in plain sight, and it ran contrary to Pete's whole life, the new one she'd built after Jack.

"Pete," Jack snapped. His expression was hard-edged, the mask in place, waiting to see if she'd give in to his demands.

"Yes, Jack," she said with a sigh. "I'll believe you."

Chapter 9

Jack glared suspiciously at the door of Pete's flat. "This doesn't look like any bloody hotel I've ever seen."

"It's not," said Pete, peeling the package notices and the card from the estate agent off the door and sliding her key home. "It's my flat."

One dark eyebrow crawled upward on Jack's forehead. "And this is part of our arrangement how, exactly?"

Pete flicked on lights and put up her bag and coat, motioning Jack inside. "It's a very nice flat. You can have a shower and put on some of Terry's old clothes."

"Who in bloody fuck-all is Terry?"

"My ex-fiancé," said Pete shortly. "Bath's down the hall. I'll put the kettle on."

She left Jack standing and went into the kitchen, careful to keep her back turned so he wouldn't catch on she was watching him. After a moment and a spate of muttering, she heard Jack go down the hall. A door closed and water ran in the basin, rattling the old pipes like a disgruntled poltergeist.

Pete moved swiftly. She threw the bolts on the front door and locked the padlock she and Terry had never used because the area wasn't that bad, shoving the key deep into the catch-all drawer in the kitchen. All the windows were painted shut and covered with safety lattice, so he wouldn't be getting out that way. No back stairs.

Pete crossed herself reflexively, a move she hadn't performed in the eight years since Connor's death, but which seemed highly appropriate now.

She would not allow herself to think about what Jack would say once he emerged from the loo. He'd be bloody angry, but she figured that in his diminished state she could probably take him on. Plus, there were always the handcuffs.

"I'm starved," Jack announced. "Call for takeaway."

Pete jumped and silently berated herself. He was silent as a shade, just as he'd always been, appearing practically out of ether.

Jack's mouth curled into a slow grin. "Sorry. Didn't mean to frighten you."

"Not frightened," said Pete. "You never frightened me, Jack."

"Come now, Pete," he teased. "I was the scariest thing your little head ever laid eyes on."

Pete handed him a menu for the curry stand at the corner. "For a time," she said. "A very short time, until I realized what was standing just behind you, in shadow."

The grin vanished and Jack's grim set returned. "And you didn't stick around long then, did you? Ran right back to Daddy and safety."

"Saffron rice or naan?" Pete said quietly.

Jack gauged her, seeing if his pinprick had drawn blood. Pete didn't let him know that ever since he'd appeared back at her shoulder all the old wounds had slipped their stitches. She was bleeding in the open, her scars exposed.

But fuck if she'd let Jack and his new, persistent hostility see it.

And she succeeded, because he shrugged in an elaborate display of apathy and said, "Rice, I guess."

One of these days, she'd ask him about that rage he carried like a stone on his back. Pete dialed for takeaway and ordered two curries. If Jack ate, it would be a good sign—not all was lost if he ate.

She turned from the phone and saw him examining the photograph of herself and Terry on the fireplace mantel. Pete had laid it facedown, but Jack picked it up. "This the bloke?"

"That's Terry," Pete confirmed.

"He looks like a git."

"Thank you for the assessment," Pete said. "You look like a transient, but we won't delve into that comparison, will we?"

"Ouch!" Jack said with what may have been a faint admiration. "You bloody well learned to go for the bollocks, didn't you?"

"I may have picked up a skill or two since you last knew me," Pete agreed. Jack slouched on her sofa and flicked on the telly, changing until he found a Manchester game. "You got any lager?"

"Not for you," Pete said. She crossed her arms, uncrossed them, brushed her straight black hair behind her ears, where it promptly fell free again. How could Jack Winter be *sitting* there, watching telly and waiting for takeaway and demanding a drink? She'd seen what Jack could do with little more than a thought and a muttered word or two of the old language, and she had entrapped him into her flat, her home.

Was she *mad*?

A knock made her start. Jack barely stirred, asleep within seconds once he relaxed.

"That'll be curry," Pete said. Jack snored, familiar and at the same time as alien as if she'd invited Frankenstein's monster to sleep on her sofa.

Pete paid for the takeaway and tried to eat, but she kept craning over the sounds of Manchester winning to see if Jack was awake. But he slept, still as a breathing corpse, until Pete dumped her dinner into the bin and sat down to write reports on the two missing children that Jack was supposed to help her find. Two days now, when it faded to black outside her windows. Two days—hardly any time at all.

She could wake Jack up, but what purpose would that serve? And if she were completely honest, would a part of her admit to a certain *rightness* at Jack being in her flat, at Jack being alive at all?

Pete felt her eyelids drift down, dreamily, and she let herself sleep lulled by Jack's rattling breath and the receding waves of sound from the telly. She woke to the ITV logo bouncing around the screen and Jack's incensed expression, his knotty hand on her shoulder, shaking her.

"Let go!" She brushed him off.

"Open the bloody door!" he grated.

Pete yawned and blinked, not intending to appear indifferent, but she did, and Jack kicked at her scatter rug. "Fuck it, open up!"

"What could possibly be that important at this hour?" Pete said, rubbing her temples. Purely rhetorical, because she knew without having to ponder. It was the only driving force junkies obeyed.

"Well, let's start with you sodding locking me in!" Jack said.

Pete stood, flexing her foot where it had gone to sleep. "It isn't a safe neighborhood, Jack." Flimsy. *Didn't Da teach you to be a better liar than that?* She prayed, another habit that she'd mostly excised since Jack and Connor had died. *Please, let this work out in my favor. Don't let him see how afraid I am of what he can still do.*

"I'm leaving now," he said, shoving his hands into the pockets of his jeans. "Thanks for the curry and the washup."

"You've only just gotten here," Pete protested, in what to her ears sounded like a fairly innocent manner. "And you didn't eat a thing."

"I've just . . . got to go," Jack said. "Open the door, please?"

He was begging. Fuck all, the heroin must have its jaws around him tight to make Jack Winter resort to that.

Pete drew in a breath through her nose. She met Jack's eyes and said, "No."

They narrowed and hardened to ice chips, and his pleasant visage peeled back to show the beast under the skin. "What d'you mean, 'no'?"

"Just what I said," Pete replied with a sigh. "It's late. Whatever-it-is can wait till morning."

Jack grabbed the picture of Pete and Terry and hurled it at the opposite wall. Glass shattered into snow fragments, blanketing the wood floor.

He rounded on Pete, and she tensed. The blue light flamed up in his eyes and he gripped her by the upper arms, face inches away. She could see that he hadn't shaved, that he had a faint scar vertically along his right cheek—*he didn't have that before*—and that if she didn't yield to his drive to get a fix, he would have no trouble at all killing her.

"Let. Me. Out," Jack said slowly.

"Won't do it, Jack," Pete whispered. "We can stand here until the sun comes up."

He squeezed and Pete bit the inside of her cheek. His misery made him bloody strong. "If you don't get me my fix," Jack said, "you can forget about our little bargain to save poor innocent Patrick and Diana. You'll have killed them over me. Now me, I could live with that on my head, but I doubt you can, Pete. You're far too good and pure."

"You don't know me so well any longer," Pete said. Jack sighed, looking at the floor between them, shaking finitely all over his body.

"Don't know what you're doing to me, do you? Probably the closest you've ever come to it is renting the *Trainspotting* video." He leaned in, their mouths and skin millimeters apart. "Pete, you don't know. You have no idea what it is to need this. Please. I'm *asking* you now. Let me out to get my fix, so it doesn't all go horribly wrong."

"I've been with the Met long enough to know what it is to be an addict," said Pete, pulling her chin back, because proximity to Jack did strange things to a person. "And I know when a bloke's trying to manipulate me. No, Jack. Nothing will go wrong and the answer is no."

One fist went up. "Open the fucking door before I bash your *fucking face.*"

Pete felt her jaw tighten and her lips compress. All her patience for this new Jack ran out like water. A dozen years of regret and feeling the hole in her heart, and this was what she got?

Pete used the rage of her wasted nightmares to fuel the snarl in her voice. "You won't do any such thing, Jack, because you're a fucking coward. And sod your deal, by the way. I said I'd get you washed and fed. I didn't agree to anything about your smack."

His upper lip twisted but under the surface of his sneer the fire flickered and burned out of his eyes.

Pete gripped the hand bruising her arm and twisted just enough to throw the joints out of prime. "Bollocks!" Jack yelped. Pete gripped his wrist and elbow in a control hold, propelling Jack toward the bathroom.

"Now we're going to get one thing straight," she said, shoving Jack into her old claw-footed bathtub and spinning the cold tap open all the way.

"*Fuck!*" he shouted, collapsing in a heap. "You fleabitten whore! That freezes!"

"I don't care what sort of a problem you've developed in regard to me," Pete said, ticking off on her fingers. "I care about Patrick and Diana and finding them alive and well. And you are going to help me, and you're going to do it without the assistance of your sodding heroin, or so help me, Jack, I will personally beat you senseless and deliver you to the lockup at the Yard."

He glared up at her, his bleached hair dribbling into his eyes like sodden straw. Pete glared back, watching him shiver and trying to ignore the pity shredding her intentions to be hard.

After a long rotation of the clock hands, Jack wiped a hand over his face and reached up to turn off the tap. "All right, Caldecott," he said finally. "You got yourself a deal."

Chapter 10

The children's ward at St. John's Hospital made an effort to paint a cheery face on things with bright furniture and murals on the walls, but it had the same effect as a syphilitic prostitute smearing on expensive rouge.

Bridget Killigan's father—Dexter, *"Call me Dex, they all do"*—looked up when she swung open the door. "Inspector?"

"Is she sleeping?" Pete asked. Bridget lay on the hospital bed like a child bride on her funeral pyre.

"She drifts," said the father. "In and out." He stroked Bridget's hair back from her grave face, like she was a porcelain thing, smashable.

"Could I have a word?" Pete asked even though a word would get no results. Bridget's mind was gone as the ash on the end of a burning cigarette. But Pete needed groundwork, if she was going to find Patrick and Diana, needed facts to know that Jack wasn't simply wanking off over her discomfiture.

She needed truth, even if she blended or blurred or broke it, later on. *Start with the truth,* Connor said, *and then you can draw the map, walk anywhere you please. Go to the sodding forbidden forest if you like, but start at true.*

"Bridget?"

The girl stirred, the white marble eyes flicking toward Pete as if Bridget could still see, even though the doctor in A&E had assured Pete she was totally blind. "Who is it? Mum?"

"No, love," said Pete, gripping the rail of Bridget's bed. Cold and straight, inhuman. Strength. "No, this is Detective Inspector Caldecott. You can call me Pete."

Bridget's forehead creased. "Pete's a funny name for a girl."

"I know," Pete agreed, breathing deep and keeping her tone steady. "It's bloody—er, very funny. You think that's a burden, my sister's name is Morning Glory."

Bridget made no reaction.

Pete chewed her lip. "Bridget, I need to ask you about the person who took you."

Bridget's father pressed his palms together, lips moving silently. Bridget let out a small sigh, as if she'd repeated her story many times.

"We went to see the old Cold Man. He lives down the murky path, just around the bend."

Pete took Bridget's hand. Her skin was cooler than the air, dry like parchment. Bridget was a shadow child, a thin husk with nothing beating beneath the surface.

"Bridget, where is the murky path? Where does it go?"

"I think you've done quite enough," Dexter Killigan said abruptly, standing and placing his hand protectively on his daughter's shoulder. "She can't tell you anything."

"Bridget," Pete said again, squeezing the girl's papery hand. "Bridget, what did you see when you went down the murky path?"

She rolled her head toward Pete and fixed Pete with those white eyes, dead pearls in her tiny corpse-face. "We saw the bone tombs. The dead places where the dreamers go. He strides in the shadows and he reached out his hand to me."

The hospital room was warm, nearly stuffy, but Pete felt a cold that cut to her bones. Bridget's calm monotone recalled images just beneath the rippling surface of Pete's own memory, black smoke and skeletal phantoms whispering close to her ear.

"And what does he do, Bridget?" she finally managed. Her voice came out dry, as if she'd been smoking for twenty years hence. "What does the old Cold Man do?"

Bridget was still for a long moment, breath shallow, pulse beating in her translucent throat. Pete leaned in. "Bridget?"

The little girl's hand latched around Pete's wrist, touch like frost. Pete jumped.

Bridget whispered sibilantly. "He's touched both of us, Pete Caldecott. Backward and forward, up and down the years, he sees. And he waits."

Black pools spun in front of Pete's vision as her blood dropped groundward. "What did you say? How do you . . ."

But Bridget was gone again, still and silent and asleep. Her father shook himself and then pointed at the door. "Get out," he told Pete shakily. "Get out and don't come back. Leave my daughter alone."

Pete moved for the door faster than she admitted to herself. She needed to be outside, and needed a fag, not necessarily in that order. "I'm sorry," she said to Dexter Killigan before the door swished shut on the tableau in the hospital room.

He didn't answer, mourning Bridget with his stillness and his unblinking, distant stare.

Chapter 11

At the door to her flat, Pete paused and listened, catching not a sound from inside. "Bloody hell," she muttered. Relief, not worry, that. She'd left Jack cuffed to the headboard of her bed, after he'd passed out on it, and by the sound of things, he'd stayed there.

Pete believed it, right up until she opened the door. The rug in the front room was crumpled and her hall table had been tipped over. "Shit." Then, "Jack?"

He'd be gone, and the only question would be how many of her pawnable possessions he could carry.

Pete jerked a Parliament out of the pack and stomped into the kitchen for a light. She passed the bathroom on her way. Jack lay on his side next to the toilet, the sweat beading on his face the only sign he was alive.

The unlit fag dropped from Pete's mouth. "Damn you, Jack," she hissed. Then she was on her knees, turning his head, feeling for a pulse, pulling his eyelids back to examine his ice-chip eyes for shock. They were bloodshot but the pupils flexed at her intrusion, and Jack swatted at her weakly.

"Go 'way."

"Jesus, Jack," Pete breathed, sitting back on her heels.

Jack rolled on to his back and moaned, throwing a hand over his eyes.

"*He's* got fuck-all to do with this. I'm bloody dying. You're an evil spawn of witches, Pete Caldecott."

Pete rolled a clean towel and slipped it under Jack's head. "You may be a lot of things, but dying isn't one. And the next time you call me a name, I'm putting my foot up your arse and leaving it there."

A smile flashed, the devil-grin. "Same little firecracker. Always liked that you weren't afraid of me."

"I—" Pete started, but Jack's face twisted, and then he lunged for the toilet and was violently sick.

Pete put a hand between Jack's shoulder blades, feeling the bones grind under the skin as he retched. He was burning hot, but his sweat was like ice water.

"I just need a little," Jack pleaded as he pressed his forehead against the porcelain rim. "Just a little to take the edge off. It's been *hours,* Pete. Fucking *days.*"

"No," said Pete without hesitation.

"Fuck you!" Jack screamed, driving his fists into the tile floor of the bathroom. His knuckles left bloody smears.

"Fine," Pete said, standing. "You'll either pull through it or you won't. But you did this to yourself, Jack, and if you wanted to keep spiraling down toward the rock fucking bottom, you should have kept your bloody mouth shut about Bridget."

Jack glared at her, mouth opening to spew another curse, but his jaw slackened. "Pete," he said softly. "Pete, move out of the way."

Pete glanced behind her, feeling a twinge of ice on the base of her neck. Jack's pupils dilated until his eyes were wormholes rimmed with frost. "Did someone die in your flat?" he whispered. "A man, your height, dark visage and eyes?"

Because it was Jack, and not anyone else, Pete found herself nodding as the frost fingers spread out to grip her spine. "Yes, but that has to be forty years ago now."

Jack's thin chest fluttered as he sucked in a wavering breath. "Get away from him," he told Pete. "He's hungry."

Pete's sensible ballet flats were rooted to the tile, and even though her instincts were screaming in concert, a million pinpricks over her skin and psyche, she couldn't move.

"Behind me," Jack rasped. "Move your arse, woman!"

She'd never heard Jack so dead serious, and it snapped the frozen spell. Pete scrabbled across the sweat-slicked tile and crouched behind Jack against the shower curtain, which rustled like a gale had just blown through the bathroom.

Nothing was behind her. Pete felt instantly ridiculous, the ice on her skin replaced by the flush of a paranoid caught out. "Jack . . ." She sighed. "Bloody hell, don't do that to me."

"*Shut* it," he said urgently, still fixated on the corner near the door. "Oh, yes. You're a nasty one, aren't you? Been starving and starving all these years, you fucking shadow with teeth. Well, bollocks to you."

The sense of evil just over the left shoulder returned full-force and Pete saw the air in the spot where she'd stood *shimmer,* as if something were trying to push into the realm of sight through sheer malevolence. "Oh, God," she said, because He was the first powerful thing that jumped to mind.

"Forget about that," said Jack. He dipped an index finger in the ruddy smear he'd left on the tiles and began to draw, a radius filled with swirling symbols that shifted and blended into something strong and binding, like the iron scrollwork on a castle's gate.

The air crackled and rippled, and blackness began to crowd in through the seams in the walls, the drain and faucet of Pete's bathroom sink, a shadowy smoke-ether that brought with it whispers and fluttering cries, phrases that twisted just out of hearing.

Jack's jaw set, bone jumping under the skin. "Think you're a smart bastard, do you?"

"I don't think this is working," Pete murmured. Jack was expanding another set of symbols, barely integral when drawn with his shaking fingers.

The smoke filled the bathroom, always at the edges of Pete's vision, narrowing it down into a tunnel the size of a shilling coin. The babble of unearthly voices was joined by smells, and feelings—turned earth, blood-spattered sheets, tiny fingers on Pete's skin and sliding through her hair.

She gripped Jack's shoulder. "For fuck's sake, Jack, I do not want to die on the floor of my loo."

And his hand stopped shaking, and his breathing calmed, and with that the circle resolved as bright and solid as if it had been carved into the tiles. The shimmering malice dissolved like dust motes in a bar of sun, and fast as they'd seeped into the realm of the real, the whispers and the smells and the tiny grasping fingers and fangs were gone.

Jack slumped. "Bloody hell. You couldn't have brought me someplace safer, like, say, the fucking Tower?"

"I . . ." Pete pressed her hands over her nose and mouth and forced herself into a mold of composure she felt ill suited to fit. "I have no idea what that was."

"*That,*" said Jack, "is what happens when I don't get my fix."

"You . . ." Pete looked at the corner where the presense had spread its oily sheen, and back at Jack. "You see . . . whatever that was?"

"Shade," said Jack. "Ghost, if you want to be pedestrian about it. A poxy one allowed to hang about for far too long.

Bugger all, didn't you have this place cleansed before you moved in?"

"It never occurred to me," said Pete, although more than once on nights when rain blurred the streetlamps outside into nightmare gloom or the telly turned on by itself, she'd thought about it. The circle of protection Jack could chalk, and grow strong as iron. The five-pointed silver circlet Mum had always worn at her throat.

Jack rolled on his side, eyes half-closed like he'd just taken the purest hit of his life. "Christ on a motorbike. I'm bloody exhausted. If I get back in the bed, could you restrain your kinky self from handcuffing me again?"

Having seen what she had, just then, Pete simply nodded. "You won't try to run away?"

"Pete, I'm two breaths from shaking hands with the reaper. Don't be fucking stupid."

"Back to being a git, I see," said Pete. "Maybe there is hope, after all."

Jack slept for a long time after Pete laid him back in her bed, and she sat at awkward angles in the wicker chair next to him, attempting to make sense of departmental e-mails on her laptop and ignore the fact that they had perhaps a day and a half left if the kidnapper worked according to method. Every time she tried to focus on the pixels, her vision shimmered and blurred just like the shade that had almost appeared.

Just as nebulous were her thoughts, the tails and fragments of questions that wouldn't be answered. Jack moaned in his sleep, his fever dreams gripping his body and causing his hands to lash out under the sheets.

Pete put a hand on his shoulder. "All right. No one's here except me."

Dreaming, he didn't have the wherefore to offer venom in return, and Pete found herself curiously saddened by this. She might never find out what had intervened to make

Jack hate her, and this illusion was all she had, until Patrick and Diana were found. If they were found.

The thought stirred a blacker feeling in her than the aura of any shade.

Chapter 12

In Pete's dream, Patrick and Diana reached out to her with black and sticky fingers, their mouths smeared with offal as they feasted on the long-dead bodies of those who had come to this tomb before her. Pete tried to run but every way was bricked over, a blank wall rife with spiderwebs and scrabble marks dug by human fingernails.

The shadows at the far end of the tomb rippled and parted and the crowned figure, robed in bloody and rotted burial shrouds, floated forward.

He sees you, Pete Caldecott, whispered Bridget Killigan. And he held out his hand, curled around something that fluttered and oozed blood between his knotty fingers. "Take it. Take what was always yours, tattered girl. Be mine, and whole."

Pete pressed against the wall, grit working its way down her neck, tiny bugs and specks of graveyard dirt. A rush of wind blew through the crypt, the ends of the robed thing flapping on white bone joints, revealing armor washed clean against his rotted skeleton. Patrick and Diana looked up in concert. Smoke boiled across the floor and coalesced into the form of a man, a man with burning silver eyes that seared Pete's mind, not with heat but with a cold that could stop her heart. She felt a delicate shattering behind her skull, and then her mobile started to ring.

Pete's laptop slid to the floor as she bolted awake, her mobile trilling and dancing on the bedside table. Jack reached out in his sleep and swatted at it.

"Hallo," Pete mumbled, trying to sound like she hadn't been nodding. Dreaming.

"Well, you're hard enough to get hold of!" Terry snapped.

"Terry." Pete wondered that she was relieved he'd called. He'd woken her up. That was what mattered.

"I've faxed the new papers to your desk."

Pete checked on Jack, whose trembling had ceased for the moment, and slipped into the hallway, shutting the bedroom door. "I'm not at work, Terry."

She could hear the sneer coming down the line. "Then where on earth are you? It's not like you to go anywhere off your little track from flat to work and back again."

"Oh, for fuck's sake, Terry. Grow up." Pete slapped her mobile shut. Jack groaned, and she returned to the bedside, feeling his pulse and his hot, gleaming forehead. The worst of the withdrawal was past him, *please, God, let it be over,* and when he woke he'd have raging flu symptoms and a craving like iron claws in his skull, but he'd be sober, and help her, before Patrick and Diana were lost.

Pete used a washcloth to brush Jack's sweat-soaked hair away from his face, and went into the sitting room to let him sleep for as long as she could allow. She tried to eat what takeaway hadn't gone dodgy. Cold aloo gobi did nothing for the state of her stomach, nervous as a pacing cat. Ollie called, and she let her mobile ring through to voice mail, because she didn't have any answers for him.

Pete swept up the broken glass from Terry's picture just to move, and after a second of consideration dropped the snapshot into the bin. It had been taken the day after Pete was promoted to detective inspector, and the day before

Terry had asked her to marry him. A moment when things were right and good, and they were so no longer. The picture had no place now that Jack had reentered her life, and her flat.

She straightened up Jack's other messes but she couldn't calm down. Sleeping in the middle of the day had put her at odds, plus the slumbering but screaming presence of the man himself in her bedroom.

Finally, when she knew she'd go mad if she spent another second pacing the floor, back and forth past the bedroom door, she made up the sofa and lay in the twilight, watching the hands of the clock tick toward midnight.

Chapter 13

The sofa wasn't conducive to dreaming, and Pete was glad. She awoke at the first rays of the sun and put the kettle on, collecting Patrick and Diana's case files.

She pushed open the bedroom door with her foot. "Jack?"

He was curled on his side with the blankets kicked back, shaking and sweating as if he were being held to an invisible flame. He'd gotten worse, inexplicably so. Pete felt frustrated tears building and blinked them away.

She juggled her two mugs and armload of folders and shook his shoulder. "Jack, wake up."

His eyes flicked open and then he pressed his fists to his temples. "Jesus, *listen* to them all . . ."

"Brought you some tea," said Pete. "I thought we might go over the case files, see if you can glean anything?" The words hung in the air, fragile, and Pete felt the tension shatter them.

"There's a woman screaming," Jack muttered. "Over and over, screaming and rocking while she clutches the stillborn to her chest." He ground his teeth together and shouted, "Fucking *shut up,* the lot of you! You'll drive a man mad!"

"What do you hear?" Pete asked.

"Everything," Jack moaned. "Every dead thing that I

could shut off with a hit is in my head and it's going to *explode*."

Pete sipped at her tea because she didn't know what to say and burned her tongue. "You've always seen things, Jack?"

"Always," he agreed, panting as his fever fluctuated between arctic and hellfire.

"How did you shut it out, before?" Pete asked. "I know you weren't using when we knew each other."

"Wasn't as bad," Jack muttered. "Wasn't as *loud*. I'd get flashes, see shades, kiddy stuff. Nothing . . . nothing like this fucking *bombardment* until . . . that day we were together."

"What happened in that tomb, Jack?" Pete asked quietly. "What did we do?" Cloudy memories that she'd written off to trauma threatened to burst through, shadows that stained her real and normal existence crept in from all corners. Pete gritted her teeth and did her best to shut it out.

Jack stared past her into nothing, eyes floating and empty. Eventually they fluttered and closed, and his breathing smoothed into sleep. "Bollocks," Pete muttered.

Jack spent the day and most of the night in and out, wandering between worlds, muttering snatches of disembodied conversations. Sometimes he sobbed, or shook, and Pete could never be sure if it was the drugs or what he was seeing.

The unpleasant realization of *If he dies, it's on my head* made itself known after the third time Jack had thrown up in as many hours, barely more than bile and a little blood. He hadn't eaten since the curry the first night.

"Jack," she whispered, touching his arm. It was dry now, smooth and cool, like a dead man's skin that had lain outside under a winter moon. He jerked under her, clawing at his own throat and chest.

Pete gripped Jack's bicep and bent close to his ear. "If you die on me again, Jack Winter, you'd better believe I'm coming into hell after you."

She started as Jack wrapped his fingers around her wrist, eyes open in the dark and shining blackly into hers. "That which you do not understand is not yours to offer," he rasped in a voice not his own. Then he fell back onto the mattress, and Pete jerked awake.

Finally, when dawn rolled over the edge of the window and through the gaps in the shades again, Pete staggered to the sofa, which seemed remarkably welcoming now, and collapsed on her side, weariness permeating down to her bones. She slept a little, hearing the daylight rattles of the flat and the sound of lorries and people in the street, the weak interplay of cloud-shrouded sunlight stroking across her eyelids every so often.

The springs in the sofa defeated her, finally, and Pete muttered curses as she went to forage for caffeine.

Jack sat at the kitchen table wearing denim and one of Terry's polos, bulging around his wasted torso, drinking a cup of tea and smoking a fag. Pete blinked once to ensure it wasn't just another dream.

"You're awake," Jack said helpfully.

"And you're unpleasant," said Pete. "Of course I'm awake."

"There's some hot water left," Jack said, exhaling. Pete cast a glance at the packet on the table.

"Are those my Parliaments?"

Jack nodded, dragging deeply. "Can't expect me to live a life completely free of vices, luv." His hand was almost steady. A person would have to be looking to catch the tremor or see Jack's graveyard pallor for sickness rather than affectation.

Pete snatched up the packet and shoved it in the pocket of her bathrobe. "Where did you get these?"

"From your bag," said Jack. He extinguished the butt on the table, leaving a long coal-colored streak on the vinyl.

"If this is what you're like off the junk," Pete said, "it's no wonder you did it for all those years."

"I apologize," said Jack with a bitter twist to the words. "It was bad and rude of me to go through your things. And to use your fine furniture as an ashtray." He held up one palm with fingers splayed. "Next time I'll use me hand."

White scars, ragged circles, dotted Jack's left palm and wrist. Pete nearly lost her grip on her tea mug. "God, Jack, what did you do that for?"

"Various things." He shrugged. "Got pissed, did it for a laugh. For a while pain was the best way I could think to keep the talent under control."

"That's what lets you see dead things?" Pete lit a Parliament of her own. "Talent's a funny word to use."

"So is 'mage,' but I'm that, too."

Pete exhaled. "I'm glad you're feeling better."

"Not really," said Jack. "Usually when I quit I nick some methadone or poppers off one of the other layabouts at the squat, makes things a bit easier. You're a real hellcat, making me go cold turkey like that."

"It was the only way you were going to help me," said Pete.

"Yes," agreed Jack. "And for being utterly cold as coffin nails, you get my grudging respect. But don't you make the mistake of thinking I'm fond of you, or we're squared with each other. Not after you tricked me like that."

"Any trickery I probably learned from you," said Pete. "Now, this isn't a hotel, so what are you going to do to help me find Patrick and Diana? We've got less than a day."

Jack narrowed his eyes at her, rocking his chair back on its hind legs. Just as Pete was getting ready to scream at his inscrutability he said, "Got a pen?"

She handed him the one from her message pad silently and he scribbled on the back of a Boots receipt. "Go here and get me the *Grimoire de Spiritus,* Hatchett's *Dictionary of Unfriendly Entities,* and the black briefcase that's hidden behind the LP of *Dark Side of the Moon.* Understand?"

Pete looked at the Bayswater address. "Why do you need some dodgy books and a briefcase? Can't you do what you did with Bridget?"

"This *is* what I did for Bridget . . . well, most of it at any rate. Look, do you want to find the sodding brats with all their vital parts or not?"

Pete sighed and ran water over her cigarette to extinguish it. "All right. Back in an hour."

Chapter 14

The address belonged to a set of flats thin and sooty as a Victorian chimney sweep. The crinkled moon face of an old woman stared at Pete from the second floor before a sad floral-sprigged curtain twitched shut.

Pete climbed five flights that smelled of smoke and too many cabbage dinners until she found the door to number 57. She'd expected a shriveled old man, a gnome with a Gandalf hairdo and a sage twinkle in his eye, so the large Rastafarian who opened the door raised her eyebrow. Just a little, though.

He looked Pete up and down, flashing a gold front tooth. "May I 'elp you?"

"I . . ." said Pete. Then, with a thrust of her chin, "Jack Winter sent me."

"Jack Winter," said the Rasta. It came out soft and heavy with thought. *Jahck*. Pete desperately hoped that the man wasn't someone Jack had managed to get after him during the time he'd been away.

"He asked me to get some books for him," Pete elaborated. "And a briefcase."

A grin split the Rasta's face. "You much more beautiful than the last one who come around on Jack Winter's orders, miss. Come you in."

Pete stepped over the threshold, feeling inexplicably comfortable when she did so. The flat was spare of furniture and had only one rag rug on the scarred floor. The narrow windows were leaded and let in a weak trickle of light. What the flat did have was a proliferation of oddities that would cause P. T. Barnum to spasm with joy—jars and boxes on the wall-to-wall cases, books piled to Pete's chin in the corner, books on every surface, along with rows and rows of vinyl records and an old '78 turntable. Connor had listened to Elton John's early albums on his. It was in the hospital room when he died, needle ready to drop on "Goodbye, Yellow Brick Road."

"What he send you for? You want tea maybe, and a sausage roll?" asked the Rasta, peering at Pete around the doorjamb leading deeper into the flat.

"No, no, thank you," she said. "In a bit of a hurry, you know."

"Have your look, then." He gestured at the bookshelves. "I have business to attend to."

"I . . . well, thanks," Pete called as she heard a door close deeper in the flat. After a moment a luxurious scent, dark and secret-tinged as a lover's trysting place under ancient trees, drifted into the main room.

Pete found the books easily enough, and after digging through a pile of LPs on the bookcase found a scratched copy of *Dark Side of the Moon.* Behind it, sitting dusty and patient as a faithful retainer on the shelf, was a plain black briefcase. Something rattled like knucklebones when Pete picked it up, and she decided not to get unduly curious until she had her privacy.

She straightened up and found herself face-to-face with a head in a jar. It looked like it had been in the jar for at least a hundred years. The skin was sallow and pickled, and the eyes gazed at nothing through their cataract film. "You bloody owe me, Jack," Pete muttered. She shouted, "Got everything, thanks!" to the silent flat. No one answered before she took her leave, but she could swear the head was grinning at her.

Chapter 15

She called, "I'm back," to the silence of the flat when she opened her door again. Jack was sacked out on the sofa, his blond head dipped to his chest, light tremors running through his shoulders all the way down to the tips of his fingers.

Pete dumped the books and the briefcase on the floor by her front door and hurried over, kneeling down. "Jack? Jack, what's wrong?"

"Her wrists are bleeding and bleeding," Jack muttered. "It's sliding down her arms in little red rivers, swirling away down the pipes, and we're all drinking it, we're all watching and waiting for her to raise the blade and cut again."

Pete grasped his shoulders, giving a shake. "It's not real, Jack." She would have to hunt down the estate agent who sold her and Terry this flat and bloody strangle the man. First the shade and now this, some bird who had slashed herself in Pete's bathtub.

"I can hear her crying," Jack whispered.

"I got your briefcase," said Pete desperately. "Jack, please just talk to me."

He rubbed his hands over his face and with great effort met Pete's eyes. "Lawrence didn't give you any trouble?"

"His manners far exceed yours," Pete said, handing Jack the books and the briefcase.

One side of Jack's mouth curved. It was a far cry from the devil-grin, but Pete took what she could get.

"Right," said Jack, running his fingertips along the scarred leather of the briefcase. His caress revealed the case was locked and bore no combination knobs, just an engraved plate that depicted a snake, eating its own tail.

"What's in there?" said Pete.

"Something of mine," said Jack.

"Seems like you don't want anyone inside," Pete observed.

"Oh, them that know, know better than to go into anything *I* own," said Jack. "This bloody lock was from Marius Cross, the previous owner."

Pete had a good idea of what had happened to Marius Cross, locked briefcase or no. "Did you take it from him?"

"From his cold body," said Jack. "Believe me, luv, he had no need of it."

"Let's just get on with this," said Pete, ignoring the gnawing in her gut, the same as when she'd stood in the circle on the tomb floor.

"Be a luv and get me a needle, or a sharp paring knife . . . something to prick meself with," said Jack. Pete spread her hands out, already shaking her head.

"No, Jack. No more blood." Did he think she was stone stupid, after the last time?

"Every second you spend arguing with me is another one that the precious hope of our nation's future has lost," said Jack sensibly.

"You're not supposed to make even a little sense," Pete muttered. She rummaged inside her ottoman's storage for the sewing kit and handed Jack a needle. "It's disconcerting."

"Seamstressing is never a hobby I pegged as one of yours," said Jack. He pricked himself without a wince or a sigh and rubbed his bloody finger pad along the lock. The snake uncoiled and the case gave three clicks.

"It was Terry's kit," said Pete. "His shirts were hand tailored, so he mended them if they got damaged."

"Ponce." Jack snorted. The briefcase lid popped up, ominous as a crocodile's mouth.

"Just because someone can put things back together instead of breaking them down to shambles doesn't make that someone a ponce," Pete snapped. "You're a real sod, Jack."

"That's hardly news, luv." He looked at her over the battered leather of the case. "You're doing a deal to defend some bugger that you dumped out on his arse."

Pete rubbed her thumbs against her temples. Jack took a flat mirror and a velvet sack out from the case. The sack rattled again, like a snake.

"For your information," she said quietly, "Terry left me."

"Not surprising, that," said Jack. "I just guessed you'd be the one to do the leaving, since you seemed to be a hand at it when I knew you last."

"Oh, *bugger* you," Pete snapped. "You and your little bag of marbles." Just when Jack seemed to be letting his rage go, it burst forth again, like an infection of bad spirit.

"It's not marbles," said Jack. He set the mirror on the ottoman and shook the bag once, giving Pete a grin that made her feel cold rather than comforted.

"What is it, then?"

"Bones, luv," said Jack. He dumped out the sack. The white chips hit mirror glass with a death rattle. "It's a bag of bones."

Pete flinched away from them instinctively, feeling a frisson of cold crackling intensity from the bones, each one round with a black center where the marrow had been picked out. They had been polished to a high shine and made a sound like beads as Jack gathered them up and rattled them between his fists. "Always feel so bloody silly doing this. Marius was an old *vaudun,* and they do like their theatrics and their headless chickens."

"Please tell me we don't have to kill birds to get a result," Pete muttered. She was starting to feel foolish rather than bothered by Jack and his shaking of the bones. This was a scene she'd watched in too many silly films for it to carry the least hint of sincerity.

"Don't be stupid," Jack said. "Just get the brats' pictures and put them on the mirror so I have something to focus on, and stand bloody well back."

Pete extracted the wallet-sized snapshots of Patrick and Diana from their case files, and placed them carefully on the mirror, which was rimmed with a black wooden frame and was as cold as mercury in arctic air. The spine of fear, from the deep place in her mind where her nightmares lived, pricked Pete again and she drew back, as far as she could without making it outwardly obvious she was having doubts.

Jack started to shake the bones faster, the clacking blending into a low whir, and Pete thought his eyes had rolled back in his head until she realized he was still looking dead ahead, and white was rubbing out the blue of his irises, stealing out from the center of his eyes like frost.

"Jack?" Pete said hesitantly. She felt as if the air were pushing in on her, something inexplicable *rising* in the room as Jack's head tilted back and his hands rattled like he was seizing.

"Jack!" Pete cried as he stiffened and then with a spasmodic gasp flung the bones down onto the mirror and the pictures of the children.

The bones stayed where they fell, as if they were magnets. Pete thought she caught a glimpse of a dark reflection in the mirror before Jack sighed and rotated his head from side to side. "Fucking trances. Always give me neck a cramp."

The reflection flapped its wings and disappeared. It would have been less than a single frame of film. Pete allowed herself to be sure she'd imagined it. Jack's witchfire and his visions were his things. She did not see them, and she did not want to.

"That's it, then?" she said. Her voice came out weak and soft and she swallowed to make it hard again. "That seemed awfully simple."

Jack gave her a skewering glance before he hunched to examine the bones. He'd started to shiver again. "Well, it wasn't, so sod off."

"You can use that blanket on the back of the sofa if you like," said Pete. Jack sneezed, and used a corner of the blanket to blow his nose.

"Cheers." He passed his hand over the bones, fingers splayed, once, twice, three times. "Ah," he said at last, the syllable acres from pleased.

"No good?" Pete deflated inwardly, space containing the wild hope that Jack could repeat his magic with Bridget on the new missing children, that his pithy pronouncement would roll forth and everything would be real and simple again, collapsing.

"It's bloody good," said Jack. "But you're not going to like it. Got a city map?"

Pete fetched the battered one from her desk, marked in several places with notes from old cases. Jack tried to unfold it with his shivery fingers, managed it on the second try, and jabbed his finger at a spot near the heart of the city. "The kids are there."

Pete squinted to read "Brompton Cemetery." "I know the area," she said. "Not too far from where I grew up, that." She looked at Jack. "You're sure?"

"'Course I'm bloody sure," Jack muttered. He sniffled and rubbed the back of his hand against his nose. His eyes were red-rimmed and every few seconds he shivered as though a winter wind were cutting his flesh, but his cheeks weren't as yellow and sick as they'd been half a day before, and his movements had more life—less a listless marionette, more of the Jack she remembered. "All right," said Pete. She dug in her bag for her mobile and started to dial Ollie Heath. "What's the part I'm not going to like?"

Jack made another finger-pass over the bones, and another breath of cold trailed up Pete's spine. "There's black magic around the children," said Jack. "More specifically, them that make use of black magic. Sorcerers."

Pete kept her expression composed. "I think I can handle a few gits in black capes drawing pentagrams, Jack."

"You don't understand." He sighed, as if she'd just told him London was the capital of France. "If sorcerers took the children, something is moving. You said Bridget Killigan was blinded?"

"She's got a kind of amnesia, too," said Pete.

We went to see the old Cold Man. He lives on the murky path, just around the bend.

"Ah, tits," Jack muttered. "Be prepared, Pete—the people that snatched the brats are dangerous and probably won't be in the best humor when we find them. Something's up, mark my words. I can feel it shifting in the lines—there's a darkness clustering around these kids, and the first one, too. Only scried for her because the ghost voices were cutting into the fix and I was trying to make 'em shut it." He rubbed his arms, up and down, rhythmic unconscious strokes. "Any idea how strong a shade has to be to break through an opiate high, Pete? Strong enough to light up the O2. Whole land of the dead is buzzing, and it's the thunder of the oncoming storm." His eyes were bright as he talked, and his body vibrated like a string, the frantic energy of a street preacher.

"What d'you mean 'when we find them'?" she asked Jack. "You're bloody well not coming along on an open investigation."

Jack smirked, lacing his hands behind his head. A little sweat gleamed on his forehead, and he coughed, but he'd stopped shaking for the time. "Planning to be cavalry all by yourself?"

"I very well could be," Pete said. "I'm not an incompetent."

"Yeah, but you won't go on your own," said Jack. He stood up, swaying but walking, and pulled his jackboots on. "You know that I'm right, and there's bad magic running through this entire thing. You'll take me along because you don't want to be staring into the night alone."

Pete started to protest, but Jack stopped lacing his boots and gave her a pained half-smile. "It's not a weakness, Pete—nobody wants that."

If it were anyone else, she would swear he was trying to be a comfort.

It would be far less disconcerting if Jack weren't so often right about her thoughts and secrets, but she *didn't* very well want to go bursting in on kidnappers alone, in a graveyard, at night. Newell would have her arse for going at this off the book. "Why do you care about these kids?" she demanded. "You didn't even want to help me. Just listening in to ghosts, isn't that right? Nothing selfless about you, not an ounce."

Jack shook his head. "We're not on about me, now." He lifted one bone-sharp shoulder. "If sorcerers are in the mix I might have a laugh, at least. Tick-tock, Inspector. You're the one banging on about time running out."

"I hate you," Pete mumbled, grabbing her coat from the hook and a torch from her hall table. After a moment's debate she also plucked her handcuffs out and hooked them to her belt. Feeble protection against what she thought might be waiting for them even in her own mind.

Jack shrugged into his leather, chains rattling on pyramid spikes, and followed Pete out of the flat. "I'll live with you hating me. At least that way, we're even."

Chapter 16

The section of Brompton Jack led her to was small and personal, fallen out of use as London marched ever forward, forgetting its left-behind dead. Back gardens and leaning brick flats crowded in against the mossy walls.

"Some Goth freak has his dream view, eh?" said Jack as he rattled the padlock on a rusty crypt gate. "You got a wrench in the Mini? I know a few blokes who'd pay cold hard sterling for ground bones and graveyard dust."

Pete pinched between her eyes. "I'm not even going to dignify that."

Jack flashed her a closemouthed smile. "Good girl. Guess that's why you're the copper, eh?"

"I have moments," Pete agreed. She walked again, pushing aside waist-high weeds as the path narrowed and the tombs leaned in, crumbling from their foundations. Jack caught her wrist.

"Oi. What do you think you're doing? I'll go first."

"Sod off, it's not the bloody Victorian era," said Pete, swatting away tiny branches clawing for her face and hair. Muttering, Jack followed her through a trampled gap.

Before them, headstones tilted crazily from dead grass, a path to the two crypts at the back of the plot overgrown with stinging nettles. Pete felt the breath of ghosts brushing her cheeks, the sighs of the long-forgotten dead disturbing this silent patch of earth. She shivered. It had been much better not knowing.

Jack winced and rubbed his hands over his eyes. "You should've let me have the heroin, Pete."

"Be quiet," Pete hissed. Though it was almost invisible under the misty glow from the streetlamps, she was sure candlelight flickered from the mausoleum on the left. She touched Jack's arm. "Someone else is here."

An itchy feeling started between her shoulder blades, that of a convenient setup. *Anything* could be waiting in the sagging brick structure, none of the possibilities pleasant or inclined to let her go alive.

Jack squinted at the candlelit crypt. "Got a fag?"

Pete handed one over. Jack's face flickered briefly skeletal as he lit the Parliament. "Right. Let's go get your bloody brats."

"Wait!" Pete whipped him around a full one hundred eighty degrees when she snatched at his arm. She'd forgotten for a moment how light he was.

Jack glared and Pete explained, "We're not just going to rush in. Procedures to follow, plus we don't know what's in there."

"Black magic," said Jack. "Whole place stinks of it. Feels like cobweb on your face."

"Whatever the case, we should use caution," said Pete. "In the interest of not getting our bloody heads blown off."

"Whoever has the kids isn't going to give us a written invite," said Jack. "Sorcerers understand force, Pete, so I'm going to give it to them."

"But we don't know how many of them there are!" Pete whispered as Jack jerked free and strode across the brown grass crackled with early frost, crushing it under his soles.

"Damned stupid impulsive arrogant sod," Pete hissed, running after him.

Jack met the door with a planted foot, black wood shattering under his kick. Dry rot and dust swirled around Jack, turning his skinny dark-clad frame to a ghost in its own right.

Pete fetched up at his shoulder, shouting "Police!" belatedly, praying that in addition to whatever occult trappings the kidnappers carried, they hadn't gotten their hands on guns.

The two men at the center of the crypt were young— Pete noticed that first. One still had a rash of pimples up his right cheek, and their faces weren't hard or cold enough to hide the rush of guilty fear in their eyes. In a restaurant or club, they'd be any two university students trying too hard, in expensive black jackets and black denim, silver charms dangling around their necks, identical spinning-wheel shapes that looked like poisonous spiders.

One found his voice, anger twisting it. "Who the fuck are you lot?"

Jack smirked. "I'm Jack Winter, and I'm here to make your worst bloody nightmares come true."

The two black-clad boys looked at Jack in askance, then each other, questioning. The bepimpled one shrugged ignorance. Then they both laughed in Jack's face.

Pete placed a hand on Jack's shoulder. He shook under her, a leaf raging in the face of a gale. "What have you done with Patrick Dumbershall and Diana Leroy?" she asked evenly. "I warn you, lying at this juncture is only going to make me angry enough to hurt you. Both of you. Badly."

Looks traded again, a nervous shuffling of feet on the stone floor of the crypt. The sound unpleasantly evoked Pete's dream. *Take what is yours, Pete Caldecott.*

"Go bugger yourself," the second spoke up. "We ain't doing anything wrong."

"I'm an inspector with the Metropolitan Police and my associate has identified you as the kidnappers of two children," said Pete, stepping forward. "Those two facts plus you lot hanging about this tomb add up to me arresting you. Hands on heads, and face the wall."

Before she could move, Pete felt electricity roil upward from her gut, through her spine, exploding against her brain like a hit to the temple. *Power.* Like she'd felt only once when she faced Jack across the clumsily chalked circle twelve years before. In her second of hesitation, the sorcerer's magic slammed into her.

Wind, like a wall, like seeing the closed lid of the empty coffin at Jack's funeral, snatched Pete and sent her tumbling backward to land in the dirt at Jack's feet.

The sorcerer smiled, folding his hands together like a gun and drawing in a breath to say words of power.

He never got the chance.

Jack held out his right hand with fingers splayed, like he was framing a photograph. Then he twisted his hand, and the sorcerer on the right dropped to his knees, face twisted in supplication.

"I . . . what . . ." His words degenerated into breathless gurgling.

Jack took a step toward the fallen boy, and Pete felt the second sorcerer draw on the black well of magic that swirled just beyond sight and sound. She closed the distance between herself and the sorcerer and put a right cross into his half-shaven jaw. A twinge of separation stabbed her between her first and second knuckle. The sorcerer sat down hard, eyes swimming. Pete flexed her hand and said, "Stay put unless you want to take your means through a plastic straw for the foreseeable future."

The victim of Jack's attention clawed at his throat, whimpering. Pete perceived a darkness hovering over Jack and the sorcerer, like the thing in the scrying mirror, a hooded and robed figure who stared impassively with obsidian bird's eyes.

Jack spoke and shattered the vision. "I've stopped your

heart, you little cunt-rag. Would you like me to make your blood come out of your eyes next? Your coffin will be closed and padlocked when I'm done." Jack clenched his fingers again and the man screamed, trails of blood oozing from his nose, his mouth, red tears forming and sliding down his face.

"Still laughing at me now, you boss-eyed wanker?" Jack snarled.

"Jack," said Pete. The expression of rage on Jack's face she'd never seen, not even when he'd hit a skinhead in Fiver's with his microphone stand during a brawl. Not that the Nazi hadn't deserved it. Not that the kidnapper didn't, now. But watching Jack torture the boy turned Pete's stomach, and she gripped him hard at the elbow. "Jack, *stop*."

He blinked at Pete, almost like she'd just turned visible. "Fine," he muttered. "No fun any longer, anyway." He snapped his fingers, and the sorcerer jerked and went still.

Pete felt as if her own blood had drained right along with the boy's. "Jack," she whispered, papery. "Did you kill him?"

"Hm? Yeah, probably," Jack said with a thin smile. "Not a great loss to the gene pool, trust me."

Bloody hell. Bollocks, bugger, and fuck-all to that, Pete's logical half screamed. Jack, innocent and angry Jack, had killed another human being.

A kidnapper. Someone who would blind an eight-year-old girl. Bridget Killigan turned her face to Pete, and hissed at her to let the sorcerer die.

"Tell me where the fucking children are before he does worse to you," Pete said aloud to the sorcerer she'd punched. Later, when she was alone and safeguarded, she could break down. Now, Patrick and Diana had no chance without her, the cold and unflappable detective inspector.

"G-gods . . ." the sorcerer quavered, looking like nothing but the frightened boy that he was. "We didn't . . . I mean, you can't just . . ."

"Your gods are not here for you," Pete rasped. *"Tell me now."*

The sorcerer did what many other criminals of Pete's acquaintance had done before him—he scrambled to his feet and ran, catching his shoulder on the door of the crypt, falling, up and running again for Old Brompton Road.

Jack raised his right hand and Pete felt power pull against her mind like a tide. "Let him go," she said. Jack considered, the blank slaty look back in his eyes. *Coldhearted,* Pete identified it. She should chase the git herself, but then she'd leave both Jack and the dead sorcerer unattended. Pete flexed her fists in frustration as she watched the live specimen clear a garden wall and disappear from view.

"Yeah, all right," Jack said. "Run on, little man. Let him tell all his mates what went on here when they're buggering each other at the disco later on. Or applying eyeliner, or whatever it is those black little bastards do nowadays . . ."

"Will you shut up!" Pete shouted. Something skated across her hearing, just beyond her range. A dry, strangled cry. Sobbing, from under the stones. "They're here," Pete breathed with relief. "Patrick and Diana."

Jack blinked at her, a few tendrils of ice-white curling back from the color in his eyes. Then he was himself. "I don't see anything in this musty place."

"Under the flags," said Pete by way of explanation, casting around for the trapdoor to the lower level of the crypt.

"Here," said Jack, bracing himself against a sarcophagus carved with the relief of a small girl, smaller than Bridget Killigan or Diana. Pete joined him and pushed. Something in her back gave and she tried not to think about the next time she'd have to chase down a suspect.

The sarcophagus moved with a groan and a rending of stone. A huff of stale air greeted Pete, the essence of the long dead rushing into the wider night.

Crying continued, dry heaving sobs from a body whose

tears had long since dried up and was too shattered to speak.

"Patrick? Diana?" Pete shouted. "It's the police. Call out if you can hear me."

Nothing greeted her except the whispering sobs, and Pete cursed as she crouched and dropped herself into the darkness. The fall was longer than she expected and she landed hard, going down on one knee. "Bugger all!" Back, knee—she'd be in fantastic shape the next time something nasty showed up while she was helpless in the loo.

A blue shine blossomed above her, and Jack's face slid over the gap in the ceiling, witchfire dancing lazy ballet around the fingers of his right hand.

"Thanks," Pete whispered. The bottom level of the crypt was old, lichens and cobwebs undisturbed, warnings to trespassers that no one except the dead resided.

In the corner, chained to the ancient slabs by a pair of rusty manacles, Patrick and Diana crouched, naked and crying. The relief that coursed through Pete was indescribable, a slackening of muscles and a quickening of the heart.

Then she saw their eyes. They were gray in the witchfire, but under a good bulb they would be white. Blind. Drained.

Pete pressed her palms to her face. "Fuck it," she said quietly enough that no one except her and the angel and demon on her shoulders would hear. She had found the children, but their monotone whimpers told the same tale as Bridget Killigan—the fracturing of a mind and the ruination of a life.

"Anyone alive down there?" Jack called. "I'm going to feel awfully silly having topped this git if it was for nothing. 'Course, he did deserve exactly what he got . . ."

"I'm going to throw you my mobile," Pete said. She swallowed her defeat in a hard ball that scraped down her throat, and made sure she was in control. She was *Inspector Caldecott*. Finder of lost children. Logical. Unemotional.

And again, too late . . .

"Call the number in the memory for DI Heath and tell him you're with me. Give him the address."

"You're not going to bring the kids up?" Jack said, snatching her mobile out of the air when she threw it. He poked suspiciously at the keypad.

Pete bit her own lip hard enough to bleed it, steeled herself for the sight and turned back to the blinded children. "No. Not until someone brings the bolt cutters."

Chapter 17

"Bloody hell," said Ollie Heath. He passed a hand protectively over his thinning crop of hair and regarded Pete with pity. "We're not having much luck with this, are we, Caldecott?"

The ambulance carrying Patrick and Diana to A&E had long since pulled away, leaving police and forensics to go about their grim business. Pete patted herself down for a fag. The packet was empty. She cursed.

"Er, don't take this wrong," said Ollie, lowering his voice, "but who's the dodgy bloke you were with when you called in?" He inclined his head toward Jack. Jack was slouched against the outside of the graveyard gate, under the arch with the last of Pete's Parliaments in his mouth, eyes closed. Smoke drifted up and wreathed his face. He might have been a ghost himself.

"He's the tip," said Pete. Ollie's eyebrows crinkled his expansive forehead.

"Thought you said that was nothing."

"It turned into something."

"Not like you to hang about with an informant, Caldecott," said Ollie with concern.

"I know him," Pete admitted. "He's an all-right bloke." A lie, one that came without thinking. Nobody had asked probing questions about the dead sorcerer yet, and Pete intended to be the one to have the first attempt at Jack on that score. For all of Jack's hostility, she'd thought him harmless, and now the sorcerer's blood was on her.

"Listen, I'll finish up here if you'd like," said Ollie, laying a hand on her shoulder. Jack's eyes, hooded and black under the sodium light, focused on Ollie and Pete felt a distinct vibration, like a spirit had just breathed on the back of her neck.

"Thanks, Ollie," she said, ducking out from under his hand. Ollie Heath was truly harmless, slow and dedicated to the job. Pete wouldn't be unleashing Jack on him. "Ring me as soon as the hospital will let us talk to the kids, yeah?"

"Right," Ollie agreed. "Go get some sleep, Caldecott—you're chalky."

I just saw a ghost, Pete thought. She smiled at Ollie for appearances, and went to collect Jack.

"No one's yet asked about the dead man," she told him. He shrugged.

"I'll just tell 'em you did it. You're allowed to do stuff like that. Line of duty and all that shit, yeah?"

Pete pressed her lips into a line. "You won't be telling anyone anything, because we're going home." For once, Jack was silent and he slouched obediently back to the Mini. Pete couldn't decide if it was providence or bad luck that Jack was staying with her a time longer.

They drove through Chelsea's midnight streets in silence. The Mini's lights barely sliced the fog, and more than once Pete saw black shapes move among the swirling gloom. Her spine danced as the Mini bounced over cobbles in the old, walled part of the city, the cold heart hushed and damp as a shallow grave.

"There's something out there," she said aloud, not really knowing why the words came, but knowing she was right.

"Yeah," said Jack, leaning his forehead against the glass. "There is."

"You killed someone tonight," said Pete. "We should get it clear now—don't you dare do a thing like that again while you're on my watch. Do you want to land us both in jail?"

Jack sighed and managed to look mightily annoyed with his eyes closed and his head tilted back. "Anyone ever mention you're a terrible nag? You're going to put a husband straight into an early grave."

"I bloody well mean it, Jack!" Pete cried. "What gives you the right to be executioner?"

Jack opened his eyes and sat up. "Pull over."

"You all right?" asked Pete. The Mini's headlights illuminated windowless flat blocks and closed-down shops. She wasn't stopping unless there was a dire emergency.

"Just pull over and don't argue!" Jack snapped. Pete jerked the Mini to the curb and set the brake with a squeal. "What?"

Jack pointed to a tumbledown doorway with an unassuming lit sign over the frame: ROYAL OAKS PUBLIC HOUSE. "If you insist on moralizing at me about the dead toerag, I need a drink." He unfolded his skeleton from the Mini's passenger seat and stepped into the street, crossing in front of the car. Pete felt the passing urge to press on the gas and run him over, but instead she shut off the engine and dogged his heels into the pub.

It was low and smoky inside, but older than Pete realized—the long bartop was carved from the trunk of a single tree, all the knots and scars, and mellowed paneling held in ancient cigarette smoke. Concentric rings stained the plaster ceiling and a jukebox that looked like it had weathered the Blitz burbled out Elvis Costello. The basso bounce of "Watching the Detectives" blanketed conversation in secrecy.

Jack landed on the nearest stool with a clatter of feet and bony elbows. "Pint of bitters," he told the publican, "and a whisky."

"Just the whisky," Pete said, digging for her wallet. The publican was big and shave-headed, Latin phrases in ink cascading up both of his arms under his cutoff shirt. He grunted when he caught sight of Pete's warrant card as she paid the bill.

"Mother's milk." Jack sighed as he downed the whisky.

"Don't think you can get pissed enough to avoid talking to me," Pete warned.

"Fucking hell!" Jack said, slamming his glass on the bar. "What d'you want me to do, Pete, rush up to midnight mass and confess my sins? Would it help if I sent a tin of biscuits to the wake? What?"

"I'm not saying he didn't deserve it." Pete sighed. "He kidnapped those two children, and he was going to give us a bad time. Jack, I can't tell you how often I've wanted to do just what you did, to some wankstick or other I find on the job. But you can't—"

Jack's hand snaked out and wrapped around Pete's wrist, drawing her in until she could smell the old Parliaments and the new whisky that drifted off his skin. He squeezed until her bones grated and Pete cried out, attempting to pull free. But for that second, Jack was strong again, his eyes burning with the fire that consumed whatever it touched.

"Can't what, Pete?" he whispered with a snarl. "Can't go around killing people? Can't because that's what's good and right and proper? Well, Pete, I'll tell you a secret." And his eyes went from flaming to the deepest dark, inky and wicked. "We're not dealing with everyday thieves and killers any longer. This is the world of magic. People murder in this world, and people die, and it's the bloody way of things. I'm not sorry for putting a cold fist around that git's heart and he wouldn't be sorry if it were the reverse. Magic kills, Pete. *Get used to it.*"

After a long moment when all she heard was her heartbeat, Pete said, "You're hurting me."

Jack made a disgusted noise and released her. "'Sides, was I supposed to let those tossers laugh at me and do nothing? My name used to *mean* something to those demon-buggering gits. Bloody kids should learn some bloody respect."

Pete's hands still shook from the memory of the boy's face. She wrapped them around the whisky glass and downed her drink in a swallow. "Bit late for that, seeing as how one is on his way to the morgue."

"I mean," Jack continued, speaking more to his pint than to Pete, "in a way they were doing me a favor—I didn't realize until tonight how bad of a state things were in. I've been sodding *forgotten*, Pete! Do you have any idea what that means?"

"No fans accosting you in lifts?" Pete ventured. The whisky spread warm fingers through her and she was able to tamp down the tangle of fear and incomprehension that Jack's actions of the night had birthed.

Jack's mouth twisted upward on the left side. "You really had no idea, did you? About what I did before."

"No," said Pete honestly. Vaguely, she'd been aware that a lot of Jack's friends were older and more serious than one would typically suspect fans of the Poor Dead Bastards to be. And that Jack's tattoos never seemed exactly the same twice, and that when he was around the air tasted different, like just before a lightning storm.

"Makes no difference now, apparently," Jack grumbled in disgust.

"I'm just having a bloody hard time believing those two kids arranged this entire thing, and had the stomach to blind three children," said Pete.

"They didn't," said Jack. "Sorcerers are the outsourced

labor of magic—where there's a sorcerer, there's something jerking the strings and often as not it's something hungry and not human."

"Who would they be working for, then?" Pete said. "Tell me what I need to know to catch this bastard, Jack."

He drew on his pint and wiped his mouth on the back of his hand before he spoke. "I will say, those two were a deal more experienced than your bottom-level eclectic who stumbles into magic because he read some dusty book out of the library and is slagged off at life. The one who set you on your arse had talent."

"Wasted talent, seeing as he's *dead*," Pete muttered.

"Bugger, Pete, are we back to that already?" Jack rolled his eyes and emptied his pint, catching the publican's eye for another.

Pete made herself consider: If the sorcerer had been a Russian mafiya thug with a black-market gun, and he'd shot at Jack, would she have hesitated before she took the gun away and spent three shells in the man's heart? She would not. "I'll let it go for now," she told Jack. "But that better have been the first person you did in, Jack. If I find out this is a habit . . ."

"The first in a very long time," said Jack, holding up a hand to stop her. "Death follows me and I do my best to keep a hand's-breadth ahead, but it doesn't always work. You've seen direct evidence of that."

Pete nodded. "For the time being, I'll take that as at least partial truth. Who do you believe is giving the orders to snatch the children? And why children?"

"Aside from the fact that they're small and fit snug in the boot of a car?"

Pete glared at him. Jack's mouth curved on one side. "You need to grow back that amputated sense of humor, Inspector. The Yard's got it locked in a box."

"Talk, Jack," Pete snapped. "You don't enjoy my

company—you've made that much clear—so let's get this done as quickly as possible. Someone-or-thing who likes to mutilate children is still out there." How she would convince Ollie and DCI Newell of that fact was a bridge she'd build later.

"Fine, fine," he said. "Children are life. Vitality. Innocence. What have you. Some things, some hungry eldritch things, feed on it. They take away everything that keeps a child's soul unstained and when they've sucked the husk dry they take that vitality and they use it to make themselves strong again. Like taking all the blood and life from an unwilling donor, with side effects black enough to drive the donor mad."

We went to see the old Cold Man . . .

"What could it be, Jack?"

"Could be a lot of things. A more powerful sorcerer's flesh construct. A psychic feeder—someone who has the sight like me, but they give a touch along with their look." He rubbed his chin, making a sandpaper sound with his fingers against the dark stubble there. "But if it's taking children, it's probably an entity. A nonhuman, which means that you don't fuck about with it unless you want your sanity and soul siphoned out."

"Insane" would be Pete's definition for the entire evening up to this point, but she merely nodded because Jack seemed so relaxed and sure of his words, for the first time since she'd seen him again. "How do we find it? And stop it in its tracks?"

"Not easy," said Jack. "But I'll do it all the same. This beastie, this ghostly twat, seems to think that I'm awfully easy to tromp over and kick into the gutter for the sweepers. Tosser." He slammed his empty pint glass down. "It's my own fault, but no more—now I'm on the bloody warpath. Nobody dismisses me that easily."

"Why did you start looking for a fix?" Pete asked abruptly.

"If things were so sodding wonderful, why did you chuck it?"

Jack regarded her for a long time, not with the burning fury of before but with a sadness, the expression of someone looking back through a photo album of much happier times. "I was alone, Pete. Alone with none but the dead for company. At the time it seemed like the only way to keep meself from going insane," he said. "And it still does."

Pete felt an uncomfortable prickle down her spine as she saw the desire for a fix pass over Jack's face and alight in his reddened eyes. Here he was, wielding something akin to an Uzi with the flick of his fingers, and she had just kicked away his remaining support. Was she bloody insane?

No, she firmly reminded herself. No, Jack had survived suffering before, and he would again, because the alternative ended with Pete in a bloody mess on the floor of her flat while Jack roamed the streets of London with his sanity in long tatters and heroin burning a path through his blood.

"I'm on now," Jack said, his high dudgeon restored. "I'm not resting until I kick this cock-smear back into beyond the beyond." He raised an eyebrow. "If you're up for it, Pete, I could use the assist."

Pete laughed, and to her surprise carried on laughing for several moments. "You? You want *my* help?"

Jack swirled the dregs of his drink, shoulders hunching. "Don't see what's so bloody amusing."

Pete rubbed her forehead. No one in Scotland Yard would ever believe this was the real reason behind the blinded children. But it was what it was, and it also wasn't like she could let Jack go gallivanting off on his own. Who knew what kind of dark territory he'd go toward, on the warpath as he was?

"Thought you hated me," Pete said to him. "Thought the very sight of me made you sick, or some rot. That's what's funny, and also begs a question: Why should I put up with your shite a moment longer than I have to?"

The corners of his mouth twitched. The lager and the

whisky had made him more expansive. "Not every woman will fetch a sorcerer a punch across the gob when it gets thick. You could tell me to fuck off if you like. I'd probably deserve it."

"Make that *definitely*." Pete tapped her fingers on the knotty wood of the bar, knowing that she should leave Jack to his path and go back to her life.

But if she left him now, it would never be finished. She'd have her nightmares until the day she died. "But you helped me," she continued. "And I still have a case to close. So yes, I'll stay with you for now."

Just like time had flickered on a faulty circuit, the devil-grin spread over Jack's face and he was young again. "Brilliant. Knew you would."

Chapter 18

Just as before, Pete stood in front of the bleeding shrouded figure and he extended his hand, the waxy flesh dripping red as the thing in his fist beat desperately to be free.

"Take what belongs to you, Pete Caldecott," he hissed. "Take it before it destroys your tattered heart."

"I don't know what you want!" Pete cried desperately. She was very cold and looked down to find herself in her nightdress. So much for convenient dreaming.

"Take it," said the shroud-man. "It belongs to you. It has always belonged."

"She won't listen," purred a second voice, and from over the shrouded figure's shoulder the smoke rolled, gathering around Pete's ankles and forming into a human figure. "She won't see or hear. She's taken out her own eye with a hot poker made of memory. She's blind and dumb to us forever."

Pete knew it was impossible for a column of smoke to grin, but this one did, and its voice grated against her brain, like a thousand tiny screams echoed beneath it. "Run while you can, little girl," the figure hissed. "Run far and fast and don't ever sleep."

Then he reached for Pete—she knew instinctively that slit-throat voice and long grasping hands made it a *he*—and she screamed and fell backward, the ridiculous Victorian nightdress tangling her feet, sending her down into the grave-yard earth. It was soft and dozens of rotting hands wrapped around her arms and legs and *everywhere*. The shrouded figure drew a sword from the belt of his bloody armor and tried to save her, but she was pulled inward, into the grave, and the last thing she heard as she woke was the wicker man, the smoke, laughing and laughing and laughing.

"Pete!" Jack was shaking her, hard enough to snap teeth together.

She blinked, saw her flat, saw her sitting room, which really needed a good scrubbing. Cobwebs hung in all the corners.

Jack let go of her. "You were screaming in your sleep."

Pete pressed her fingers against her eyes. "I was dreaming about something worth screaming at."

Jack pressed a businesslike hand against her forehead. "You're burning up, luv," he said. "Sure it was a frightening dream and not a hot one?"

Pete swatted him on the arm when the mischief showed in his smile. "You're a great bloody help, you are."

"Can't have you keeling over in the middle of a dustup, can I?" said Jack. "However I may feel about you personally. Not worth seeing you get your time card punched when my arse is on the line."

Pete slammed her feet onto the floor, curving her hands in what she guessed was a subconscious desire to strangle Jack. "What the *bloody hell* is your problem with me, Winter?"

He snorted and swung his eyes to the window. The sun was high, catching motes of dust across the panes, and Pete knew she was already late for work.

"Like you don't know," Jack said finally with a shrug so disaffected Iggy and all of the Stooges would have burst into tears of envy.

"That's just it," said Pete. "I *don't* know, Jack." She stood up and he met her, looked down with that bitter quirk to his mouth that warned of rage just beneath. She shouldn't press, but Pete did, because she was damned if she let Jack linger on with his contempt and his silence. "What happened that day, in the tomb?" she asked softly. "I've thought and dreamed about it so much, Jack, but I never really remember. What happened that made you hate me this much?"

Jack's lip curled and his eyes blackened again, and Pete steeled herself for something, she didn't know exactly what, but the air between them had charged.

"You really don't remember?" Jack said, that predatory cold flickering in the depths. Pete shook her head, throat dry.

"How about that," Jack murmured. "If you're telling the truth."

"What reason would I have to lie?" Pete said.

"You know more than you're admitting to yourself," Jack said. "You saw him, same as me. You were *there,* until you let go." The last two words could have cut flesh.

"I have no idea what you're talking about," Pete said automatically, although images of the smoke man flamed behind her eyes.

Jack considered her for a moment, as if he weren't sure what to do with an inconveniently dead body, and then his anger slipped back over his face and he threw up his hands. "Then bloody well figure it out, Pete," he snarled. He went into the toilet and slammed the door.

"Bollocks," Pete swore, slumping back on the sofa and pressing her pillow over her face.

Chapter 19

Pete waded through the day of papers and questions and frowning stares from Chief Inspector Newell and took the tube home next to a beautiful Indian couple who smelled of sweat and spices.

"Home, Jack," Pete called reflexively as she entered her front hall. The flat was dark and she saw the glow of a cigarette tip coming from the sofa. Jack exhaled a cloud of smoke and it shone blue-white in the reflection from the streetlamp.

"About time," he said, swinging himself upright. "We've got places to go."

"Where?" said Pete. She didn't flick on the light. Talking to Jack, seeing only the ember of his fag and the flash of his eyes was oddly appropriate, a mirror of hundreds of dreams where he appeared as nothing more than shadow with bits of substance.

Jack grinned and she saw the ivory gleam of his teeth. "You'll see."

They took the tube at Jack's insistence. He jumped the gates and then threw up his hands when Pete glared at him and swiped her Oyster card twice. "Come on, Caldecott, don't give me that look."

"Where are we going?" Pete asked again as the train roared through the tunnel, slicking back Jack's hair. They were the only people in the Mornington Crescent station, alone under the flickering fluorescent tubes with smoke and graffiti on the tiles.

"You'll know when we get there," said Jack, holding the door for her. The tube rattled past Euston, on into stations that were barely lit, the humps of dozing bums flashing past, leather-clad youths staring out into the tunnel with shining animal eyes, transit police wrapped in blue nylon armor like weary sentinels. Pete wrapped her coat around her, crossing her arms across her stomach.

"Don't worry about them, luv," Jack whispered. "I'm here."

Pete turned to look at him in the intermittent flashes from the tunnel lights, each exposure imprinting Jack in stark relief. "That's why I'm worried, Jack."

He sighed and threw his head back, worrying an unlit cigarette between his lips. "We're meeting a friend of mine."

"Are you and this friend on good terms?" Pete wondered. Jack lifted one shoulder.

"Last time I saw him, probably a decade ago, he and I had a slight difference of opinion."

"About what?" said Pete, feeling the cold breath from the train window on the back of her neck.

"Long story," said Jack with a lazy grin. "But it involved two nights in Liverpool and a dancer named Cassidy. She did this bit where she put her leg up over her head . . ."

Pete held up a hand. "Is he going to try and bash our skulls in?"

"No," said Jack. "Not his style."

"Thank God for small favors," said Pete.

They got off the tube at Charing Cross and walked up the center of a nearby mews, the slick cobbles ringing under

Pete's boot heels. Big Ben chimed eleven o'clock in the distance, amplified in the mist so that it echoed from every direction. Pete could smell the Thames, the wet rotting atmosphere that soaked into brick and clothing and hair.

"This way," said Jack, his Parliament springing to life without the aid of a light. Pete blinked. Jack exhaled and held out the fag. "Care for a taste?"

"I'm quitting," Pete said perversely. Jack laughed, and it turned into a cough.

"Bloody hell. I hate this fucking wet weather."

"Move to Arizona, then," Pete snapped. The row houses got older, arched and leaded windows staring out black and blank into the night. Pete caught movement in the corner of her vision and whipped her head to the left. A woman in black latex that gleamed like bloody skin and a man in an Arsenal jersey disappeared into an alley.

Jack snorted. "Didn't peg you for an easy shock, Caldecott."

Pete stopped in the street and crossed her arms. "I'm not, Jack. I came after you, didn't I? And on that matter, I am not going another step until you tell me what the bloody hell is going on."

Jack rolled his eyes at her, taking a long drag on his cigarette. "Anyone ever told you you're too damned stubborn for your own good?"

"Constantly," said Pete. "What is this?"

Jack sighed. "Pete, I told you the night you found me that I only had one condition for doing this, yeah?"

"You did," Pete agreed cautiously.

"I asked you to believe me," said Jack. "So believe me now when I say I can't tell you where we're going and who we're meeting. You're just going to have to hold your knickers on and see." He turned with a ripple of fog and tobacco smoke and kept walking. Pete swore under her breath and followed, trying to ignore the roiling in her stomach that told her dark things were on their heels, just outside the pools of streetlamp light.

Once or twice she heard a snuffling and squealing, nails clacking on paving stones. She kept her eyes on the uneven blond spikes of Jack's hair and didn't look back.

Then Big Ben chimed midnight.

Pete stopped and cocked her head, listening to the bell ring through to twelve and telling herself she was crazy, or the clock was faulty, or that *something* logical and sane was going on here.

"You heard it," Jack stated. Pete sighed and stopped trying to pretend. Clocks that chimed midnight at half-eleven and shadow creatures were what Jack asked of her. So be it.

"I did." She nodded. "What does that mean?"

Jack dropped his Parliament to the stones. It hissed and went out as he ground it under his heel. "It means we're here."

Chapter 20

Jack led Pete up a side passage, not even wide enough for the Mini to squeeze through, to a squat stone building with a red door bound in iron.

"They expecting an invasion?" Pete said, gesturing at the entry.

"The three bands means this is neutral territory," said Jack. "The iron is to keep out Fae."

"Fae," Pete echoed. "You mean fairies."

"Kindly folk," said Jack. "Shining ones. Unseelie. Call 'em what you will, nobody here wants the treacherous little buggers in their pub."

"And just where is 'here'?" Pete asked.

Jack took her lightly by the shoulders and looked into her eyes. Calm, they were icy as a glacier under a cloud-covered sky. "We're in their place now, Pete. It's nearly always midnight and the things from your nightmares are crawling in the shadows."

"And I'm supposed to be frightened, after seeing you murder somebody casually less than a day ago?" Pete demanded, moving his hands off her ungently.

He grabbed her again, and slammed Pete against the outside wall of the pub hard enough to make breath leave her lungs. She struggled, and Jack locked his bony fingers against her flesh, more than enough to bruise. "This is not the daytime world that you know, Pete," he said, his voice grating like he'd just smoked a pack of unfiltered. "This is the Black. It is a hard realm with little mercy for the unprepared. People die here, Pete, and it's usually because someone else has decided to kill them. It is *the way things are*. If you can't stomach the truth then go back now."

Pete's heart danced, scraping her rib cage with panic. She allowed none of it to show on her face, raising her eyes to the sky and inhaling a sharp, cold draught.

Above her, something with stone for skin grumbled and settled itself more comfortably on its perch, ugly dog face serene.

Pete forced herself to look only at Jack. "I told you, I'd do what was necessary to catch this child-stealing bastard. That we'd end this. Not you, all alone striding into the darkness. We. Now get your bloody hands off me before I have a boot between your balls."

Jack let go of her arms and lifted the gryffon-headed knocker on the pub's door. He let it fall three times, and the red door swung open with a moan of ill-oiled age. Jack made a courtly gesture to Pete. "After you, luv." He grinned as she stepped into oil lamps and noise and smoke. "Welcome to the Lament Pub," Jack said. "And welcome to the Black."

Pete stepped over the threshold and felt a prickle, not on her skin but across the reflective surface of her consciousness, like a smooth stone stirring ripples in a pool. Ambient power drifted and swirled differently here, the air molecules arranged out of order and the light and shadow slippery. Her eyes refused to focus. She felt an overwhelming pressure on her skull, as though her senses were all overloading at once, smell and taste and sound rising to levels that threatened to drown her. This was worse than when her intuition knifed her mind. Worse than her dreams, than the tomb itself, full of ghosts and darkness. The magic of the place reached inside Pete's skull and clawed it clean, leaving her trembling.

Jack's hand closed on her wrist, a touch that was steadying but not rough. "Easy, luv. It's always worst the first time you cross in."

Pete shut her eyes and breathed, just as she'd breathed the first time she'd encountered a corpse. A drowned man, a homeless drunk bumping against the pilings on the Thames. Pete shut her eyes and fixed what the pub *should* be in her mind, just as she'd seen the corpse as it was against the backs of her lids, no life in the black glassy eyes. She gritted her teeth and slowly opened her eyes again.

The low thread of conversation in the pub bubbled, just beyond hearing the words of the individual voices, and a cloud of cigarette smoke hung low over the clusters of small round tables and bowed heads, and the massive ebony-topped bar. A man sitting with his back to her flexed his shoulders and Pete saw, just for a moment, the long reach of bone wings before they glimmered and vanished beneath a glamour of a rat-eaten coat. A dance floor and a jukebox with the original 45s crouched awkwardly in one corner, out of place in the old pub, which should have had Shakespeare and Marlowe bending their heads together in a dark nook.

And it was all slightly odd, and very usual, with none of the blurring heart-racing *wrongness* that had engulfed Pete when she stepped inside. The cries of magic softened, and retreated, taking the pain in her head with them. The staring faces, a few with pointed teeth, turned back to their drinks and conversation.

She glanced back to see Jack with a contemplative half-smile on his face. "Thought you'd adjust," he said as if he'd bet against Pete with himself.

"Who's this friend we're here to see?" said Pete.

"The third time you've asked me," said Jack. "If I were the devil, I'd be compelled to answer." He helped Pete out of her jacket and threw it on the curled iron hooks just inside the door. There were several others—a motocross leather, a woolen cape, a fur with the skull of the unfortunate wolf still attached.

"Yes, but you'd take my soul in return," Pete said with her own smile.

Jack stared past her into the middle distance before he returned her gaze. His was clouded and almost mourning. "What makes you think I haven't, luv?"

Pete rolled her eyes. "I'm getting a drink." She took a stool and gestured to the publican, a palely beautiful young man with black spiked hair and silver piercings cascading up both ears and gleaming in his nose. He dipped his head to acknowledge her and Pete saw flashes of Celtic warriors, branded and painted for sacrifice and battle.

"What'll you have, luv?" he intoned with a slow-burning smile and a bare muscled arm placed on the bar in front of Pete. His skin was whiter than alabaster, white as dead skin, and it fairly glowed against the dark bar top.

"I'll . . . a pint of . . ." Pete blinked. His eyes were black . . . a moment ago they'd been green.

"A pint of what, miss?" Amusement crinkled his mouth and lit those black stone animal eyes. Pete's throat, when she tried to swallow and speak, scraped painfully.

"A . . . I . . . lager on tap?" The necessary connective tissue for a complete sentence eluded her.

"Would you like mead? Or maybe an oaken ale," said the publican. He leaned in and Pete could hear the drums, smell the smoke of the Beltane fires and the bloody screams of the rival tribesmen who had died under his blade.

"Oaken ale," Pete murmured, thinking with that sensation of being outside herself that she was very, very close to a man whom she didn't know at all, thinking wild savage thoughts about him, and that she couldn't be arsed to care, because he was beautiful. Wild. "What's that?"

"Something you don't want," said Jack, leaning on the bar next to her.

With an audible snap, whatever was holding Pete in the publican's eye broke and she sat up straight, her cheeks hot.

"I was just having a bit of fun, mate," said the publican with an amused look that telegraphed unbearable smugness. "Didn't know she was spoken for."

"You do now," Jack snarled. "And the next time you try to pass off your bloody Fae nectar on a human, I'll shove your little horned head up your arse and hold it there until you stop twitching."

"No harm done!" the publican exclaimed, holding up his hands. "Didn't realize she was mortal. Take your ease, old-timer, and have something to drink."

Jack's hand flashed out, like a fatal serpent, and gripped the publican by the throat, fingers digging into his voice box. "Do you know who I am, you sodding barn animal?" he hissed. The publican gurgled. "I'm Jack fucking Winter," Jack said, releasing him with a push that rattled clean glasses on the bar back.

The publican bleached even paler than he already was, if it were possible. "I—I didn't know, sir. Forgive me, mage." He dipped his head again, this time to avoid eye contact with Jack.

"Give me two pints of the Newcastle," said Jack, "and piss off."

The publican filled his order and retreated to the opposite end of the bar, where he assiduously pretended to polish glasses.

"Creepy wanker," Pete muttered, shaking off the last vestiges of the publican's cold, ancient aura.

"Just a satyr," Jack said. "Walking bollocks with a brainstem attached. Pay that one no mind."

"Please tell me he is not who we are here to see," Pete

muttered. She felt like she'd touched rotted meat, or a brick wall slick with mold and moss.

"No." Jack gestured over his shoulder. "He's back there, alone. As usual."

Pete's gaze was drawn to the back corner of the pub, where roof beams and lamplight conspired to create a slice of shadow. A solitary figure sat, fragrant green-tinged smoke from his pipe rising to create the shape of a crown of young spring leaves before dissipating.

Jack nudged her arm. "Come on." He picked up the two pints of Newcastle Brown and started toward the table with a measured step. If Pete didn't know better she'd call it reluctance, or a sort of respect.

The man seated alone and smoking was unremarkable, as far as men went. Pete would pass him boarding the tube or in a queue at the news agent's without a glance, although he did have lines of mischief at the corners of his mouth and eyes, and they glowed pleasantly brown. He was older than Jack, wearing a well-trimmed black beard and a soft sport coat patched at the elbows.

Jack set the pints down on his table and grinned. "Been a long time, Knight."

When the man turned to look at them, Pete heard a rushing sound, as if a spring wind had disturbed a sacred grove, and with great clarity she saw a tree, ancient, branches piercing the sky while the roots reached down and grasped the heart of the earth.

"Well," said the man. "Jack Winter. I next expected to see you lying in state at your premature funeral, yet here you are disturbing my evening. Well done."

Shaking his head, Jack gestured between the man and Pete. "Detective Inspector Caldecott, Ian Mosswood. Mosswood, this is Pete."

Mosswood raised one eyebrow in an arch so critical

Pete felt the urge to stand up straight and comb her hair. "Pete. How frightfully unusual."

"You know, Mosswood," said Jack, slapping his shoulder, "in this ever-changing world, it's good to know you're still . . ." He gestured to encompass Mosswood's jacket. "Tweed."

"I presume," said Mosswood, eyeing the pint of ale, "that since you came over here and bothered me you have some reason." He turned his pipe over and tapped it out against the table's edge. Fragrances of grass and cut wheat filled Pete's nostrils.

"Bloody right," said Jack, pulling out a chair and straddling it backward. "I need to pick your leafy brain, Mosswood. Brought you the requisite offering and everything, just like a proper druid. Sorry for the lack of white robe and virgin, but Pete's sheets are all striped and I wouldn't presume to guess as to her eligibility for virgin."

"Sod you," Pete responded, flicking Jack the bird.

Mosswood picked up the ale and sniffed it with distaste, his prominent nose crinkling.

"Get off it," said Jack. "You know it's your favorite."

"It is a sad day when a Green Man's allegiance can be bought for an inadequately washed pint glass of malted hops and stale yeast," said Mosswood with a disapproving curl of his lip. "But such is the way of the world, sadly. I accept your offering. What the bloody hell are you bothering me over, Jack?"

"Problems," said Jack. "Got a nasty, nasty ghost or hungry beastie on the prowl—some misty tosser with an appetite for little children. I need to find him, and find a way to hurt him bad before I exorcise the bastard back to the Inquisition."

Mosswood looked up at Pete, who stood awkwardly by his elbow, not sure she was invited into a conversation that had obviously picked up just where it left off the last time the two men had seen each other.

"Sit down, my dear," he said with a small smile. "Don't let this foolish mage's ramblings inhibit you."

"Oh," said Pete, "I don't." She pulled out the remaining chair and sat. "Thank you."

"She is considerably lovely," Mosswood told Jack. "And polite. What in the world is she doing with you?"

"Funny, you git," said Jack with a humorless smirk. "How about telling me what I need to do to flush out this bugger?"

Mosswood relit his pipe, taking tobacco that smelled like shaved bark from a leather pouch and tamping it down carefully with his thumb. The pipe was carved from a black wood, slightly glossy, the nicks from the knife that had wrought it visible, a tiny story along the well-rubbed stem and barrel. "What you want to begin your search is a Trifold Focus. I do not know of any in existence, but I'm sure one of your other . . . sources will be more than happy to oblige the information for the price of an immortal soul or two."

Jack drained his Newcastle and gave Pete a satisfied grin. "I told you he'd come through."

Chapter 21

They walked out of the fog and found the Mini waiting. Big Ben chimed midnight once more and Pete said a silent thank-you to be away from places where the air was not the same and she could feel invisible eyes on her all the time.

Jack sat closemouthed during the ride and he was chalk colored by the time they reached Pete's flat. "You all right?" she inquired when he stumbled and fetched against the wall just inside her door.

"Yeah . . ." Jack's jaw set. "No. No, I'm not." He made a run for the bathroom and Pete heard him retching miserably.

It was so easy to forget, when Jack was sarcastic and smoking a Parliament, throwing out smiles and pinning her with his hard eyes, how she'd found him less than a week ago. Skinny, wasted, and his body still screamed for a fix even now.

Pete hesitated for a few more seconds, listening to Jack choke, then nudged the bathroom door open with her toe and crouched beside him, placing a hand on the back of his neck. Jack's skin was cold and slick, like he'd just been pulled from a pool of oily, lifeless water.

"Don't . . . don't . . ." he gasped, finally managing to draw a breath. The loo stank of old ale and sweat with an undertone of something darker, burned from crossing a barrier that flesh was not meant to. "I'm all right," Jack muttered, sitting back on his heels and wiping the sweat away with the flats of his palms from his face. "It takes a lot out of you. Crossing to and from the Black. I'd forgotten how fucking difficult that is."

"I feel fine," said Pete quietly.

"Well, aren't you bloody well special," Jack snapped. Pete stood and held out her right hand, trying not to let it shake with anger that Jack might take for timidity.

"Give it to me."

"Give what to you?" Jack muttered, leaning his head back against the tile wall and breathing through his nose. He hadn't stopped sweating even though rain was washing the windows of the flat with intermittent sleet and Pete's fingers were cold because the radiators were turned down.

"Your goddamned stash, Jack!" Pete bellowed, picking up her container of hairbrushes and clips off the basin and flinging it at him. Her anger rushed up from the iron-banded box where she kept it through her workdays and ever since Connor had died. Really, since Jack had died for the first time. She threw the pink ceramic cup at his lying face and felt relief, like she had just destroyed the visage of an oppressive stone idol.

Jack ducked and was pelted with clips and pins. "Oi!" he shouted. "What the in the seven bleeding hells is your problem, woman?"

"You're my problem!" Pete shouted. "You're a fucking junkie liar is my problem!" She grabbed his jacket from where it lay on the floor and dug into the pockets, her fingers shaking and still slicked with Jack's sweat.

Pete prayed again. She prayed to find nothing, to be irrational and tired and overloaded from the graveyard and the blind children and walking down the cobble street where it was always midnight.

Her fingers closed around an empty cellophane bag,

gritty with a powder that felt like ground glass and a capped syringe, full of cloudy cooked heroin that three long years as a PC pulling junkies off the street prophesied she would find. Pete dropped the baggie on the tiles next to Jack. "God damn you," she said quietly. "You've been fixing the entire time."

"No," said Jack, pulling himself up and bracing one arm against the wall. Fine purple webs traveled up his forearm, spread out from red-black pinpricks, bloody spiders living under the skin. "No," Jack repeated. "That was my last dose, and my first shot in five days, which is why I'm vomiting my fucking guts out now and could do without you screaming at me. Harpy."

Pete poked Jack in the chest with her index finger. Fever heat rolled off him in a whisky-scented wave. "Don't you ever sodding lie to me again, Jack, or I will jam my boot in your arse so far I'll knock out your back teeth."

Jack dropped his head. "You asked me to *see,* Pete, and if you knew what crossing the Black without something to dampen my sight meant, you wouldn't have asked me. You wouldn't make me nip off to a dodgy pub loo to shoot up. You'd prime the needle and put it in my bloody arm."

"I don't want to hear your sodding excuses," said Pete. She put the tips of her fingers under Jack's chin. "Have you told me anything that's true? Anything?"

"Doubtful, luv," Jack said. He tried to smile but Pete saw a death mask. "That's all I am, a liar and a sinner."

"Did you know what would happen in that tomb?" Pete asked quietly.

Silence pulled the air between them thin. "I've always known I was going to die," said Jack eventually. "That I was going to die young, and that I was going to die badly."

"I mean about me," Pete said. "Did you know about me, Jack? What would happen if I went in there?"

"You never give up, do you?" he shouted, angry again as

quickly as lightning flickered. "Sod it, Pete, realize it's not always about you and your trite little middle-class daddy-love issues and leave me alone!"

He grabbed the jacket out of her hands, so hard and quick her fingers burned from the friction of the leather.

"Where are you going?" Pete demanded. Jack shoved her aside and stomped out. A minute later the front door of the flat slammed and there was the echoing quiet left by rage and half-truths in Jack's wake.

Chapter 22

No one wanted to look at Pete when she pushed open the door to the MIT room in New Scotland Yard the next morning. They all bent their heads, pretended papers and computer screens were important, and only looked at her from the sides of their eyes. Whispers weighed heavy on the air.

"What the bloody hell is everyone in here waiting for?" she asked Ollie, once she'd made an extra-large mug of tea. "Is it common consensus I'm going to whip out a rifle and start shooting?"

"You haven't been about," said Ollie. He hunched himself up against his too-tight tie and collar, and refused to meet her eyes.

"Meaning what?" Pete said, narrowing hers.

"Meaning . . ." Ollie sighed. "I like you, Caldecott, so I'll say it right out: There's some here that think you're not able to handle this thing with Bridget Killigan. And after the other two kids were . . . well. There's talk, is all."

"This is because of Jack, isn't it?" Pete demanded. "Because I brought him into the case and because I haven't been handing in my reports to the guv every day like I'm in sodding fifth form. Is that what you're saying?"

"That's part of it," Ollie agreed. His fat fingers were splayed on the desk they shared, and he stared at them, not at Pete. "You're not yourself, Pete. Everyone sees it. Except you." He pushed back from the desk and stood. "And that's the whole of it." Ollie walked away and Pete sat in her own chair, hard enough to send electricity up her spine.

Jack and Connor gibbered at her, reminding her that she was blinded to all but herself, blinded as surely as Patrick, Diana, and Bridget Killigan. Connor stared up at her accusingly from his hospital bed, his eyes peeling her skin back to the fault underneath. Jack proffered his bruised and bloodied arms, a supplicant even as he depressed the plunger of the disposable syringe.

Connor wasn't a man given to fancy. Therapists and pills were his answer to Pete's nightmares, when she'd lost Jack. MG was the one who wanted to see magic, and never could, whose silence spoke volumes as Pete choked down small chalky Xanax and tried to pretend everything was normal.

"When you see a nightmare," Juniper Caldecott said, resting her hand on Pete's head, *"you just look it right in the face and you make it go away."*

For the first time since she'd packed her two teal Samsonites and left Connor, Pete, and MG, Pete wished her mother were still about. Juniper with her altars and her sage scent and her smiles like warm scarves on cold days could have exorcised these ghosts.

"Typical," she muttered, shoving case files around in an effort to occupy her hands if her mind insisted on wandering.

Pete was only aware of DCI Newell standing over her with his long and disapproving shadow after he'd said her name several times. His face was pinched when she finally looked up.

"There's been another kidnapping, Caldecott," he said, holding out a jacket. "I need you to interview the victim's mother immediately."

Pete slid her chair back a bit too quickly, stumbling over her own feet. "Yes, sir. Right away."

Newell studied her, with a stare he probably imagined was penetrating. It had all the effect on Pete of a moth against her cheek. She had that feeling of floating, one she recognized now as the aftereffect of any time in Jack's presence. When she'd walked in the fog with him something had *released*, a spyhole in the battlement of something immense and still and floating, that Pete had run her fingers through but never immersed in.

She was half in and half out of Jack's world now, and the real one seemed pale beside it.

"Caldecott," Newell said, "if you don't wrap this nasty business up rather quickly, I'm going to be forced to suggest a leave. And may I remind you, you've already used up several days' worth of personal time gallivanting with this informant of yours."

At least he didn't also hint that if Pete were put on leave, she'd be making an involuntary appointment with a psychiatrist. Pete ripped the file out of his hands and shoved it into her tote. "My report will be in your box as soon as possible, guv."

"Inspector . . ." Newell started, but Pete was already banging aside the swinging doors, running out as blindly as Jack had the night before, that immense stirring in her head brewing into a storm.

The file said the missing girl was called Margaret Smythe, and her picture was candid and unsmiling. Straight hair framed a heart face and immense eyes the color of an angry tiger's.

Pete read the single sheet three times, committing it to memory before she cranked open the Mini's door and mounted the steps of the Smythes' semidetached home. She was on a quiet street in Bromley, would not be here were it not for Margaret's strange, invisible, and inexplicable disappearance from within a brick house with all the windows and doors locked.

She stilled herself, mind and body, and let the imitation brass knocker fall twice. The door opened after someone scrabbled with dead bolts for a few seconds. Margaret Smythe's mother was blond and lovely despite deep blue half-moons painted in the skin under her eyes and fine lines of desperation wrought at the corners of her mouth.

"Mrs. Smythe," said Pete, flashing her warrant card and badge. "DI Caldecott from the Metropolitan Police Service. May I come in?"

"It's Ms.," said Margaret's mother, her eyes roving past Pete and out onto the pavement, searching for any shadow out of place. "Ms. Smythe. I don't understand, the police were already here . . . I gave my information and they did fuck-all and went away again."

"Yes, I know the local bureau have already been around," said Pete with what she hoped was a soothing demeanor. She didn't think she managed it, because Ms. Smythe's face pinched.

"We've had similar cases in London," Pete went on. "Ms. Smythe, your daughter is missing and time is of the essence. Please, just let me in for a moment."

Margaret's mother hesitated for a second more, looking Pete up and down. She would never stop being suspicious of people at her door, at footsteps behind her on the pavement. Pete stepped toward her, putting one hand flat on the mesh that separated them.

Ms. Smythe stepped aside. "Come in, then. Make it quick. I have a news conference in a little more than an hour."

Pete stepped over the threshold and something parted the air in front of her, light like the brush of fingers against a fevered cheek. An inkling of the power that burned when Jack was in a room.

"Could I see Margaret's bedroom please, Ms. Smythe?"

Ms. Smythe gestured up the stairs and went into the sitting room, slumping on a sagging sofa in front of a console television that showed a fuzzy rerun of *Hollyoaks*.

Shock does funny things, Pete repeated, although it was hard to reconcile the saucer overflowing with cigarette butts and the plastic cup half-full of whisky with a distraught mother. Ms. Smythe began to apply lipstick and rouge, crooked in the dim light.

Margaret's door supported a hanging hand-painted sign covered in drooping daisies and her name in crookedly precise letters. A newer, larger sign on pasteboard proclaimed KEEP OUT — THIS MEANS U. Pete pushed it open and examined the purple satin bedspread, the white desk and dressing table that were still little-princess while the rest of the room was older, darker.

She sifted through the drawers and paged through the dresses hanging in Margaret's closet, most of them some variation on bruise-colored satin and silk. A sticky stack of photographs had been shoved to the back of the desk, Margaret and a dodgy-looking bloke with a wisp of ponytail that he would believe was a lot hipper than it was. "Ms. Smythe?" Pete called. "When did Margaret's father leave?"

Her mother mounted the stairs and came to the door of Margaret's room, but kept herself carefully outside. "Two years ago. All in the report those other police took down."

"Divorce," Pete said, more of a hope than a question.

"He's doing a hitch in Pentonville," Ms. Smythe said, her eyes fierce. "And we're still married, I suppose."

Pete set down the stuffed penguin that sat on the center of Margaret's bed. The penguin was wearing a black mesh shirt and his feather ruff was purple. "What did he go in for?"

"That has nothing to do with this," Ms. Smythe snapped. "My husband never wanted the bloody kid in the first place."

Pete crossed the distance between them and bored into the other woman until she dropped her eyes to the ratty pilled carpet under her bare feet. "Your daughter is *gone*, Ms. Smythe. She has been stolen from you without a trace of anyone coming in or leaving. She's vanished, and if I don't find her, she is going to suffer horribly, just like the three other children. You have five days, starting from last night. That's how long . . . he . . . keeps them." She stopped herself from using *it* just in time. "Then they're blinded, and muted, and returned to you just a husk."

Ms. Smythe swallowed a sob, her chin tucked to her chest. Pete said, very softly, "Is that what you want?"

"God help me," Ms. Smythe whispered. "I always knew something would happen to that child. She's . . . she's not all right, you know."

"She was abused?" Pete wondered if that might be the link between all of the children, some psychic thread that attracted hungry entities.

"No!" Ms. Smythe rounded fiercely on Pete. "I never put up with anything of the sort under my roof—you check, with your smug London smirk you're giving me. I had one of my boyfriends put away for having that very idea, last year. It's in the records. You *check*."

"Fine, fine. I believe you, ma'am." Pete put her hands out. "What, then? What's wrong with your daughter?"

"Who said anything was bloody wrong?" Ms. Smythe cried helplessly, then vanished down the stairs before anything else could be said. Pete smelled the tang of cheap fags and more whisky and heard the telly volume go back up.

"Crazy bint," she muttered. Ms. Smythe hadn't ejected her from the house, though, so Pete went back into Margaret's bedroom and looked out the window, down into a tiny overgrown garden that looked like a thorny green maw, a Fae place that would swallow little children. In front of her face, a ghost of a spiderweb swayed in the air. The spider had long since vacated.

Behind Pete, in the reflection of the glass, something on the far wall shimmered and twisted under her eyes, and made the center point of her forehead twinge like the symbol Jack had drawn in blood when the shade appeared.

Pete touched the spot on the wall and found it slightly warm, and took out her penknife and scraped a little bit of the paint away. Oily black stuff flaked onto her shoes, roofing tar or old motor oil. "Ms. Smythe!" Pete shouted in a tone that brooked no argument. "I need to speak with you for a moment longer!"

She took her pocketlight and shone it at an oblique angle to the wall, and the shape under the paint jumped into sharp relief. It didn't hurt, like the things Jack painted in blood . . . it was solid, like pressing your forehead against a cool iron bar on a warm day.

Ms. Smythe appeared with a snuffling and a cloud of smoke. "What is it now?"

"You painted over something here," said Pete, pointing to the spot she'd scraped off. "Who did this?" She'd take a rag of paint thinner to the wall herself, if it would lead to whatever was taking children. She'd go wrestle Jack out of whatever gutter he was napping in and shove it in his face until he'd be forced to give her help.

"Margaret did it."

Pete froze, felt the prickles over the backs of her hands and the underside of the instincts that she tried to ignore, the electric fence that sparked to life when she got too close to things that were malignant. "Why on earth?"

"She were a silly child, Inspector. You have to understand that. Always seeing things where there weren't any. She said it was to keep them out."

Pete looked at the wall. The lumpy sign didn't feel *wrong,* it was just overwhelmingly present, on a plane that wasn't the three dimensions Pete's mind was accustomed to. She followed the line of sight, to the narrow leaded window overlooking the garden, replete with cobwebs and dead oak leaves. "Keep who out, Ms. Smythe? Margaret thought someone was trying to hurt her?"

"Something," Ms. Smythe muttered. "But you have to understand, she were just given to fancies . . . too many books, or not enough friends, and I fully blame myself for that part of it; if she were a normal little girl she wouldn't do those things."

"Ms. Smythe . . ." Pete rubbed at her forehead. It was starting to throb dully, and it had nothing to do with the magic-thick air of the bedroom. "Who? Who or what was your daughter afraid of?"

"She said . . ." Ms. Smythe took a large breath and let it out in a rush. "She said it were to keep the fairies out. The garden folk that lived down below. She said they whispered to her and kept her awake because she was bright and they were twilight—her words, not mine, Inspector—and they wanted to take her away." Margaret's mother's eyes glimmered and Pete saw that she'd been wrong, that real grief and desperation were hovering underneath the booze and the television interviews. Things had been wrong in the Smythes' world long before Margaret was taken. "If only she'd been a normal little girl . . ."

"It's all right, Ms. Smythe," said Pete, patting the taller woman on the shoulder. "Margaret has time yet, if we're dealing with the same individual."

"She always read books—thick grown-up books, with more of those symbols in them," said Ms. Smythe. "She'll be terrible bored if they're not treating her well and giving her a bit of telly and something to read."

"I'll find your daughter," said Pete with a conviction she

neither felt nor believed. Ms. Smythe just shook her head and slumped slowly downstairs, and Pete followed after she shut her eyes to block the feedback from the sign on the wall out of her mind.

Chapter 23

After she finished in Bromley, Pete once again drove through the rain-grayed streets of Southwark, searching every bowed face for Jack's familiar planar cheekbones and burning glacial eyes.

She ended up in front of the rotting row house where she'd found him and realized he wasn't a phantom, a remnant of nightmare given flesh. Something tapped on her window and Pete's heart leaped along with her body. "Bloody hell," she muttered, rotating the handle to roll the glass down. The youth in the jacket leaned into her face, breathing out sausages and sour mash whisky.

"You on a bust?"

"You think I'd tell you?" Pete arched an eyebrow. He grinned wider.

"Jack's your mate. He told me, you came around, that he was in the Four Horsemen 'round the corner."

"Thank you," said Pete, more to get him and his sausage stink away than anything. She didn't want to see Jack nodding in the back booth of some cut-rate goth club. She didn't want to see the fresh needle marks. But she set the parking brake and locked the Mini and walked down the damp bricks to the small black door of the Four Horsemen.

It wasn't like she could do anything else. Jack drew you in, inexorably, like the orbit of a dying star. And besides, she owed him a smack for running off.

The pub—it was a pub, not a club or a dodgy bar—was dark and smelled like damp rot with an overtone of grease baked onto every surface. Jack's bleached head flashed under the half-dark fluorescent tube lights, dipping toward a glass. A bird's bill and a bird's body in the shadows, dark-feathered wings and gleaming eyes.

"Another girl is missing," said Pete without preamble when she reached his table. Jack raised his head, red-shot eyes and a blurry smile swimming into view.

"Knew you'd come looking for me."

Pete took the glass out of his hand, the gesture feeling as if it were carved in granite. "You're drunk."

"Very good, Inspector." He grabbed a green bottle with a black label and swigged directly. "I am pissed, in body and spirit, and I will continue to crawl inside this whisky bottle until that bloke in the corner with the slit throat shuts up about his mother."

Pete glanced over her shoulder. The corner booth was empty. "You're not fixing."

"Aren't we the bright penny," Jack slurred, taking another drink. Pete grabbed him by the arm, but he slipped it and batted at her. "No, Inspector, this time we're not making any clever deals. No threats and no banter. You shot your bolt with me and while in a moment of insanity I may have asked for your help, I now fully agree that I am worthless to the world at large. You've put me in my place, right and proper."

Pete grabbed Jack's bottle and upended it, letting the whisky flow out into his lap. He yelped and jumped up, the amber stain spreading like a gut shot. "Stop sodding crying," Pete told him. "Another girl is missing."

"So?" Jack muttered, slumping squishily back into his seat. Pete waved at the lurking publican.

"Coffee. Black and hot as you can make it. *So,* Jack, she was like you. Or at least had the potential to be."

As if she'd dropped him in a porcelain tub of ice, the unfocused sorrow flowed out of Jack's face and the edge, sharp as a flick-knife, returned. "Are you sure?"

"I wouldn't be in this bloody place if I wasn't," Pete said. "What in bugger-all is that *smell?*"

"It's kidney pie every lunch hour. Specialty of the house," Jack said. "The girl. How old?"

"Ten," said Pete. "Her name is Margaret—"

Jack cut the air with a finger. "I don't care what her name is." The publican slammed down a dingy cup of coffee in a saucer with sugar and cream packets tottering at his elbow. Jack swigged it and made a face. "Bloody hell. Could strip paint off your motor, that. What's really important is the significant."

"What's a significant?" Pete said.

"Novices usually have something around them, an animal or a piece of the earth, a physical piece of the magic that they can cling to. Anything in the room, feathers or odd rocks or a pet poisonous spider?"

Pete closed her eyes and rotated slowly through Margaret's room, the pink bedspread worn thin, the secondhand desk. The little girl's mobile over the bed, gently drifting make-believe constellations that repeated in paint on the ceiling.

"Stars," she said. "A star. They were on everything. Pink, mostly, if that makes a difference."

Jack swore into his coffee. "What kind of star?"

"Five-pointed," said Pete. "Just a usual star."

"Not usual," said Jack. "The star is the witch, a white practitioner and a channel for pure energy. A bloody open line to the white side of the next world."

"I'm not going to like where this is going," Pete stated. Already she felt it, the dark undertow of magic against her skin. The thing that blinded children, that ate their memories and their life force, laughed at her quietly from the corner of her dream crypt. "The girl was drawing symbols on her walls. She said Fae were after her."

Jack lifted a shoulder. "Probably are, but this thing isn't a Fae. They have their rules and their ceremonies and their love of shine and innocence, but what's taken the girl isn't Fae, and we've got bigger problems now than those little bastards. If whatever is out there starts feeding on Megan—"

"Margaret."

"Bloody whatever. It will gain energy like there's no next minute. It will infuse itself with pure magic until it's bright as a dwarf star and then I won't be able to do fuck-all with an exorcism, and we're all buggered."

"Mosswood told you how to find this thing," said Pete. She raised her index finger when Jack opened his mouth to object. "I *know* that you can find it, so why aren't we looking right *now*? Before Margaret ends up blind and spiritless?"

"It's not that simple," Jack grumbled.

"Oh, no," said Pete, jerking the whisky bottle away as Jack went for it again. "What happened to 'Poor me, the Robert Smith Fan Club doesn't respect me, now I've to prove what a big strong mage I am?'"

Jack glared at her, pursing his lips when she set the whisky bottle out of reach. Finally he said, "Anyone ever tell you you're a stubborn little bit?"

"You," said Pete. "And I knew it already. Come on, then." She took Jack by the elbow and helped him out of his chair. He stumbled against her and Pete snaked an arm under his. "Don't you dare try to get a feel."

"I don't even like you, remember?" said Jack. Pete grumbled under her breath as they came out of the tavern into dim silver sunlight.

"Let's walk for a bit," said Jack when she pointed them toward the Mini. "Clear me head."

Pete nodded. Jack turned them to the river, the salty, laden air seeming to soothe him. He still leaned heavily on Pete and she let the silence stretch, allowing herself to think for a few footsteps rung on brick that there were no missing children, no ghosts. Just her, and Jack, together in a day full of mist.

"This isn't going to be easy, you know," Jack said. His hand on Pete's shoulder tightened for a pulse beat, and she looked up at him. Jack caught her eye and curled his mouth in a not-quite smile. He looked to Pete as if he were smiling at a story of a grimly ironic death.

"Mosswood said all we needed was the Trifold Focus thing," said Pete. She didn't like the smile. It shot straight to the same black place where the daylight echoes of her nightmares resided. Her skin chilled where it touched Jack, like she'd brushed the hide of something swampy and old.

"Mosswood says a lot of things, but in all the years I've known him, I've never heard the whole truth," said Jack. "The Trifold Focus is a scrying tool, not a magic wand."

"You use magic wands?"

"Don't be a smartarse," Jack said. "The fastest way to find a ghost is to ask something that traffics in them."

"Some*thing*?" Pete demanded.

"A mage on his own could spend years sorting through all the pathetic bits of spirit left behind from suicide and traffic accidents and bugger knows what else," said Jack. He stopped at the rust-bubbled iron railing at the edge of the Thames, the slimy bricks breathing sea smell over the boiling brown water. "Mosswood's given me a direct line."

"Will you stop being cryptic?" said Pete. She put her hands on Jack's shoulders and said, "Tell me what I have to do to save Margaret Smythe. Whatever it is. I'll do it."

Jack shook his head, staring at the water. "You call in a favor, Pete. You ask what's already on the other side, the things that crawl in the tunnels between the veils. You call up a demon and cut a deal."

Pete's carefully practiced expressionlessness, the mask she wore just like Jack wore his devilish smiles, slipped then. She felt her lips part and knew the disbelief had started in her eyes. "You did say demon. We're talking *Faust.* 'The Devil and Daniel Webster,' Dorian bloody Gray . . ."

"The Devil," said Jack. "The Devil doesn't exist, Pete. He's the fear in our reptile brains. *Demons* exist. The Trifold Focus is used to call them and compel them into your will."

Pete pressed a hand to her forehead and turned her back on Jack. The Thames stirred gently, black ripples shivering like raven feathers.

"I can't let you do this," she said finally. "There's got to be another way."

"No," said Jack. "And if you really believed there was, you'd be able to look me in the eye." He walked over to her, swaying just a little. The air around Pete crackled. "Was a time I did this sort of thing often," said Jack quietly.

"Was there a time when you asked me to help you?" Pete whispered. Jack sucked in a breath, then sighed and sat down on the curb. Pete watched him light a Parliament and draw deep. Blue smoke drifted out of his nose to mingle with the haze above the river.

"Not that time," said Jack. "Or any other. Not demons. Never you."

Pete watched him sit, hunched, smoking, his platinum spikes flattened on one side from where he'd slept. She stood the same distance from Jack now that she'd stood from him across the circle in the tomb. Nothing flowed over her skin now. The ripples underneath her thoughts were quiet. Jack hadn't lied to her.

Pete went and sat down next to him, pulling out her own pack of fags. "All right, then," she said, lighting hers off the end of Jack's. "How does one call a demon?"

PART 2

The Black

"It is the eve of St. George's Day. Do you not know
that tonight, when the clock strikes midnight, all the
evil things in the world will have full sway?"
—Bram Stoker, *Dracula*

Chapter 24

Pete took Jack home, put the kettle on, and made two mugs. "Sugar. No cream."

Jack accepted the mug and took a sip, then yelped. "Bloody hell, that's burning hot!"

"It's just come off the boil, ninny," Pete said, blowing across the surface of her own tea. Jack pulled a pout.

"'M not a ninny."

Pete stirred her own mug. "I'm sorry, I must have been thinking of another mage." She let herself smile, and felt a jump against her rib cage when Jack returned it, a brief flicker like a kiss of flame.

Jack dropped his eyes and dug in his jacket pocket, finding a scrap of vellum paper and a pencil. "Going to need some things for what's ahead. You'll have to take me to the Kings Road."

A memory of a basement shop fragrant with spices and spiderwebbed with intermingling magics stirred. Pete swallowed and nodded. Margaret. Bridget, Patrick, and Diana. Forget the rest. "Fine."

"And there's the matter of getting my hands on a Trifold Focus," Jack said. Pete stopped her tea mid-sip.

"You don't have one?"

Jack laughed. "No, Pete. No, I don't happen to have one of those lying about."

"What's so bloody amusing? How do we get one?" said Pete. "Buy it?"

Jack snorted. "Would that it were that simple."

"Mosswood made it sound simple," Pete muttered. Mosswood was straight ahead and trusting, solid as an oak. Jack shifted his gaze to his list. He was movable as Mosswood was still, the wind through the sacred grove.

"The only Trifold Focus I know of is in the private collection of a bloke called Travis Grinchley," Jack said.

"Grinchley not the lending type?" Pete guessed. Jack smiled, a predatory showing of teeth.

"The last man who stole from him floated up in the Thames two weeks later, with his eyes and his tongue missing."

"Could be worse," said Pete gamely. Jack stuck his pencil behind his ear.

"They cut out his tongue to make room for his heart to be shoved in."

"Oh."

"Yeah."

"So what's your grand plan?" said Pete. The sitting room had darkened as the fog outside turned from daytime silver to nighttime velvet. She flicked on the nearest lamp and shadows sprang to life on the walls.

"Grinchley will never give it over willingly," said Jack. "And you'd be mad to fuck with a collector of dark magics. So that leaves outright treachery and low dealings."

"You look awfully happy about that," said Pete.

Jack smiled, dropping her a wink. "As if I'd be anything else, luv."

"Still haven't told me the great trick to get the Focus away from this Grinchley person." Pete lifted an eyebrow, her motherly gesture, used on teenaged shoplifters and errant schoolchildren. Jack scribed a circle in the air with his finger.

"We'll just twist him, luv. Give him a bit of street magic and shift the thing right out from under him. A minor entity of some sort should do the trick."

"More summoning." Pete felt a ball of something hard and unpleasant grow just under her heart. "Jack . . ."

"Pete." He closed his hand into a fist. "This is what I did, very well, for quite a time before I met you. Let me do my work. You promised."

"I promised to listen to your rot," Pete shot back. "I didn't promise bugger-all about this idiotic idea you have to steal from a man who slices out people's hearts."

"Translocation," said Jack. "My idiot idea is transloca-tion. I never have to get within a hundred meters of the man and I'll be done with the Focus before Grinchley even realizes it's missing. Devil knows he has enough arcane shite in his musty old house."

Think of Margaret, Connor whispered. *Think of every night after you find her dead and cold if you don't listen to Jack.* "I just hope I can," Pete muttered.

"What?" Jack said distractedly. He stood up and sorted through the armload of books Pete had brought to him, paging through the index of the *Dictionary of Unfriendly Entities.*

"Nothing." Pete sighed. She set her tea aside. "I'm going to go do paperwork while you do . . . whatever it is you're doing."

"Research," said Jack. "Got to figure which sort of en-tity will be willing to trade with me for this favor. Imps might do it. Imps love sneaking about."

"You don't just . . . know?" Pete asked. "They don't make you memorize that stuff, like?"

Jack shook his head. "There was no 'they,' Pete. I didn't go to some bloody school and get instructed by gits in robes. You either die quickly because your talent overwhelms you, or you learn quickly and stay a step ahead of whatever wants to chew on your arse." He thumped the thick black book. "Research is a mage's best friend. Why would I carry all that dusty knowledge around when I can just rely on the sods who came before me?"

"Fine." Pete held up her hands. "Like I said, I'll be upstairs in the office closet. Nothing personal, but the very idea turns my stomach."

"You'll get used to it," said Jack. "You got any chalk in case I need to set a protection hex?"

"In the kitchen drawer with the cling film," said Pete. "And no, I won't get used to it."

She turned and left Jack in the shadows and went into her tiny office—more of an artist's garret than anything, up a flight of stairs barely wide enough for two feet side by side. Her desk and her computer were wrapped in a thin film of dust. Pete clicked on her scrollwork lamp with its bright reading bulb, turning the window facing into the street to a sheet of onyx.

Jack shifted something in the sitting room, and Pete smelled the chalk dust clear as if she were next to him. That dark stirring of deep, old things pushed against the front of her skull. She searched her desk for aspirin to deal with the persistent headache, but found none.

Pete pressed her forehead against the chilled windowpane. Fog thickened and everything past the glass was invisible and gold-tinged, until the streetlight at the end of the block winked out.

She drew back and saw ice crawl across the glass where her breath met it.

Beyond the pane, the fog swirled and parted, as if Avalon were about to reveal itself. Pete felt her body and mind become entranced, the cold seeping down from her bones into her blood and her skin, ice crystals weighing her eyelashes.

Noise and sensation faded, and the fog outside swirled and twisted back on itself and coalesced into a woman's face.

Something whispered, from that dark wellspring that rippled and chattered when Pete touched things not entirely made of earth. A tiny tug on her mind, beyond the cold and the pale, pale face with eyes closed, body clothed in robes of purest silver mist that floated in the night outside.

The whispers rose to the pitch of a scream in the back of Pete's mind, a flock of tiny mouths crying out in concert. *Peril.*

Pete gasped, taking in air so cold it burned her chest like a gout of flame. The pale face outside opened in a soundless scream, fangs the color of old bone showing beneath lips stained with blood, warm and steaming against the thing's frozen skin.

Pete let out a scream of her own. "Fuck me!"

The garret window shattered, throwing a snowstorm of glass inward, and Pete fell, tangling her legs in her chair's and going down hard on her left shoulder. Pain, disorientation, a sensation of *fullness* in her head, like she'd caught the feedback of an amplifier turned on full.

Frozen obsidian claws raked her back and the silver mist poured into the room, forming three of the female shapes. The one who broke the window hissed, staring down at Pete with empty black eyes that seemed to stretch to the bottom of the world.

Pete opened her mouth to yell for Jack, but was deafened by a scream that went straight through her, rending flesh and piercing bone.

The mist-woman closed her mouth, blood bubbling down her chin, and hissed, "Where is the crow-mage? The man called Winter?" Her voice was sibilant and split Pete's ears until she was sure she was deaf, hearing the mist-woman's voice through the echo inside her skull.

"I don't . . ." she said, or thought she did. She couldn't hear, not even her own heartbeat.

The mist-woman's robe smelled of marsh water and the blood of ancient battlefields. It slithered over Pete's face as she lay at their feet, body stiff and chilled, head ringing. *Jack.* She had to get Jack. Warn Jack.

"Where is the mage called Winter?" they demanded again, a concert of moans and sighs. Their hair floated as if they were submerged, black as muddy reeds. Behind their shoulders, a line of light glowed, the edge of the door. "The mage called Winter!" the bansidhe screamed. They looked like every one of Juniper's stories, down to the black claws that curled from sodden, wrinkled hands.

The first bansidhe swooped and brought her face close to Pete's. "Give him to us!"

Fear coiled, sprung, wrapped itself around Pete's heart like a rusty iron chain, but she met the bansidhe's black eyes, and snarled with all the pain and fury she could expel. "Go back to Hell." She rolled, wrenching all the already painful parts of her body, and wrapped her hands around the lamp, swinging it through the bansidhe's drowned corpse face.

The bansidhe howled, claws raking at its face where Pete hit, the skin melting and running over a skull alive with maggots. Stinking marsh water spattered on the floor.

Pete broke for the door. "Jack! Jack, there's trouble!"

Behind her she felt them, as if she were extending invisible fingers. She felt their blackness part the air as they flew, claws and hair lashing, catching Pete's shirt and yanking her backward.

She fell, twisting, down the last stairs, rolled on her side and got up again. The bansidhe's howling cracked her skull, caused the hall lights to flicker.

Jack appeared in front of her, eyes flaming, his hands sparking with chalk dust as the mist covered them both. "Jack!" Pete gasped, or screamed. She didn't know, only the vibration in her throat even told her she was speaking. "Jack, they're behind me."

Jack's irises expanded and he let go of Pete's shoulders. He saw them. "Pete." She saw his lips move. "Pete, get behind me."

"Winter!" screeched the bansidhe, and Pete heard them perfectly. "Crow-mage! Surrender yourself!"

Jack drew in a breath and witchfire blossomed on his palms, hot as the bansidhe's skin was icy. "Bugger to that," he said. "You're not welcome here, and this is a very bad time to make me lose my temper."

The bansidhe drew back their lips from their razor-wire fangs. Their leader raised her right hand and drew her left set of talons across her wrist. Blood oozed from the cuts, and where it hit the walls and the floor smoke rose, black as the coal haze that drifted over London a hundred years ago.

Pete choked as the smoke roiled and grew. It was too much like her nightmare, and where the smoke touched her skin ice crystals appeared. The entire hallway of her flat was frozen over with ice the color of oil.

"Surrender, or the companion dies," snarled the bansidhe woman. "We have cause, crow-mage!"

"State your cause, then!" Jack snapped. "I serve no Unseelie master and you can't compel me with your bloody Fae laws!"

"A price has been paid and a bargain set." The bansidhe smiled, or what a smile would have been wrought in her hissing rictus of a face. "Your life has a value, crow-mage. For the one who ends it, your talents are the reward."

Pete choked as she felt the ice work its way down her throat, and caught hold of Jack's hand. His body was humming like a guitar string, but he showed none of it, stock-still, the witchfire melting the ice around him quickly as it grew.

"Leave now," Jack told the bansidhe with a terrible still anger that Pete had only ever seen from Connor, "and maybe I'll decide not to rip your wretched carcasses out of the ether and turn you to mud as a repayment for this trespass."

The bansidhe screamed at the insult, and Pete staggered, but the pain slowly lessened inside her head, almost as if she could dial down the volume now that she was growing used to the sound. She dug her other set of fingers into Jack's collarbone and felt him still his shaking in return.

"This is no warded place or churchyard!" the leader screeched. Pete's small cluster of photographs tumbled to the ground under the noise, their glass shattering. "This is neutral ground, mage, and we demand your surrender! Give yourself over . . . or live to see your thighbones picked clean." Her shadowed spirit eyes flickered with delight.

Jack slid his gaze over to Pete, all the rage run out. He was skinny and old too soon again, and Pete saw from the tight lines along his mouth that Jack was afraid. "Run," he said. "Get to the lift."

"What are you doing?" Pete said. She could hear again, the pain almost entirely dissipated. She would not let go of Jack, not leave him for the sighing and screaming bansidhe.

"Not sure," said Jack. "Time was I could bolt for holy ground, but I've accepted that I'm not as young as I used to be. They've been given cause to take me away, by some git who cuts deals with Fae—I'm gaining the feeling rapidly that I'm rather fucked."

"My lift is holy ground?" Pete tried to arch her eyebrow but was shivering too uncontrollably. Jack cut his hand across the air.

"No, but it's steel, I'd guess. Not cold iron, but it'll keep them out long enough. Might as well save yourself, Pete."

The bansidhe rippled and swirled like a phantom wind had stirred her and then appeared inches from Jack's face. Pete lost feeling in her exposed skin, and saw blue veins crawl into being along Jack's cheeks and neck.

"Do you surrender, crow-mage?" the bansidhe demanded, her voice low and jagged as an old scar. "Or do you choose to die at my hand?"

"Jack," Pete hissed. "Jack, I may have something."

Jack looked at Pete, back at the bansidhe, staring the creature eye to eye as if she were another hooligan in the pit at Fiver's, inconsequential. "You sure?" he murmured.

Pete squeezed his shoulder hard as she could, until the bones creaked. She wasn't. They could die, and the only difference would be what room of her flat was taped off for the crime scene investigators.

The bansidhe howled and raised her claws to rake Jack's face. Pete jerked him backward. "I'm sure!"

She dragged Jack away, turned and ran, taking up his hand. Skidding on the ice, her heart thrumming like a faulty motor, she fell into the bathroom. Jack tripped over her legs and landed on top.

"The tub," Pete rasped. Trying to speak normally, she found her throat raw as if she'd stood on the Channel cliffs in a winter storm and screamed.

Jack understood and ripped the curtain off its hooks, pulling Pete after him until they landed in a heap in the basin of the old claw-foot.

And the bansidhe came, raging and screaming as if their newborn children had been ripped away, flying hair cutting like stinging nettles and their icy breath clouding the air in the bath. Pete's door fell off the hinges and the mirror and tiles cracked as they howled. She ducked her head below the lip of the tub and prayed, wordless with fear even inside her own head.

On top of her, Jack muttered, over and over, in Irish that sounded like last rites, "*Cosain mé, cosain sí, a fhiach dhubh, cosain sí.*"

The bansidhe howled on, and slowly their cries of rage turned into a high keening of pain. Pete raised her eyes over the lip of the basin and saw the leader ripping out her own hair, clawing at her flesh, bits and patches flaking away from decaying black bone.

"You are a deceiver, crow-mage! May you burn in hell!" the leader cried. Then a whirlwind left a slick of snow that smelled like seawater, and the bansidhe vanished into smoke.

Pete exhaled. Her hands and throat and skin were tinged with pink frostbite, and her bones hurt. The cold had cut all the way down. She groaned. "Jack, get off me."

He hauled himself out of the tub and sprawled on the tile. "Old flat. Iron tub. Iron sink and pipes as well?"

"I—I guess so," Pete muttered shakily. She sat back and then screeched as bright fire lanced between her shoulder blades. Jack was back next to her, peeling back her bloody shirt.

"Bollocks," he hissed when he saw the claw marks. "They got you, Pete."

"Cunts," Pete muttered.

"You don't know half the story." Jack sighed. "Come on, luv. That'll need cleaning, if not stitches." He offered his hand. Pete clasped it, but held on when he tried to lift her.

"You're being awfully solicitous for a man who hates me."

"Saved my arse," said Jack. "Least I can do is put yours back together." He pulled Pete to her feet and she felt a wire inside his arms that hadn't been there when she'd found him in Southwark.

"Those women," she said, sitting on the lid of the toilet while Jack searched for peroxide and gauze.

"Bansidhe, luv. The only way they resemble women is in their charming personalities. Unseelie bitches."

"Be that as it may, Jack. They called you 'crow-mage.' What does that mean?"

Jack poured peroxide on a pad and dabbed it against her back, and Pete yelped. "It means nothing. The Fae are fond of names that should be spelled out in portentous capital letters."

He dropped his eyes as he smoothed a bandage over Pete's back, not even trying to hide the lie. Pete opened her mouth, then shut it again. She hurt. Her skin, her mind, gristle and bone were all weary. Someday soon, she'd find out what the bansidhe had meant, but not now.

"Why'd you tell me to run?"

"No point in both of us getting our blood spilled and drunk up, was there?" he grunted. Pete began to say that she knew something else had moved Jack to try and save her, but that would be disastrous—*he'd* run and she'd never see him again. So she sat in compliant silence as Jack taped down the gauze, his hands free of tremors for the first time.

"Thank you," she said, when Jack pulled her torn shirt back over her shoulder blades.

"Yeah." He dismissed it with a shrug, and left the room. Pete sighed and tried standing on her left hip. It shot tongues of fire up and down her leg when she put weight on it, but she hobbled into the hallway, hissing as she stepped on a piece of crushed glass. "Jack, do me a favor and get my shoes from the entry?"

"Don't have time to clean up." Jack reappeared with one of Pete's duffels in hand and a fistful of Terry's hand-me-down clothing in the other. "We've got to get moving before more creatures of the night try to tear our flesh off the bones."

Pete swallowed, looking at the wreck the bansidhe had made of her flat. "Why did they come? What did you do to them, Jack?"

"Quick to blame me, aren't you?" he snapped, shoving his clothes into the duffel. "And I don't know *why*, Pete." He sighed and shoved a hand into his hair, spiking it downward over his eyes. "Fuck. I should have realized something would bollocks this up. Sounded so simple—find the kids, get clear of you, go on with me life. Should have *known*."

"Your personal angst aside, for a moment," said Pete. "The bansidhe were *after* you, Jack. Knew you by name."

"Which is precisely why we need to go!" he said. He turned and strode into the front entry, bringing Pete's workday shoes back to her. "I wasn't strong enough to ward your flat when I came here, Pete—and the bansidhe broke whatever barriers may have naturally occured. *Anything* can come inside, and trust me, there are things out there that make the bansidhe nothing more than a dream-shadow on the wall."

Pete stepped into her shoes. She *knew* Jack was right, in that solid and unexplainable way of magic that she was beginning to recognize when it dropped into her mind like a single raindrop into a deep well. "I promised to believe you," she said, "but I'm stretching, Jack. Close to breaking. Where can we possibly go?"

"Let's just get to the car and drive," Jack said. "I'll tell you when we're there."

Chapter 25

"Whitechapel," said Jack as Pete guided the Mini through the midnight streets. "No place like it."

"No," Pete agreed as they slid past a human dealer, slouched on a corner with a windcheater turned up against the damp. Furtive eyeshine glinted at her from farther back in the shadows. "No, there isn't."

"Up here," said Jack, and she saw his body loosen from the wire tension for the first time since the attack. "Park on the street. We'll take the fire stairs."

A four-story brick structure with arched windows, slightly Gothic, a bit of rusted ironwork added at some point when the façade became shabby, stared back at Pete with darkened windows. Jack egressed the Mini fast as she'd ever seen him move and started for a rusted set of iron stairs bolted to the bricks, leading up and up into the dark.

"What is this place?" Pete asked as they climbed, the treads under their feet shuddering and groaning like the ghost of Marley. Rust flakes rained onto Pete's head.

Jack stopped at the fourth-floor landing and produced a key from the chain around his neck. He unlocked the French windows in front of them, not without resistance from the rusted latch. "This is my flat."

Pete paused on the sill, startled. "Flat? You let it?"

"Own it. Bought and paid for ages ago," said Jack, flicking a light switch. Nothing reacted. "Ah, tits," he said. "Well, can't blame the power company, really. I don't think I ever paid a bill."

"Jack," said Pete, fighting the urge to bang her forehead against the nearest hard flat surface, "if you own a flat, why the bloody hell were you crashing in a squat miles from here?"

Jack fumbled in the darkness, broken only by the skeletal arches of his flat's windows. His lighter snapped and a moment later his face was illuminated with candle flame, hollow as a death mask. "Nobody knows about this place," he said. "I bought it from a hearth witch named Jerrold. Mad as a hatter, last stages of dementia. I think he thought I was paying him to take a boil off me arse."

"You con a helpless old man out of a flat and then don't use it," Pete muttered. "When it comes to you, Jack, that almost makes sense."

"Hang about with me a bit longer, Pete, and you'll learn the value of having a place no one knows you go to," he said. "Close the shutters. You're letting all the warmth out."

Pete stepped inside, feeling a pull against her skin as if she'd brushed cobwebs. Jack watched her circumspectly for a moment and then nodded, lighting more candles off the one he held. A mantel, fireplace, and bare wood floors flickered into view along with burial mounds of furniture that smelled like dust and rot.

"What did I just touch?" Pete rubbed her arms, hugging herself.

"The flat's protection hex," Jack said. "If you'd been unfriendly you'd experience pain unlike anything I can describe, if you were human. If you were demon, or Fae, well . . ." He held up his hands and made a *poof* motion. "When it comes to home security, it does not pay to fuck about."

"You would have just watched me fry." Pete turned her back on him. Tired, sore. Nearly killed inside her own home, and now on Jack's turf completely. *Wonderful way to keep in control of your situation,* she could almost hear Connor scolding.

"If you'd been out to do the same to me? Absolutely," said Jack. Candles lit one after the other now, sympathetic flames springing to life of their own accord, and they threw a glow of ancient bonfires against the walls of the flat. Pete shivered. They did little to warm.

The only furniture to speak of was a plaid sofa with springs popping out of the armrests, but there were books everywhere, on the built-in shelves to either side of the fireplace and stacked high as Pete's waist under the windows. Boxes and crates were clustered in a corner, and she squinted to see glass jars, grimoires bound in leather and iron, and the white of bone. She looked away before she caught sight of something that she didn't need to see.

A little over a week with Jack now. She was learning what to do when he put her into these situations.

"I'm going to sleep, if I can," she said. "Any beds, or is that reaching for the stars?"

"I think I've got a blanket or two and a mattress that doesn't have anything living in it," said Jack. "Bedroom's down the hall. Good night."

Pete took a fat black candle off the mantel and guided herself to the door, watching Jack for a moment over her shoulder. He went to the window and looked out at the street, silent and pale as a saint's statue waiting in vigilance.

The shrouded man, and Pete felt sure this time that the figure had been a man once, held out his hand, squeezing so tightly to contain the beating thing within that bone showed through his knuckles. Blood, thickened and hot, seeped through his grasp and into the graveyard dirt below. "Take it," said the shrouded man. "Take it before it dies and goes to dust."

"I . . ." Pete started to tell him *I can't,* because she knew that no matter how natural it might seem to stretch out her hand, she could never contain the beating thing in the man's fist. In her grasp, it would gasp and shatter into a thousand pieces because she was weak.

Before she could speak, though, the smoke came out of the shadows and swallowed everything. This time it was in her throat, siphoning off her air and replacing everything with the hot, desert blackness of oblivion.

Pete knew she was dying, that only taking the shrouded man's offering could repel the smoke, and that she could do neither thing. She could just stand and let herself be replaced by the shadow-figure, filled and consumed body and mind by the malignance living in the smoke. It was pain, a slipping away of something that Pete tried to hold, until it tore the skin from her.

The blankets wrapped around Pete when she clawed to the surface of the waking world, smelling of pot smoke and cinnamon, mellowed and musty with age, were damp with her sweat. Her heart thrummed for the seconds it took her to realize she was awake, sun cutting across her face from unshaded windows.

"Christ on a motorbike!" She sighed, falling back and forgetting she had no pillow. "Ow! Bugger all!"

Jack stuck his head through the door, hair distinctly more spiky on the left side than the right. "Everything five by five, luv?"

"Bad dream," said Pete, rubbing her palms over her face. She had broken into a fresh fever sweat, despite seeing her breath on the air and her skin prickling.

"I've got breakfast on," said Jack. "Come into the kitchen."

Pete followed him, padding on bare feet that quickly went numb. "Thought the electric was off."

Jack snorted. "Think I need electric for a simple fry-up?"

Pete conceded he had a point. The kitchen's pink-sprigged wallpaper and clean white countertops reminded Pete of summer visits to her grandmother Caldecott's trim house in Galway. A kettle on the old-fashioned enamel stove radiated heat, steam roiling out of the spout. A frying pan sizzled with eggs and sausages.

"You're awfully chipper," Pete noticed as Jack fussed with mugs and tea that came from a plastic convenience-mart bag. "Your sight quiet? I find it hard to believe nobody died in a building this decrepit."

"Not that," said Jack. "It's this place. Whitechapel." He set a mug with a cartoon purple cow in front of Pete, and shoveled some eggs onto a plate for himself. Jack looked her over, like she was keeping a secret. "Can you feel it?"

Pete didn't like the way Jack was looking at her. It was that cold look, the one that calculated exactly how much your flesh and spirit were worth in his currency. "Feel what?" she said neutrally, sipping at her tea. It burned over her tongue.

"Whitechapel has a dark heartbeat," said Jack. "It breathes out malevolence and draws in them that need blackness to survive. Dampens the sight, like living under a bridge."

"But there are shadows under a bridge," Pete said.

Jack grinned, without humor. "Just so."

Chapter 26

"I'll still need to call an imp for the task at hand," said Jack later, his back turned as he did the washing-up. Pete was smoking a slow Parliament, mostly watching it burn in a saucer, taking a puff every few minutes as a token effort.

"You found out which one, then," Pete stated.

"Managed before the bloody bansidhe interrupted me," Jack said. "The *Dictionary* is shredded, though. Lawrence will kick my teeth in for that. Man treats his books like ruddy babies." He shut off the water and dropped the mugs and plastic plates into the rack to dry. Pete saw him shake once, and grip the counter edge, but the heroin tremors were barely visible any longer, like moth's wings fluttering.

"Look," Jack said. "Go get a *Times* and find a little café to read it in. I'll be done by the time you get back. I know how you feel about it, all that—"

"I want to watch," said Pete. The bansidhe's cuts stung her skin as she squirmed at the thought.

Jack blinked. "Pardon me?"

"I'm staying," Pete repeated. "Do what you have to do, Jack. I'll be here."

He shrugged. "Suit yourself. I'll be in the sitting room."

Pete followed after a moment. Jack was on his knees scratching an uneven chalk circle into the wood floor. In the daytime the flat was shabby in the way of an old woman on pension—faded and stained but not without a grace. The ceilings were twice as high as her own flat, the windows arched like a church with sills a fat cat could curl on. Crown molding, rotted away in places, marched around the ceiling and the lamps were Moorish iron, glass globes sooty from their previous life as gaslights. The building might have been even older than the Blitz, judging by the cracks in the plaster and the leaded panes.

"Bugger!" Jack shouted as his chalk snapped in half. He spat on the marking and erased it with his thumb. The circle encased a five-pointed star and scribbles that looked like chickens had run through a bakery. The whole affair was hopelessly lopsided and scrawled, and Pete put a hand to her mouth to hide a small smile. Jack snarled at her before he went back to drawing.

"I'm sorry," she said. "It's just . . . I imagined the whole thing would be much more sinister."

"It's been a long time since I've done this, so you can bugger yourself," said Jack. "I could go find some black cats and chicken's blood, if that would improve your experience, milady."

Pete sat on the sill, pressing her back up against the glass and letting the sunlight warm it. "Quit being childish and get the bloody imp up here. We're wasting time we could be using to help Margaret. Three days, Jack."

"All right, all right," Jack muttered. "Hold your bloody horses." He got up, dusting off his hands, and went to root around in the kitchen. He returned with a few white packets in his fist and emptied them into a red puddle at the center of the circle.

"What . . . ?" Pete started.

"Catsup," said Jack. "They're mad for it. I think it's the acidity. Imps eat sulfur, in the pit. Wager this tastes a deal better."

"And now I know more than I ever wanted about the preferred snack food for denizens of the underworld," said Pete, tilting her head back and shutting her eyes. "I feel so broadened."

"Hell," said Jack. "Not the underworld. You're talking about the land of the dead. Hell is another prospect entirely. It's a rather terrible insult to suggest that they're the same."

"Because God knows, the *biggest* concern I have right now is insulting a demon," Pete muttered. She was being snarky mostly because she could feel the pull against her skin and her mind, that same prickle that had overtaken her in the tomb long ago. Nervous twitches sprang to life in her gut.

"Jack," she said. He flicked his fingernail against a twist of paper and a slow ember started, curling a little smoke into the air. He dropped it inside the circle and the smoke curled and spread but never crossed the boundaries.

"Jack," Pete said again, louder. Jack glanced up at her.

"Yeah?"

Pete fidgeted. The circle vibrated a little at the edge of her vision, caused a ringing in her ears. "This will be different, won't it?"

Jack's irritation sluiced away and he gave her a regretful smile.

"Yeah, Pete. This time will be different. You have to trust me, right?"

To believe *you,* Pete thought. *Trust is another thing.* But she didn't say it out loud. Jack hadn't earned that, in spite of her dependence on him now that her flat was destroyed. It was just her feeling, the same one that let her know she was walking down a bad alley and would do well to turn around.

"Hrathetoth!" Jack said, not shouting but definitely commanding something. "Hrathetoth, the offering has been placed upon the consecrated ring and I command thee, at my will, appear." Jack sounded as if he were reading off a tube schedule between High Barnet and King's Cross, but the lack of ceremony did nothing to put Pete at ease. That was how it had started, before.

Something sparked and popped in the center of the circle, over the pool of catsup. "Come off it, Hrathetoth!" Jack snapped. "I compelled you; now show your weasely little face. It's not as if you have a *choice*."

A screech like a cat in the jaws of a bulldog stood the short hairs on Pete's neck on end, and then a snarling, twitching, fur-covered blob materialized in the circle, growing cohesive and gaining tiny horns and clawed toes and a pair of glowing yellow eyes.

Hrathetoth the imp looked, on the whole, like an angry dust lion grown to unusual size and gifted with teeth and limbs. "Crow-mage!" it shrieked when it caught sight of Jack. "Explain yourself!"

"Cut that out," Jack said, flicking another catsup packet at Hrathetoth with a bored movement. "We both know this is the most excitement you'll have in a decade."

Hrathetoth blinked his lanternlike eyes at Pete. "Who is she? She is pretty. Pretty and dark, like a starless sky, or the inside of a rhinoceros."

"You'll forgive him," said Jack as Hrathetoth decimated the packet and began licking up catsup. "Demons don't really grasp the concept of metaphor and simile."

"Is she going to heeeelp you?" Hrathetoth grinned widely, showing too many rows of spiked needle teeth. "Because you know you can't save yourself, crow-mage, and—"

He let out a gurgle as Jack's hand flashed out and wrapped around Hrathetoth's throat. "Listen here, you piece of deception given form, I'm not in the mood. I need the Trifold Focus and I need it now, so bloody go get it."

"Can't be done!" Hrathetoth squeaked. "Grinchley wards

his house against intruders! Strong wards, with nasty mean teeth."

"Then *find a way around them,*" Jack growled, and the witchfire flared to life in his eyes. His grip on Hrathetoth started to steam and the demon squealed in pain. Pete rapidly came and put a hand on his shoulder.

"Jack, maybe he's telling the truth."

"He's a bloody demon, Pete. They don't understand truth—just how much flesh they can take off your hide in exchange for the favor." He shook the imp. "Isn't that right, Hrathetoth?"

"Yes . . . yes . . ." Hrathetoth agreed. "Villainy and deceit down all the days! But Grinchley is guarded, crowmage, by things bigger and hungrier than me and I can't change it!"

Jack jerked Hrathetoth closer to the edge of the chalk. "I told you to fucking quit with the 'crow-mage'!"

"No!" Hrathetoth screamed. "Don't break it!" Pieces of his fuzzy black fur dropped off and burned away as they touched the chalk.

"Afraid of dying? Then get me the Focus!" Jack bellowed. "I *command* it!"

"If you break the ring, not only will it be me, but the pretty darkling, too!" Hrathetoth rasped. "She did not cast it. She is not protected from what breaks through."

Jack looked back at Pete like he'd just remembered she was still about. "So she isn't," he said after a long moment. He breathed in, nostrils flaring, and the witchfire went out. "All right, you fuzzy little bugger, you got me on a technicality. But don't think we won't be speaking again." He let go of the imp and said in a bored tone, "I release you, return no more until you are called."

Hrathetoth vanished with a pop of palpable relief. Jack rubbed his hands over his face and got to his feet. "Sodding Hellspawn."

"So there's no chance, then," Pete said. "This Grinchley has the Trifold Focus and the next time I see Margaret, she'll be like the others."

"The girl will be *dead*," said Jack. "The beastie will suck her dry. The other children, there wasn't much there except innocence and maybe a few echoes of talent from some great-great-ancestor to feed on. Molly—"

"Margaret," said Pete.

"Whatever. She's one of us."

"Us." Pete arched an eyebrow. Jack waved a hand.

"I mean like me. With her significant, she's likely a witch—if she were touching dark magic she'd be skinning cats and setting other children's jumpers on fire."

"There's a difference." Pete was honestly surprised. " 'Mage' and 'sorcerer' not just a semantic thing?"

" 'Course there's a difference," Jack snorted. "Different as punk and disco."

Pete started to say how that was a pretty poor analogy, but Jack held up a hand. "Simply: Witches work with light energy. Sorcerers work with nightmares."

"And mages?" asked Pete.

"Mages dip in both," said Jack. "We're in the shadows, but not the dark." He shook his shoulders, as though he'd just taken a hit of speed. "Calling Hrathetoth was quite the workout. Energy's still up. Want to see a trick?"

"No," said Pete, feeling her lips twitch. Just for a second, she glimpsed the Jack from a dozen years ago, without the long shadow that lay across him in the present.

"Come on," said Jack, taking her hand. "Humor me a bit. Take your mind off the missing girl."

"Nothing will do that," Pete said from experience. She'd dreamed of victims for months afterward—battered wives, stolen children, decimated spirits that clung to her, tearing at her hair and hissing all through her unwaking hours. Pete woke screaming so often that Terry had invested in earplugs.

Jack cupped her hand, palm upward, and conjured a spurt of witchfire in his fingers. He blew a breath over it and the fire flared and drifted upward, settling like milkweed into Pete's palm. It turned the shape of a daisy, then a tiny, perfect oak tree, and finally a duck.

Pete bit the inside of her cheeks and looked up into his face. Jack was grinning at her. "How can you be dour when you've got a tiny duck?" he asked.

She laughed, short, but it was the first real laughter that had come since she'd found Jack again. "You're bloody weird, Jack Winter."

"I'm that," he said. "Ask anybody." The fire duck snapped its bill and ruffled its wings. Pete held her hand out, watching the witchfire burn, when suddenly the duck blurred and lost cohesion as if acid had been poured over it. The fire began to *seep,* to travel inward, through her skin, lighting it from the inside so the bones of her hand stood out as if she'd been struck by lightning.

A heat like a crematory furnace raced up Pete's arm, into her head and heart, and she screamed before everything exploded behind her eyes and she collapsed, the only sensation the shrieking feedback inside her skull.

The black bird spread its wings before Pete, and she knew this wasn't like the other dream. She was cold, and the spider-legged sensation of being in the wrong world crawled over her.

No longer in the Stygian darkness, she stood on the hilltop of a windswept battlefield, hundreds of bodies inkblots against blood-sodden grass.

The crawling of magic resolved into a hooded figure with wings and a dark face. The bird cried, the force of the cold and the malevolence in its voice pushing Pete backward. She found herself pinned by glowing yellow eyes and a woman's red mouth parted to show a raven's beak.

This is not your place. You are unwelcome here.

The black bird's talons closed around her heart and Pete tasted her own blood frozen on her tongue, and in her ears, cawing laughter fell.

"Take it." The shrouded man's tatters whipped in the wind from the black bird's wings, which beat up smoke from the burial fires all around, swirling it faster and faster until Pete could feel herself being swept away, body replaced by the smoke-man and voice by the horrid screech of the black bird.

"Take it," said the shrouded man, thrusting his fist toward Pete. But she couldn't breathe, couldn't speak, and watched as her own hand dissolved into smoke.

Pete screamed and jerked awake into Jack, who toppled over backward. "Fucking hell! You scared the shit out of me, Caldecott!"

Panting, feeling droplets on her skin like she'd been scalded by freezing rain, Pete wrapped her arms around herself. "What . . . what the *hell* was that? *That* was your parlor trick?"

Jack crouched on his heels, ignoring her sputtering, and took Pete's chin between his thumb and forefinger. "You've got a ghost on you," he breathed. "It's right there, in your eyes."

"I'm . . . possessed?" Pete pulled away. She was freezing, and Jack's words caused gooseflesh to break out on her arms. "Shouldn't I be screaming, or levitating, or spewing obscene Latin phrases backward?"

"Not a possession," said Jack. "A spirit rider. Like . . . you've been touched, by someone with blood on their hand, and they've left fingerprints on you. They follow and watch and whisper in your dreams."

Her breath misted when she exhaled, and Pete shivered. "It's the spirit. The one that's feeding on Margaret?"

"It's a good guess," said Jack. He rubbed a hand over his

face. "Bollocks. I should have guessed, with your night-mares . . . should have bloody known."

"Don't blame yourself," said Pete. "*I* didn't know they were anything but bad dreams." And she didn't volunteer the other part of the dream—the shrouded man, and the beating heart, and the advent of the black bird. That was hers, and not Jack's, to know. "Nothing good ever comes from the Black," she murmured.

"This one, this isn't from the Black," Jack said. He patted down his pockets and then conjured a fag. "Coming to you in your dreams, sinking claws into your soul, it's living in the in-between."

Pete rubbed her palms over her arms and felt the heat of friction. "Wherever it's bloody from, I wish it hadn't picked me."

"The in-between, the thin space. The realm between life and death." Jack exhaled a halo. "There's not many living that touch the cold space, Pete. Be glad it didn't try to pull you in."

"I'm still alive," Pete said. She felt the small sharp-toothed gnawing of the craving for a smoke of her own. "Can't snatch my soul out from under me."

"Soul's a tricky thing." Jack grabbed his jacket and shrugged into it. "And you can hurt, bleed, and die in the thin spaces, Pete, be you flesh, phantom, or something other."

"Just make the dream stop," Pete sighed. "I haven't slept in weeks and I'm becoming distinctly peevish from it."

"I'll get something for it," Jack promised. "You'll be all right by yourself for a few hours?"

Pete stood when he did, although the walls of the room pulsed ominously and she was dizzy. "Will *you*, Jack? You're not exactly equipped to be running around the city."

He drew back, closing off as if she'd hit him in the mouth. "After everything that's happened in the past days and you still think I'm running off to bloody score."

"Jack, it's what you've been doing for a dozen years," said Pete. "I need you to be clean and sharp when we find Margaret, and whatever has her."

"You're a cynical and mistrustful bitch," Jack said, crossing his arms.

"Yeah, and people like you made me that way," Pete snapped. She rubbed her forehead. Staying upright was a task.

"Now I remember why I walked away from you, Caldecott," Jack said. "This kind of treatment would convince a bloke to stay dead."

"Well, I bloody danced a jig on your grave!" Pete shouted, but Jack slamming the door drowned her out.

Chapter 27

The flat was silent after Jack left, suffocatingly so. Pete poked in the wardrobe in the bedroom, the kitchen cabinets, and found nothing except dust and damp. "Sod you, Jack," she muttered. He was running off, wasting time, and she was supposed to sit home. Not bloody likely.

Leaving the flat unlocked, Pete left via the front door and found herself in a narrow hallway that could have easily hosted gaslight trysts a hundred years ago. A rickety lift with a folding gate lowered her to the street and she walked until she found a bus shelter where she could talk unobtrusively. One lesson from Jack's reappearance that tickled her spine: Things didn't need to be near you to be watching you.

Pete dialed her mobile, waded through the voice directory for New Scotland Yard, and waited with her stomach flipping while the extension rang.

"Ollie Heath." Ollie sounded as though he had a mouthful of shepherd's pie.

"Ollie, it's Pete."

"Pete!" he shouted. "Where the bloody hell have you been? Newell is shitting chestnuts!"

"That sounds uncomfortable." Pete punched on speakerphone and pulled up her mobile mail client. "Look, I'm sending you a name and I want you to e-mail everything you find to my mobile."

"You got a lead?" Ollie said.

"I will," said Pete. "Once I talk to him." She tapped Ollie's e-mail into the address bar and sent the message.

"Got it," said Ollie a moment later. "Though Newell'll have my hide for helping you out." He whistled. "Caldecott, what the bloody hell are you doing messing about with Travis Grinchley?"

Pete drew in a breath. A pointed question and a good one. "He has something I need to move the kidnapping cases. And to find Margaret Smythe," she said.

"Be careful," said Ollie. "People that cross Grinchley end up in baggies. Little ones. For sandwiches."

"Just send me the information when you have it," Pete snapped, "and don't editorialize."

"All right, all right," said Ollie. "What should I tell Newell when he asks me *yet again* where you've gotten off to?"

Pete stepped out of the shelter and headed for the Stepney Green tube, weaving between taxis stopped at a red light. "Tell him I went to the graveyard."

In Hatton Cemetery, the headstones sat in neat lines, sentinels against the living. The grass stayed mowed and solitary figures and families moved among the rows, placing flowers or standing with their heads bowed.

Pete pulled a few weeds from the base of Connor's headstone. A vase of pink carnations with rotted edges sat in front, tipped over.

"MG, you sodding witch," Pete muttered, picking up the carnations and dumping them into the nearest trash can. Her sister came up from High Wycombe, always managing to miss Pete's own infrequent visits, left cheap flowers purchased outside the cemetery, but never cleaned the grave.

Connor had encased MG's feet in stone when she wanted to fly, with peyote or boys or music. Pete's adventure in Highgate hadn't helped matters. MG never forgave either of them for clipping the wings of her wild, carefree, imaginary life.

"I know you wouldn't approve, Da," Pete murmured, smoothing the turned earth over the grave. "But I know you wouldn't have me leave a little girl to get murdered, either." She sighed and stood, brushing the graveyard dirt from her knees. "What I'm saying is, if I don't come around for a while . . . Jack will take care of your spot. I think I can at least count on him for that."

Her mobile burbled, and Travis Grinchley's address and relevant personal details appeared onscreen. Pete stood for a moment longer, reading Connor's epitaph. *May angels usher you on to paradise.*

"I'm sorry, Da," she said, and left between the rows of headstones before she lost her nerve.

Chapter 28

Travis Grinchley's narrow Camden house was three stories of red brick veined with climbing ivy and granite-block bones. Someone had spray-painted NO FUTURE across the bricks at eye level.

"Bloody hooligans," said a reedy voice from Pete's left. A wizened man in a frock coat and spats clutched a cluster of plastic shopping bags filled with takeaway cartons.

"You live here?" Pete said, finding both the fact that Grinchley had a butler and that he dressed the poor man like *this* vaguely unbelievable.

"I'm Mr. Grinchley's manservant, among other functions," said the gnome, pulling himself upright with a creak of spine. Pete stepped in and took the bags from him, flashing her warrant card with her free hand.

"It's imperative I speak with Mr. Grinchley. Is he in?"

The butler coughed once, in what may have been a laugh a few decades and a few thousand packets of cigarettes ago. "Mr. Grinchley is always in, Inspector. Mr. Grinchley hasn't left his home in nearly fourteen years."

Pete blinked at him, words failing. "Well," she said finally. "Then it will be convenient for me to speak with him."

"I doubt it, miss," said the butler. He took an old-fashioned iron ring from the pocket of his coat and unlocked the double front doors with a skeleton key. "Mr. Grinchley hates being disturbed."

Pete mounted the steps after him, putting on her brightest official smile. "I promise not to be a bother."

The butler grunted and stepped aside to let her in. "Police are always a bother, miss. Usually, they make appointments. Out of respect for Mr. Grinchley's status in the community."

"No offense meant," said Pete, "but Mr. Grinchley's *status* is exactly why I came here." She stepped over the threshold and extended the bags, but before the butler relieved her, pain hit like an iron pipe across her skull.

Pete dropped to her knees on the Persian carpet in the front hall, head bulging with agony. It was as though everything she felt and heard, all those little inklings of magic that she tried to push away, were hugely amplified and splitting her forehead apart.

A pair of black leather driving shoes drifted into her field of view, rapidly blurring as she clutched her head, trying to shut out the avalanche of whispers, the sheer pressure of power causing a trickle of blood from her right nostril.

"Those are my home's protection hexes," said Travis Grinchley. "Designed to keep out unfriendly persons and things."

"I know what a protection hex is," Pete ground out.

One of the shoes, smelling of hide and polish, went under her chin and lifted Pete's face to gaze into Grinchley's. He wore spectacles and had the jaw of a matinee idol. "Interesting. I must say, you don't look terribly unfriendly, miss. Does she look unfriendly to you, Perkins?"

"The inspector asked to speak to you on a matter of some import," said Perkins. "And I got your curry for tea, sir."

Grinchley shoved his spectacles up his nose and reexamined Pete. "An inspector. Goodness. A vast improvement over the last clod the local constabulary sent out." He smiled, lips closed, stretched and bloodless. "In that case, Inspector . . . do come in."

The scream of feedback in her head ceased immediately, and Pete went on all fours, feeling sweat along her back sting the scratches left by the bansidhe. "Are you this hospitable with all of your visitors, Mr. Grinchley?"

He took her hand, laid a kiss that crawled along her skin on the back of it, and helped her to her feet. "Only with lovely ones."

Pete took her hand away too quickly and shoved it into her pocket. "Is there somewhere we can talk in private?"

Grinchley's eyes glittered darkly. "Of course. Perkins, bring in a tray when the tea's ready."

Perkins inclined his head and shuffled away like the macabre monster given life. "That makes you the mad doctor, then," Pete whispered at Grinchley's back as he led her into his study. A fire burned in the grate, gas whooshing in the closed space, heating the low-ceilinged room to incubatory temperatures. Grinchley kept his curtains drawn. They could be anywhere, in any time or place. Pete felt her skin dance with chill despite the fire.

"Something stronger than tea?" Grinchley held up a crystal decanter and a cut glass.

"I'm on duty," Pete lied. Grinchley poured himself a tipple.

"Pity." He swirled the whisky and swallowed. *All he needs is a bloody monocle and tailcoat,* Pete thought. "What did you want to speak with me about, Inspector?" said Grinchley. "I can hardly have witnessed a crime or been privy to confidential information. As you can see." He gestured at the dark oak bookshelves filled with artifacts and leather tomes. Jars and animal skulls shone in the firelight. "I'm quite comfortable within my four walls."

"I'll be blunt," said Pete, turning her back on the rows

of curiosities. "Four children have been snatched in the past three weeks. Three have turned up blinded and traumatized beyond speech. The fourth is still missing." She pulled Margaret's picture from the pocket of her jacket and thrust it at Grinchley, who took a disdainful step back. "This child is ten years old, Mr. Grinchley. A close friend of mine believes you have the means to assist in finding her."

Grinchley frowned, a studied gesture with just the right crinkling of skin between his eyes and thoughtful concern twisting his mouth. Pete saw it then—the flatness behind Grinchley's blandly handsome face. Jack did something similar when he lied, but the difference was that Jack *did* feel, underneath his calculated masks. Grinchley was simply empty.

"You know what a protection hex is and you haven't asked me about anything in my collection that would indicate your unfamiliarity with the arcane, so I can hardly play innocent, Inspector. How can I help with your esoteric problem?" Grinchley inclined his head.

"Your Trifold Focus," said Pete. "Give it to me."

Just for a moment, Grinchley tensed, the lines around his eyes growing darker. Then he smiled again, easy and predatory. "Why, Inspector. Someone's been telling you tales. I'm a collector, it's true, but I don't possess anything on the magnitude of *that* particular item. I can only wish."

"Leave out the act, Grinchley," Pete snapped. "Unlike you, my friend isn't a liar . . . not about things of this nature, anyway. You have it."

"Your *friend* should check his sources," Grinchley said, his smile fleeing. He downed the last of the tumbler and slammed it on his desk. "Now I believe I've accommodated you long enough, Inspector. Please leave."

Pete breathed in, and out. *Margaret,* she reminded herself. "No," she said.

Grinchley froze, his face twisting into a thunderous

frown. "No? Inspector, I can assure you that contradicting me is a very stupid move. Did your friend tell you that as well?"

"Give me the Focus and I'll leave," said Pete, calm as if she were ordering a pint. At the base of her spine, fear uncoiled and crawled upward. "I'm quite serious about this, Grinchley."

He crossed the space between them so quickly Pete barely saw his shadow, gripping her by the shoulders and pushing her against the nearest set of bookcases. The jars and lacquer boxes rattled over Pete's head as her skull slammed into the edge of the shelf. "What does a pretty, simple girl like you want a Trifold Focus for, hmm?" Grinchley murmured. "Such a unique item would only be of use to a sorcerer, or a cheap mage with delusions of power. So which is your *friend,* Inspector? Is he a true student of the blacker arts, or is he a pathetic conjure-man on the street corner with cards up his sleeve, dreaming of a power he cannot hold?"

"He's the type that would melt flesh off your bones for that insult," Pete choked. She wrapped her hand around Grinchley's wrist, which felt like a slender tree trunk, and exerted the pressure points. Grinchley grunted, lips peeling back from his teeth.

"You fight. Stirring effort, but it won't help you." He lifted his other hand to touch Pete's cheek. "I'm not surprised he picked you—the worthless mage. Beautiful, not too delicate, but easily broken by terror or sorrow." His eyes blazed, like Jack's, but their fire was gold and terrible as an angel falling in flames. "Someday he planned it, of that I'm sure. He wants to shatter you, Inspector. Pity I got there first." He reached over Pete's head and brought out a length of rotted and frayed rope. With a flick, he wrapped it around her neck.

"The Dead Man's Snare," Grinchley murmured, reverently as any curator. Pete choked as the smelly thing contracted of its own will, wrapping around her neck so tightly she felt instant bruises on the flesh beneath.

"This particular specimen was collected and cursed at Tyburn, after its length had stretched thirteen murderous bastards on the hanging tree."

The rope grew and grew, rewrapping itself around Pete's neck each time, twisting a hangman's knot. She tried to shove her fingers under the moldy cord, but to no avail. Black started to creep around the edges of her vision.

"It still hungers, Inspector," Grichley said, stroking her face. "And the more you fight, the lustier it will be. So by all means, dance. Dance the dead man's jig. Every movement you make prolongs your death."

"How will you . . . explain . . . killing . . . a police officer?" Pete managed. Grinchley raised one shoulder.

"It wouldn't be the first time someone in a position of authority has come sniffing at my collection. I deal with the most faithful and esteemed servants of the Black, Inspector. I am discreet."

She wasn't getting out of this with mere talk, then, and the blasted rope was so tight she could barely speak. *You'll know when the time for talk is past,* Connor said. *You'll know it and you'd better take swift action, girl, lest you want to end life dirty and bloody and broken.*

Pete drew up her knee and with the last of her air planted a kick squarely between Grinchley's legs. He moaned and doubled over, and Pete reached out and swiped what looked like a bone-handled athame from a low display. She shoved it between her flesh and the Dead Man's Snare, and the ancient strands parted, recoiling from the metal and freeing her air.

"All right, Grinchley," she said. Her voice was barely a whisper. She touched her throat and the flesh was tender and rigid with forming bruises. "Get over behind the desk."

The skin of an affable older gentleman had slipped away entirely and Grinchley staggered to the desk under her guidance. He was lumpy and ill formed, like a golem, and his eyes and teeth glittered in the low light. Pete knew this was what Grinchley's last thief must have seen, just before he ended his nightmare in the Thames.

She tucked the snare into her back pocket, and then unplugged the telephone and tossed the cord to Grinchley. "Tie your legs, and use a real knot."

"You really think you can do anything, *command* anything of me?" Grinchley hissed. "My magic will tear you limb from limb and then—"

"Firstly," said Pete as she pulled out the cord of a lamp and tied Grinchley's arms behind him. "If there's one thing I've learned in the past week it's that real mages don't ramble on, they just do it." She secured the knot with a tug. "If you had magic other than tawdry rope tricks, you would have *used* it, you silly git."

Grinchley started to spit invectives, but Pete picked up a wadded message slip from his desk and stuck it in his mouth. "Secondly, I'm leaving here with the Trifold Focus, and I am out of time to fuck about with you, Grinchley, so either tell me where you keep it or I start slicing." She raised the knife and let it catch the light of the fireplace.

After a long moment of staring into her eyes, Grinchley grunted and spat out the paper. "You're made of less breakable porcelain than it appears at first glance, Inspector."

"Lucky, lucky me. Where's the Focus?" said Pete, keeping her voice flat. All she needed to hurt Grinchley, to bleed him, was contained in the memory of Bridget Killigan, of the bleeding tracks in Jack's skin, and the invisible pressure of a Fate measuring off the last moments of Margaret Smythe's existence. But she'd let the threat do the work unless he pressed her. She was still the detective inspector, not a thug.

"The Focus is in my vault room." Grinchley sighed. "In the cellar, at the back of the house."

"There," said Pete. "Isn't being reasonable a simple thing?"

"You'll pay," Grinchley said as she left him tied. "You'll pay in blood for this, little Inspector. Not today and not tomorrow and perhaps not until the end of your time on this earth, but you've put your hand in a wolf's mouth and you'll—"

Pete slammed the library door shut on him and followed a dark broad hallway toward the rear of the town house. The cellar door wasn't locked, and Pete paused at the foot of the stairs. Connor would have said this was too easy by half. Grinchley should have fought harder. He should have locked his doors, at the very bloody least.

Her footfalls were nearly silenced on thick Persian carpet over the stones and it was only a draft against her neck that warned Pete of someone behind her. She spun to see a huge man in an undershirt and black trousers swing a massive fist at her face.

She ducked, but not fast enough and the blow glanced off her skull. Pete fell and the air sang out of her as she hit the floor. The man hulked above her. A line of stitches paraded across his neck and around his right arm at the shoulder, purple and infected. His eyes were mismatched, green and blue, and he grinned at Pete through bloody teeth. "Trespasser." The word ground out from a throat that might have been patched together after a cutting.

For a few precious seconds, Pete was unable to do anything except stare. It cost her any chance to get away—the golem grabbed her by her collar and simply dragged her along, ignoring Pete's kicks and shouted curses except for a grunt.

They turned a corner and the smell of bleach invaded

Pete's nostrils as she slid along a floor of worn linoleum. The golem hauled her to a stop in a scrub room, brightly lit as the rest of Grinchley's town house was shadowed.

"I'd so hoped you wouldn't cause any trouble, Inspector." Perkins sighed. His frock coat was missing and a dishtowel was over his shoulder. "But it appears you were rash. Take her into the operating theater, if you will."

The reanimated servant grunted and picked Pete up again. "It takes orders from you . . ." she said. The thickness in her head lifted a fraction and she saw past Perkins's stooped shoulders and sagging skin. "You're the sorcerer."

"Of course," said Perkins. "One of Mr. Grinchley's objets d'art, if you will. He does pay handsomely for my services, and my brethren benefit from Grinchley's expertise in antiquities of an . . . impure nature. Now I don't believe I'll bore you with the details, Inspector. We've all watched a James Bond film or two." He nodded to the servant. "I'll be down momentarily."

The servant half dragged Pete to a metal security door and worked the handle clumsily with his free hand. One limb was small and boyish with manicured nails and the other was flat and scarred; a dock worker's hand.

The operating theater was a catacomb, buried long before the town house sat atop it, slimy stone steps leading down to the round killing floor. Pete skidded and fell the last three steps, landing in a heap. The servant kicked her in the stomach, rolling her along like a lumpy carpet.

Pete felt something prick her as she hit the opposite wall of the stone chamber. A numbness spread over a patch of skin on her hip and she slipped her hand into her trouser pocket. The syringe she'd taken away from Jack greeted her, cap loosened and tip dripping. The golem dragged a heavy pair of shackles from their bolt in the wall toward her, moaning softly to himself.

When he came near, reaching for her arms with a grasping gesture, Pete rolled over and jammed the syringe into the inside of the golem's thigh, where a fat artery would have pulsed in life.

The golem shuddered and let out a choked sound that was almost a sob. He took one more shambling step and collapsed backward.

Pete pulled herself up on the ragged blocks of the wall and checked for injuries. She was bruised but not bleeding, her knees and the back of one hand scraped from the fall. She made the executive decision that she'd live, and stepped over the downed creature to fix on a door.

The operating theater had iron shackles bolted into the walls at intervals along the curve of the stones and a modern drain set into the floor over a steel autopsy table. Blood trickled down the table's grooves, an insistent hollow dripping against the damp stone.

On the tabletop, a half-assembled golem blinked milky eyes as a spinal cord waiting for hips and legs twitched like a tail. Pete skirted it as widely as she could, but the eyes still rolled after her and teeth unfettered by a tongue chattered.

Just beyond the table was a door, iron bubbled with rust and age. It had no visible handle that Pete could see, and she pried her fingers into the cracks at the edge and only succeeded in bloodying her nails. "Sod your aunt," she hissed in frustration.

The ceiling of the theater had no skylight or vent, and the walls, for all their age, were bricked tightly with mortar and moss. The golem on the table hissed at Pete, jerking its arms as it tried to reach for her.

Pete leaned against the wall and shut her eyes, trying to keep her panic in check enough so that she wouldn't scream. She'd be all right. One way or another, she'd be all right.

Jack, should have listened to Jack, should have known that you running off would go this way. Now what will you do? All of the normal whispers and shivers of magic that Pete had come to recognize in her renewed time with Jack faded in the operating theater and her skin felt slick with something else, cold and silken as spoiled milk.

This is the Black. People die here, and usually because someone's decided to kill them.

"Shut up, Jack. Since when are you bloody right about anything?" Pete muttered. She tried her mobile, got no signal underground, and paced a few times, keeping clear of the golem. She was truly, properly fucked. Trapped in here until Grinchley or Perkins decided what to do with her.

"They'll find my bones when they knock this place down to make a motorway," Pete said. The golem keened and hissed. "Be quiet!" Pete shouted at it, because it was better than crying in frustration.

A groaning and scrabbling began from outside the iron door, and Pete steeled herself for anything, but Perkins appeared, pushing open the massive gate with some effort.

He caught sight of the first golem, still and spent on the floor. "Oh," Perkins said. "Oh, dear."

Pete snatched up a scalpel from the rolling tray by the surgery, which also held bundles of half-rotted herbs and a black candle smeared in blood alongside the precise row of instruments, and stepped into Perkin's view. "He was a lightweight."

Perkins turned to her, his eyes glittering. "Do you have any idea how long it takes to animate one of those, you stupid girl? You've cost me *months.*"

Pete allowed herself a smirk that she did not feel. "Well, it's not exactly a model airplane, is it?"

Snarling, Perkins raised his hand, black mist crackling with ice trailing from his fingertips. "Pain," he said simply, and Pete felt every muscle, every tendon and joint in her, seize with the worst kind of agony. It was fever-pain and torn muscles and a dull rusty nail in her flesh all at once.

A high buzzing scream cut the air, hers, and she fell back against the surgery table, vision blacking out. The half-golem on the table latched its teeth around her wrist and the cold pressure against her bones sent her into panic.

Pete heaved against the golem, and the flesh of her wrist tore as the golem went flying through the air with a hiss, landing on Perkins like a sack of lead pipes. Pete scattered the herbs and the candle, feeling her hand grow slick and warm as blood pumped out of the tear in her skin. The cold wet magic in the room shifted, loosened, and the golem let out a scream of victory.

Perkins fell over and the golem clawed at his face and chest, latching its teeth to his throat and gnawing with fierce desire until Perkins's neck artery fountained blood and he gurgled, going still. The golem continued to eat, blood flowing through it and onto the floor through its loose-ended entrails.

The pain Perkins had laid on her lessened slowly after he died, not at all like Pete would have expected from a spell, but it did lessen and she did climb the slippery stone steps back into the too-bright scrub room, which she saw now also held an altar of bones and pickled bits of skin and flesh in jars. A skull grinned at her from the center of an omega symbol wrought into clay. Pete wished fleetingly for Jack, he'd be able to tell her what she had to do for sure, but she settled for kicking over the altar and was relieved to feel the familiar prickles along her neck and scalp return as the flow of magic pulsed into the emptiness left by Perkins.

A tremble in her knees warned Pete that she was losing too much blood, and she saw her wrist was still pumping. "Bugger all." She tore off the bottom of her T-shirt and wrapped it tightly around the golem bite. It wasn't bleeding enough to have nicked a vein, but it hurt and there was a film of greenish spittle on the wound. "I'd bloody well better not start craving brains," Pete said, trying the door that led away from the upstairs of the house.

It opened smoothly and led Pete down another flight of slanted stone steps into a catacomb that paralleled the operating theater. She only had to listen to the groans and cries from behind the tiny barred doors on either side of the hallway to realize that it wasn't a catacomb—this was a dungeon.

Hands reached for Pete as she stepped into the shadow, some human and emaciated, some stiff and black with final-stage decomposition. Skin and blood sloughed off and regrew, and rats scattered and hissed farther back in the dark.

Someone latched on to the arm of Pete's jacket. "Help . . . me . . ." A man dressed in bum's rags clung to her, face drawn into a rictus of desperation.

Pete recoiled. "Human?"

"Yes," sobbed the man. "Oh, God, yes. They offered me a hot meal . . . took me off the street . . . he uses us for *parts,* don't you see? *Spare parts.*" He proffered his other arm to Pete, severed at the elbow with a clumsily cauterized wound.

The door of the man's cell wasn't locked, just bolted from the outside. Pete slid the bolt back and said, "Run. Don't stop."

The man didn't thank her. He staggered out and back along the gauntlet of shrieks and snarls, crying and stumbling until he vanished up the stairs.

Remains of Perkins's magic stared at Pete from behind every door she passed, all the way down the deceptively long corridor until she reached the end, the rear of the house. Men and women, young and old, most of them clumsily reanimated to spit or cry, some of them chewing on their own limbs, or each other. The air was rank with decomposition the farther Pete walked.

Some of the subjects had symbols or sigils painted on the doors of their cells and Pete rubbed them out when she could, hoping fervently that she wasn't turning off any electric fences designed to keep in rabid dogs as she did.

"Bitch!" something hissed from behind one of the doors. "I'll pull your eyes out and roll them on my tongue!" The hiss started up a cacophony of other noises, curses and threats filtered through ruined tongues and toothless mouths.

"You're welcome, you wanker," Pete muttered, moving on rapidly to the corridor's end, lit with an old-fashioned oil lantern.

The vault room was locked with an iron key that hung on a nail next to the rusty hinges. Pete started to scoff at Grinchley's idea of security, then realized that no one could be expected to walk along the trail of nightmares behind her to actually get here except Perkins and Grinchley himself.

Pete turned the ancient lock with no small amount of effort and went inside. The vault room was packed with cases and compact shelving, everything arranged in no particular order. Three human skulls of varying size and age grinned at Pete from the nearest cabinet, and a stuffed Feejee mermaid perched in a gilt birdcage. Every inch of the room was crammed with objects of magic and vileness, human and animal body parts, books bound in skin, statues whose eyes followed Pete as she moved among the shelves.

This is useless. Connor came into her head unbidden. *Going to stand there like a flytrap with your mouth open all day, girl? Organize. Categorize. Find the piece that don't fit.*

Pete thought of the dark rooms in Grinchley's house, how everything was arranged to frighten, to misdirect.

Someone with an ego the size of Grinchley's wouldn't hide his treasures, except in plain sight.

Her eyes drawn back to the largest shelf, the one with the skulls, Pete discerned a sheen of silver behind the smallest skull's eyes. She picked up the thing, half expecting it to bite her, and saw a flat black box bound in silver bands lying on the shelf.

Covered in dust and unassuming though it was, Pete knew this was what she was looking for. It shone in the Black, magic raw as a nuclear spill. She reached out carefully with a finger and flicked the latch, laying the box open.

The Trifold Focus lay wrapped in a black silk cloth, smaller and plainer than Jack had made it out to be, just a silver circlet with three interconnected spirals at the center, flat and more like a drink coaster than anything.

Pete touched it and a jolt of static raced up her arm. The Focus's metal strands shifted and curled beneath her hand, recoiling, and Pete quickly pulled it away. They settled immediately. "Thank bloody God," Pete muttered. Searching the rest of the vault room would be on her list of preferred activities straight after walking into traffic on the M-25 wearing nothing but her knickers.

She put the box with the Focus into the pocket of her coat and saw a door with a gleam of light around it at the far end of the room. Anything to not have to walk back through Grinchley's torture chambers.

The doorway led to a real basement, with a furnace and a collection of musty cricket equipment. Pete paused and turned the dial on the ancient oil furnace to maximum. It began to shudder and clank as she cleared the street.

Pete pulled out her mobile and dialed 999. "This is Detective Inspector Caldecott reporting a fire at the Grinchley residence, 14 Mornington Crescent."

She heard the wail of sirens as she walked to the cross

street and hailed a taxi. The fire brigade would go where no warrantless police officer could. Considering what Grinchley had put her through, Pete thought she was being extraordinarily kind.

Chapter 29

"Jack!" Pete shouted as she opened the door to the flat. "Jack, you need to keep your door locked. This isn't a good neighborhood."

"Pete!" Jack came rushing from the kitchen, Parliament dangling from the corner of his mouth. Smoke trailed behind him like a cluster of familiars. "Fuck all, Pete, where the bloody hell have you been?"

"Are you all right?" Pete said, taking him by the chin and examining his eyes. Jack's pupils were large and wide, glimmering like glass.

"Maybe. Yes. I don't know." Jack rumpled his hair and then slumped. "I thought you'd gone off."

"I just went to run an errand," said Pete. She grabbed Jack's right forearm, examining the tracks for fresh bruises. He jerked it away.

"I didn't bloody use. I took some uppers. Couldn't focus."

"Oh, for the love of sweet infant Christ," Pete shouted. "Jack, first you despise me and then you pop pills the minute I'm gone from sight! What *is* it?" She formed her hands into fists, released them, because hitting Jack wouldn't make him tell her.

"Jack," she said softly. "I'm not moving from this spot until you answer what it is I did to you to make you this way."

He pinched the spot between his eyes, creasing a furrow in the skin. "You left me, Pete," he said. "You just fucking left me, that day. The only person I let in a little bit and she leaves me on the floor of a fucking grave and never shows her face again. Felt bloody marvelous when I woke and realized that, thanks."

Pete looked at her feet. A splash of blood from Grinchley's operating bay sat like a teardrop on the toe of her shoe. "I thought you were dead, Jack. You were just *lying* there . . . you were *gone.*"

"And you never bothered to find out differently, did you?"

"I never did *anything,*" Pete said desperately. "I ran out of the cemetery and all the way home and I locked myself in my room for two days and cried until I couldn't breathe. But I never told a soul, because there was never a soul I could tell. Da eventually figured out we'd been seeing each other—didn't tell MG, thank all that's holy—and he lit into me right proper.

"Da told me . . ." Pete chewed on her lip for a moment. She'd long since forgiven Connor for the lie, but she couldn't be sure Jack would. "Da told me you died, Jack. And that it would be best to forget you."

"Cunt," Jack muttered.

"Well, he never did like you," Pete said. "You shagged his oldest and put his youngest into a blind fit."

Jack dragged on his Parliament and refused to look at her. "I waited around London for a fair time after I got out of the hospital. I guess I was hoping you'd show up looking for me."

"I did," said Pete. "Every face on the street. Every day. For all the time until I went away to university. Eventually, though, I listened to Da. I tried to believe what I saw wasn't what happened, and that you *were* dead and I should put you out of mind, and I am *sorry* for that, Jack, but it was what I had to do to go on."

"And then you were able to sweep me neatly into the 'Mistakes of My Youth' category with *Terry*'s help," Jack snarled.

"*Terry* has nothing to do with this," Pete snapped. "So leave it out." She took a breath. Imagining saying these things, speaking them to Jack's dream-ghost was easy. This—this was like scaling the White Tower barefoot.

"I got it, finally," Jack muttered. "When you didn't come. You were a sweet kid but you were slumming. No future. Nothing with me."

"Jack," Pete said. She took his hands in hers, trying not to flinch at how close to skeletal they still were. "I was a child, and I made a child's choice. I dreamed about you, up until the day I saw you again in that terrible hotel. Knowing that you were alive was probably the best day of my life." She took out the box from her pocket and opened it and folded the Trifold Focus into Jack's palm. "I went to get this for you. I'm back now. I don't leave anymore, and I won't try and forget any longer."

She stepped past Jack and went into the loo, locking the door and sitting on the tub's edge, pressing the heels of her hands into her eyes. Only a few tears came, because she was too battered to really cry.

After a long while, as Pete sat and watched the shadows move across the floor from the wavy-glass window, Jack knocked on the door. "Pete. I went to the Costa."

He pushed open the door, cradling a cardboard cup and a fresh fag in his free hand. Pete's nose crinkled. "Jack, you hate coffee. You told me so the night we met."

"Need to sober up," he muttered, taking a sip and wincing as if he were having his toenails pulled off. "We've got work to do."

"The summoning," said Pete.

"The summoning," Jack agreed. "But first, you're going to tell me how you got the Focus out of Grinchley's house.

He's not going to burst in here and bash me kneecaps in, is he?"

Pete stood, wiping away the last hints of moisture from her face. "I went, I tangled with his pet reanimator and I got the Focus and got the bloody hell out of his freaky basement."

Jack frowned. "Reanimator?"

"You wouldn't sodding believe the scene in that place, Jack." Pete thought about the cages, the hands, the golem on the surgery table and shivered again. "I still feel as if I need a hot shower."

"Don't let me stop you, luv."

Pete reached out to slap at him, but her heart wasn't in it and Jack sidestepped. "In all seriousness, now—Grinchley is animating corpses?"

"His butler is," said Pete.

Jack blew out a breath. "A necromancer? Really? Haven't run across one of them since the Stone Age."

"Perkins looked as if he were *from* the Stone Age," Pete said.

"That's odd, to be certain," said Jack. "Necromancy and flesh-crafting are dying arts. No one apprentices to them any longer. No need, with infernal servants being as easy to compel as they are in this day and age."

"Grinchley set this on me, as well," Pete said, drawing out the desiccated Dead Man's Snare from her hip. "Thought maybe you'd have some use for it."

Jack whistled. "Nicely done, Pete. Powerful little bit of conjuring on this one." He pushed it back at her. "But you keep it."

"I really don't think I'll ever have need of this. I *hope* I won't, at the very least," Pete said. "Maybe you could use it to break the ice at parties or something."

Jack sipped his coffee and grinned. "You won it fair and

square in sorcerous combat, Pete. Keep it. It's yours. And when I did parties, I usually called up a few poltergeists or minor demons. Bit more flash. Speaking of which, I could use some help with this bit if you're not too knackered."

"Show me what to do," said Pete, shutting the bathroom door behind her.

"Come into the kitchen and have one of these over-priced pastries and I'll explain things," Jack said.

After Pete had stirred a cup of espresso for herself, Jack slid into the seat across from her and held out a black velvet sack. "Got this for you, too."

Pete slid out a small crescent charm on a plain silver chain. It was cool to the touch and when she held it the constant undertone of magic that hissed to the hidden part of her mind quieted.

"It's a talisman for dreamers," said Jack. "It will keep you safe from sundown to dawn."

Pete admired the way the half-circle caught the light. "Will it."

"That's the theory, anyway," said Jack. "Really, it depends on you."

"How do you mean?" Pete said. She put the charm around her neck and felt the silver kiss her clavicle. It felt like dipping a hand into cool water, with cool stones beneath and the moon reflected above.

"Do you *want* to stop dreaming?" Jack asked.

"This particular dream, yes," Pete said emphatically. "And I could do without being haunted, as well."

Jack's mouth quirked. "I'm afraid while you hang around me there's always a bit of ghost-light about," he said. "But the bugger shouldn't be able to get to your mind so easily with that."

"Ta," Pete said, smiling a bit herself. Jack looked pleased, like he'd picked out a birthday gift in the proper size.

"Kid stuff. Don't mention it." He extinguished his Parliament in the remains of his coffee. His hands shook but a little, and he collected a pen and started drawing on scraps. "Now, this is what calling the demon should entail, and what I need from you . . ."

Chapter 30

A few hours later, Pete followed Jack through the aisles of a DIY shop, collecting supplies from the hardware department. "You're joking, right?" she said. "This is where we get the supplies for a demonic ritual?"

"Some of it, yeah," said Jack. "Magic isn't all eye of newt or skinning black cats."

Pete jerked her trolley to a stop. "I am not killing a cat."

"Dagon in a rowboat, Pete, relax. The demon we want doesn't accept animal sacrifices. It would be terribly offensive."

"Facts I'm sure will come in handy in my day-to-day life," she muttered, following Jack as he picked out a roll of copper wire.

"Will if you keep on with me," Jack said with a shadow of a grin. He picked up a box of roofing nails and tucked them into his jacket pocket. Pete cleared her throat vigorously. Jack gave her an exasperated look, one dark eyebrow cocked.

Pete pointed to the trolley basket. "In."

"They're fifteen quid!" Jack protested. "For a box of ruddy nails!"

"I'm sure all the girls at Fiver's would swoon over your criminal behavior," said Pete. "But if we get pinched we're never going to track down this ghostie or beastie or whatever in time, so put the bloody nails in the trolley and grow the bloody hell up."

Jack glared at her, but he dropped the box in the basket and stalked off, leaving Pete to pay for everything.

"Where are we going now?" Pete demanded. She was trailing Jack through the Kings Road, passing between tourists with cameras and pimply children in tight black jeans and Mohawks trying to grasp on to the heyday of punk outside what used to be Sex.

"Picking up a few last odds and ends," said Jack, turning down a narrow flight of steps to a nameless shop with a black door.

Pete stopped just short of the entrance. "Jack, this is a dodgy porn shop."

"Among other things," he agreed, opening the door, causing an obscenely pleasant bell to jingle.

"Bloody hell," Pete muttered, following him inside.

"I got what I needed from the spellcrafter's supply when I bought your talisman," said Jack. "Just need to see a friend about one last thing."

The shop was gray—gray carpet, walls that had once been white but lay coated with a decade's worth of grime, grim fluorescent tubes overhead like a morgue. Even the covers of the magazines and videos looked deflated and drained of color, posters on the walls curling up at the edges and exposing mildew.

Jack went straight to the counter and slapped his hand on it, waking the snoring clerk so abruptly he slid off his stool. "Oi!"

"Mmph?" said the clerk. "Wotcha want?" He had a ponytail, sad and greasy like a rat's and, if it were possible, was even skinnier than Jack.

"Where's Mr. Towne?" Jack said. "I know he still owns the place so don't bother to lie."

"T-Towne?" said the clerk nervously.

"Towne, Melvin," Jack snapped. "Manky Mel, the sultan of snuff, wizard of wanking, whatever bloody silly thing he calls himself."

"L-look," said the clerk. "I don't want any trouble with the coppers . . ."

Jack grabbed the clerk by the ponytail and jerked him down to eye level. "I'm not a copper."

"*She* is," the clerk squeaked, pointing at Pete. "And *you're* probably just here for the money Mr. Towne owes to Left-handed Dick."

Pete cocked her head at Jack. "This friend of yours got in with a gangster who calls himself Left-handed Dick?"

"Trust me," said Jack, tightening his hold on the clerk's ponytail. "If you knew him you wouldn't be the least bit surprised. Now where is he, you sodding little piece of wormshit?"

The clerk sighed in an almost resigned manner. "He's on the set, in the back."

Jack released him with a little push. "Obliged."

"What's gotten into you?" Pete muttered as she followed Jack through the musty rows of dirty books and bins of toys. "Is your sight channeling Guy Ritchie?"

"You'll see," Jack murmured. His eyes glinted like winter sun on a glacier. "Now if you value your dignity, keep your mouth shut and stay close to me in here. And for the sake of whatever god you believe in, don't try to be Miss Detective Inspector Caldecott of the Metropolitan Police. It'll just get us both beat to shit and dumped in some gutter."

Pete started to ask what, exactly, the history between Jack and Towne entailed, but Jack banged through a fire door and shouted, "Melvin! Look who's back from the dead!"

A heavyset redhead in ill-fitting PVC squealed and covered herself with a sheet, and a voice from Pete's left shouted, "Fuck! Cut!"

Melvin Towne was nearing Pete's height, which put his eyes roughly even with Jack's chin. He had run to fat but his hands were large and soft, arms straining the pristine white T-shirt he wore. At one time, Pete would have hesitated to attempt an arrest on him by herself—Towne was powerful still and the creases on his brow and at the edge of his expressive hazel eyes leaked violence like a ruptured chemical drum. "Jack Winter," he rasped. "Don't you ever stay dead?"

"Not as of yet, you great cumstain," Jack replied genially. "I've come for the limb."

Towne crossed his twin hams of forearm. "Threw the sodding thing away."

"You're a liar, Melvin," Jack said easily. "Not only a liar, but a filthy liar, a dog-fucking liar even."

Melvin sniffed, deep and wet like he had a bad cold, or put roughly a gram of coke up his nose on a regular basis. Pete bet firmly on the latter.

"I don't have your bloody limb," he said again. He walked over to the redhead and jerked the sheet away from her. "I don't fucking pay you to sit on your fat arse with your legs crossed." The girl obligingly resumed the pose she'd been in when Pete and Jack interrupted, wrapping a silk noose hanging from the sprinkler pipes above around her neck and posing on a battered metal dinette chair.

"Choke," Melvin directed. "I want to see the eyes popping out of your fat head when you come, bitch."

Pete would have hesitated, alone, but she wasn't alone now.

She walked over to Towne, picked up his high-end digital camera, and dropped it hard on the cement floor. "Jack asked you a question," she said calmly, making herself look Towne in his pockmarked moon face.

"You fucking cunt!" he exclaimed. "I ought to ram that

camera up your arse until I've shot three grand worth of video, because that's what it'll cost to replace!"

Pete pulled out the Dead Man's Snare and wrapped it around Towne's neck, less gracefully than Grinchley had managed, but the effect was the same. "You are wasting our time," she snarled. "Give Jack his fucking limb before I use my other hand to tear your bollocks off, *cunt*."

"She'll do it, mate," Jack said, fishing a packet of Parliaments out of his jacket. He offered one to the plump girl, who silently shook her head.

"Bad for your health."

"Speaking of which." Pete grinned at Towne and dug her nails into his sweaty chin, forcing him to look at her as he wheezed. "Ever shot a brain aneurysm in one of your little faux-death films? I wonder, will you be a twitcher? I think you're too fat. You'll probably just gurgle, shit yourself, and die."

"In the lockbox!" Towne shouted. "For fuck's sake! The key's in my pocket."

Pete tugged at the Snare, and it uncoiled, folding back into her hand. She smiled at her feet, unaccountably pleased. To Towne she said, "Good man." To Jack, "*You* are getting the key."

Back on the street, Pete snatched the brown-wrapped parcel out of Jack's hands and tore it open. "Oi!" he shouted. "That's me personal property, I'll have you know."

The parcel contained a plastic box, sealed with packing tape. The box was clear and inside . . . Pete nearly dropped the box on the pavement. "Jack, this is a human hand. A *mummified* human hand."

"Towne's wife," he agreed. "Caught her cheating about fifteen or twenty years ago and chopped off bits and pieces until she was sorry. Filmed it all. Was his first big hit, as I recall."

Pete stopped walking and thrust the box back into Jack's hands. "Is this your way of telling me you *enjoy* the company of people like Towne?"

"I'm not that oblique, luv." He grinned. "Saw the video, noticed with my sight Towne had an Egregor, a demon of rage, hanging around him. I bargained the Egregor back into the Black and compelled Towne to give me this as payment."

"But it's a *hand,*" Pete reminded him.

"It's desire," said Jack. "Desire for pain and desire for revenge and desire for love so powerful that it destroyed what it touched. This is a powerful temptation for any demon, Pete. They trade in desire—breathe it. I'm sure every infernal thing in the greater London area has got a hard-on already."

"How reassuring," Pete muttered. Jack turned into the Fulham Broadway tube station.

"We can go home now. We've got everything we need."

Chapter 31

At home in the sitting room, Pete watched Jack lay copper wire out in a circle and nail it down at the four corners with the iron nails. He chalked symbols at the four points, punctuating the northernmost with a black candle. He drew another, seemingly random set of symbols inside the wire and then said to Pete, "Be a love and get me the table salt."

Pete handed him the carton they'd bought at Tesco and Jack scattered a liberal handful inside the copper. "Earth," he said, and then took out his flick-knife and cut the tip of his finger. He squeezed a few fat blood droplets into the circle, as well. "And spirit."

Jack opened Grinchley's lacquer box and took out the Trifold Focus, holding it in the palm of his hand as if it were a dead, dried butterfly. "The best thing for you would be to go in the other room, Pete," he said without taking his eyes off it. "This probably isn't going to be pretty."

"If I wanted pretty I would have become a bloody decorator," said Pete, crossing her arms. "I'm staying."

Jack wanted to object, she could tell, but he pressed his lips together and then said, "Fine. But you stand against that wall. No talking. No matter what happens, no flying off the handle and threatening to rip someone's bollocks off. Got that?"

"Towne deserved to have them ripped off," Pete muttered.

"That he did," Jack agreed. "I've never seen you so fiery, Pete. I rather enjoyed it." His grin suggested exactly how much.

"Shut up and get on with this," Pete snapped. "This thing has had Margaret Smythe for nearly three days, and your reputation in the Black isn't getting any better."

"Your wish is my command, or some rot," said Jack. He placed the box containing the late Mrs. Towne's hand near his feet and stood at the bottom edge of the circle. He gripped the Focus and Pete heard the slide of metal on flesh as twin spikes flashed out from the bottom of the flat metal disc and drove into Jack's palms.

He didn't make a sound. Milky pale rolled across his eyes and they slowly went back in his head, exposing tiny crimson veins like spiderwebs inside his skull.

"Jack?" Pete said, alarmed. She started to go toward him but a shriek cut the air and went straight through her, all the way to the bone, and Pete stumbled back, crying out. "Fuck!"

The shriek crested and stabilized into a low whine and then with a strained *pop* Pete felt a *give* in the air, the shifting of something from one world to another.

"Jack Winter," said the demon. "Why do you call upon me?"

After a heartbeat Jack's eyes flicked back to blue faster than Pete could see. He shook himself and spoke. "To seek that which is lost." There was ritual behind the words the demon and Jack were speaking, and the demon gave a pleasurable shudder when Jack answered correctly.

"First we will strike an accord, a promise of tasting blood if the oath is broken. Only then do I seek your lost object."

"Fair enough," said Jack with a shrug. "Here." He thrust

the box with the erstwhile Mrs. Towne's limb closer for the demon's examination. The demon caressed it in a hand with odd-shaped nails and uneven fingers of every color, patchier even than Grinchley's flesh golems.

"I grant you the product of man's strongest desire," said Jack, yanking the box away from the demon's ministrations. "To honor Talshebeth, the keeper of lost things."

Pete saw that the demon—Talshebeth—had a stitched-together scalp with wildly disparate patches of hair. He was hunchbacked and clothed in castoff rags sewn into a bright coat and had bowed legs swaddled in what appeared to be a thousand pairs of stockings. Wedding bands, dozens of them, rode his thin fingers down to the first knuckle. Across his neck stretched a crude string of baby teeth.

"As all things lost are my domain," said Talshebeth, blinking ragged lashes over a pair of chipped glass eyes. "I accept your payment. Tell me what you seek."

"The wandering spirit of Margaret Smythe," said Jack. "And the name of the one imprisoning her."

Talshebeth laughed, the sound of a carefree child with an amusing pastime, tinged in tears for what could never be retrieved. "And for this, crow-mage, you call a named demon? You have indeed fallen prey to human time's passage. You are old. *You* have lost your prime."

"Don't start up that shite with me," Jack snapped. "Tell me where the girl is or the only way you'll get the hand is when you're wanking off to it with all of the other sodding old-timers, while it lies safe and sound in my loving care."

Talshebeth's eyes turned on Pete. "And you, young and unspoiled," he murmured. "The weight of loss hangs heavy over your tiny bones. Connor Caldecott," he recited suddenly, as if a faded memory had just been washed clean. "Beloved father. Born 2 March 1941, died 12 January 2003. *May angels usher you on to paradise.*"

"Pete," Jack said, "don't listen to it. *You*," he snarled at Talshebeth, "deal with *me*."

"But of course," said Talshebeth with a wide smile made entirely of rotted and rusted wood and ivory false teeth. A maggot worked its way into one of the gaps, but Talshebeth did not seem to notice. "I live to serve, crow-mage. However, a search of this magnitude requires some expenditure of power, so if you were to release me from this crude circle . . ."

"Forget it, you hunchbacked devil," Jack said. "You can work just fine inside the circle, where the nice copper barrier keeps your sodding teeth out of my flesh."

At the street four stories down, the fire escape rattled and a few chips of plaster floated down around Pete's head. Her senses pricked her, and she was distracted from Talshebeth long enough to feel the encroachment of something black and otherworldly send ripples through her feet and up to the center of fear in her stomach.

"Jack . . ."

"Quiet, Pete!" he hissed. "My concentration's shot to hell as it is. You're not helping."

Talshebeth chuckled quietly. "She makes you lose things, crow-mage. Your composure, sanity, maybe your life. I fancy her."

"Tell me where Margaret Smythe is," Jack warned, "and do it in the next five seconds or I am going to take out an already extraordinarily shitty day on you."

The fire escape rattled again, and before Pete could grab Jack and force him to pay attention, the dark sensation was *there*. And then something smashed through one of the arched windows, striking the floor and setting off a flash like a phosphorous grenade. Pete shouted and leaped away from the wall as the rest of the glass exploded inward and five black-clad hooligans in masks and leather coats came through.

One of them went straight for Jack and he dropped the Trifold Focus as the far larger man slammed into his back.

"Get out of here, Pete!" Jack shouted just before the man fetched a punch across his head.

Pete did run—she went straight for the kitchen, one drawer left of the sink, and pulled out Jack's squat cast-iron frying pan. One of the hooligans came chasing behind her, and she swung at him, missing his head and glancing the blow off his shoulder.

He was holding something black and fat-barreled—a tranquilizer gun, Pete thought—and he pointed it at her with the arm she hadn't hit. "Cute trick, bitch. Bad luck for you that after your stunt with the bansidhe they sent humans."

He took aim at Pete. "Cold iron doesn't work on us. Stupid cow." He whispered words of power under his breath and Pete's body tensed of its own accord, anticipating pain.

No dart slammed into Pete, and it wasn't a gun, either—it was magic. Ice-cold and like slamming into a lorry head-first, it swept Pete up and tumbled her end over end until she hit the far wall of the kitchen and slid down it into a crumpled heap.

The sorcerer came to her, pointing the sleek black wand between her eyes. "Got anything to say, mage-whore?"

Pete grasped the edge of the counter and tensed. She had to make the single second she would receive count. "I say I'd take that wand and shove it up your arse, except you'd probably enjoy that."

The sorcerer snarled and raised his wand again, and Pete sprang, twisting his arm and driving it backward into his stomach. The spell fired a half-second later, and the sorcerer screamed. A pit of flesh exploded at close range, as though the sorcerer had just collided with a car.

Pete left him to bleed and ran to find Jack.

Two of the masked men were holding him down and a third was hitting Jack in the face, cursing at him unintelligibly. "Pete . . ." he managed between blows. "Pete . . . get back . . ."

Pete hit the closest with the frying pan, every ounce of her strength behind the blow. The man didn't shout or scream, he just crumpled with a crease in the side of his skull. The one hitting Jack turned and swiped at her with a skinning knife that appeared from his sleeve. Pete ducked the blade and planted her foot in his gut, and when he doubled, slammed the iron into the back of his head.

"Stop!" The man holding Jack held his wand to Jack's head. His was spindly and brown, like a piece of root. "Leave off or I spread his brains like jelly, you tart."

Pete's eyes flicked to Jack's face. Her heart was slamming into her breastbone and she wanted nothing more than to beat the men who'd beaten Jack until they were pulpy sacks of flesh.

"Listen to him," Jack mumbled through a split lip. "They're sorcerers, they mean it." His hand worked into the pocket of his jeans as the sorcerer glared at Pete. She ignored him and frowned at Jack, ever so slightly. He stared back and then dropped her a wink, so quickly Pete wondered if she'd imagined it.

She dearly hoped she hadn't.

"Are you deaf, missy? Drop the kitchenware and get your arse over here!"

"You'll wish you'd taken your chances with me," Pete said. She dropped the frying pan.

"Move!" the sorcerer snarled. To Jack he said, "I'm going to fuck her before I kill you. She's tasty, Winter, I'll give you credit for that."

Pete sighed. "That was the worst thing you could have said."

Jack's flick-knife sprang open in his pocket, and he pulled his hand free. A little bit of blue fire burst around him, more spark than flame, and when Pete looked again Jack had slipped the sorcerer's grip.

The man stared, slack and confused for a breath too

long. Jack's hand whipped out and he drove the thin blade into the sorcerer's throat to the hilt. "Last thing, too," Jack said, and then his legs went out from under him and he sat awkwardly on the floor with a thump.

The sorcerer gurgled and fell back, his wand rolling away and blood pulsing out of the wound in time with his heartbeat. Pete knelt down next to Jack, lifting him up with a hand behind his head. Her fingers met a sticky cut.

"Oh, God," she said. "Jack . . ."

"'M all right, luv," he mumbled. He spat blood and sat up, wiggling his jaw experimentally. "Nothing broken, a few sexy bruises . . . all in all, could've ended much worse."

One of Jack's eyes was blacked and he had a triple set of cuts along his cheekbone overriding his old scar. Blood trickled freely down his chin, but he managed to grin at Pete, even though he gave a soft grunt of pain.

"You look like you just faced off against the entire starting line of Man United," she said. "And the bruises are *not* sexy."

"That's what your lips say, but your adorable little blush tells me they are," Jack said.

"I was *worried* you had been *killed*," Pete said severely. She worried her lip with her teeth. "Something's bothering me . . ." She couldn't make it come clear with all of the adrenaline from the fight still in her veins, but it roiled her stomach nervously.

"Don't tell me 'It was too easy, Jack,' because there's nothing about five sorcerers busting into my flat and working me over that's bloody easy," Jack said.

Pete's stomach flip-flopped like she'd gone over the edge of the world. "Bollocks. Five of them."

The fifth sorcerer unfolded from a dark corner of the sitting room in a swirl of black, freezing smoke. He aimed a revolver at Pete and Jack. "You're a fucking wonder with the magic, Winter, but I'm willing to bet even you can't stop a bullet."

Jack looked at Pete. "He's right."

"I *told* them," the sorcerer said. "Told them that we should have found you and plugged your junkie arm with an overdose when we had the chance, but no. You weren't a *threat*. I can't tell you how happy I am that you finally managed to become one."

Jack heaved a sigh. "Sonny boy, do I *know* you?"

"No," the sorcerer said, a grin spreading under his mask. "But soon everyone in the Black will know me—they will turn when I go by and whisper, 'There goes the killer of Jack Winter, the murderer who stood on the body of the crow-mage and claimed his magic for his own.' You've held your talent and your gift long enough, Winter. Time to give up the ghost."

He started for Jack and Pete, thumb pulling back the hammer of the revolver.

"Wait—" Jack started as the sorcerer's foot displaced the copper wire of the circle. Faster than Pete could see, Talshebeth fell upon the sorcerer, blunt teeth pulling and tearing at the skin, consuming the sorcerer's flesh while his magic was absorbed into the folds and crannies of Talshebeth's form.

"—mind the circle," Jack finished.

"Oh, yes," Talshebeth breathed. "So much rage. So much shadow inside him." The copper wire at his feet glowed molten and the circle broke, running into the cracks in the floor.

"Ah, tits." Jack reached out and shoved Pete behind him without taking his eyes off Talshebeth, with more strength than she would suspect a man twice his size of.

"Oi!" she protested.

"Shut it," Jack said in a low voice, his eyes on Talshebeth. The demon took one step over the liquid copper, then another, placing his mismatched human and cloven feet right together with a sigh of happiness.

"It appears our bargain is void, crow-mage," he said, tongue darting out to taste the air.

"If you know what's good for you, you'll take the hand and leave," Jack said. Talshebeth laughed, gutturally now, pure pleasure in pain.

"Why would I take your offering, crow-mage, when I can have *you*?"

Jack grabbed Pete's wrist. "Run," he said. "Fast and far as you can, and don't look back, don't *come* back no matter what you hear or feel."

"I'm not going anywhere," Pete muttered. "You're no good to me dead."

"Good woman," said Talshebeth. "Loyal, brave, and shining to a fault. Stay, little one. Watch what becomes of the crow-mage when he faces a truer evil."

Jack backed up, almost stumbling over her, and Pete went with him. "You should have run for it," said Jack. "Demons aren't like Fae or like us—they're of another world and there's not a bloody thing I can do to stop him once he's free."

Talshebeth raised his hands as though he were trying to stop a lorry and a greenish aura of magic blossomed around him. He was no longer awkwardly ugly and misshapen. Freed, he was inhuman and terrible to behold.

Jack threw up a hand in turn and Pete felt the crackle of air around him, the energy that was achingly familiar. Jack turned his head and met her eyes. "I'll protect you," he said in an almost earnest tone.

Talshebeth showed his teeth and sent a wave of the sickly green forward, blotting out all the light in Pete's field of vision.

She heard Jack yell and felt the energy around him shudder under the blast. Twisting in his grip on her wrist, Pete grabbed his hand, blind. She wanted to tell Jack so many things and they would all sound trite now. She didn't want to die. She didn't want to be helpless, letting a junkie mage be her human shield when *she* should be shielding *him*. She was the bright one, the protector . . . and she was helpless to stop Talshebeth's fury of toothsome, shrieking magic.

This is the Black. People die here . . .

I don't want to die, Pete thought, bell clear and solid in the face of the ethereal hurricane. Jack's shoulder shuddered under her cheek where she pressed her face low to keep her eyes off the demon, and like a stinking river rushes through a broken dam she felt his magic give, cracking under the demon's. *I don't want to die I don't want to die Idon'twantJacktodieagain . . .*

In the hand holding Jack's, it started, a vibration as if she'd sat on her hand for a few hours and then abruptly released it. The numbness spread up her arm and where Jack's skin met hers heat like red iron burned.

Light exploded in front of her eyes, and she heard Jack yell, *felt* his magic gather and rush outward, and when she opened her eyes Talshebeth was consumed by something gray-black and dense, a flight of magic that reduced him to ashes until his screams blew away on a conjured wind.

Jack slumped, sitting down hard and taking Pete with him.

"What the bloody hell just happened?" she demanded. Jack turned on her.

"You tell me, darling! One moment I'm barely holding off a demon from gnawing flesh off my bones and the next he's a little pile of matchsticks on my floor!"

"I may not know bugger-all about magic," said Pete slowly. "But I know that was not normal." She unclenched her hand from Jack's. The bones creaked in protest and a vivid red imprint of his fingers remained on her palm. "It happened when we touched, then and when you called your witchfire," she told Jack. "Whatever it was."

"Nothing," said Jack. "Nothing, is what that was."

"It was not *nothing*." Pete sounded more outraged than she meant to, or even knew she was, underneath the crushing relief to still be breathing. "You kept your promise—this was different from the last time, because last time you didn't incinerate a demon. Jack—"

"Pete, *it was nothing!*" Jack shouted. "Let it bloody well go!" He got up with difficulty and paced away from her, rubbing his left forearm.

"Why won't you just tell me what happened?" Pete said quietly.

"Because sometimes, Pete, you don't need to know everything," Jack snapped. He grabbed his jacket off the hook and unlocked the door of the flat.

"That's no kind of answer! Where are you going?" Pete demanded. "You can't leave—I need your help still to find Margaret! We're out of time!"

"In case you missed the five armed psychopaths who just burst into my flat, and the sidhe bitches before them, someone is trying to kill me," said Jack. "And I can't find out who's passed down the order dragging a square copper along with me."

"Jack—"

"Let it go, Pete!" he shouted.

"Fine." Pete threw up her hands. "You want to keep playing your little secrecy game, that's fine. But before you go storming out of here, might I point out the matter of the five bodies on your sitting-room floor?"

Jack grinned crookedly. "Bodies? All I see are some bundles of rags." He went to one of the crates stacked against the wall, rooted, tossing out a stack of vintage dirty magazines, a pair of tattered leopard-print pants, which Pete picked up and examined in horror, and finally yanked out a tightly wrapped cloth bundle. "Stand back. It's about to get hot."

He unfurled the canvas and held up a bundle of smoky-smelling herbs, whispering *"Aithinne."* The herbs swirled up and out from his palm, catching the bodies alight and burning them from the inside, like the spent end of a cigarette. Soon there was nothing but rags, just as Jack had said.

"See? No fuss," he said. "Although that was my last batch of inferno weed. Practically extinct now. Very dear."

Pete watched ash drift up from where the bodies had lain, wordlessly. "It's so very simple in your world, isn't it, Jack?"

"You'd think that," he said, grabbing his jacket from the hook. "But little things like staying alive? Not simple in the least. Now I'm going out to find out who wants to stop me from doing that. Got any more objections?"

"Jack . . ." Pete started.

"Good," he said, walking out and slamming the door in her face.

Pete slumped down against the wall again. "Bugger."

Chapter 32

After Pete swept up the ashes of Talshebeth and the sorcerers and binned them, and put the kettle on, and made a cup of tea, she finally realized that Jack wasn't coming back.

Her mobile rang as she was struggling with the bin bag and she grabbed it up. "Hullo."

"Pete, I'm very patiently waiting for you to sign the revised offer papers. I faxed them to your desk at the Yard *days* ago. Have you quite taken leave of the last vestiges of your so-called responsibility?"

"It's just hit where I am, Terry. I don't have time for this—" Pete started.

"You know something, Pete, you are going to *make* time for me," Terry fussed. "You're the one who couldn't let the disposition of our assets go on in a civilized manner, and now you can't be bothered to face up to the mess you've caused. I, for one, think—"

"Terry, perhaps I'm not making myself clear enough about this," Pete said softly. Terry paused.

"Please elucidate."

"*Sod off!*" Pete yelled into the mouthpiece, and then threw her mobile across the kitchen. She hauled the bin bag to the rubbish cart behind the building and it was as if nothing had ever happened in the flat, except for the distinct ebb and flow of the Black, just out of the corner of Pete's eyes, the aftershocks causing tiny ripples in the underground pool of magic.

How long had she been able to feel the Black, Pete wondered, and denied it for bad dreams and shadow? How long had Jack and everything that floated around him been standing just out of view?

Existential ponderings aside, the one fact Pete knew was that she was immeasurably tired, and wanted nothing more than a kip, but curiosity, and Jack not being about to stop her, drove her to stay awake to do a bit of snooping.

The shadows were stretching on to evening. Pete lit the oil lamp and went to get a blanket from Jack's bedroom to wrap up in.

Thick robes of cobwebs trailed from the ceiling in Jack's room, and the floor was littered with musty books and papers. A lone chest of drawers in the corner was the only furniture besides the mattress and scarred wardrobe.

She put a blanket around her shoulders, and crouched to illuminate the stack of books nearest to the mattress. Most of the spines were in languages she didn't read, nor did anyone else who'd been alive in the past five hundred years, but two were in English. *Theories of Energy Magic* and *Practicum of Lesser Spirits and Their Uses*. Pete moved on to the next stack. "Mages couldn't use bloody textbooks, like everyone else," she muttered. Whatever had happened with Jack before he stormed out would not happen again, not if Pete could help it. The feeling of being the transformer on a live wire was unpleasant enough to last several lifetimes.

Pete lofted the lamp to look for more books, catching a Poor Dead Bastards poster with curling corners on the wall opposite. She tried the drawers of the chest, found them open. "Let's see what you keep hidden," Pete muttered, half convinced that Jack would hear her, wherever he was.

He had that odd prescient knowledge of a clever devil, one that appeared when you spoke his name.

Herbs and crystals on leather thongs, shriveled birds' feet, a collection of vellum scraps covered over with Jack's scratchy handwriting crumpled in one corner, a marijuana pipe, and a slide whistle made up the entirety of the drawer's contents.

"Nothing," Pete muttered. Nothing that would show why Jack had run away, again. Or why he refused to admit what had gone on when they vanquished Talshebeth.

She sat down on Jack's dusty mattress and sneezed. It smelled like him, whisky and Parliaments and that slightly burnt scent that was his alone.

Pete realized that all the fear and rage had left her and her limbs were lead. She scanned the pages of a few more books, making a go of it, and then gave in to her body's shouted signals to catch a few hours of sleep. If she wasn't on her game, she wouldn't be of any use to Margaret or anyone else.

Shoving a pile of Jack's clothes off the mattress to make a space for herself, Pete heard something crackle inside the pocket of his leather jacket, the same one he'd worn the first time she'd met him. Pete pulled out a many-times-creased piece of vellum, greasy and frayed at the edges.

PETE CALDECOTT
221 CROYDON PLACE, #32
LONDON

Pete's hand shook as she recognized her old address, the one she'd lived at with Connor until he'd taken sick, but hadn't moved to until several years after she'd lost contact with Jack. The paper was worn enough and the ink faded to believe it was a decade old. Jack had found her and held this scrap, but he'd never come to her, never written or called. He'd just kept this little bit of information near his heart.

She stared for a moment longer, and then Pete threw back the blanket. She was tired, of Jack's contradictions and his secrets. She pulled on her shoes and coat and left the flat, leaving the door unlocked as usual in case Jack came home.

Chapter 33

Pete walked through Spitalfields, feet ringing off the cobbles that the Ripper's shadow had stalked one hundred twenty years before. She let herself be pulled from street to street, through pocket parks and alleys until she fetched up at a rusted iron gate. A padlock dangled limply from a chain that was nearly eaten away, and a swift kick sent it clattering.

Inside the gate was unlit night. Pete wrapped her coat around her more tightly and walked into it.

She would swear up and down that the pub Jack had taken her to the first time was in an open street, bright red door banded with iron facing out, but now it was simply *there*, at the other end of the alley.

Music drifted out when Pete pulled on the great iron handle, and a bouncer who hadn't been about the last time stopped her with a large hand, nails lacquered black. "Going somewhere special, miss?"

Pete drew in a breath. The man was massive, shaven-headed with Maori tattoos crawling over the bare flesh. He grinned and displayed a missing front tooth when she gaped at him. "I'm looking for Mr. Mosswood," she said finally, willing herself to be firm.

"You got business with the Green Man." The bouncer

raised an eyebrow in surprise, but didn't question her. He stepped aside and Pete walked in.

The band onstage could have been playing an Irish folksong, or "God Save the Queen" . . . the music dove and dipped, never more than a snatch intelligible, but it was still beautiful and at the same time left Pete feeling stricken, as though she'd left pieces of herself scattered everywhere to be picked over by the crows.

"The eponymous Lament," said a familiar voice. Pete spun to see Mosswood sitting cross-legged at a table, chewing on the end of his pipe.

"Mr. Mosswood."

"Just Mosswood," he said, blowing a lazy smoke ring.

"Lament for who?" Pete said. "Or what?"

"You've heard of Nero, surely, and the music he played while the empire burned," said Mosswood. "This is the same music. The music that played when Cain slew Abel and the sound that will be at the end of the world."

Even though a fire was roaring in the pub's wide grate, Pete shivered. Mosswood indicated the chair opposite him. "You are obviously troubled a great deal to come here without an escort, Miss Caldecott. Please. Sit down."

"I don't need an escort," said Pete reflexively.

"I suppose you don't." Mosswood knocked out his pipe against the edge of the table and took his leather tobacco pouch out of his coat. "You wouldn't have been able to find your way here again if you were not touched by the Black."

A cup of tea appeared on the edge of the table, a tiny hand sliding back below eye level, and Pete started.

"Thank you, Nora," said Mosswood. "And another of the same for Miss Caldecott. Sugar?"

"No sugar," Pete said, regarding the small earthy-colored creature with an arched eyebrow.

"Brownies," said Mosswood when Nora had scuttled

away. "Not very intelligent, but love menial tasks. Useful for housework, if you need someone to come in."

"I'm here about Jack," Pete said, putting her palms flat on the table.

"Oh, I doubt that." Mosswood blew on his pipe and smoke sprouted as the tobacco lit of its own volition. "You are here about what's happening to you, my dear. Jack is merely a side effect of all this."

"I don't—" Pete started.

"How much has Jack told you about this? The Black? The magic that he works?"

Pete sighed. "Not much, and before tonight I didn't want to know. I'd convinced myself a long time ago that all *this*"— and here she gestured at the pub, the music, and brownies scuttling under tables—"wasn't real. But tonight . . ."

"Tonight was different," Mosswood said, examining her with a penetrating gaze. For all of his well-groomed shabbiness, the patched coat and sleek beard, Mosswood's eyes were inhuman, black and flat like stones. "Tell me."

"I . . . Jack and I were trying to get rid of a demon— that's a long story, entirely separate—and I touched him, really touched him because I was scared, and all this power just . . . *appeared*."

Mosswood scratched his beard and sucked on his pipe. "More power than the irredeemable Mr. Winter usually commands. Impressive."

"What's so impressive about that?" Pete said.

"Mages, in the great order of the Black, are candle flames," Mosswood said. "Jack Winter is an acetylene torch turned on full. Do you see?"

"I just want to know what happened when I touched him," said Pete.

"Afraid of it, are you?" Mosswood nodded. "Bright girl."

"I'm not *afraid* of anything," Pete snapped. "If it was just my life, I wouldn't be here. There's an innocent child at stake and I need to know that Jack is telling me the truth, when he decides to tell me anything. Whatever happened could affect my ability to help her. Or anyone."

"Jack Winter telling the truth," Mosswood mused. "There's something I'd like to see."

"Listen," Pete said. "I'm not stupid. I *know* something happened that wasn't meant to the first time Jack and I tried magic together. I don't think mages make a habit of working rituals that leave them on Death's doorstep. And now, the *same thing* almost blew his flat to smithereens earlier tonight."

"It is not a thing," said Mosswood. "Magic is not an object."

Pete dropped her eyes at the rebuke, wishing she'd never come. Being in the Black made her feel as if she were half in and half out of icy water, displaced and distracted.

Mosswood finally sighed. "I can only venture a guess, you understand . . ."

"Anything," said Pete with relief. "Wild speculation, baseless rumor . . . I've already spent over a decade thinking I'm crazy for believing any of this."

"Many thousands of years ago," said Mosswood, "there was a class of magicians, used by the old gods to speak for them . . . druids, priestesses of the Morrigan, a class of the Celt's battle shamans . . . you see?"

Pete nodded. The brownie set a cup of strong hot tea at her elbow, and she sipped reflexively. The way Mosswood spoke, it was easy to imagine sitting at the foot of the great standing stones, watching hooded figures dance in the starlight.

"The term 'magician' is a fallacy, really," said Mosswood. "They were called 'Weirs,' in the old tongues. Shapers of magic."

"Weir." Pete tasted the word, swallowed it down with her next swig of tea. "And what did the Weirs do, Mr. Mosswood?"

"Just Mosswood," he said again. "Weirs are odd and frightening, Miss Caldecott, because . . ." He sighed and sucked his pipe. "I fear I am doing you a disservice by saying this, but . . . Weirs escape classification. They do not tend toward magic the same way mages and sorcerers do. They are transformers, amplifiers, able to perceive the truth in dreaming, and if they are connected to a mage or sorcerer, terrible, terrible things have happened."

"What sort of things?" Pete drained her mug to the bottom, bitter tea leaves touching her tongue.

"Well," said Mosswood, "you don't think the *Hindenburg* explosion was really an accident, do you? Or Three Mile Island? Or the Tunguska meteor?"

Pete sat back, rubbing her arms. The cozy pub had become freezing cold. "So if I am . . . a Weir, and I've connected with Jack . . ."

Mosswood blew a ring of smoke, his eyes murky. "Then may whatever god you believe in watch over you both. Someone of Jack's abilities, amplified by a Weir, would be like a storm sweeping from the netherworld to flatten everything outside the Black."

"Weirs amplify mage's talents?" Pete felt her heartbeat slow in numb anticipation.

"Of course," said Mosswood mildly. "Why do you think virgin girls were so popular with magicians in the old times? It wasn't for their conversation."

A low shudder started in Pete's stomach and worked its way toward becoming a clear thought. She saw Jack, in his torn T-shirt and black jeans, jackboots and metal bracelets gleaming in the candlelight. Standing across the circle from her, inside the dark still tomb. Reaching out, to take her by the hand.

Afraid, luv? Don't be. I'm here, after all.

Pete stood up, knocking her chair away with a clatter. "I—I have to go. I'm sorry, Mosswood. Thank you . . ." She turned and managed to navigate out of the pub and back down the alley, fingers closing around the cold lumpy metal of the gate and pushing it aside. A black border closed around her vision and finally the street in front of her disappeared completely and all Pete saw as she spiraled down was Jack, Jack and his devil's grin.

PART 3

The Graveyard

When they kick at your front door
How you gonna come?
With your hands on your head
Or on the trigger of your gun?

—The Clash

Chapter 34

Pete shoved open the door to Jack's flat so that it hit the wall with a crack. She jumped at the same time as he did, startled to actually find him slouched on his sofa. A haze of pungent blue-green smoke drifted around him.

"Who the fuck is that?" demanded the woman on the other end of the sofa. She was rail skinny, a thatch of grown-out blond hair that still held purple dye in the tips sticking out wildly around her narrow pixie face.

"Hattie, this is Pete," Jack said. His posture instantly drew tight as he caught Pete's expression.

"'S a bloody odd name, ain't it?" Hattie said, taking another draw on her Thai stick.

For Pete's part, she drew in a breath, letting the pot-smoke smell wash over her, and then said, very softly, "Jack, I need to speak with you."

He stood, and Hattie made an unsteady move to follow. *"Alone."* Pete pinned Hattie with a glare, and the spindly girl sank back down into her seat.

"What's wrong, luv?" Jack said when Pete pulled him into the hallway and slammed the flat's door.

"How long have you known?" Pete said. Jack blinked once. His eyes were clear—he wasn't stoned, had just been playing at it. Pete found herself startled again at how quickly Jack could shuck and don different skins.

"Known what, Pete?" he asked in a credible display of innocence, but Pete knew better.

"I've been trying to figure it out, the whole walk home— did you know before that day in the tomb, or did you only figure it out when that *thing* came out at us and went straight for my heart instead of doing what you wanted?"

Jack's eyes iced over, the deep glacial blue stealing around the iris, but Pete pressed on. "And that convenient tip to the police, and you sticking around me right up until now. For your *reputation*." She lowered her voice. "Did you really think I wouldn't realize what you're doing, Jack?"

Jack spread his hands, and smiled at her. It was a warm smile, charming and guileless. "I don't know what you're talking about, luv—"

Pete slapped him, hard enough to leave a crack at the corner of his mouth that dribbled blood. "*Don't* lie to me again, Jack Winter," she hissed. "And *don't* call me 'luv' any longer. You lost that right the day you decided to use me like a fucking telly antenna, a dozen bloody years ago."

His fists curled and Pete braced herself to be hit. He probably wouldn't rattle her teeth, he was so skinny.

"You put me in danger. You knew exactly what would happen and you *used* me," she kept on. "And when you found me again, you used me again. And now that little girl is probably dead and I've spent the last twelve years trying to outrun nightmares of something that wasn't even my fault in the first place. Do you know how many nights I've wished I could make up for hurting you, for letting that thing loose? Too *bloody* many, Jack!" Shaking, she clenched her teeth to keep her voice steady and said, "I'm going home. You can't help me, or Margaret Smythe. You can't help anyone."

He let her get almost to the lift before he said, "You thought it was entirely your fault?"

"Isn't it?" Pete said. "When a Weir and a mage meet, terrible things happen. Mosswood said it."

"Mosswood doesn't know bloody everything." She heard a rustle and a sizzle as Jack conjured a fag, and then his breath drawing on it. "Listen, Caldecott, whatever happened between us before, right now all that matters is we've come to the attention of the wrong sort of people."

He lifted away from the wall and walked over to Pete, placing the tips of his fingers on her right shoulder. Pete shuddered as his presence crackled around her. "Don't touch me," she whispered.

Jack slid his grip to her arm and turned her to face him. The magic that rolled over Pete sucked her air away, just as it had the first time she'd stood close enough to touch him. "We're in danger, Pete," he said. "And if you don't stay with me, you're going to die. Later on, we can scream and throw crockery and shed tears over what I knew and how I used your talent and when, but right now, if you want *any* chance of saving Margaret Smythe from the clutches of certain death, then luv—you're with me."

Pete glared at his hand until he removed it from her arm. "Is the Hattie trollop *strictly* necessary?"

"Hattie's an old friend," Jack said. "She's not bad."

"She's a fucking junkie," Pete pointed out. Jack smiled, lips thin.

"So am I, Pete." He stamped out his cigarette and walked back down the dim hallway to the flat. "Hattie's got someone for us to meet, might have a line on those demon-wanking sorcerers who are after me."

"And then we find Margaret," Pete told him. She let him know, with the thrust of her chin, that she'd break Jack's shins and drag him with her if it came to that.

He flashed her the devil-grin, not worried in the least. "Yes. If we find them—then we find Margaret. Can't do fuck-all for the kid if we're dead, can we?"

Pete conceded that he had a point. Whatever Jack was, wrong wasn't usually it. She gestured for him to lead the way back into the flat. "Don't make the mistake of thinking this is good and settled between us."

"Wouldn't dream," Jack said, turning the knob. "You'd wake me up right quick."

Hattie jumped up when Pete came back into the flat. "Jack, what's up? Can we get out of here, already? You know being out the Black always gives me fucking hives."

"Pete is going to be joining us," Jack said, shrugging into his jacket. The screaming skull on the back leered at Pete. Hattie worried her lower lip, fingers picking idly at the hair on her opposite arm.

"Why?"

"Because I said so, Hattie." Jack stuck a Parliament between his lips but didn't light it.

Pete watched Jack, and Hattie, and the look that passed between them. Jack had shifted again, this time into an edgy, aggressive mode that made him square his shoulders and jut his jaw. Hattie folded in on herself even more.

"She don't blend in," she finally muttered. "Like a new penny in the collection box. She'll pox up the whole thing."

"Either you two leave off talking about me like I'm deaf or I can take your skinny arse to rot the night in jail," Pete told Hattie. She turned on Jack. "That goes for you, too."

"Except my skinny arse is cute." Jack winked at her. Hattie glared at Pete from under bruise-colored lids.

Chapter 35

"This might take some time," Jack said to Pete as they walked along the narrow high street outside Jack's flat. "We're going to have to go into the Black." He looked down at her. "Not that you seem to have a problem with that any longer."

"I do what I have to," said Pete shortly. "You wouldn't tell me the truth."

Jack laughed once. "I have to remember you're not sixteen any longer."

"Not for some time," Pete said. She felt a breath of wind and then suddenly it was full night and they were walking past grated and boarded-up storefronts, hunched shapes sleeping on the grates that vented the underground. A prehensile tail twitched out from under a ratty red blanket.

"It's just up here," Hattie called from ahead of them.

"That was easy," Pete remarked.

"In-between places," said Jack. "Those alleys that no one ever looks down. All of Whitechapel is thin, makes it easy to pass back and forth."

"I'm just telling you now, we don't have much time," said Pete. "Less than twelve hours if it's keeping to the same line as with the other three children."

"Time goes differently in the Black," Jack said. "Slows down, goes backward or forward."

"Is that supposed to make me feel better?" Pete asked.

Jack reached the metal security door that Hattie was standing in front of, her hands and shoulders twitching.

"No," Jack said. "Once I came in for a pint and walked out at breakfast time three days hence." He slid the door back on its rollers and gestured Pete inside. "After you, luv."

They walked down, on a set of slippery metal stairs through air that smelled like piss and sweat, droplets of moisture shaken from pipes overhead by throbbing bass.

"What exactly are we hoping to accomplish by coming here?" Pete asked Jack, raising her voice to be heard over the muffled music.

Hattie threw open the door and a profundo remix of "Don't Like the Drugs" smacked into Pete like a brick.

"An impression!" Jack shouted, and then they were inside.

The basement room could have been Fiver's, with the walls painted black and the tiny raised stage space replaced by an emaciated DJ and blocky turntables. And the people, close together in sticky knots, sliding up and down to the clotted beat of the music—they were different.

A hand closed around her wrist and she looked over to see Jack grimacing. "Are you all right?" she mouthed at him. A ring of white had appeared around his lips and his eyes were almost colorless.

"Too many bodies," he muttered in her ear. "Too many spirits. Wasn't ready for the sight."

Pete glanced around and perceived nothing but a mass of sweating and mostly pasty humans clothed in shades of black and black.

A strobe flickered across her vision and for a moment she caught flashes of horn and bone, long teeth arching over cloven lower lips as a tongue snaked toward her. Flash again, back to skin and cloth. "Come on," she said, tugging against Jack to pull him away from the dancers and their swirling auras.

Jack swayed just a little, sweat beading in the hollow of his neck and stippling the collar of his shirt. Pete reached up and brushed it away. Jack started at her touch, and the white in his eyes deepened back to the usual blue.

"I'm here," Pete mouthed. Jack squeezed her wrist.

"Ta."

Hattie was already bent over a tall glass of whisky, sucking on a borrowed cigarette held out by a Mohawked man with a bare chest and studded jacket.

"Hattie." Pete indicated the glass with her chin. "Give it here."

"Oi," said the Mohawk. "I paid for that, you tart. Leave 'er be."

"Excuse me," said Pete, reaching across Hattie's nonexistent chest and taking the tumbler, "but kindly bugger off back to 1985 and leave us the bloody hell alone."

Jack tilted the whisky down in one swallow, coughed, and then settled on the nearest barstool with a sigh.

The Mohawk looked at Jack, at Pete and Hattie, and then held up his hands. "Didn't realize she was with you, mate. Apologies."

"Fuck off," Jack said plainly. The man left.

"This the sort of impression you were after?" Pete shouted-muttered under the throb of the music. She kept her back to the bar, her hands at her sides, and wished she had something other than wit and fists at her disposal.

Jack faced the body sea with his elbows on the bar, a serene smile playing between his lips and his eyes. "You ever shill at cards, Pete?"

"I went into the Met straight out of university so . . . no," said Pete.

His fingers twitched and produced a card from his sleeve, a tarot picture of the Hanged Man. "You lose a few rounds at first," said Jack, still roving his gaze across the club. "You chum the waters with your weakness. You stand back and you let them get close, close enough, and you jam the knife in so tight and deep they never stop bleeding." Jack made the card disappear again, witchfire eating it into nothingness.

Pete eased near enough to speak into Jack's ear. "So who's getting close to us now?"

A girl in a satin slip adorned with roses, thorny twists of vine when Pete blinked, a dress again when the lights flared, grinned at Jack with needlelike teeth as she slipped past. Jack lit a cigarette and let the smoke trail out through his nostrils. "The wrong kind of people." His magic no longer crackled, it rolled off him in the slow honeyed way that made everyone in the club with the least sensitivity turn to look at him. Pete felt it cling to her and shook it off. If Mosswood was right, she was going to have to find a way to shut off the hum, the ripples, and the cries that seemed to resonate through London.

"Wrong for what?"

"Wrong for me to bring around someone like you," said Jack. "But oh, so bloody right for what we're trying to do." The houselights went down, and in the sudden blackness Jack's eyes burned blue.

"Bloody hell," said someone from over Pete's shoulder, sotto voce, but in order to be heard over the music you practically had to scream. "Jack Winter, isn't it?"

"You're fucking stoned," said a male voice. "Jack Winter's dead."

Jack's smile slipped down the scale to predatory. "See?"

Pete and Jack turned in concert to face a pair of young, pale, serious faces, boy and girl, both staring at Jack sidelong.

"If so," Jack said to them, "I'd say I managed to make one bloody attractive corpse."

The girl clutched the boy's arm, tearing a hole in his

fishnet sleeve with her dead-blood nails. "By the Black! Arty, it's really him."

Arty regarded Pete and Jack through hooded eyes, bloodshot with whatever was in his glass. He sneered when Pete returned his stare. "Yeah. Guess he hasn't kicked."

He swung himself to face Jack, limbs heavy. Pete shifted herself to the balls of her feet, ready to deal Arty a punch to his pointy chin if he moved in on her or Jack.

"Do you know there's a bounty out on your pretty little Billy Idol head?" Arty slurred.

"Why, son?" Jack said. He curled his lip slightly, carrying on with the reference. "Are you going to collect?"

"Oh, *don't* mind him," the girl gushed, dealing Arty a shot to the ribs. "My brother's a bloody idiot when he's in his cups. I'm Absithium, and he's Artem, but you can call us Arty and Abby." She extended her hand palm down, as though she expected Jack to kiss it, and he did. Hattie grunted at the gesture, her blotchy forehead crinkling.

"Jack Winter," Jack told Abby, ignoring Hattie as if she were a lamp or a hatstand.

"I *knew* it was you," Abby simpered. "Arty and I . . . we're twins, but I'm an intuitive and he's got other talents."

Pete noticed a ripple in the crowd around them. A shifting of heads and eyes, when Jack said his name. "Chumming the bloody waters," she muttered, taking Hattie's fresh glass of whisky and draining it herself.

Abby jerked her chin at Hattie. "I've seen you before, too. At Millie Child's?"

"Yeah, whatever," said Hattie. "I spent a few nights there last month."

"The new moon sex rituals," said Abby sagely. She looked Pete over and dismissed her in the space of a heartbeat. "May I ask you a question?" she demanded of Jack, tilting her heavy black beehive to one side in an expression

that Pete supposed would be coquettish if Abby hadn't been
made up like a dead porcelain doll.

"Anything, my dear," Jack said.

"Where have you *been,* all this time?" Abby chewed on
her thin lower lip. "I mean, we *all*"—she gestured at the
dancers—"have our theories."

"And wagers," said Arty with a shift of interest. "Personally, I say you were pinched by the common police and spent
the last dozen years being buggered over at Pentonville." He
took a swig of his pint, face knobby with belligerence. "So
where'ye been, Winter?"

Jack leaned close to Arty, meeting the boy's kohled
eyes. He held there, his lips parted and barely an inch from
Arty's ear, until Arty stilled completely.

Then Jack breathed, "Hell."

He slung his arm around Hattie, picked up Arty's pint
and drained the remains. "But now I'm back, and I'm bound
to raise a little infernal noise of my own." He kissed Hattie,
hard, smearing her lips apart and probing with his tongue.
Hattie yielded like an understuffed doll.

Pete became aware that the music had faded to the end
of the track and the club was largely silent, everyone waiting to see what Jack would do next.

Arty cast his eyes at a few fellows of comparable size
and thickness. "Sure, Winter. Play your set. Let all of them
see what a bad man you are." He slid from his stool like a
small mountain moving. "Hell or not, hasn't helped you
much. You look bloody wasted." The other boys came to his
shoulders.

Pete pointed her finger at Arty. "Don't," she warned.

"What are you going to do, curse me?" he sneered.

Pete looked to Jack, who was fondling Hattie with a
bored expression as he glared at Arty. His eyes flicked to
hers for a second, and he was still Jack. *Make an impression.*

Arty grabbed the lapel of Pete's jacket. "I asked you a question, you slag."

The DJ began another song, and Pete hit Arty in the jaw, in the soft spot just above the bone that snaps the head around and brings unconsciousness.

She raised her eyes to the other boys. "Jack doesn't need your meddling and I don't want you breathing my air. Piss off."

Abby jumped in between Pete and the boys. "They didn't *mean* it!" she cried. Arty groaned and sat up, shaking his head. "How could you?" she hissed at him.

"Winter's not a sorcerer!" he said defensively. "How's I supposed to know he practices bloody black magic?"

"I practice whatever I bloody want," Jack said. He slung his other arm around Abby. "Let's leave off these cunts and find someplace private, eh, luv?"

Abby fairly glowed. "Of course! I know just the place."

Jack, Hattie, and Abby walked through the room, dancers parting like a furrow, and Pete followed before the passageway closed and she was trapped. Every set of eyes in the room bored holes in her back until the door boomed shut behind her.

Chapter 36

Abby took them to a turreted Victorian, black with red light shining from every window. She lifted the iron knocker, a fanged nymph's head, and let it fall once.

"What is this place?" Pete stopped at the foot of the steps.

"Mad Chen's," muttered Hattie. She let Jack half drag her up to the door. Pete looked up and down the street. Dead trees and dead leaves bent and scuttled toward her, a winter wind pushing behind.

"Pete." Jack jerked his head at her as the door opened and a hooligan in a silk jacket peered out. He looked at Abby, nodded, and then stepped back.

Mad Chen's was lit by gaslight, red as new blood spilling, burning some sort of alien fuel. Thick wispy smoke drifted toward the tin ceilings, painted over with spray-can slogans, and under the smoke a garden of beds lay scattered across the wide rooms.

The beds were of every description—day lounges and iron institutional frames. All made up in silk or satin, no filthy mattresses like where Pete had found Jack.

Most of the beds were occupied, and slow-moving, doe-eyed women passed among them holding long boxes and trays with pipes and small sticky globs of pungent brown in wooden boxes. Their breasts and nipples, ringed or studded or tattooed, gleamed in the low red light.

"Up here," said Abby as they passed through the main part of the den, and she led them up a spiral staircase and into a narrow hallway.

Some of the doors had a key sticking out, and some were locked, with cries or silence coming from behind. Abby turned a key in the second door on the left and went in, slouching down on a sofa. "Fuck, I'm bored. Should we ring Mad Chen to bring up some poppy and absinthe?"

Hattie flopped next to her. "I'd murder a hit of anything right now."

Pete remained standing. "I have to go to the loo." She narrowed her eyes at Jack before she slipped back out the door and went down the hall, trying doors until she found a narrow closet with a toilet and a bulb on a pull chain.

She shut the door and leaned against the wall, and realized once she was still that her legs were shaking. The Black pulsed against her, and she swore she could feel it on her skin, like the opium resin, sticky and visceral.

"It never really gets better."

Jack opened the door and slid into the closet with her. Pete had to turn sideways to accommodate him.

"Jack, what in all Hell are we doing here?"

He leaned his head back against the wall and produced a fag, lit it, and took a deep drag. "Abby and her twit of a brother are sorcerers. If they don't go blabbing to whoever's trying to get rid of me before this fag's gone, I've no sort of currency left with this lot at all and I might as well chuck myself off of Tower Bridge and be done with it."

Jack smelled like whisky and rain, like lightning had just struck earth. Pete breathed in him and the tobacco, closing her eyes.

A pressure on her shoulder, as Jack closed his free hand around it. "Thank you, for going along. Probably would be bleeding internally in some dank alley if you hadn't smacked that bloody Arty." He half grinned at her. "Where did a sweet little girl like you learn to throw a punch, anyhow?"

"I was never particularly sweet, Jack," Pete said. "You would have found that out, if you'd stuck around."

He smiled humorlessly, around the cigarette. "Regrets get you nothing except a bloody face and a broken heart if you're lucky, Pete." He cracked the door of the closet and peered out. "Should be enough time for Abby to tip off whoever her master is and end this idiot idea they have of chasing me all over the bloody city. Let's get back."

He brushed past Pete, their full length touching, and then in a flutter of her heartbeat, he was gone again.

Pete pushed back against the pressure under her mind, the pressure that Jack said never really got better, and she followed him.

Chapter 37

"Mad Chen's got some shit in from the Golden Triangle," said Abby when Pete and Jack came back. She reappraised Pete when they entered the room together. "Your *friend* going to take part?"

A wavy glass bottle full of slightly luminous green liquid had appeared on the table, and Jack took a tumbler, filled, and downed it.

"*She* won't." He coughed. "Then who would there be to knock about anyone who irritates me?"

"Why do you keep mundanes around if you're not fucking them?" Abby asked with genuine curiosity.

"This absinthe tastes like a bloody tramp pissed in a gutter and had it bottled," Jack said. "And has anyone ever told you that for such a pretty slip of a thing you ask a lot of silly sodding questions?"

Pete went to the window and watched the street, but nothing except shadows and the crooked skeletons of bare trees stared back. She drew the velvet curtains. Dust shook out of their folds, old dust that smelled like vellum and bone, and she sneezed.

Hattie watched her mournfully. "You like, a bodyguard then?"

Only one door in and out of the room, and no closet she

could see—just overstuffed furniture and an old peeling sleigh bed with a ragged coverlet. Pete nodded absently at Hattie. "Something like that."

"Ever met David Beckham?" Hattie said. She looked like a sad leather-clad raggedy doll, with her featureless skinny limbs and chopped-off eggplant hair.

"I only ever looked out for Jack," Pete told her. "I'm a detective inspector with the Met."

Abby's head snaked around. "You're a what?"

"Trust me, darling, if I was going to take you in I would have done it long before you opened your mouth," Pete said. "Drink your mixer and behave yourself."

"Jack . . ." Abby started, but he glared at her over his second green tumbler.

"Pete's with me. Shut it." He gave her a cool smile when she pouted. "Besides, I need your help now, Abby. Need to pick that black little head of yours."

"Is that so?" Abby glared at Pete in vindication as she downed her second drink in one go.

"Yeah," said Jack easily. "Ran into some blokes a few days ago, sorcerers like you, but nowhere near as lovely."

Abby snorted, poured herself another glass, sipped it. "So?"

"So, what's a smart little sorcerer up to these days?" said Jack. "I know something big's gearing up, so don't bother to lie. You lot have been twitchy as jackrabbits ever since I dove back into the scene." He went to Abby and brushed the stark black hair out of her eyes, cupping her chin between his thin fingers. Pete felt her stomach give an uncomfortable cramp.

"Come on," Jack murmured. "You can tell old Jack Winter. Whisper it in my ear. Always had more of an affinity for your kind of magic, anyway. It wouldn't even be a betrayal, luv."

Abby swallowed, a petal flush creeping into her porcelain

cheeks. "They say . . . well . . . they say that something big is right on the other side of the veil. A spirit, or some such thing . . . and, well, some of us are offering service. Letting it gather power, and helping it, because when he comes through, he'll reward us."

"He," said Jack. "You have anything more specific for me, darling?"

Abby gulped the rest of her third helping of absinthe. The dry scent of licorice permeated through the smoky air. "I could have my throat cut for telling you that much, mage." She hiked her black hobble skirt over her knees and cast a languid look in Jack's direction. "If the questions are over, do you want to—"

Then Abby choked, her pale slender fingers scrabbling at the hollow of her throat, her eyes going wide and the irises expanding with effort.

Hattie moved away from her, with surprising speed. "What's her problem, then?"

Abby gagged, her pale pink tongue protruding between lips that were bordered in blue. She really did look like an animated corpse, jerky and lifeless as black spittle dribbled from the corner of her mouth.

Jack looked at Abby, looked down at his own empty glass. "Oh, fuck me." He dropped the tumbler with a splinter of crystal and dove for a decorative basin in the corner of the room, shoving his finger down his throat.

Pete grabbed Abby, who convulsed as if she were on a string, leaving ragged red streaks along her neck as she tried to claw the obstruction from her windpipe. Pete pushed the girl's hands away from her flesh—Abby's strength was no more than that of a housecat—and laid her back, turning her head to one side and shoving index and middle fingers down her gullet to clear an airway.

In the corner, Jack vomited violently into the basin, skinny shoulders hunched as he retched and shook.

Viscous black closed around Pete's fingers, seemingly gallons of the stuff, flowing from Abby's mouth and filling her throat. An all-over shudder, a death rattle, Pete would think later, and Abby went still, black swimming up to cover her eyes in opaque film.

Hattie spoke from around a fist thrust into her mouth. "That was some bad shit, I think."

"Nothing you could have done, Pete," said Jack weakly, wiping the back of his hand across his mouth and spitting into the basin. "Not that you'll ever lose sleep over failing to save a treacherous little bint like her."

Pete sat back on her heels, the black stuff staining her fingertips. She brushed it on her jeans. "What in the hell was all that, Jack?"

Jack took Pete's discolored fingers in his and sniffed. "Morgovina mushrooms," he said finally. "Fae plant. Melts you from the inside out. Nasty little way to die."

"The absinthe disguised the scent," said Pete, noticing the half-dusty, half-rotted stench rising from the pool of liquid under Abby's head.

"Brutal but not clever," said Jack.

"You were bloody stupid to drink anything in this place. Think you'd never heard a folktale in your life," Pete said. Jack raised an eyebrow at her.

"I'll have you know that my near-death experience has left me rather fragile and your attitude is not helping." He shrugged out of his jacket and draped it across a chair, then lit a Parliament and set it in the ashtray on the small table. "And more to the point, find a place to hide, because who-ever poisoned the booze will be up to make sure the job is done any minute now."

Hattie heaved what may have been a resigned sigh and disappeared down the hallway to the loo. Pete lit on a wardrobe open to display a collection of antique opium pipes and closed herself in it.

"Lucy in Narnia," she whispered.

Jack leaned against the wall behind the door, hands in his pockets, looking almost bored.

"Not up to your usual standards of excitement?" Pete said through the keyhole.

"This isn't excitement," said Jack. "Never could fathom why sorcerers thought sitting about cutting your forearms and doing Victorian drugs was such a great laugh." He rolled his neck from side to side. "Unless there's magic, blood, or disgustingly attractive women involved, I couldn't care bloody less at this point in me life."

"So the last week has been a complete loss, then," Pete said.

Jack looked at her, and even through the small crack in the wardrobe Pete felt the snowy chill of his eyes on her skin. "Not a complete one," he said after a moment. "Not in a few ways that matter . . ."

"Still yourself," Pete hissed, though she was rue to interrupt him. "Someone's coming."

Footsteps creaked along the corridor and a hand tried the knob, pausing in surprise when the owner found the door unlocked. Slowly, it swung wide and revealed a sallow-faced man and an olive-skinned woman dressed in plain black, witchfire burning plum-colored in their hands.

The man jerked his chin at Abby's body, and the woman clicked over on precise stiletto heels and felt for a pulse. She shook her head, and the man stepped over the threshold.

Faster than smoke, Jack stepped out from his hiding spot and banged the door shut. "Evening, girls."

"Winter," the man hissed.

Jack gave a wide grin and a nod. "Observant cunt, aren't you?" He picked up the cigarette he'd lit and had a drag on. "Though I have to tell you—and take this as constructive critique, by all means—the poisoned absinthe? Tacky, mate. Look, you killed your own lapdog."

The woman, still crouched with her back to Pete, worked a small curved blade out from the cuff of her jacket.

"Jack!" Pete shouted, banging open the wardrobe and grabbing the closest weapon, an ivory opium pipe. She jabbed the carved and pointed tip in between the woman's shoulder blades and the sorcerer arched back with a cry.

The man brought his hand up, the witchfire changing color into something sulfurous and corrosive, but Jack hit him before the magic could form into anything useful. Blood shot from the sorcerer's split lip, and he dropped after swaying for a moment.

Jack reached over and grabbed Pete's hand. "Now we have to run, luv."

"What about Hattie?"

"Hattie will be happier locked in the loo, trust me."

Pete followed him down the hall, her heart jackhammering like she were back outside the door of her first bust, sweating inside her stab vest. Jack kicked open a thin door leading to stairs upward.

"Stop!" The male sorcerer appeared in the door, a fan of blood and spittle on his chin and down the front of his shirt. He pressed his hands together and muttered a stream of guttural Latin, and black smoke boiled from around his feet to form two small lithe shadows, that in turn gave birth to a twin pair of their own.

"Bollocks," Jack hissed, taking the stairs two at a time.

"Are they ghosts?" Pete shouted as she pounded after him.

"Worse!" Jack shouted. "Thought-forms! Shadowy blood-hounds!"

They crossed the attic, tumbling over trunks and bundles, and Jack used his elbow to smash a window that had been painted shut. "You first," he panted. "Out."

Pete looked at the street fifteen meters below, back at Jack. "Are you *quite mad*?"

The smoke-shadows flowed under the door, through the

cracks in the floor. They had grown steel claws and teeth, and darker hollows for eyes.

Jack opened his mouth to cajole, or yell, but Pete held up a hand. "Never mind. I'm going." She hoisted herself through the broken window and onto the slippery roof, but instead of letting go and plummeting for the street she gripped the gutter so hard she thought the skin on her knuckles would split and climbed toward the ridgeline.

She watched the shadows swipe at Jack, catching the leg he still had inside the window and leaving lines of crimson. "Bugger!" Jack yelped. He spread his fingers wide and exhaled, and a flock of smoke-crows blossomed from his palm. The crows cawed and swooped, catching the sorcerer's hounds with their talons and bills.

The shadows screamed and vanished, the crows with them. Jack grinned. "Couldn't sustain his will when someone co-opted his trick. Probably has a small cock, too."

"Come *on*," Pete yelled, nearly losing her grip. She pulled herself up onto the flat square top of Mad Chen's turret roof and helped Jack, who flopped over with a wheeze.

His coughing turned to chuckles, then to laughter. "Bloody hell. I'd forgotten how much fun this is."

Pete cocked her head. "Fun? You've got a fucking strange idea of fun."

The wood next to Jack's head exploded, driving splinters into Pete's arm. Another sorcerer appeared out of the shadows, the yellow clouds oozing corrosive fumes from his hands. "How many of these wankers are there?" Pete shouted. The sorcerer stopped just short of her feet and smiled in the manner of a small boy who likes to burn ants.

"Looks like I get your skin and your talent, Winter, and the chance to get over." He grinned.

Jack rolled on his side and stood, ducking the sorcerer's reach. He grabbed the shorter man by the back of the neck. "You'll get over something, that's sure." He rotated his grip and tossed the sorcerer off the edge of the roof. The man screamed until a sound like a breaking tree trunk cut off the cry.

Pete peered over the edge, saw the broken doll shape and a dark stain spreading. "Think he's dead?"

Jack lit a Parliament, drew once, and flicked the rest after the sorcerer. "About to wish he was."

The man was conscious, groaning, when Pete and Jack climbed down to the street. "If more are coming after us," said Pete, "we're a bit exposed."

Jack gripped the sorcerer under the arms, struggling against the stocky weight. "'S why we're getting the fuck out of here." He attempted to pull the moaning sorcerer along the pavement. The man's leg was twisted, a lump of displaced bone under his skin, and he yelled. Jack wheezed and dropped him. "You need to get on a diet, boyo."

Pete rolled her eyes and banded her arm across the sorcerer's chest, a lifesaving carry on dry land. The door of Mad Chen's banged open and the male sorcerer appeared, trailed by his renewed thought-forms, which seemed to have grown a few dozen more steel teeth since Pete saw them last.

"Bollocks," she said, dragging the sorcerer along the pavement. "What the hell happens now, Jack? I don't think your little trick with the birds will be quite as scary out in the open."

"Never fear, Pete. Our chariot awaits." Jack stepped into the street and let out a piercing whistle. "Taxi!"

One moment the street was empty and the next a gleaming black cab, smooth lines and lantern headlights, something from the black-and-white era, sat idling at the curb, stopped in a swirl of leaves and winter wind. The rear door swung open of its own accord.

Jack grabbed the sorcerer's legs. "Get him in."

Pete folded the quietly sobbing man into the back of the cab and scrambled inside, sliding on butter-colored leather seats. Jack knocked on the partition and told the shadowed driver, "Sodding floor it!"

The cab lit out with a squeal of tires, taking the corner with a lurch that threw Pete against the door, the handle thudding into her gut.

"One thing about the Black," Jack said as they roared through empty nighttime streets. "You can always find a cab when you really need one."

The driver turned his head slightly. "What destination, please?" His voice was smooth and bell-like, more suited to an angelic choir than a slightly threadbare cab. It gave Pete a warm feeling in the pit of her stomach.

A gas streetlamp caught the driver's eyes, and they shone silver.

Jack grunted softly and held his forehead. "Fae," he said through clenched teeth.

"Driving a cab?" Pete raised an eyebrow.

"Fae love human devices," Jack muttered. "Plays hell on the sight, let me tell you." To the driver he said, "Whitechapel, Mile End Road, number forty-six."

"Right away, sir," purred the Fae. His teeth, silver like his eyes, were a row of needles.

The sorcerer moaned, his eyes flicking weakly between Pete and Jack. "Where are you taking me?"

Jack thumped him on the crown of his head. "Shut it. No questions from you."

"What *are* we going to do with him?" Pete whispered. "Can't very well leave him on the street to be picked over."

"Who says I can't?" Jack muttered. "Tosser tried to kill me. But no, I've got something in mind."

After a time the cab glided to a stop in front of Jack's flat and he jumped out quickly, leaving Pete to drag the sorcerer onto the curb. She banged the man's broken leg against the running board and he screamed.

"Sorry, mate," Pete apologized. "But you did rather bring

it on yourself." She leaned back into the cab. "How much do I owe you?"

Jack grabbed her by the collar and yanked her back out. Pete struggled furiously, and reared back to slap him. He caught her hand, fingers squeezing her wrist bones together. "Don't you know better than to make deals with the Fae?"

"He's a bloody cab driver!" Pete protested as the taxi disappeared at the end of the street, taillights winking when it rounded the corner.

"*Never* offer to repay a Fae," Jack said tightly. "And *never* allow them to strike a bargain with you. The cab is on my account. I'll pay up when they decide my debt is due and not a moment before."

"I'm truly sorry. I didn't know," Pete said. "Now let go of me before I fetch you a smack."

Jack heaved a sigh and pushed his hair every which way with his fingers. "You wanted to learn the Black, and how to survive in it . . . consider that lesson the first." He dropped her wrist. "Sorry if I hurt you."

"'S all right," Pete muttered. Her skin was slightly pink where Jack had touched her.

The sorcerer managed to haul himself onto his elbows, attempting to crawl away down the street. "Will you look at this git," Jack exclaimed. He pointed a finger at the sorcerer and muttered, *"Sioctha."* The sorcerer jerked, all of his limbs going rigid. Pete put her face in her hands.

"Did you explode this one's heart, too?"

"Nope," Jack said triumphantly. "Just stiff. A little magic rigor mortis until he tells me what I want to know. Get his other arm."

Together they dragged the sorcerer up the creaking fire escape to the flat, and once inside Jack rolled the man onto his back and put a boot in the center of his chest.

"Get the frying pan, or a phone directory—something

heavy to bash him in the good kneecap if he gets smart," he said to Pete. "Right," he addressed the sorcerer. "You know who I am, and what I can do, and I'm going to let you go now with the provision that if you try any tricks, what's left of you will fit inside a syringe. Got it?"

The sorcerer tried to speak, huffed breath through his nose and his immobile lips, eyes going wide.

"Good," Jack said conversationally. *"Bí scaoilte."* The sorcerer shuddered and relaxed. Jack pressed down harder with his boot. "Who are you bloody working for?"

"Roast in hell, Winter, you doped-up has-been!" the sorcerer shouted.

"Oi," Pete said. She picked up a heavy bookend from Jack's shelf. "What's your name?"

"Roddy," the sorcerer spat. "Roddy Post."

"Well, Roddy Post," said Pete. "Are you going to answer my friend's questions?"

"Go bugger yourself!" Roddy moaned. His face was pale, twin stains of crimson in the hollows of his cheeks.

Pete knelt, lifted the bookend, and brought it down on Roddy's right hand. He howled. Jack raised his eyebrows.

"You've got issues, luv."

"Fine . . ." Roddy sobbed. "Fine, I'll sodding tell you whatever you want."

"Like a cheap notebook, you are," Jack said. "Folding when she only tapped you with that thing."

"Don't be too hard on him," Pete said, giving Roddy a thin smile. "You'd be amazed at what a couple of broken knuckles will do for a bloke's outlook."

Jack's expression went from amused to something darker, deeper, as if he were taking Pete's measure. "All for the sake of the child, eh?" he asked her.

Pete looked at Roddy, his pale drawn face. "Of course," she murmured, and set the bookend down because it was suddenly very heavy.

"Now, then," said Jack. He went into the kitchen and brought back a chair. "Pete, help the bloke to sit up."

Pete heaved Roddy into the seat and Jack stood in front of him. "Talk. Who's trying to kill me and why?"

Roddy's ragged breathing smoothed. "I can't tell you."

"Bloody hell . . ." Jack muttered, raising his palm and opening his mouth to speak another word of magic.

"I can show you," Roddy said sullenly. Jack cocked his head, as if weighing Roddy's sins to decide if he lived or died.

"Well, all right then," he finally said with his old grin. "Pete, let's bear up poor Roddy's leg and let him lead the way."

Chapter 38

They drove through stone canyons, the old parts of the city, strongholds of visiting royalty, reclaimed as hotels and bars, neon hidden in crevices between the hand-hewn rock walls.

"Here," Roddy muttered. "Pull over here."

Pete eased the Mini to the curb on Ironmonger Lane and looked up at the stone edifice. "What's here?"

Roddy looked at his feet. "The Arkanum."

Jack choked. "You're not *serious*." He craned out the window to look up at the building. "Incredible."

"What's the Arkanum?" Pete asked Roddy.

"The Arkanum is the collective of darkness, the society of secret and shadow. We see and do what you only dream of, and we pull the strings of the bright, living world." Roddy muttered all of this, his voice blurry with pain and resignation.

Jack rolled his eyes and popped the door open. "A eighteenth-century collective of sorcerers wiped out by witchfinders and who never got the bloody hint." He leaned back in. "How many in there, Roddy?"

"None," Roddy said miserably. "There's not many of us these days and you've killed near half. The rest are out looking for you."

Jack checked the street and then motioned Pete out. "We take him with us."

In the lift, Roddy's pungent sweat made Pete's nose crinkle. "So you people just hang around thinking of ways to kill Jack? Seems silly. Completely."

"Thought he *was* dead," Roddy muttered. "Only in the last couple of weeks, the Black started to talk about seeing him again."

"But why?" said Pete. "He didn't do anything to you."

"Right here," said Jack as the digital numbers ticked by. "Not bloody deaf, either."

"Do you have any idea what it would mean to be the sorcerer who killed the crow-mage?" Roddy demanded, and his face sparked back to life. "You would be legend in your own time, with more power than any before. Feared, hated, and respected—the tenets of the Arkanum."

"*Why* do you people call him 'crow-mage'?" Pete asked. The lift came to a stop.

"Don't answer that, Roddy, 'less you want it to be the last coherent thing you ever say," Jack said, throwing a glare over his shoulder as he stepped into a narrow hallway, lit with brass sconces. One door stood at the far end.

Roddy limped after him at Pete's prodding. "Just through there," he said, slouching against the wall opposite the lift. "Everything you want is in there."

"Good man," said Jack. He shoved Roddy aside and put his hand on the door, jiggling it. "It's locked."

"I haven't a key," said Roddy with a thrust of his chin, before Jack could turn on him. "The High Sorcerers control the access."

"No matter," said Jack. "Pete, you got a hairpin or a bra wire or something?"

"Do I look like I have a hairpin, Jack?"

"Never mind," he said, digging a skeleton key out of his pocket and working it into the lock. He leaned against the keyhole and breathed, *"Go n-iompaí an iarann agus go ligfeadh lean ar aghaidh,"* in a whisper meant for a lover. Pete heard ancient tumblers groaning.

"Racking up felonies by the minute, I see," she said. Jack gave her a wide grin.

"Not breaking in if you have a key."

"You think you can enter our sanctum with such a crude tool?" Roddy muttered.

The lock clicked and the door popped open. Jack rolled his eyes. "Apparently I can, sonny boy. What about it?"

"Don't be waiting, then," Roddy said sullenly. "Burst in and save the day, Winter."

"All right, keep your shorts on," said Jack. He put his hand on the knob, but before it turned, pain like she'd just smacked into a ledge hit Pete. The Black rushed up at her, magic that was barren and unforgiving, nothing like the dancing fire of Jack's talent or the icy slickness of her dream. She gasped as she touched it, and Jack stopped and turned to look at her.

"What's wrong, luv?"

"I . . ." The pain intensified, the magic crouching, leaping, digging teeth into her brain. "I . . ." She couldn't speak, just felt the magic pressing down on her. Her Black-fueled intution rocketed through the pain and she grabbed for Jack's hand on the door, trying to make him stop, turn back, before he became broken and bloody and still again.

"Sweet Lilith . . ." Roddy cursed. "They know! They—" He was cut off as Jack spun around and grabbed him by the neck.

"What have you done, you slimy little cunt?"

Roddy began to smile, and then to laugh. "It was so easy," he said. "I'd heard so many stories about how good you were, Winter, how quicksilver and clever. And look, a broken leg and a sob story was all it took for you to swallow it."

"Jack," Pete ground out. She tried pushing against the

feedback from the Black, and the pain lessened, though not by much.

Roddy grinned at both of them unpleasantly. "You came in here obedient as dogs."

Demonstrating far more strength than Pete would have guessed a man of Jack's size to have, Jack lifted Roddy onto his tiptoes. "What did you and your shit-sucking Arkanum mates do? Tell me before I break you in half and jam you together backward."

Roddy laughed, shaking his head. "It doesn't matter now, Winter. I did my job. I'll be seeing you on the other side . . . and her . . . and all the rest." And Roddy fell forward against Jack, and shoved them back together, through the door into the Arkanum's sanctum.

The spell hovering over the flat snapped into place and Pete could move again without the feeling of ice picks being driven through her eye sockets. She was up and moving for Jack and Roddy before her mind caught up. She could *see* the spell, a thicket of thorns and prehensile vines that wrapped themselves around both men with blood-hungry quickness.

"Jack!" she screamed, as a shadow lashed his face and caused a line of blood droplets to erupt. "Jack, tell me how to stop it!"

"Get this fucking fat tosser off of me, to start!" Jack bellowed, shoving at Roddy, who fought just as wildly to hold him in place. The shadows, thick as they lay on Jack, fell twice as heavy on him, wrapping Roddy up in a hungry cascade of magic and malice. The sorcerer's clothes began to disintegrate, and the skin beneath, flaking off like ash from a dead fire. Roddy's face went stone, grim—he would die to keep Jack from escaping the spell's embrace.

Pete reached for Jack, between the twisting vines of magic, and felt a lash like a thousand thorns on her skin.

Blood erupted everywhere the shadows touched, and she drew back, cursing.

Jack punched Roddy in the face, ineffectually. "Get . . . off . . . me . . . cunt!"

From an archway deeper in the flat two more sorcerers appeared, and two more—four figures all burning the poisoned purple witchfire in their palms.

"Hold him, Roddy!" one shouted. "We'll take care of the bitch."

Jack's clothing began to flake away, like Roddy's skin— a patch of his jacket, a chunk of his pantleg, the sole of his jackboot. "Pete, watch it!" he yelled as one of the sorcerers came for her, a telescoping police baton upraised.

"You think I'm not worth your magic?" Pete cocked her head.

"Mage groupie? I *know* you aren't worthy," said the sorcerer. Pete sighed.

"You're wrong. So very wrong." Before the sorcerer could puzzle that, she kicked out and drove her heel into the man's knee.

The sorcerer crumpled over, dropping the baton, and the other three hurled clusters of the foul-smelling offensive magic at her, giving distance in the face of their cursing, crying compatriot. Pete took a dive, landed elbows first on the parquet floor, and slid out of range, ignoring the pain that returned all through her when she hit.

She could barely see Jack any longer, obscured as he and Roddy were by the writhing mass of the spell. "Jack," she moaned, for just a moment not able to contemplate anything but the sight of his newly dead body. Toerag that he was, as much as he'd made her life a pit of misery over the week he'd come back, Jack being dead again was something that Pete knew would send her straight around the bend.

The spell hissed at her when she drew close, and a

thorny limb lashed out to slice her flesh. *Shaper of magic. I am a shaper of magic.*

Then Jack's echo, *Mosswood doesn't know bloody everything.*

"He'd sodding better on this count," Pete whispered, and then inhaled, held out her hand, and *pushed* against the mass of the Black around the spell. She pushed like she'd push on a thousand-pound beam across her chest, like she'd push to go through a door with something terrible but necessary on the other side. Feeling as if every blood vessel in her would burst with the effort, Pete held against the tide of black magic that kept the spell alive, moving it, shaping against it until with a great groan of defeat a hole appeared, pinpoint at first but tearing open to body size.

Jack's face, plus a few hundred scratches and a smearing of ash materialized, his expression genuinely shocked. Pete stuck out her hand.

"I can't hold this!" She could already feel herself begin to tremble under the strain of pushing back the spell, and another ball of energy lanced by her head to remind her that her troubles were far from over.

Jack's own hand, slicked with his blood, lanced out through the magic's gap and grabbed on to her, and Pete hauled him out, inch by inch. Roddy's hand latched on to Jack's ankle in turn, half skeletal and locked in a dead man's grasp. Jack brought his other heel down, the steel of his jackboot snapping off the encrusted bones.

Roddy gave a scream like Death itself had just wrapped a hand around his heart and yanked it free, and the spell collapsed in on him, enraged and starving and consuming.

Jack patted himself over frantically. "Ah, tits. I lost me flick-knife."

"Forget the bloody knife. Are you all right?" Pete demanded.

"No," said Jack insistently, as the sorcerers began to get

closer with their spells. "I need blood . . . *fresh* blood," he snapped when Pete started to point out the thousands of shallow cuts all over his exposed skin.

Pete found her pocket knife in an obscure corner of her jacket and grabbed Jack's palm, slicing it deeply as she dared. He yelped. "Bloody hell, woman! When did you get so violent?"

"That should be sufficient, yeah?" Pete said, indicating the warm crimson stream that flowed freely over Jack's palm.

"Good *gods,* yes, *quite* sufficient if you want me to *die!*" Jack said.

"Give over with your drama and do something about these cunts before they finally manage to aim!" Pete shouted, ducking another blast.

Jack swore at her, but smeared the blood on the floor in front of him and said, *"An t-ok, tabhair do dhroim."*

The spell began to expand, revealing the ashy bones of Roddy, and lit across the flat, over the walls and the floor, digging in to every crevice and engulfing the three remaining sorcerers before they could react to the mass of magic that slammed them backward into the walls. The air filled with ash and the floor tilted crazily as Jack's magic met the spells living in the bones of the flat, the concussion jolting Pete down to her marrow.

Jack grabbed her arm. "Time to run again, luv, I'm afraid."

"I agree," Pete said as a massive section of the outer stone wall fell away, exposing the skyline of London, twinkling serenely in the late night. "Fucking move!"

She and Jack ended up having to jump for it as the front room of the flat collapsed, roaring in on itself with beams and stone, making an abattoir for the four men within.

Pete rolled over and sat up, dizzy, Jack swimming back into focus above her. A warm nettle of pain cut across one cheek and she touched blood. "I felt it," she said. "Before

Roddy pushed you through the door." Her voice was thick and far away.

"I know you did, luv," Jack said, dabbing at her cheek with his sleeve. He glanced back at the ruin. Two of the bodies were half out of the rubble, frozen in tableau. Their eyes stared at Pete with the stony hatred of the dead.

"He played it very well," said Jack. "Didn't tip off."

Pete glared back at the bodies. "Broken knuckles don't hurt *that* much."

"I don't know about you," said Jack, helping Pete to her feet and offering her a Parliament, which she accepted, "but I'm about through playing with these bastards."

"Through, and thoroughly bored of this Sturm und Drang," said Pete. "We need a new plan, Winter."

Jack worried his thumbnail as he exhaled a cloud of smoke, and then said, "First thing we need to do is find a set of pliers."

The Arkanum's kitchen was largely intact except for cracks in the floor that let Pete look through clear to the ground story, and half the cabinets gone. Pete located a toolbox under the sink and gave Jack a pair of needle-nosed pliers, while he went to an overturned apothecary desk and rooted in the cubbies until he came up with a black bottle of liquid.

"Let me guess—the blood of virgin brides and plump, innocent babies," Pete said.

"Ink," said Jack. "Black number ten. You've become very morbid." He took a shallow stone dish, the pliers, and the ink and went to the nearest body, gripping the sorcerer's index finger and working the pliers under the nail.

"Mage's manicure, then?" Pete asked. Jack grunted and yanked, and with a wet sound of torn paper the man's nail came off. Jack examined it.

"A bit sticky, but it will do," he pronounced. He set the bowl on the floor and told Pete, "Find north."

Pete peered out the massive gap where the wall once was and located the Thames. "That way." She pointed out a rough north, over her shoulder.

Jack oriented himself and poured the ink into the bowl, then dropped in the nail. It floated, tiny tendrils of sundered flesh disappearing into the black viscous pool.

He blew on the ink and muttered, *"Amharc."* Jack's breath made ripples in the ink. The nail began to spin, lazily at first and then faster and faster, carving a trough in the liquid.

"The Black sees him," Jack muttered, ink from the center of his eye spilling across the blue. Pete felt that electric prickle on her skin as magic took hold.

"The ghost?"

Jack nodded grimly. "He's touched this bloke. Touched all of them, if what Abby said held any truth at all. It's tied to them, and now I can see it right back."

Abruptly, the fingernail stopped spinning and sat deathly still, pointing directly northeast. The surface of the ink quivered ever so slightly as the magic pulsed.

"You know what's northeast, don't you?" Jack asked as he stood, his eyes flickering plain again.

Pete nodded once, over an icy knot in her gut. "Highgate Cemetery."

Chapter 39

Pete had never walked through the cemetery gates again after the emergency responders had taken her out through the small stone arch on the day of the ritual. She'd passed them hundreds of times, though, always aware.

But she'd stayed on the outside. Never walked in. Never broken that unspoken barrier between her nightmares and the reality she'd constructed after Jack's death and her break with feeling anything, believing anything except what the light showed her.

"You're sure this is the place?" Pete said. "I mean, 'northeast' is a rather general classification."

"The scrying medium said northeast," Jack said, "and there aren't any other great bloody haunted cemeteries in this direction that I know of."

The wind kicked up and Pete shivered, although it was a late-autumn wind, not a cutting winter gale. Jack stopped walking, his boots crunching on gravel. "You going to be all right, Pete?"

"Of course," she said. She took out her mobile, hoping it made her look brisk and businesslike—anything but afraid, which she was, and hating herself for it. She couldn't shake afterimages of black smoke and flickering candle flames, and the echoes of Jack's screaming.

"Ollie Heath, please," Pete said when New Scotland Yard's operator picked up. Ollie had just mumbled "Hullo" when Jack snatched the mobile from her and shut it off.

"Oi!" Pete protested, but he shushed her.

"Hear that?"

Pete listened, heard nothing but the wind twisting through the trees and through her hair like the searching fingers of a ghost.

Twined with the wind, a cluster of whispers fluttered against her mind.

"Something's awake," Jack muttered. "Awake and walking, and ten to one it's our boy. Hold off on the copper brigade just for now. Don't want those nice blokes' wives collecting their pensions because they got eaten, do you?"

Pete shook her head. The whispers weren't audible, not really; they just filled her skull from the inside like razor blades, multitudinous and harsh. "Right," said Jack, starting to walk again. He moved slowly, with a noiseless control, and looked much younger and fitter than his scars and sunken cheeks. "Ghost-killing, first form: You can't. Don't try—don't shriek or throw rocks at it or try to send it on to its final reward. If little Maggie—"

"Margaret."

"Close enough, aren't I? If she's still alive you grab her and you run like the fucking legions of Hell are snapping at your heels."

"And what do you do, while I'm running?" Pete asked.

Jack lit a cigarette with a click of his tongue and inhaled. "Distract it long enough to fill my end of our deal and get my arse back to a normal sort of existence."

"So in just a few minutes, we'll be all through?" Pete felt her forehead wrinkle. "I don't think I like that, Jack."

"Plenty of unlikable things in life," he said. "Save the sorrys for when we actually make it away from here with our souls and sanity intact. If the ghost is strong enough to compel living humans to snatch children and then feed off them, it had one hell of a temper in life, and death is piss-poor for softening your impulses."

"How do we hold it off?" Pete swiveled her gaze through the shadows. The headstones tilted and faded and grew older, granite and angels with their arms and wings fallen off. The path narrowed, for pallbearers and mourners instead of automobiles.

"We're alive," said Jack. "We belong here. It doesn't. So there's that, and I've got a shield hex if things get uncivilized." He looked Pete over and she felt calculated and weighed again, Jack still testing her worth. "I won't lie," he said. "If you were an experienced Weir you'd be a real help directing my magic, but as it is, just try not to leave your arse in the wind."

Pete bristled, the quick sting of accumulated intolerance from her fellow inspectors and now from Jack sending her anger to the surface. "I am *not* helpless."

"Neither is the ghost," Jack said. "And unlike you, it has the benefit of already being dead."

Pete didn't respond. She thought about the children's blank white eyes, and tried to force her feet to move forward and follow Jack.

He stopped, and came back and took her hand. "Be fast. Be strong. Don't look it in the face," he said. "That's the best and only advice I can give."

"Not like the last time," Pete said quietly. Jack shook his head.

"Nothing like it. Come on, let's get the girl and get out of here."

As they walked, toward a pool of silver light growing around a bend in the path, Jack didn't let go of Pete's hand and she didn't try to pull away.

The whispers crested and dissipated as they rounded the corner and found themselves faced with a half-collapsed mausoleum, two sorcerers fidgeting to either side of the entrance, and between them—

Pete choked as the air went out of her, and she felt the buzz-saw whine of magic all around her. The ghost was a column of black smoke, vaguely human, burning silver sockets where eyes should be.

"I told you not to look at it!" Jack hissed, digging his nails into her palm. The air rippled and a shield hex blossomed in front of Pete, heavy and gleaming.

"Oi, you!" one of the sorcerers shouted. "You, get out of here!"

"Fucking hell," said the other. "That's really Jack Winter. He came."

Slowly, the ghost coalesced into a figure made of shadow wisps and dark, the eyes topping a cruel mouth that curved in a black slit.

Jack Winter, it hissed. Pete's body was numb, stiff with shock.

"Jack," she said. "It's from my dreams . . . that's the thing . . . I saw it." No response came, and she became aware that Jack was no longer holding her hand.

"Jack?"

He was staring at the ghost, shaking his head slowly back and forth. Jack's eyes had gone white, whiter than Bridget Killigan's, a snow-driven color that was icy and depthless. "No," Jack murmured. "No, no, no. I sent you back . . ."

Pitiful words, crow-mage, for one arrogant as yourself, the ghost said. *I will feed on your spirit and sculpt your bones.*

"Let's give 'em some room," said one of the sorcerers.

"What about the bloody kid?" hissed the other.

"Leave her, 'less you want to get mage guts all over you!" the first shouted, as the ghost let out a howl that ground Pete's teeth together. "Let's sodding *go!*"

They vacated the entrance to the tomb and Pete saw

Margaret Smythe crouched, with her arms around her knees, eyes blessedly brown and impossibly wide peeking over the tops.

Pete looked back at Jack. He stared at the ghost, and the ghost grinned at him, gaping and toothsome. *No more chatter, crow-mage? No more pithy words from the old tongues to expunge me?*

"You're not him!" Jack shouted. He held up his hand and the shield hex became like a wall of heavy water, rippling and impenetrable. "Now piss off!"

The ghost laughed, a scrape against Pete's mind that hurt so much she staggered. It turned, its face sliding along the smoke column of its body to regard her.

Your dreams are most intriguing, young miss. The pity lies in the weakness of your flesh.

"Not weak," Pete ground out. She held out her hand. "Margaret. Come along, luv."

"No!" Margaret shook her head furiously, scooting backward into the mausoleum.

She has grown fond of me, you see. Children are sometimes so very foolish, the ghost murmured, like the moan of a dying mother.

Pete turned on it, careful not to meet the silver orbs distorted by the shield hex. "I swear to everything above and below that if you've hurt her I'll follow you all the way down to the underworld and find a way to kill you again."

The ghost snarled and raised a smoke-hand tipped with black claws. Pete made a dive for Margaret. She felt the swipe, felt it grab the ends of her hair and the seams of her shirt, barely missing skin, the magic burning as if she'd touched supercooled metal.

She had the thought *I should be dead* as she hit the ground, snagging Margaret's hand and pulling her close, balling up her body around the little girl and rolling away from the shrieking spirit.

When she opened her eyes Jack stood above her, both hands extended, the shield hex glowing blue-hot around the edges as the ghost struck it again and again. Jack wobbled under each blow, and Pete saw a ribbon of blood begin to leak out of his nose.

"Not *exactly* like you remember, is it, you wispy cunt," he ground out. "Pete, run," he said. "Run for your life."

The light of the shield hex reflected off the ghost's teeth and Pete shook her head. "Not leaving you. Can't."

Margaret was sobbing, but in relief, not terror. Pete reached out her free hand and laid it on Jack's arm.

"Pete . . ." he started, but she gripped his hand before he could protest.

"I know what I'm doing," she said. It was a complete lie, and it didn't seem to appease Jack, but by then it was too late.

Just as with Talshebeth, Pete felt the dial on her senses pushed to maximum—the shriek of magic and the burning of Jack's skin on hers, the same wind roaring through the well-kept trees and between the tombs. The storm discorporated the ghost, all except a black skeleton that thrashed and howled as the gale of shield magic pelted it.

Jack pulled both of them away, scooping Margaret up in one arm and dragging Pete with the other, although he told her later that he'd had to half carry her because as soon as the ghost's silver eyes winked out under the assault of Jack's talents, Pete blacked out and woke up on Jack's mattress, in his flat, alone.

Chapter 40

"Inspector." A hand gripped her shoulder, tentative and shaky. Not Jack. "Inspector."

Pete opened her eyes, though the light seemed very bright, and ached, forcing her to lower her lids and peer at whoever-it-was through a forest of eyelashes.

"Ollie."

Ollie Heath sat back on his heels, the tight set of his jaw loosening when she spoke. "Thank God. Thought you'd gone and punched your ticket."

"No," Pete said, soft and brief out of necessity. She felt as if she'd drunk up all the alcohol in London, and then vomited it back up and drunk some more. Her tongue was cottony and her skull pulsated steadily as if one of those cymbal-clashing monkey dolls had her head in its grasp.

Pete saw milling figures in somber blue outside Jack's bedroom door, and two in green carrying a paramedic's case.

She bolted up. "Margaret."

"The girl's fine, just fine," said Ollie. "I called the bus for your friend, actually. He could barely stand upright, and he's got himself some nasty burns on his hand . . . scratched all to Hades too, all over his body. Strangest bloody thing I've ever seen."

Ollie propped pillows against the wall, staying crouched

next to Pete as she craned to see into the rest of the flat. "Margaret is safe."

"Safe and sound and gone home with her mum," Ollie confirmed. "Now, I know DCI Newell is waiting to hear you tell exactly what the bloody hell happened and where you've been for the last three days, and I have to say I wondered myself—"

Pete clasped her hand around Ollie's wrist. "I can't. You have to just trust me, Ollie, and not breathe a word to Newell."

Ollie nodded slowly. "I'll always want to know how you found that child in time, Pete."

"You wouldn't believe it," Pete assured him. Ollie stood. "Likely not. I'll go let Mr. Winter know you're awake. He was troubled when he called. Claimed you passed out."

"I did," Pete said. Everything after she took Jack's hand was an inkblot on the narrative, obscured by folds of pain and ghostly hisses. "Wait," she said as Ollie walked out, the belated truth breaking through her foggy mind. "Jack called you?"

"Took your mobile and did it," said Ollie. "He was terribly concerned over you and the fate of the girl."

"How about *that*," Pete mused. She could only imagine Jack's conversation with Ollie when he called to report the missing Margaret Smythe found.

"Seems an all-right bloke, if a bit on the shifty side," Ollie observed. "Want me to send him in?"

"Please," Pete said, pulling her hair into a knot at the base of her neck and attempting to work the kinks out of her arms and shoulders. Everything hurt, as though she'd run for kilometers beyond measure and then gone a few rounds with a drunken Chelsea fan on game day.

Ollie disappeared and a moment later Jack replaced him, not hurrying or rushing in but just there, as if Pete had willed him into being. She blinked and then narrowed her eyes. "One day you're going to tell me how you do that."

"Do what, luv?" He pulled the straight-backed chair up to the mattress and leaned down to put one finger under her chin. "You look a bit worse for wear." The corners of his mouth crinkled a little and his eyes darkened to a deep-sea color with what Pete would classify as relief, if it were anyone but Jack.

Pete examined him in turn. Except for neatly wrapped bandages on his palms he was untouched, rumpled, and smelling of day-old tobacco. As usual, and Pete couldn't have been more grateful.

"If it wasn't for your hands I'd believe I dreamed the ghost, everything," she said.

Jack's eyes rippled again, slate. "You didn't."

"I know," Pete said quietly. "What have you told the police?"

"Not a bloody thing," said Jack. "I've taken a pinch before, Pete. I can keep me mouth shut."

Pete tilted her head back and shut her eyes, the solid and the real finally seeping back into her skin. "Then it's over. I'll make up a story for Newell, and you'll corroborate it, and it will be over."

A silence stretched, and Pete opened one eye. Jack was staring out the window, past the telephone wires and the chimney pots on the opposite block of flats, watching as slivers of mist collected and filtered the sun to a tarnished sheen that turned his hair molten and his skin paper.

"It's not," he said finally. "It's not finished."

Pete swung her legs over the side of the mattress and sat up, even though dizziness rocked her like a ship in high wind. "What do you mean, Jack?"

He stood up, knocking the chair over, and paced away. "Come on, Pete!" he snarled. "Don't play the sweet schoolgirl with me. You *know* what that thing was in the grave-yard! You saw it."

"I don't," said Pete, shaking her head once. "I was focused on Margaret. And you. It was from my dream. That's all."

"From your dream because you've *bloody seen it before*." Jack slumped. He looked like a doll with cut strings, disjointed and laid aside. Pete got up and made her unsteady way to him.

"Whatever it is, Jack—just tell me."

"It's worse," he said. "It's about to get *much* worse. That ghost . . . I swear I sent him back, Pete. I *did*." Jack's voice threaded with frustration, as if he'd reached into his top hat to produce a dove and found a dead cat instead. "He can't have existed in the thin spaces for a dozen years on his own."

"Well, obviously he *did*," Pete murmured. "I have a notion feeding on children helped with that."

"*No*," said Jack firmly. "No, it doesn't work that way, Pete. He should have been called back into the land of the dead. For him to linger, to get so strong . . . he's had assistance, of the most grievous kind."

"Don't like the sound of that," Pete said.

"And you shouldn't," said Jack. "Whoever would keep *him* close to this world . . . there's a nutter with black plans, mark my words."

"Got a theory?" she asked, and Jack rubbed at the point between his eyes as if he were trying to erase something.

"Haven't a bloody clue. I swear, Pete," he said again, more to himself than to anyone present. "I sent him back."

"Who is he?" Pete asked, rising and stepping around Jack to face him. Jack closed his eyes, rubbing his hands over his face. In the direct foggy sunlight, all of his scars and premature lines were stark. Jack looked old, hollowed out and collapsing.

"His name is Algernon Treadwell," Jack said finally,

from behind his hands. "And he's what I summoned out of the tomb twelve years ago."

"Pete." Ollie stuck his head into the bedroom. "We're clearing out—you'll need a lift back to your flat, yeah?"

"No," Pete said faintly, not taking her eyes from Jack. He looked resigned, dragging the toe of one boot back and forth across the dust on the floorboards.

"No," Pete said louder. "I need to stay here for a bit."

"Well . . . ring me when you're in," said Ollie. "I'll be at the Yard doing up the reports."

Pete nodded, and Ollie backed away. A few seconds later the front door banged shut.

Sighing, Pete went to the window and leaned her forehead against the glass.

"Jasper Gorson," said Jack. Pete didn't move. She felt like a column of ice, frangible and nerveless.

"Don't tell me this is the one time you're not going to ask 'Who's that.' " Jack sighed. "You want to know what happened, I can see it."

"I want to know?" Pete murmured. She saw that limestone door scaled with moss roll back, and felt the cool dry breath of the tomb on her face. She had made a circuit and come back to stand in front of it, a dozen years hence. There was nothing to do but face up.

"I suppose I do," she said. "I would like to know the hours of my life that I've spent in nightmares since you did this, Jack. I would know how long I waited for you to come back, and tell me it was all a terrible mistake. I would like to know, because then I could quantify exactly how much of my suffering *whatever* you were hoping to accomplish was worth to you."

Jack's jaw knotted. "I was a stupid kid, Pete, the same as you. I didn't know what would happen."

"The hell you didn't," Pete hissed, stepping in and jabbing a finger into his chest. Jack took a hasty step back.

"When things went wrong you bolted without a glance backward. All that rot . . . 'Oh, Pete, I waited for you for so very long . . .' Pure rubbish. You didn't bloody care what happened to me! I should bash your bloody face in, you fucking bastard!" The high ceiling rattled echoes back and Pete realized she was shouting.

"Fine. I didn't, when I started," Jack said. "And when Treadwell came after us, you ran away and left me for dead."

"I thought you *were* dead—"

"And then you were able to shut out the Black, and I hated you for it. But I know now, Pete, so do you want to hear it or not?"

Pete nodded tightly, knotting and unknotting her fists to keep from hitting a wall, or Jack.

"This is how it was," Jack said softly. "Back then the two most reputable mages in the Black were me and Jasper Gorson. Gorson had been bragging for weeks that he'd raised a black spirit, flashing this grimoire it had supposedly transcribed for him." He produced a Parliament and chewed on the end before an ember flared. "So me back got up, and I went looking for a spirit to raise and tap into, as well."

"Jack, did it ever occur to you that Gorson may have been a fucking liar?" Pete asked.

"Of *course* he was a liar," Jack snapped, "but try telling that to the stupid sods who hang around the Lament pub."

Pete thought of Arty and Abby, and Hattie Page. "Go on."

"I got the books and I looked and I found him," Jack said. "Algernon Treadwell." He shivered and sat down, resting his elbows on his thighs and his head in his hands. "He was a sorcerer, the worst of his time. Feared. Tried, tortured, and killed by witchfinders in the winter of 1836. I paid off a groundskeeper to show me Treadwell's tomb, and then . . ." He looked up at Pete, smoke drifting from his nose and mouth. "Then your bloody sister brought you to see me play at Fiver's."

"Did you know what I was?" Pete asked quietly. "Was it that from the first minute?"

"No," Jack said. "No, it took me a few days to realize why I always felt like I was grasping at power lines when you were in the room."

"And then you wasted no time at all." Pete clapped her hands together. "Bravo."

"Pete, you have to believe I didn't mean—"

"I believe you," she said. "I believe that you didn't want to get killed." She went to the hooks in the entry and took her coat and bag.

"You can't leave!" Jack exclaimed. "Treadwell is still about!"

"What's he going to do?" Pete snapped. "Rattle chains and write REDRUM on the mirrors?"

Jack crossed the room in a blur of bleached head and angry burning gaze and grabbed Pete's arm. "Bugger all, Pete, stop being so fucking righteous. I'm sorry you got involved again, but you *are,* until Treadwell's back where he belongs."

"And you are a bloody fucking *expert* on that, aren't you," Pete said. Jack winced, and finally went silent. "I'll be at home," said Pete. "Don't come find me. Don't call. In point of fact, Jack, I don't want to bloody know of your existence *ever* again."

He didn't try to stop her when she walked out, and slammed the door hard enough to rattle every ghost in the building.

Chapter 41

Pete didn't go home. She walked through the fog, into the City, listening to her footsteps ring and eventually came to St. James's Park. She followed a gravel path until hedgerows and mist hid her from all human eyes, and then stopped, her face tilted back, feeling the cold sprinkle of rain on her cheeks.

In a day as damply vibrant as this one, it was difficult to believe a sorcerer's spirit bent on mayhem had an eye out for her.

It was even difficult to believe that Jack had used her.

Afraid, luv? Don't be.

She'd *trusted* him, that was the thing that finally made Pete shiver, not with cold, and blink twin tears down her cheeks that were not rain. Things that she'd rather forget were swimming near the surface, about Jack. About the day. About everything.

And finally, for the first time since she'd run screaming from the tomb, Pete let them come.

She had trusted him to be with her and keep her safe and she'd gone with it when he'd lit the candles and guided her to the foot of the circle, natural, like it was an everyday thing.

"So what dark pagan gods are we invoking?" she joked, standing on her tiptoes to keep Jack's hand tight against hers across the circle. Jack chuckled when his invocation finished, and snapped his lighter closed, snuffing the brighter flame and leaving just the flickering faerie light of the candles on the floor. The carvings on the tomb's wall threw long shadows, scraping fingers and grasping mouths.

"No gods. That's next week's exercise. Today we're just testing an academic theory."

"Share with the class?" Pete's feet hurt from the long up-hill walk from the tube in her school shoes and she fidgeted.

"It wouldn't be a surprise then, luv." Jack smiled, thin and white, his thumb circling the hollow part of her palm. "You want to be surprised, don't you?"

"Not sure," Pete said honestly. It was cold inside the tomb, and unnaturally dark when contrasted with the strong sun outside. Jack held his free hand out, palm down over the circle, and Pete's stomach did a nervous flip-flop.

The blood they had both spilled began to move across each line of the circle, turning the crooked chalk marks crimson. Jack twisted his fingers, cat's-cradle, until the blood spread and pooled at the very center of the mark.

"It's working," he whispered, a boyish grin breaking out. "Bloody hell, it's working."

The crimson began to fade, and Jack cursed. "Fuck it. Not enough . . ."

Pete watched him, and she didn't know why she spoke up again, because never in a million days would she, Connor Caldecott's sensible daughter through and through, believe so outlandish a thing, but the words flew out. "This is real."

Twin points of witchfire sprang to life in Jack's eyes. Harmless, beautiful witchfire that she'd seen him conjure before, only now it burned Pete hot enough to melt her under the force of Jack's gaze. "No bloody kidding," was all he said, before he pulled his flick-knife with his free hand and cut his thumb again. Three drops of his blood landed in the center of the chalk lines.

They disappeared, sucked inward through the stone floor. A sensation of wrongness crept up Pete's spine, as if the floor had tilted underneath her feet just slightly.

"Don't move," Jack ordered, licking the remaining blood off his palm. He repeated the cut on her hand as well, dropping her blood onto the stones next to his and Pete coiled in on herself, knowing that if she moved now things would go even worse than they already had.

Jack held on to her, their blood mingling and slicking her skin. "Look at you, still holding strong. Don't let go, yeah?"

"Never," Pete whispered.

Jack shut his eyes, face tilted upward into the dark. Pete could picture him in a gold circlet and a white robe just then, at the head of a coven in a circle of stones.

"Eitil dom, a spiorad," Jack muttered. *"Eitil dom, a spiorad. Tar do mo fhuil beo."* He opened his eyes and spoke aloud. "Algernon Treadwell. Hound-sorcerer. I command you into my circle, spirit and soul. *Tar do mo fhuil beo.*"

For a long minute, the only sounds to Pete were her own breathing and the faraway rush of traffic through the afternoon. "Come on . . ." Jack whispered. "You ruddy bastard. Come to me."

The skin on the back of Pete's neck twinged as though someone had dropped ice cubes down her collar. With a shivering sigh of magic black smoke began to issue forth from all the walls and flagstones of the tomb, creeping through the crevices and forming in the air, the shape beginning to breathe.

Transfixed, Pete watched as smoke grew hands, and fingers, and a soundless mouth. When it spoke, no real sound slipped into the small echoing space, but Pete heard it just the same and it made the space behind her eyes hurt.

Who might this be, who has so rudely called?

Jack's shoulders dropped, the tension wire cut when the

thing spoke. "Jack Winter." He grinned broadly. "Jack Winter compels you, hound-sorcerer."

The smoke drifted around to face Pete as if on a spindle. *Not entirely, it seems.*

"Oi," Jack ordered. "Leave her out of it."

But why? She is deliciously vulnerable, an uncorrupted conduit. Open and willing. The smoke was smoke, but Pete swore that its hollow mouth smiled. *I believe I see why you protect this one, Jack Winter.*

Jack's jaw knotted but his voice remained steady and low as ever. Maybe, Pete thought, the smoke-man couldn't see the twin flames in his eyes because the smoke-man appeared to have none. "Get off it. My circle *compels* you to obey me."

It would, the smoke agreed, *it would if properly drawn. Your filthy marsh-mouthed language betrays you as a trainee of the* Fiach Duhb. *Your hag's blood holds no sway. Stand aside if you value your scrabbling misery of a life, mage.*

And the smoke-man walked. It came straight for Pete, one hand with trailing wisp-claws reaching for her. Jack went to his knee, chalked a hasty symbol on the floor with his unencumbered hand, and the smoke-man slowed, but Pete was rooted and stilled even though she *wanted* to run, far and fast as her legs would take her. She could not move, not against the assault of cries and the raw, heavy power, like iron buried deep within frozen earth that the smoke pressed down around her.

Jack said, "Fuck," and pushed the toe of his boot over the circle's outer line, smudging the symbols within beyond recognition. "Go back!" Jack ordered loudly. "Return to the city of the dead and no more with the living will you be. Your time here is at an end, hound-sorcerer."

Just as it had gathered the blood, the chalk star began to gather the smoke, pulling the ghost inexorably downward. It let out a scream that bled Pete's eardrums, swiping at her wildly and close enough to leave ice crystals on her brow.

This is NOT the last, Jack Winter! it howled. *If I must return to the bleak spires then you return as well!* The smoke-man thrust out his one remaining hand and seized Jack, pushing talons made of black ice through his abdomen. Jack grunted and doubled as the black smoke flowed into him.

"Stop!" Pete screamed. Jack tried to motion her away, but he was atrophying, his skin paling to blue-yellow, dark lines sprouting in all the crevices of his face, dead dull gray growing from the roots of his hair. As the ghost flowed into him Jack's life flowed out, his cheeks and eyes sinking and his body falling to the floor.

Their hands broke apart. Pete could not move, could not even work her jaws to scream.

A spout of crimson blood, the color of rose petals against his sallow sunken face, dribbled from Jack's mouth.

"Go back," Jack ground, barely above a whisper. Night-shaded smoke drifted out in lieu of breath when he spoke. "You are shapeless and shadow. You are dead, and you belong with the dead. The living world holds no place for you. Go back."

The ghost shrieked, and clutched at Jack. More and more blood poured from his mouth, his eyes, his nostrils.

Seeing Jack's life leach out of him broke her paralysis, and Pete picked up the black candle, because it was the only thing within her reach, and flung it at the ghost. "Go back!" she echoed Jack, feeling tears on her cheeks. "Leave him alone!"

Jack coughed weakly, and went still. Pete let out a cry. "He's not! You haven't killed him!"

The ghost hissed, arching back as if in agony, and then with a rush it disappeared completely, the chalk lines of the circle vibrating with displaced power.

Jack was still, silent and bloody. The light of the guttering candle threw the shadow of an enormous crow, stooped and spreading its wings around Jack to embrace him. The crow became a girl, a woman, a hag. All bent to touch Jack's blood-smeared forehead, their gestures those of disbelieving and mournful lovers.

Pete didn't run to Jack, because of the hopping, sentient shadow and because the thought of him dead—as he surely was; she'd been to enough funerals to know cloudy eyes and dead stillness—became too much to bear. She ran instead, screaming, through the cemetery until she found the visitor's hut, pounding on the door and scraping her knuckles free of skin.

Connor told her Jack was dead, when she finally decided she had to talk to *someone,* days later. And she cried. Relegated him to her nightmares, until she'd seen him again in the Montresor Hotel.

And never, ever admitted to herself that she'd been the one to let go.

That was it, Pete realized as she shivered under the chill from the overcast and fog, and started the walk back to the street from the footpath. She had *seen* Jack die, known that the ghost killed him before she broke the candle.

Pete sighed as she turned back toward the Mall, Whitechapel invisible at this distance through the fog. She'd never be free of Jack Winter. But now, unlike then, she wasn't running away.

Chapter 42

She pounded on Jack's door three times with the side of her fist. "Sod off!" he shouted.

Pete knocked again. Jack threw the door open, a frying pan in his hand. "Listen, you bloody—"

"I want to know how you came back," Pete said. "You were dead. I saw Death hunched over you that day, the bird's form. I want to know how you survived it."

Jack's expression flickered at that, but he pulled the door wide enough for a person and motioned her in. Pete folded her arms, and nudged the door shut with her foot. "So. How did you?"

"That bit is a story for another day," said Jack, eyes darting. "What made you come back?" He went into the kitchen and tossed the frying pan into a cabinet, and lit the burner under the kettle.

Pete had asked herself the question repeatedly as she walked back to Whitechapel. "I guess I can't walk away from you. Even though I should."

Jack's mouth quirked. "Make it difficult, do I?"

"Don't take it that way," Pete warned. "The way I see it, you didn't put Treadwell back where he belonged before, and I have no reason to think you're up for the task this time."

Jack rubbed his gut in mock-pain. "You do go for the vulnerable spots, luv."

"We're going to find out what Treadwell wants," Pete said firmly, pulling the kettle off the burner when it squealed. "And then, that other day is going to come, and you're going to tell me how you survived him the first time."

"Is there ever anything you're not absolutely certain of?" Jack added sugar to his mug.

"Any number of things," said Pete. "None of which have to do with you."

"I don't know what Treadwell wants." Jack sighed. "He's been hovering between this world and the land of the dead for a dozen years, just gathering rage, and power with no rhyme or reason behind it."

Pete sipped her tea. It was stale, and the water tasted like minerals. "He's seen you now. He knows you're still about."

Jack's eyes gleamed, like midnight ice. "Good. Been an age since I had a decent fight."

"Treadwell is a *ghost*," Pete said. "Like you so helpfully pointed out, he is *already passed on*. I seriously doubt a few lines of Irish and some witchfire are going to put a dent in his plans. Assuming angry ghosts have plans."

"Without a doubt," said Jack. "Haven't the foggiest what they are, but I don't think it involves rainbows and leprechauns doing a jig."

Pete put her mug into the sink and held out her hand to Jack. "What?" he demanded suspiciously.

"Give me a fag," she said. "I need it if I'm going to help you."

Jack conjured a Parliament, but held it back. "Pete . . . you don't have to be involved. Treadwell doesn't want you—I'm the one who called him, challenged him."

"Jack Winter," said Pete, "if you expect me to believe you

have gone altruistic and noble at this late date, you must be around the fucking bend."

He handed her the cigarette and she lit it from the burner. "Can't put much past you."

"No," Pete agreed. She inhaled, exhaled, felt the slow burn down her throat. More cases solved over fags and tea than she cared to count. This should be no different. She shouldn't be panicking, but her stomach bounced as Jack rubbed the point between his eyes and sighed.

"Why did you?" she asked. "Why try to give me an out, after all that yelling you did about having to work with me in the first place?"

He smiled, grim. "Pete, I've gone to a lot of funerals. Forgive me if I didn't want to spend another Sunday in a wet graveyard and choke down warm pasta salad in some pub, because I *know* that flaky sister of yours wouldn't kick out for anything decent at the wake."

Pete dragged, watched the column of ash grow long and gray, and said, "You think I'm going to die."

Jack shrugged. "Someone is, luv. This isn't one of the times that there's a happy ending."

"Is there ever?" Pete muttered. She stubbed out the Parliament and threw it down the drain. Jack watched her, eyes narrowed.

"You having second thoughts?"

Pete turned on him. He wasn't calculating her any longer, wasn't weighing. His face was folded shut, but his eyes gleamed with a light Pete had never witnessed.

"I'm thinking that at least I won't die in a bed with needles and tubes stuck in me," she said, softer than a sigh. Jack unfolded himself from the wall and took up her hands. He'd gotten more solid, Pete realized, his hands heavy and the fingers free from tremors.

"It will end badly, Pete, but we'll be together this time around. I promise you."

"You're promising me, now?" She smiled a little, and the afterimage of Connor and the road she had looked down toward him faded.

"You promised me," Jack said. "Even if I'm a bloody liar, it's the least I can do."

"And are you? A liar, I mean," Pete asked. Jack let go of her and picked up his jacket.

"We'll find out."

Chapter 43

"So we just hang around Highgate and wait for Treadwell to show up again?" Pete asked as they crossed into the Black in an alleyway behind a kebab shop.

"I have a distinct feeling that when Treadwell wants his presence known, he'll send me a message," Jack said.

The Lament's red door was shut, and no music drifted to Pete's ears. "Closed on Sundays," Jack said by way of explanation.

"It's Friday . . ." Pete started, but then shook her head. "Never mind."

Jack kicked aside the mud mat, and examined the square granite flower pots on either side of the door. "Ah, leave it out. Where does that ruddy publican hide it?"

"Looking for this?" Mosswood stood in the street with a newspaper under his arm, backlit by the gaslight on the corner. He swung a small iron key on a fob chain.

"Even better than breaking in," Jack said. "Need to speak with you."

"I should think so," said Mosswood. He opened the Lament's three locks and pushed the door wide, motioning Pete and Jack in. "The Black has been a veritable hive of gossip since your and Miss Caldecott's ghostly assignation."

"What's old chilly-boy after?" Jack asked.

"Why, your suffering, I imagine," said Mosswood. "Algernon Treadwell was not known for his humor in life, or his mercy. I once saw him put out a man's eyes for daring to meet his."

Mosswood stalked across the main floor and led Pete and Jack to a private room done like a club in leather wingback chairs and Persian rugs. Bookshelves lined the walls and an ornate fire grate nested in the corner. Mosswood muttered and green flames sprang to life.

Jack paced, examining the books, but Pete sat opposite Mosswood. "Thanks for your help."

"And who said I was helping you?" Mosswood raised his eyebrows and began to tamp tobacco into his pipe.

"You don't have a choice," said Jack with an unpleasant smile. "Treadwell will know I came calling on you. He won't believe you *didn't* help me, so you might as well."

Mosswood sighed and looked at Pete. "I see you made the choice to continue. Regretting it yet?"

Pete looked to Jack, who reiterated the question with his expression. "Not yet," Pete said honestly.

"I don't know how much time we have," Jack said to Mosswood. "Mind if I get on with it? Everything on my account, as per usual."

The Green Man sighed and puffed his pipe. "Do your worst."

Jack went to a set of apothecary drawers on the other side of the snug room, drawers that made up a dizzyingly vast section of shelf with their tiny, precise labels, and began opening them at random, examining their contents with the avid enthusiasm of a fetishist in an underwear store.

"Is there anything I can do?" Pete asked.

"Not until Treadwell shows up and tries to push me heart out through my nose again," Jack said. He took two leather pouches on thongs from a drawer and tossed one to Pete. She loosened the thong and looked inside.

"Salt?"

"Earth. Life," said Jack. "Wear it when we go back to the graveyard." He tucked what looked like charcoal into his pocket along with a fresh chunk of chalk. "Got to piss. Back in a moment."

"So we just sit here," said Pete glumly, when Jack had left.

"One word of advice." Mosswood tapped his pipe stem against his teeth. "Jack is taking everything with him that he can think of. Charcoal is a focus for mage talents. He's got the salt because he doesn't believe his shield hex will protect him. But the only certain way to exorcise Treadwell is the way it's always been. Take a coffin nail and drive it into the spot where he was buried."

"That seems awfully simple," Pete said. "Are you saying Jack doesn't—"

"Jack will try to make his point before he gets down to business," Mosswood said. "He has the unfortunate human vice of pride. I'm telling *you* this in case Jack doesn't get his chance to deal with Treadwell. For your own good, accept the possibility of that occurrence."

Pete looked into the fire. She tried to imagine facing Treadwell alone, Jack gone away, and couldn't. She knew her inability made her the sad, guileless little girl who couldn't protect herself, just as before. Pete swallowed a lump of bitter acid at the memory of her own trust, and how last time it had led to the end of everything.

Not this time, she promised. *Treadwell won't take Jack away again.*

The embers pulsed, and the fire snuffed out as the front door of the Lament creaked open and brought the knife-edged autumn gale with it. "I'll go shut it," Pete said, relieved to be out of the weighty silence of Mosswood's presence.

"Don't—" Mosswood started, but Pete stepped into the main room of the pub and immediately saw her mistake. Felt it, as the dark magic wrapped around her. Three sorcerers wielding the bruise-colored witchfire she'd come to recognize stood arrayed between her, the entrance, and any possible weapon behind the bar.

"Jack—" Pete opened her mouth to shout, at the same time balling her fists. Magic be damned—she would go down kicking and punching, if that was what it took.

One of the sorcerers flowed across the floor in a haze of blue-black fire and clamped one hand over her mouth, his other arm pinning Pete in a breath-taking hug. "Don't scream," he hissed. "Time enough for that later."

"Let her go," said Mosswood. He stood well clear of the sorcerer's reach, but he looked stern and not like someone Pete would trifle with, were she in a position to.

"Bugger off, Knight." The second sorcerer sneered. "Matters of the Arkanum don't concern *you*."

"Matters in my pub do," said Mosswood. "And if you sorry lot are the best of the Arkanum I will eat my tobacco pouch with salt."

"We *just* want the crow-mage," the one holding Pete snarled. "But if you'd like to become incentive, feel free to step between us and him."

Jack appeared from the archway painted with GENTS, wiping his hands on his shirt. He stopped when he saw the tableau. "What's the matter—couldn't Treadwell come out and play? Or did a spare wind get him stuck in a chimney pot somewhere?"

"If you want her back, come to Highgate and don't try any of your mage's cleverness," said the sorcerer holding Pete.

"You honestly think I couldn't drop you dead where you stand?" Jack asked, pleasant and soft.

The sorcerer began to laugh. "Anything you do would put the chit at risk, and I don't think you want that."

"Maybe I don't care," Jack said. His eyes flamed to life.

"Maybe you should do as you're told," the sorcerer

snapped, "and maybe you'll be in time to keep your girlfriend from the touch of him."

Jack looked at Pete, and sighed. "They've got me bent over properly. I'm sorry, luv."

Pete tried to say, "What the bloody hell do you think you're doing letting me become a hostage," but she was too muffled by the sorcerer's fingers. She kicked at him instead and caused a groan but no loosening of his grip on her.

"Pete. *Pete.*" Jack held up his hands. "I'll be right behind you, luv. I promise. Believe me. No harm will come to you. Believe me, please."

He was coming as close to begging as Jack would ever come, Pete knew. And fuck, she wasn't going to die on the floor of a pub, at the hand of a reject from the Cure reunion tour.

She worked her head free of the sorcerer's grip. "I believe you." Before she heard Jack's reply, if there was one, the walls of the Lament blurred and fell away to rushing black, and everything fell away, leaving Pete dangling before she slammed back to earth.

"You like that?" The sorcerer's face was in the light now, the electric lamps of the regular world's Highgate Cemetery. "Shadow-stepping. Mages can't translocate like that. Only sorcerers."

"My knees are positively weak," Pete said. Treadwell's sorcerer jerked her arm, black petals of smoke blossoming on his other palm.

"Don't be smart. I could take your face off."

"Will it save me from having to listen to you rattle on?" Pete gave the sorcerer her worst glare as he marched her through leaning rows of headstones.

"Winter doesn't like his women mouthy. Wonder he let you stick around as long as you did."

"There's a lot you don't know about Jack Winter," Pete said.

The sorcerer barked a laugh. "As much as you did when you got tangled up with him in the first place, you silly chit?"

Pete looked at her feet for a few steps. "No," she said finally. "I knew far, far less. But that doesn't change the fact that I'm here now, stolen and harmed by you, and that because you stole me you're fucked when Jack finds us."

"Petrifying," said the sorcerer. "Move your little damsel act right along." He shoved her and she tripped over a low tombstone.

"Let *go* of me!" Pete cried, jerking against the man's grasp. He stopped her, grabbing her by the upper arms, squeezing until Pete knew most women would let tears slide down their cheeks. She stayed silent, still. She would never cry.

"You listen," growled the sorcerer. "Winter doesn't *care* about you, you understand that? He *let* us steal you away. Now, you keep your mouth shut and your head down and our master might see his way to letting you go . . . or keeping you as an amusement. That's a better future than what Winter can offer you on his best day." He pulled her along the path again, Pete's feet digging furrows in the earth as she resisted him.

They walked, or rather the sorcerer walked, dragging Pete, for a long while, clear across the old part of the cemetery. Pete smirked. "Looks like your teleporter is off prime. You should have Scotty in to calibrate that."

The sorcerer paused when they were in the oldest part of the cemetery, amid the weeds and the forgotten sunken graves. "You're not afraid of what we're going to do to you," the sorcerer stated, disappointment pulling at his face. His witchfire flared with a snap and he patted Pete down, taking away her mobile, the keys to the Mini, and anything else that might constitute a weapon.

"Jack will come for me," said Pete with a thrust of her chin. "And when he does I—far from a damsel, thank you—am personally going to make you sorry for this entire night and the rest of your wasted life." She could lie convincingly to everyone—it was her own doubts that were the problem. Jack *wasn't* here and the Black wasn't snapping and hissing in the way that meant he was near.

"You tell yourself anything you like, girl," said the sorcerer, tossing her things into the weeds. "But the fact remains, you're all alone." He turned Pete so they were pressed back to front, his arm across her throat. "Look there."

Over the humped, half-collapsed roof of the closest mausoleum, Pete could see torchlight, and hear low voices in the sort of contemplative chant that should accompany confession and absolution.

"That," hissed the sorcerer, his hand sliding up and down Pete's throat, stroking her skin and leaving a trail of shivers. "*That* is magic's future. Not Jack Winter. Not the old ways or the old gods. It's men, taking what they want. What our master started, we'll finish."

"They might," said a Manchester drawl from Pete's back. "But you? All you'll be getting is a concussion and some pretty new bruises."

Jack raised a burial urn over his head and smashed the sorcerer's skull with it, ash and bone fragments raining around Pete. The sorcerer staggered and went to the ground, raising his hand, his magic gathering.

"Don't," Jack snarled. "If you value the bits that make you a man, don't."

Pete jumped away from the sorcerer as he made a grab for her, his teeth bared in fury. She stomped on his outstretched hand, eliciting a howl.

Before she could find something to tie the sorcerer up with, Jack stepped in and snapped his head backward with a jackboot to the face. "The next time you touch Pete, I kill you where you stand," he said.

Trembling in Pete's hands and everywhere reminded her that she was still in the cemetery, that Treadwell was there, sending tendrils of ice across the Black.

Jack came to her, his chest rising and falling in time with the waves of fire in his eyes, and the icy whispers quieted when he got close enough to touch.

He took Pete's chin in his hand, turned her face side to side, brushed her cheek with his thumb. "You still got all your fingers and toes, then?"

Pete jerked her head away. "What the bloody hell took you so long?"

"I *did* have to bargain for a means of transport that'd get me here before they carved your eyes out, didn't I?" Jack said. "And let me tell you, riding with the dullahan is not something a bloke ever gets used to. The smell alone—"

"Treadwell is over there, beyond the tomb," Pete broke in. "Jack, Mosswood told me that the only way to exorcise him—"

"The coffin nail, I know." Jack waved the notion away. "I want you to stay with me, do you understand?"

"Oh, like you stayed with me in the pub?" Pete followed him between the gravestones, Jack marking a straight line, not even attempting to hide his advance. "Answer me!" she demanded. "How could you let them snatch me? I don't like being the damsel in distress, Jack. It's bloody demeaning."

Jack stopped walking, heaving a dramatic sigh. "Treadwell wanted to play with me, and he wanted to make me suffer. I could sit around wringing my hands and waiting for his flunkies to bring back sliced-off bits of Pete, or I could let him think he'd gotten one over and meet him head-on." He grinned. "So relax, Pete. You weren't a damsel. You were bait."

Pete slapped him, so hard he rocked back on his heels. Jack rubbed his jaw. "Are you quite finished?" he asked.

"Now I am." Pete nodded. "Do something like this again and I'll rip your sodding balls off."

"Received loud and clear," Jack agreed. He started walking again. "Hello, you bastards!" he bellowed. "Here I am! The crow-mage, come walking to your doorstep!"

The sorcerers of the Arkanum appeared, some blending out from the shadows, some stepping out from hiding spots. "Winter," one hissed, teeth flashing under the sodium lights.

"Ready, luv?" Jack said to her, barely a rumble in his chest.

"It's Petunia." Pete gripped Jack's hand firmly, a slow spread of warmth passing up her arm.

Jack looked at her in askance as the sorcerers conjured red witchfire, a circle of bloody pinpoints springing to life around them. "What is?"

"My name," Pete told him. "It's Petunia." She could feel Treadwell behind her eyes, pushing and guiding with fingers like living icicles.

"Dreadful," Jack muttered. "Don't blame you for shortening it."

"I wanted you to know," Pete said.

Jack squeezed her hand. "I do, Pete." He breathed in and the magic crackled around him, the Black leaching from the ether to gather and swarm.

Pete shut her eyes. Jack exhaled and said, *"Cosain."*

The shield hex blossomed, growing and spreading outward, a stone bubble that decimated the circle of sorcerers, breaking bones and bloodying faces. The hex coalesced and held, shimmering against the night light. "In my bag," said Jack, indicating a battered satchel with his chin. "Take out the hammer and the coffin nail while I hold the hex, will you, luv?"

Pete dug in the satchel, which contained any number of unpleasantly slimy and smelly things, and pulled out a wooden mallet and a large square-headed nail. The nail sent a jolt of white-heat magic through her hand when she touched it.

"Here." She nudged them into Jack's hands.

"Cheers," he muttered. "Here goes bloody nothing."

Jack closed his eyes and knelt in front of Treadwell's burial spot, raising the coffin nail and the hemlock hammer. "Algernon Treadwell!" he commanded. "I call you forth to face me. Arise, spirit!" He hit the nail. "Rise!" Again and again the hammer fell, driving the nail into the earth to the hilt.

Outside the shield hex, the sorcerers regained their feet but they simply stood, watching, burning witchfire the only sign of life.

"Jack . . ." Pete touched his shoulder. The expectancy of the sorcerers, their smiles, sent a chill stronger than any magic through her.

"Treadwell!" Jack shouted again. "Come on, you bastard! Come here and meet me!"

With a tiny sigh, a point of silver light blossomed, like a pinpoint into another world. *Petty and theatrical as always, Jack Winter.*

"No," Jack replied as Treadwell coalesced. "No, this time I'm just sending you back. Nothing petty about it."

Treadwell's hollow silver eyes fastened on Pete. *Your mage should learn to mind his hexes. As I am challenged, so I begin.*

The spirit exhaled Latin under his breath, and Jack grabbed his head, teeth grinding. The shield hex wavered and went out, and two sorcerers jumped in to pull Pete away from Jack, who went to his knees.

Treadwell raised Jack's chin, one long-taloned ice finger

digging a bead of blood out of Jack's skin. *So easy. So very disappointing.*

"Jack . . ." Pete flung herself against her captors. "Jack!"

"Kill me, if you will," Jack growled. His eyes were blue fire, no white or iris left. "But believe that I'll pull you right down into the bleak city with me, you hollowed-out misty wanker."

I believe, but you are so very wrong about me, Jack. Your death is not my desire. Contrary to all presuppositions, you have made yourself useful.

"The fuck are you on about?" Jack demanded.

Your mind is corrupted and your talents are weak and fleeting, ensnared by too many bargains, Treadwell hissed. *But your body—your body will do admirably.*

For the first time that Pete had seen, Jack faltered and looked utterly displaced.

"What the fuck are you on about?" he managed. "You dead never make any bloody sense."

It was a simple thing, Winter . . . to draw you out, and to draw you to me. All it took was a stroke to your pride, to give you a chance to best me. And you appeared, you and your form, mine for the taking.

"The bansidhe. The Arkanum," Pete whispered. Treadwell froze the air around him, and her cheeks and fingers were numb.

Lures, Treadwell agreed. *The correct ones, it appears. Not enough to stop the crow-mage, but enough wind to change his flight.*

"You think I don't have a plan?" Jack snarled at him. "That I'd just rush in any door you opened?"

I think you cannot resist the chance to prove what a wicked sort of man you are, Treadwell said. *And I do not think that you have any more plan now than you did when I killed you the first time.*

Treadwell laughed, a steam hiss across the surface of Pete's mind, and at his gesture one of the sorcerers stepped in behind Jack and drove a long knife into his kidneys.

Rebirth is painful, of course, Treadwell murmured. *Transformation is by definition an agony of the soul. But rest assured, crow-mage, I've only brought you to the brink of death—the thin place of this world.*

"Now he gets into the body," said a sorcerer. "And he'll be corporeal." A frission of excitement spread through the circle.

Pete heard someone screaming, a single "No" repeated over and over, the word running together into speechless cries. Her mouth went dry and she realized the voice belonged to her.

"Master Treadwell," the sorcerer holding her called. "What about the woman?"

Kill her, Treadwell told him. *She is polluted by the mage.*

"Oh, God, Jack, I'm so sorry," Pete moaned. Jack lay perfectly still, his eyes open, plain and staring upward. His fingers twitched ever so slightly, and his chest barely rose.

The sorcerer with the knife came toward Pete and the two holding her jerked her head back, exposing her throat. "Oi," said one. "We could 'ave a go before you cut her."

"Or after," said the other.

The sorcerer with the knife hesitated. "Be quick about it." Behind him, the others rushed to encircle Jack with chalked sigils, light candles at the five points of the star, spread their web around him. Treadwell gazed down at Jack hungrily, stroking spectral fingers over and *through* Jack's flesh, causing him to moan and convulse each time those terrible talons sank into his skin.

"Hold her arm, Hodges . . . there's a lad," said the sorcerer who didn't care if Pete was alive or dead for his business.

"I swear," Pete gritted. "If you get close enough, I'll bloody well end you."

"Shut it," said Hodges. "You're just lucky it's us and not Master Treadwell."

They laughed, Hodges loudest of all, and his grip loosened a fraction. Pete twisted down and to the side, ripped her right arm free, and drove her two longest fingers into Hodge's throat. He made a rasp like a saw and dropped to his knees.

"Bloody hell . . ." started the first.

"Forget it," said the second. "Treadwell's starting the spell. Finish her and be quick about it, 'less you want to explain to him why we weren't standing in the circle."

The circle of magicians began chanting in Latin, forming around Jack. The sorcerer with the knife made a swipe for her, but Pete grabbed the knife above the blade, fighting the sorcerer for it, gaining a hold and breaking the man's wrist.

He screamed, and Pete looked at the last, her blood racing in time with the swelling gusts of the Black swirling around them. She had to do something, with no magic and no power of her own.

Pete turned the knife in her hand, placing the tip against her own abdomen.

You can hurt and bleed and die in the thin spaces.

She might not come back from this decision, but there was nothing else. Jack had come for her, faced Treadwell, and now he was dying again. Dying not because of his pride but because he'd stayed to help her in the first place.

Pete felt the blade of the knife break her skin, just, a bead of hot blood sliding down her stomach.

"Treadwell!" she screamed, her voice coming out raw. Treadwell turned his dreadful eyes on her.

What is the meaning of this?

"If you want Jack Winter so badly," Pete said, her hands shaking well and truly now, "then you can bloody well come and take him from me." She raised the knife and drove it into her stomach, deep and with enough force to lodge it there. The pain spread immediately, a rush of vertigo that spiraled her down and down into the icy, bottomless reaches of the Black.

Chapter 44

She opened her eyes in a small neat room, painted blue. The sitting room, from her family's old flat. Pete was standing in the center of the braided rug their mother had bought in a jumble sale in the high street, when Pete was a baby.

"Quite the view, isn't it?"

Jack spoke, his back to her as he leaned against the window, his forehead pressed to the leaded glass. Pete followed his gaze and gasped.

London was on fire, as far as the eye could see—blue flames, consuming everything down to char. Steam rose off the Thames and the city was filled with the wail of air raid sirens. The sky, what Pete could see through the smoke that burned the fine skin inside her nostrils, was streaked with bloody red as a sun wreathed in flames set to the west.

"Jack," Pete rasped, trying not to choke on the poisoned air, "where are we?"

"Inside my dying moments. The last flicker of my nightmares," Jack said. He exhaled smoke with each breath. "The dark place of the soul, in between."

"In between life and death?" Pete said.

"Of course." Jack breathed more smoke. "The world, and what comes after. I'm not really here."

"No?" Pete edged backward a step.

"No," said Jack with a sigh. "No, Pete, I'm already dead." As Pete watched, unable to force herself to move, Jack's eyes flamed, and then the flame spread and became a helm, a raven's beak and a raven's sleek wings, engulfing his body, burning him away. Jack didn't scream, just looked at her, arms spread, the fire rushing across the carpet and up the walls until it was all around her.

"No," Pete muttered. "No, no, no." She ran, keeping her body low, throwing her jacket over her head to protect it from a fiery snowfall of paint flakes and ash. The front door of the flat was locked and she beat her shoulder against it until it burst open, tumbling her into bright fluorescent light and the smell of ammonia.

There was no disorientation this time. Pete would know the hospital room with her ears swaddled and both eyes put out. The slow hiss of oxygen and the almost imperceptible *plip-plip* of the IVs resounded in a space that was too small and too stale, holding a hovering, waiting Death for too long.

Connor Caldecott slept, moving fitfully as the morphine coursed through his dreams. His chest was sunken and Pete's throat parched to realize that this was the end. The red gardenias on the nightstand were the last flowers she'd ever brought to him in the hospital.

Outside the city was lit, sparkling like broken glass under full night. Visiting hours, Pete remembered, would be long over. Still, the door swished open and someone let in a brief burst of chatter from the hallway.

"See you on third shift, Shirley luv," a nurse called, and then silence fell again as the door shut.

Jack came to Connor's bedrail, his jackboots creaking on the linoleum, hair shaved into a Mohawk and blue smudges trailing under his eyes. His skinny frame exuded weariness, and he was wrapped in stiff clothes at least three days old. "Look at you, you old sod," he muttered, coming to Connor's bedrail. "Heard you were dying. Thought you were too mean for it, meself." He tossed aside a bouquet of wilted daisies and leaned on the rail. His hands shook and he glanced over his shoulder every few seconds as conversation rang in the hall, as if his nerve endings had gone on holiday and left his limbs to their own devices.

"Can't say much, really," Jack muttered. "You never liked me. Right to. Had nothing but bad intentions for your MG." He laughed once. "Least she slipped me enough details for me to be your fake son. Did you know family can come by after visiting's closed? Bet you didn't. Doesn't look like your girls fancy hanging about too much. Can't say I blame them."

"You bastard . . ." Pete hissed.

Jack methodically searched the bedside table and pocketed the dose of Percocet the nurse had left should Connor wake up, then reached down and disconnected the IV feed to Connor's morphine bag, tying off the tube and shoving the whole thing into a shopping sack. Connor groaned in his sleep, and Jack paused. "We do what we have to. Pain's transient, old man. What's eating up your lungs—that's permanence." He patted the bag. "I need this. You're on the way out."

Connor wheezed in his sleep, a kicked sound, pathetic. Pete's heart clutched.

Jack sighed, his mouth thinning. He spoke as if he were convincing himself of a lie. "Your daughters will see you again," he whispered, bending close to Connor. "Not soon, but they will."

"Stop!" Pete cried. "For God's sake, that's my da!"

Jack turned to her. He scratched his jaw under the stubble and shrugged one shoulder. He was never quite still.

"What am I supposed to do, Pete?" Jack spread his hands. "I'm not really here. You're just walking the halls, admiring the paintings."

"You dream about this," Pete stated, motioning around

the hospital room. "Stealing his painkillers. Talking to him."

"Only lately," said Jack. He began to shiver. "I only nicked from the terminal cases, me, but I suppose it don't matter. Lot that I did that'll become fuel for nightmares, I'm sure. Thanks to you."

"I don't have much time," Pete said desperately. "I wounded myself pretty badly just to get here. Where are you, Jack?"

"I'm where he keeps me," Jack whispered, voice a husk. "At the center of it all. Stay away, Pete. Wake up. Just wake up . . ."

Jack reached for her and Pete ducked him, hitting the wheelchair release for the door and backing out as Jack doubled over in a fit of shivers and coughs.

"Bloody hell, what now?" she muttered. Her voice came out hollow and she felt as if her blood had turned to stone, cold and disconnected from her body. "Damn it," she muttered, knowing she was dying, that she'd cut too deep. "Jack, for once in your bloody life reach out to me."

"He can't hear you." The man who spoke was tall and rangy, knotty little muscles warping his prison tattoos. He wore a stained undershirt and shorts and boots, and didn't speak to Pete but to the woman who cowered on the floor across the tiny sitting room, nursing a cut lip. The flat was poor, wallpaper peeling off, floors scarred, and out the greasy window Pete could see a skyline that was not London.

"Mum!" someone screamed, and a closed door across the room rattled against a padlock.

"All right, luv," she called weakly. "I'll be right in."

"Fucking hell you will," the man snarled. "Shut up, you whiny cunt!" he screamed at the sobs from the other side of the door.

"He's just hungry," the woman pleaded. "Please, Kev, he just needs a bite and then he'll be quiet as a church mouse."

"And you think I'm made of money?" Kev sneered. "You think after I latched myself on to a bloody prozzie and her brat I've got pounds to burn still? You're lucky I haven't turned you out to work and put the brat on the mercy of the council. Lord knows you're no kind of mother, laying about swallowing down pills all day instead of on the job."

"Maybe if you stopped bloodying my face I could work," the woman muttered. Kev pulled back his foot and let loose with a kick that bent the woman on the floor around his boot, pushing a moan out of her that sank claws into Pete's chest.

"Mum!" The banging against the door redoubled. Kev kept kicking, until the woman was still. Then he turned and slipped the padlock from the door.

"Here now, Jackie boy," he said, dragging a skinny brunette boy into the sitting room. "You raise all that fuss because you want to come out?"

"What did you do to her, you fucking bastard?" Jack demanded, tears streaking down his flushed face. In this nightmare, his face still held a plump gleam of childhood, but his eyes were Jack's eyes, ageless and merciless as primordial ice.

Kev dealt him a backhanded blow, a fistful of silver rings leaving a welt on Jack's cheek. "You show some respect to the man what keeps a roof over your shiftless head!" Kev hissed. "What do you do? You're too clumsy to steal and too ugly to be turned out. You're just a little lump of shit on my boot."

"I swear, if you've hurt her again . . ." Jack trembled all over, as if he were in the middle of a blizzard. "Shiftless and ugly or not, I'll turn you in. I'll run out this door and go to the police box and when you're rotting in jail I'll take all that money you stole from Mum and I'll pay a fucking skinhead to be your boyfriend until you're a fucking cripple!"

Pete, examining Jack, decided he couldn't have been

more than ten or eleven. She pressed a hand over her mouth to keep herself steady.

Kev grabbed Jack by the hair, producing a flick-knife and pressing it against Jack's throat. "Sit down, boy," he said. Soft and pleasant, like the warning hiss of a snake. "You move a hair, and I'll slit her from ear to ear, like the pig she is." He sat Jack on the couch, where the boy folded like stiff cardboard, and knelt with legs on either side of Jack's mother, pressing the knife to her throat.

"Now you keep your eyes open," said Kev. "Eyes open, and watching. I'm giving you a lesson, boy." He loosed the button fly on his shorts, the knife steady against Jack's mother's neck.

"Don't . . ." Jack's voice strangled.

Kev pushed the woman's dress up to her waist. "Did I hear a please, Jackie? Good boys say please." He grinned, sliding a hand over Jack's mother. She moaned feebly, but didn't try to fight him off. "That's the lesson," Kev said, still smiling. "Teach you again and again, if I must."

Jack's eyes went vacant, the whites crawling in to blot out the blue, and he began to shake.

"Stop." Pete reached out and grabbed Kev's knife arm, but he batted her off as if she weighed a kilo. Pete stumbled into the credenza, sending a crack pipe and some glass figurines crashing to the floor.

"*Don't* interfere," Kev said, leveling his knife at her. "This isn't your show."

Pete pushed herself up and came at him again, swinging for the hateful smile, and again he pushed her back, lifting her clean off her feet. He was so strong, the strength of a child's nightmare.

"You're not my demon," Pete said, as Kev pushed the knife tighter against Jack's mother's throat. "Jack wasn't afraid of you. Jack wouldn't be afraid of a piss stain like you, not even then."

"You're afraid of me, missy," said Kev with certainty. He looked up and started as he saw Jack standing inches from him, eyes totally white. "I told you stay put, you little freak!"

He started to say more, but his throat twitched and closed, and he dropped the flick-knife to claw at his breast over his heart. Robotically, Jack picked up the flick-knife and put the business end into Kev's neck, the arterial blood washing the wall, Jack, and his mother in a graceful arc. She let out a feeble cry and covered her eyes.

Jack crouched on his heels, watching with unblinking attention until Kev's last ounce of life ran out of him and stained the cheap carpet with wine. "You're right," he told Pete finally, his voice thin and not all present. He picked up the flick-knife, cleaned it on his sleeve, and tucked it away. "I stopped being afraid of monsters. The shadows, the transparent voices I heard . . . they told me how to keep the monsters back. And I listened. I learned. When did you first feel it, Pete? This was my day."

"You're not here," Pete said. "That much I know. Tell me. Please? I'm running out of time so fast, Jack . . ."

"I see you," young Jack said solemnly. "I see you doomed by your need to help me. You'd rush headlong in front of a train."

"Into Hell," Pete answered.

"What do I do to earn your loyalty?" Jack crossed his thin little arms. "You shine."

"You don't make it easy, that's for bloody sure," Pete said. "But nobody deserves what Treadwell plans, Jack. Not even you." She touched the little boy on the shoulder, and he winced. "You don't have such a dark heart as you think, Jack. Hope someday you see that."

Jack pointed to the locked door, now grown iron and arched, a portal bound up in magic.

"Through there," he said. "I'm there. Be careful, Pete."

"Of what?" she said, standing slowly from the ruin of glass where she'd landed.

Jack blinked his white eyes. "You look into Treadwell, not as Jack sees him, but as magic does. And when you do it, he can see you, too, Pete. All of you."

Pete put both her hands flat on the door. It was cold, a cold of old things with no space in the real. "Bloody wonderful," she muttered before she put her hands on the massive twin latches and pushed the door free.

Chapter 45

Stepping back into a graveyard caused her to stumble, because it was a calm spring night and not the boiling, fiery center of Jack's terrors she'd envisioned.

A gaslight flickered blue, casting the whole scene in black-and-white film, all shades of bright and shadow that danced in time with the flame.

Pete walked across the grass to a single headstone; crooked and tilted to one side, planted in the earth long enough to get comfortable. Jack stood, his head bowed, hair white in the light of the lamp. He stared down at the gravestone without breathing, without even a wind to move his coat. If not for the cigarette curling smoke slowly upward, he might have been a ghost himself.

Next to him, Pete stopped. "It's really you, then."

Jack nodded once, chin tucking down against his chest. Blue slivers of magic sluiced off him, burning away like sparks in the cool air. "Really here. Just like you."

The magic glowed all over him, the spirit raven a corona that Pete watched fill up with black as if something had spilled ink across Jack's ghost-form, pulsing and retreating and growing again. The taint caused a physical ache in Pete, a feeling of loss.

"We'd better hurry and get out of here," Pete said. "Wake

up, or go away from the light, or whatever it is you do . . . here."

Jack made a bitter noise in his throat. "I never asked you to come after me, Pete. You die just like the rest of us."

Pete felt her mouth open, forced it shut quickly. "Jack, I didn't endure pain and kidnapping and massive internal bleeding so that I could come here and be snarled at. Now *come,* before Treadwell finds you."

"He wants to take my body as a vessel," Jack said. He raised his head and confronted Pete with a face of hollows behind his cigarette. "Could you do it, Pete? If Treadwell wore my face? Could you kill him?"

Pete answered without thinking, too quickly. "No. I could never make my nightmare real, Jack. Not again."

He sneered. "Then what good are you?" The cigarette sailed away into the grass, trailing embers. "*My* nightmare is real, Pete. How's your grand plan to save me working so far?"

Pete looked at the headstone, realized with a start that the broad letters carved into it were familiar.

JACK WINTER
BORN 15 JUNE
DIED

But the date was scratched out. Pete faced Jack, reaching for his wrist. "You're not dead."

"Might as well be," he muttered. "What a life I've led. Every breath, every kick and scream against the pricks, all down to nothing, just a funeral no one will ever see for a man nobody cares about."

"Oh, buggering *fuck,*" Pete shouted. "You *cannot* expect me to believe that you're actually feeling *sorry* for yourself, you stupid sod! Look at me! I've fucking killed myself over you, and all that time I thought you'd already gone I carried that wound close, never let you fade all the way to memory because you were all I had to convince myself that *maybe* there was something out there beyond living and dying with just gray in between!" She grabbed Jack, shook him, fighting against fingers numb from encroaching passage to the land of the dead.

"I cared for you so much it nearly drove me mad," Pete whispered. "So, you see, you can't leave. You simply can't."

Jack sighed. "Sometimes the thing you want won't be yours, no matter how hard you grasp onto it, Pete. This is the end. You'd do well to walk away before any hope of saving you has passed. Leave me to Treadwell, and go get on with your life."

You should heed the young man. Treadwell formed out of the crackling power in the air, a sure form of a man here, simply silver and ephemeral. He wore a frock coat and his long hair was combed back from a broad forehead. His eyes lit hungrily as he gazed upon Jack.

"I don't understand," Pete whispered. "You came to fight, Jack, and now you're giving up."

Mr. Winter is both a product and a victim of his fears, as we all are, Treadwell said, folding his hands and looking pleased. *In the end he has nothing—not faith, not hope, not love. Just fear, and fear is the most powerful agent of all.*

He stepped forward, passing through Jack's headstone. *Time has come, Mr. Winter, for you to step aside and for me to step in.*

Jack nodded numbly, opening his arms. "I'm yours."

Pete cast desperately, but the graveyard was totally empty except for Jack's headstone, lone and neglected.

"Jack," Pete said. Treadwell paused in front of him, raising one palm to brush his fingers over Jack's face. Jack didn't flinch even as ice crystals grew on his brow, but he did when Pete gripped his hand. "You're not alone," Pete said, all resolve to keep calm gone. She heard her voice through a tunnel, knew she was slipping away. "That's it, isn't it—dying and more than dying, dying alone."

Keep out of this, Treadwell hissed. He raised his hands heavenward and began to chant, the incantation rising around Pete and Jack like a black mist, a swarm of dark magic.

Pete squeezed Jack's hand, hard as she could. "You're *not* alone," she told him. "If you've made up your mind to die, then I'll be with you here, until the end. I'd follow you into death if that's what you asked, Jack. Heaven, Hell. Anywhere at all."

Silence! Treadwell screamed. The smoke rose and formed, an exact replica of Jack, featureless and incorporeal. *I will gain a form. Do not test me.*

Pete held Jack's hand, barely felt herself trembling as she made her peace, let the strands already slipping through her fingers float away. *So be it.* "Anywhere at all," she repeated.

Jack shuddered and sighed, drawing in a ragged breath. "Oh, Pete," he murmured. "Why didn't you just give up on me?"

Pete smiled at him; saw a tiny lift in his shoulders. "You told me we'd see it through together. I believed you."

Fire flamed to life in Jack's eyes and he turned on Treadwell. "Thought you'd trap me in the thin space and take my body? Lovely plan, if a bit flawed in the fact that I am not going to bloody let you anywhere near me."

Treadwell smiled, the expression on him truly terrifying. *Too late for theatrics, Winter. Too late, too late, always too late.* He muttered, *Victus.* The smoke flowed into Jack, through his nose and mouth, through his eyes. Jack went to his knees, choking, gagging, and Pete saw the aura of magic around him flare and begin to change to ice-bred silver, the raven overtaken by a ravening wolf, starved and trailing spittle from its maw.

Submit to me, crow-mage, Treadwell said. *And your soul's passage to the land of the dead will be swift.*

"Leave him alone!" Pete screamed. The smoke engulfed Jack wholly, and he stopped fighting as Treadwell watched grimly, with the kind of terrible satisfaction vengeance brings over a person.

You are too late, Treadwell whispered, already beginning to thin around the edges as Jack began to strengthen, stop choking, and stand upright. *Helpless little thing. How I pity you.*

The cemetery scene washed out, the ink of nightmares running off the page, and Pete felt the cord, frayed down to a few strands, pull her backward and away. She reached for Jack, tried desperately to stay, but he stood tall now, Treadwell's magic in him.

"I'm sorry . . ." Pete called. "I'm sorry . . ."

And she woke. The pain from the knife wound was incendiary, blade still lodged in her stomach. She pressed down on the cut and pulled the knife out, wincing as a dribble of dark red-black blood came with it. Pain was good, Pete reminded herself. Pain means you are not in shock, that you have a chance to stand up and walk away. Still, she retched from dizziness as she tried to sit up, and fell again, body shrieking alarm.

Beside her, Jack stirred and then opened his eyes, sucking in air as if he'd forgotten how. His eyes were gray and ringed, shined like two-pound coins, and the smile that split his face was cruel as a straight razor.

"Treadwell," Pete said, her voice thickened with shock.

"My stars," said Treadwell softly, through Jack's lips. The voice was Jack's, but also not Jack's, the accent lilting into something musical and antiquated instead of a Manchester drawl, timbre scaling downward into menace. "If someone had told me what abominable condition the crow-mage had left himself in, I would have attempted this with another candidate entirely."

He blinked and looked all around, eyes widening. "I say, who are these people?"

Pete saw no one except the few sorcerers who had remained, all watching anxiously just out of arm's easy reach. "Master . . . ?" one said hesitantly. "Master Treadwell, is there anything you need?"

Treadwell groaned and pressed a hand against Jack's wound, slicking his palm with blood. "A surgeon, you fool. Fetch me a surgeon before I pass through the bleak gates a second time!" He shook his head, scrubbing at his eyes with the back of Jack's hand. "Who *are* these silent, staring imbeciles? Why are they permitted to bear witness?"

Pete pushed harder against her wound and spoke. "You didn't know? About Jack's sight, I mean."

Treadwell turned on her with a hiss, his eyes flaring silver. "What do you speak of . . ." And then he cried out and threw his hands over his eyes, stumbling away from Pete. "Treachery! What are you, woman?"

"You see me," Pete repeated the words of the child in Jack's nightmare, of Bridget and Patrick and Diana. "You know what I am, Treadwell."

Treadwell gasped, and pulled himself straight, staring at her with one hand shading his eyes. "A speaker for the old ones. Of course. How else would Winter have bested *me*?"

"You think about that for a minute, Algy." Pete tossed her head with a carelessness she did not feel, one that sent rolling breakers of nausea all through her. "You can have Jack—you *do* have Jack, and his talents. You can have his sight and his body that's probably going to give out on you in another ten or fifteen years—you didn't know back in the old days what long-term heroin abuse will do to a person." She got to one knee, putting all her weight on a headstone—

steady, Pete—and even though unconsciousness seemed like a blessed port she stood, and faced Treadwell.

"His sight almost drove him mad, and that was with a lifetime of practice, of years and years and bloody *decades* to try to control what he sees. With you coming into it all at once, Treadwell . . ." She managed to shake her head. "It doesn't look sunny for you, mate."

"I have seen the dead!" Treadwell bellowed. "I know what phantoms may appear! I am not frightened by death!"

"No, 'course not," Pete said. "That's why you tried so bloody hard to cheat it. You're a terrible liar, Treadwell. You see the shades even now, all around us, and you can't shut them off. *Nothing* shuts them off. Jack used the needle every day for twelve years and even that didn't *completely* take the sight away. So you're welcome to it—sit there in your rotting body and be reminded every *second* of what's waiting for you when it ends."

Treadwell's eyes narrowed and he stepped toward Pete, obvious from the set of his shoulders that he thought he frightened her. "A woman who talks as much as you is surely bargaining, Weir. What do you propose for me?"

This was the place she should have come the first time, Pete thought. The last dozen years were a borrowed echo, a desire not to see the true road to her death.

"Me," she said, her voice coming out a whisper. "Use me, Treadwell. Give Jack back the time he has left and take me. I'm strong. I have power." Admitting it nearly broke her, a final dismantlement of the careful construct she'd placed around her mind after the first ritual. "I have all the power you'll ever need, Treadwell. You can shape me any way you like. Take me."

Treadwell considered for only a second, his gaze gleaming with a hunger that was nearly palpable. "I accept."

"Master . . ." the sorcerer started. Treadwell turned on him.

"I *am* your master now! *Keep silent!*" The sorcerer cowered. Treadwell's eyes rolled back in his head and he exhaled, silver smoke running out of Jack's mouth and nose and silver tears coursing down his cheeks. It crossed the small space between them, unbelievably cold, it should be killing her, something this cold. Pete's lungs seized as crystalline chill spread across her skin, her face, and she felt Treadwell all through her, a malignant reptile mind, power and ice.

Dimly, she watched Jack shake himself awake, take in the scene, grab his hair in anguish as Treadwell's soul flowed through her, freezing and killing her. *It's all right,* Pete thought, wishing she could speak.

Treadwell laughed inside her mind, icicles growing over and around her few shreds of precious consciousness, and Pete stopped fighting.

I am a conduit, she whispered. *I am a shaper of magic.* Treadwell cried out as their power touched and sparked.

The pain ceased and Pete had the giddy feeling of standing on a precipice, toes hanging into open space. Behind her, the freezing encroachment of Treadwell traveled ever forward, and in front was something vast and deep.

Take my power, Pete told Treadwell. *Take it into yourself and rid me of it. I do not want this. I never wanted to be this. Take it, take it, take it . . .*

She touched the void in front of her, felt it flood through her being, painless but so vast it was as if all the pieces of her had blown away. She had ceased to be Petunia Caldecott, had joined into the ancient mystery of what came after life, and what had come before. The power formed and shaped and bowed and when Pete opened her eyes, she saw the shrouded man standing before her.

"This is yours," he said, and held out his hand, hot and slick with blood. Pete looked into his face for the first time, a young face, a human face, streaked with dirt and old scars on top of his chieftain's armor, washed clean of the blood of battle.

"This is no one else's," the shrouded man said, and over his shoulder Pete discerned a thousand shadows, ravens all, and below them a tall woman with eyes like marbles and hair made from feathers who touched the shrouded man's shoulder and gibbered in his ear. A single tear worked down his cheek, and he reached out and grabbed Pete's hand, uncurling her fingers to expose her frozen blue palm. "You must take it now, at last."

Into her hand, Pete let him drop the small beating bird's heart, and then the magic took away her vision and she couldn't see the shrouded man or the raven woman anymore. From the heart, warmth spread and just for a moment Pete felt right and at home here, on the edge of everything.

Then Treadwell's freezing talons clamped down around her neck, the completion of the circuit, and he took all the magic from her, drew it into himself with a cry of ecstasy as Pete felt herself husking away.

He pulled back, or tried to, and a heat rose around them, all of Treadwell's icy power going to steam. *You . . . you tricked me!* Treadwell howled.

"I didn't," Pete told him softly. She felt their two talents rubbing ragged edges against each other, Treadwell's fraying as he wailed. "But I will die to keep you from coming back."

The magic rushed into him, more and more, filling up the reservoirs, and Pete clamped her own hand around Treadwell's skeletal one, refusing to break their connection.

You are mine! Treadwell shouted. *Mine, and I will live . . . I will live . . .*

The magic did not burn Pete, but filled her, lit every corner of her, burned down into her darkest core, where all her knotted fears lay. She saw Treadwell for what he was, a shattered, tattered echo of the sorcerer he'd once been, stretched thin between too many worlds. She saw the magic for hers, and how it could not be anyone else's.

"Go back," Pete commanded, locking her grip around his wrist, watching the magic burn him from the inside, turning his shadow to ash. "You are dead, and you belong with the dead. Go back, Algernon Treadwell, and trouble the living no more."

Treadwell screamed defiance, but even as he howled he was pulled backward, away from Pete. The raven woman seized him, raked her talons through Treadwell, stared him in the face.

"Your circle has closed, Algernon. So it must be for us all."

He tried to scream, but the ravens fell on Treadwell, lifted him up and took away his eyes and his tongue and carried him through the bleak gates of iron and sorrow, the signpost to Purgatory atop their spires.

I will find another. Treadwell sighed, the last tremor of his existence in the Black. *I will find another who lives for power and cares not, and then I will come to claim you, Weir.*

"Piss off, wanker," Pete told him. "I'm not afraid of you."

Treadwell's mouth gaped wide in wordless agony and then the raven woman cawed and the gates slammed shut with a clang that sent blackness into Pete's bones. The magic faded, the vision along with it, and she felt damp grass under her knees and palms, night dew soaking her trousers and cuffs.

Jack grabbed her, held her, looked into her eyes. "Pete. Oh, bloody hell, Pete, you're all right?"

"Yes." Pete tested her voice, found it raspy, as though she'd been out in a cold day for too long. "I mean, no. Bloody hell, Jack, I'm stabbed." She hacked out a cough and saw a few droplets of blood fly forth to land on the wilted grass. "Oh . . . that's not very good . . ."

"Come on." Jack helped her up as if she weighed no more than a sack of flour. "Got to get you to a hospital. And me, too—sodding sorcerers jabbed me well and good. Probably get lockjaw."

"He's gone," Pete murmured. "Treadwell. Back . . . back into the bleak gates. I sent him away . . . to the raven woman, and she took him . . ."

Jack looked down at her, a smile playing at the corners of his mouth. "Un-bound exorcism is a nice trick, Petunia. Only met a handful that could manage it without a circle."

"Treadwell made me mad," Pete said. "And don't sodding call me 'Petunia.' Just because . . . I shared a confidence . . . doesn't make it a bloody invitation."

"Glad to see near death hasn't softened you," Jack said. "I'd be disappointed if nearly losing your soul to a hungry ghost was all it took."

The neat visitor's hut came into view a few hundred meters down the path.

"Jack . . ." Pete ground her feet to a stop, causing them both to stumble. "I touched magic. I . . . I used it. What does that mean? What's going to happen?"

Jack wrapped his arm more tightly around her shoulders and didn't answer for too long, time enough to choose what not to say, but Pete didn't care any longer, just cared that he was *there*, next to her, solid and corporeal and *Jack*.

"It means just what I thought all along, luv—you're strong. No matter what any toerag psychiatrist says, you've got a talent. And a temper."

"I tried so hard not to . . ." Pete started to cry, and choked it back with a breath that made her hack more blood, in turn.

"Pete." Jack held her, rocked her. "It doesn't mean the end of your life, luv. May seem that way, but you'll still pay your electric and go to work and eat greasy takeaway when you're too tired to cook supper. You're not cursed. You've got magic, and people will try to abuse it, but *you're* in control of it. You're holding it in your hands."

Pete swallowed and managed to nod. "I suppose I am."

Jack lifted her chin and looked in her eyes. "Oi. You believe me, don't you?"

Pete started walking again, arm around Jack's waist. She let herself lean on him, and he stumbled a bit so she let him lean on her.

"Of course I do."

EPILOGUE

The Streets

"The devil's agents may be of flesh and blood, may they not?"

—Sir Arthur Conan Doyle,
The Hound of the Baskervilles

Chapter 46

The sky spat rain as winter took hold, and Pete crouched inside her slicker, trying to hoist her umbrella over Jack's much higher head while still gaining the benefit of coverage.

"Give it up, luv," he said, taking it from her and handing it to a hobo nodding near a tube vent.

"I'm cold," Pete protested, her teeth chattering. "If I catch pneumonia and die I'll rattle around your flat for the rest of your life, throwing vases across the room and making the telly explode."

"First of all," Jack said, pushing his wet hair out of his eyes, "that's a poltergeist. You'd be a shade. Second of all, I don't own a telly."

"That bit about me dying didn't faze you at all, eh?" Pete asked. Jack shrugged.

"You haven't yet, luv."

Pete checked her wristwatch. "I should go. I have my last postsurgery checkup in an hour."

"Going to have a nice Frankenstein scar, are you?" Jack asked.

Pete unbuttoned her slicker and pulled up her jumper to show the slightly jagged line of stitches on her stomach, like an elongated Z. Jack winced. "You stuck yourself a good one, didn't you?"

"I had to be sure I'd make it over to you," Pete said. "I don't think a light scratch would have exactly done it."

"I should get you a taxi," Jack said, stepping to the curb. Pete pulled him back.

"I'll manage on the tube—I've made it a whole week without getting so dizzy I fall over."

They paused at the entrance to the Metropolitan line. Finally Pete said, "It's all right. I know you don't like hospitals." She didn't mention that thanks to her injury-fueled journey into Jack's nightmares, she knew exactly *why* he didn't care for them.

"Meet you at the Mayfair afterward." The Mayfair Arms was the pub around the corner from Pete's doctor's surgery. She nodded.

"We'll have a bite of supper. Jack, there's something I need to ask you, now that things have settled . . ."

Jack's eyes unfocused and he looked past her, down the stairs of the tube. "Oh, bugger all . . ."

Pete was spun around and into a portly gentleman wielding a briefcase as Jack shoved past her and took the stairs into the tube two at a time. Pete blinked the rain out of her eyes. "Bloody hell. Sorry. Sorry," she apologized to the man.

"Those louts should be arrested," the man huffed. Pete took off after Jack as quickly as her healing incision would allow. She'd been at her desk in MIT ever since she'd been released from the hospital three weeks ago, and it was driving her mad. Newell refused to tell her when she might be back on duty as an active inspector. Her only comfort was that he seemed to believe her story of following the kidnap suspects to Highgate and getting stabbed in the ensuing struggle. Ollie, bless him, had covered her end and made no mention of Jack in his reports.

"Jack!" she shouted over the rumble of late-afternoon commuters packing the station. His blond head bobbed behind a pillar, headed for the tracks.

Pete caught up with him just as his feet crossed the safety line and his arms reached out in a scooping motion, to pull an invisible phantom back from the spitting rails.

The shriek of the train's horn blinded Pete to everything else, and she snatched Jack by the collar of his coat and deliberately fell backward, praying her weight would be enough to hold him.

The train blew hot dragon's breath in her face as the brakes locked and it squealed to a stop. The sound mingled with a few screams from waiting passengers who had witnessed Jack's attempted swan dive.

"It's fine!" Pete shouted above the echoes of the train. She dug out her warrant card and flashed it to the four corners, keeping one knee firmly planted on Jack's arm as he struggled under her. "Metropolitan Police. I have the situation under control."

Missing a train was worse than a man almost landing on the tracks to most of the commuters around Pete, and they moved on, whispering among themselves.

"The girl . . . she went right over the edge . . . she burned up on the rails . . ." Jack's eyes were mostly white, and he twitched restlessly as if in a fever dream.

"What girl?" Pete demanded. "Jack, there was nobody going over the edge but you."

He blinked at her, and then sagged. "Fucking hell, Pete, I'm sorry."

Pete slumped when she realized that Jack had not, in fact, gone any madder than he already was. Her knife wound hurt a great deal from the fall. "Your sight."

He nodded, rubbing his eyes with his fingertips. They were their natural color when he took his hands away. "I saw her clear as day. Pretty little blond thing, couldn't have been more than fifteen. She went down those steps with such purpose . . . I *knew* what she was about, just had to be in time to stop her . . ."

Pete got to her feet with some difficulty and offered Jack an arm. He took it, and kept leaning on her. "I can't do this, Pete. I maintained while we were trying to find Treadwell but I can't anymore. I'm very sorry."

Hearing Jack speak in a defeated tone wasn't normal—it was tilt-the-sun-the-wrong-way odd, in fact. Pete looked up at him. "No, Jack."

"You should go on to your appointment," he said. "I'm going to take care of this problem. I'll be at home if you're looking for me." He grinned without humor. "Though I don't suppose you would."

"If you go get a fix," Pete said. "Enjoy it. It will be the last time."

Jack laughed, not a pleasant sound, knife-edged with desperation. "Going to chain me up in your cellar and take my demons out, Pete?"

"No," Pete said. "You and I are going to do what you *should* have done at the start of all this, and find a way to hold back your sight without sticking death up your arm twice a day."

"Can't be done," said Jack. He shook his head, speaking more, but Pete's train pulled into the station and drowned him out. She inserted herself into the line of boarding passengers, looking back at Jack as he walked away.

"Use a clean sharp!" she shouted after him, drawing any number of odd looks.

"Can't be done, Petunia!" he yelled again, without looking at her. "You can't ride in on the white steed and pull me back from the dragon's jaws!"

Pete glared at the back of Jack's head as the train moved out of the station. "Just watch me."

Chapter 47

It was nearly eight by the time Pete arrived at Jack's flat, long dark. Her wound was pleasantly numb after the shot of painkillers Dr. Abouhd had given her, clucking over the recent inflammation.

She tried the door and found it unlocked, as usual. The flat was dark and still except for the rotten ice-cold spittle of rain brushing against the high windows.

"Jack?" Pete said softly, fearing the worst. He grunted and turned on a low lamp with a red shade, a new addition since the last time she'd been. He had a new, marginally less tatty sofa with lion's feet, and a matching chair as well. "Been shopping?" It was the most inoffensive thing Pete could think to say.

Jack grunted again. "Downstairs neighbor died. Mrs. Ramamurthy. Nicked them before her ruddy son and his ruddy MP3 player blaring ruddy techno music could sell it off." His eyes were hooded and dreamy, and his voice had that underwater quality of deep sleep.

"How long ago did you take the hit?" Pete asked.

"Not long . . ." Jack murmured. "Forgot how bloody sweet it tastes."

"Then you'll have a good memory to tide you through

yet another long and painful withdrawal," Pete said pleasantly. Jack moaned.

"Sodding sadist."

"And enjoying every minute of it, make no mistake," Pete said. She patted his leg. "I'll put the kettle on and get started."

"With what?" Jack demanded, throwing an arm dramatically over his eyes as Pete switched on the wall sconces.

"Jack, you have eight billion bloody books in this place—one of them has got to have something to help hold back the sight."

"You think I haven't checked?" Jack demanded. His petulance was a relief, much closer to normal.

"I think that I am going to check to satisfy myself," Pete said. "And that you are going to help me."

Jack moaned and sank back on the sofa again.

Pete put the kettle on and went to the wall of books. They were in no discernable order she could see, the volumes in languages she could read few and far between. *Wasn't this a brilliant bloody idea?*

"Have you thought about tattooing?" she said a good time later, after Jack was sitting upright and had poured three mugs of hot tea and a glass of whisky into himself.

Jack shrugged. "Got a few. Tattoos protect you from the physical, though, hexes and the like. The sight is a doorway between this land and the land of the dead."

"What if you, I don't know, forced your will into them or something?" Pete asked. "To hold back the sight?"

"I can't hold it back to begin with," Jack said. "Magic tattoos—can't believe I'm bloody considering this, by the way. I sound like a New Age git. Bespelled tattoos aren't unheard of, but it takes an enormous charge to make the magic stick, here in this world, under the skin." He downed the dregs of his tea. "Much as it pains me to admit it, more power than I have."

"Not more power than I have," Pete said, but Jack was already shaking his head.

"No, Pete. You don't know how to control yourself, even if it did work. You could melt the flesh off me bones."

"I don't see any difference between that chance and the chance you take that your sodding smack dealer slipped you a bad hit because he was running low on protection money this month," Pete said, folding her arms. Jack recognized the posture and threw up his hands.

"Forget it! Not going to happen, Pete."

She sank down, holding the old dusty book that outlined symbols of protection, where she'd gotten the idea for the tattoos. "Do you *want* to keep on this way, Jack? Do you like being an addict, or a madman?" She took a deep breath. "Tell me now. Please. Before I break my heart against you again."

"'Course I don't," Jack muttered after a long moment. "But there is no other way, Pete. I can either wander the streets not knowing what's real and what the sight is showing me, or I can poison myself and keep a grip on what little life I have left. I choose that. So hate me if you want. It'd be better if you left now, I think."

He lit a cigarette and moved to go into his bedroom.

"If the tattoos don't work," Pete said, "you haven't lost anything. And it's not like you have a needle phobia."

Jack's eyebrows went up. "There you go, morbid again."

"You're a bad influence on me," said Pete. "Jack," she said impulsively, when his back was turned. "We were interrupted this afternoon, but there's really something I need to ask you about the cemetery, about what happened . . ."

He sighed. "Don't tell me that sodding Inspector Heath has been after you with more questions about 'What *really* happened.'" He made finger quotes around the phrase.

"No, it's not that," said Pete. "Ollie's taken care of it. It's about . . . it's something I saw, when I was in-between with you. When you were standing in front of that headstone, you were . . . well . . . sort of glowing and the glow was . . . unpleasant."

"Aural echo," said Jack. "My spirit and magic outside my body. Not unusual for mages caught in-between."

"I *know* what an aura is," said Pete impatiently. "MG was always on about auras. This was different." Thinking about the inky flames that covered Jack's spirit being, the raven shape so similar to the woman who had watched Pete receive the heart, made her skin crawl, the way the animal mind backs away from something utterly alien.

"What did you see, Pete? All of it. You're hiding something."

"The woman . . . the one who took Treadwell back to the land of the dead. She spoke to him like she knew him."

Jack got up, paced a few steps, came back to the sofa. "The raven woman, you called her when you woke up."

Pete nodded. "She was. Black feathers for hair. Cruel bird's eyes, staring right through me." She waited for Jack's scoffing, but it didn't come. "What is it?"

"Nothing," Jack muttered finally. "Probably nothing. But Treadwell *did* have help to stay for so long and her being there, so close . . . it just crawls my skin is all."

Pete came and sat next to him. "Who was she?"

"She was exactly who you said she was," Jack murmured. "The raven woman. The Goddess of the Morrigan. Death's walker in the Black."

"Does me seeing her mean some horrible omen?" Pete guessed. Jack shook his head.

"She won't be bothering you again, Pete. She came for Treadwell because you called her. You spoke to her with the magic of a Weir, and she took back a spirit that had more than outstayed his welcome. More than that . . . I don' know. She's a treacherous companion, the raven woman."

"Let's work it out, then," said Pete. "Let's summon, or read books, or ask Mosswood . . ."

Jack held up a hand. "Pete. One lesson you learn quickly if you live any length of time with magic is that you leave the old gods to their old ways, and don't meddle." He worried the fringe on the arm of the sofa. "The Morrigan is the patron of the *Fiach Dubh,* the sort of magic I learned to work in. I'm not afraid of you seeing her, but I sure as bloody fuck-all wouldn't go looking for her to have a spot of tea. Unless you've got some reason to be concerned you've offended her, Pete . . . we're letting go of it."

"Have you always had that shadow over you, the crow?" Pete said. "Because of her?"

Jack nodded. "Yes. It's what I am—the crow-mage. Can't change that. Not something you volunteer for."

"If you're sure it's all right . . ." Pete murmured, pushing down half-formed suspicions that croaked underneath her thoughts, about Treadwell and his screams and the Morrigan and her multitude of black shadow-crows. She stood, collected more books to give her hands something to do. She wouldn't tell Jack about her dreams. The shrouded man. The bird's heart, and the merciless gaze of the Morrigan. How Pete still saw it against the backs of her eyes when she shut them, inhuman and indescribably ancient. Because Jack would worry more than he already was, and she was trying to protect him, wasn't she?

"What about you, Jack? What I saw in your nightmare, the black around your spirit-form? Don't tell me that was right and natural as well, because it wasn't. I felt it, and it was rotten and evil."

Jack came and put his hands on her shoulders, sliding them down to grip her arms. "Pete. I'm going to ask you something and I want you to do it, with no questions, and no argument. Understand?"

"Perhaps," said Pete, trying to shrug him off. He held her arms harder. "Ow! All right!" Pete cried. "Let go before I smack you one in the gob, Winter."

"For your own good, Pete. Do as I say."

Pete rolled her eyes. "Fine." She glared at him until Jack dropped her arms.

"*Forget* what you saw in the nightmarescape," he said. "What you saw around me, and for me. Put it out of your memory and out of your dreams."

"I've been trying," Pete said.

"I'm serious, Petunia."

"So am I, Jack."

He ruffled his hair, not looking entirely satisfied, but it was the best he was getting. Damn Jack if he thought he could order her about, anyway.

"Right," he said finally. "Let's go see if we can find a tattooist still doing business at the late hour, shall we?"

"We want two of these," Pete said, opening the heavy volume of Parnell's *Spells, Signs, and Symbols of Greater Protection.* The tattoo artist sneezed when he leaned in to examine the twin wadjets, the eyes of the peregrine falcon glaring back from the page.

"Oh, sure," he said. "Egyptian stuff. Pretty common, yeah? Where you want 'em?"

Pete turned to Jack, who was sitting sourly in the canvas chair next to the table full of needle packets and pots of ink.

He shrugged, pulling off his black knit jersey. "Wherever you can find room, mate."

Pete had only ever seen Jack's arms, which were both banded with ink in no real pattern—Celtic knotwork, a raven's feather, a black band of letters on his forearm that spelled out NEVER MIND THE BOLLOCKS. His chest and back were also partially inked, his back with an enormous Celtic cross twined with an oaken garland and his stomach with a grinning skull that chewed on a snake.

"Collarbones?" the tattooist asked. His sign proclaimed his name as HAL NUTTER, FINE ART TATTOOS. Hal Nutter himself was rather round and pale, like a collection of small moons rotating around a great central body wrapped in an ink-stained T-shirt touting Journey's 1978 tour.

"Fine," Jack agreed.

"One light, one dark," Pete reminded Hal. "For Thoth and Horus." Jack muttered something rude under his breath and she kicked him in the ankle.

"Right you are," said Hal, giving the pair of them a skeptical look. Jack sighed impatiently.

"I've got some heavy drinking waiting on me down at the pub, mate. Could we get on with it?"

Hal Nutter made quick work of the basic tattoos, one a black eye and one a pale outline. Pete touched them both after the last of the excess ink had been wiped away. "One for the land of the living. One for the land of the dead. You're in between. A door, like you said, but now it has a lock and key."

Jack took her hands and placed the full palms, gently, against his chest. "Only way this idiot plan of yours has a chance of working, luv."

"Er, I should really put some cream on those . . ." Hal Nutter started, and Pete glared at him.

"Give us one bloody minute, will you?"

Nutter held up his hands and backed off a pace.

Pete put her attention back on Jack. Now that she was here, so close to him, the plan seemed utterly ridiculous. Jack exuded power, like a transformer throwing off sparks. How could she hope to push against that?

"It's all right, luv," Jack whispered in her ear. "I'm here."

Pete thought about the first time she'd seen him, on stage at Fiver's, and later, again, on the floor of the squatter's house by the river. She remembered the shade in her bathroom and Jack's wide-eyed journeying into the land beyond.

Come back to me.

Again, a feeling of standing on the edge of a vast and windy chasm. Her hands began to burn and Jack said, "Fuck me!"

Stay with me, Jack. See what walks as a living thing and what floats on spare sorrow as shade.

Stay.

Because, Pete thought, that was what she wanted more than anything else. To know that she could knock on his door and he'd answer, or be rung up on the telephone if she felt like talking to him. To know that if he walked out the door, he'd walk back in again someday, however far later it might be.

Stay.

"Pete," said Jack after a long moment. "That's done it." He stretched and examined the tattoos in a hand mirror. "Not half bad, Nutter."

"Er," said Hal Nutter, who was on the far side of the shop, looking as if he wished he could fade into the walls. "Yes. Yes, quite right. That'll be one hundred twenty pounds fifty with VAT."

"Are you crying?" Jack asked Pete, examining her face as he put his shirt on.

"Not a bit," Pete said, truthfully. She felt almost a gleam on her, the vibrations of power still feeding back through the Black, through her bones.

"Good," Jack said. "Nothing to be upset over. Ink is charged. Doubt they'll hold anything back except maybe a bad hangover, but you did bloody well for someone with no training." He pulled his jacket on while Pete wrote Hal Nutter a check.

"Fancy a pint?" he asked. Pete took his hand, and he

started to pull away but then slung his arm around her.
"You all right, then?"

"Yes," said Pete, deciding she was as they walked outside and she felt the rain on her face. Jack had stayed.
She'd done it, this time. "And yes. A pint would be gorgeous."

Jack hailed a taxi, and Pete let it whisk her away through
the rain-washed streets, secure just for a moment that she
was with Jack, rather than chasing after him, trying to catch
a half-glimpsed phantom between her fingers.

Chapter 48

Two and a half weeks to the day later the cabbie—a human, Pete was quite sure—let her off in front of Jack's building reluctantly, staring out the windscreen with plain suspicion. "You sure the young man's expecting you, miss?"

Pete hauled her two suitcases and trunk out of the cab's boot, panting. "No."

"I don't think much of this neighborhood," the cabbie warned her as Pete paid him the extra for transporting herself and an inordinate amount of luggage from her old, now-sold flat to Whitechapel.

"It has its charms," Pete told him. She hoisted a duffel over each shoulder and gripped her wheeled trunk, making the four-flight journey to Jack's front door in only slightly less than a decade.

This was patently insane, she reminded herself once more. She should just find a hotel, or take up Ollie Heath's offer of a spare bedroom until she could rent a new flat, in her price range and her name only, until her half of the sale proceeds came through and she could afford to eat something other than cheap takeaway and noodles.

I'm just checking on Jack, she compromised. *With all of my things that I could stuff into Terry's old luggage.*

Perfectly reasonable. She knocked. A sensation of power

a whisper against the part of her mind that dwelled in the Black, answered. That hadn't been there before.

"Got a new warding hex on," said Jack, opening the door. He was wearing torn denim and a black button-down shirt stained with some kind of white phosphorescent powder, a cigarette tucked behind his ear. "Lot cheaper than an alarm, and I think that ruddy son of Mrs. Ramamurthy's has begun cooking speed in his dear departed mum's kitchen. Fucking criminal element's everywhere these days."

He took in her suitcases, and the sheepish expression Pete knew she was wearing. "Going on holiday? Need me to water your plants and feed the cat?"

"You know I don't have a cat." Pete couldn't look anywhere except the toes of her shoes.

"I do," said Jack, "but I'm at a loss as to why you're on my doorstep, so I figured small talk would be the route to take."

"How are you holding up?" Pete blurted. Jack shrugged.

"Can't complain. Those tattoos are bloody effective, except for the one incident with the cursed monkey doll. Who would have thought it?" He smiled at her, the full force of the devil-grin. "We both know you didn't come here to check on me, Pete, so why don't you just spit out the real reason."

Pete started to turn around, to leave without another word, but Jack caught her arm. "Pete. Tell me."

"The flat's been sold, and with everything going on—work, being back to field duty, this idiotic dedication ceremony I had to go to so they could open my da's memorial auxiliary parking structure—I haven't been able to let another place," Pete rushed out. "It's not that I don't have a little savings—I do, but it can't be just anyplace and I know this is terrible and last-minute and that the worst thing for you would be to have some pushy woman intruding and me especially, seeing as how I can't really hold any kind of control over my talents, and well, I guess I just thought I'd ask you if I could stay. Just for a few weeks."

Jack blinked, and then took the cigarette from behind his ear and stuck it in his mouth. The ember glowed. "I keep odd hours," he said.

"Police inspector," Pete reminded him. "Not a nine-to-five job, either."

"I've been on a kick for the Anti-Nowhere League and I play them loudly."

"Love them," Pete shot back. Jack grimaced.

"You're bloody mad to pick me out of all the possible sofas you could sleep on, Caldecott. I mean—"

"I've accepted that, Jack. Nowhere I'd rather be."

He sighed and stepped away from the door, pulling it wide. "Then you're welcome, is what I was going to say if you'd let me finish."

Pete grinned at him, and he finally grinned back, shaking his head. "You mean it?" she asked. Jack nodded once.

"I mean it. Come in."

Read on for a preview of

Demon Bound

by Caitlin Kittredge

Now available from St. Martin's Paperbacks.

Jack Winter has a problem. Thirteen years ago, as he lay dying on the floor of a tomb in Highgate Cemetery, Jack called up a demon and bartered his soul for his life. Now the debt has come due, and the demon has appeared to take Jack to Hell. Trouble is, Jack has finally found a reason to live. Her name is Pete Caldecott.

Pete saved Jack from himself—she got him clean, helped him control his psychic sight and with her help, he's making a living cleansing ghosts and minor supernatural annoyances in the greater London area. Jack also finds himself falling in love with Pete-- against his better judgment. Pete doesn't know about Jack's bargain, but she knows that something is wrong. Something vast and terrible is moving out of the supernatural realm of the Black. A magical cataclysm, and she won't be able to stop it without Jack's help...

PART 1

Clockwork

Listen to the army march across my coffin lid
Fire in the east and sunrise in the west
I'm just a dead man, walking with the rest.

—The Poor Dead Bastards,
"Dead Man Marching"

A crow sat on the dead branch of the dead tree that watched over two gravestones in the corner of Brompton Cemetery. It watched Jack Winter with its black eyes like beads, and he watched the crow in turn, with eyes that most people called ice, but that he simply called blue.

Jack drew a Parliament out of the air and touched his finger to the tip. He sucked a lungful of smoke and blew it at the crow, which flapped its wings and snapped its beak in irritation. "Fuck off, then," Jack told it. "Not like I want you hanging about."

"Leave that beast alone," said his companion. "If the map I got from Tourist Information is right, the graves should be around here, very close." Her circular ramble through the graves came to a stop next to Jack. "Oh."

"Mary and Stuart Poole," Jack said, flicking the end of his fag at Mary's headstone. "Who says the gods don't have the occasional bout of humor?"

Pete Caldecott gave Jack what he'd describe as a dirty look, and not in the manner that led to being naked and sweaty. She strode over and picked up his litter, shoving it into her coat pocket. "You're a bloody child, you know that? Emotionally twelve."

"I've been accused of worse," Jack said. He felt in the

inside pocket of his motorbike jacket for another Parliament, but thought better of it when Pete put a hand on her hip.

"We've a job to do, and if we don't do it, we don't get paid, so are you going to stand there all day with your thumb in your arse or are you going to get to work?"

Pete was, at the first look, nothing to write your mum about, but Jack knew better. Shorter than he by a head, big green eyes straight from the Emerald Isle, Snow White in torn denim and an army-green jacket. Lips plump like rubyfruit, a body that a bloke could spend hours on and still feel like he was starving for it.

But right now, she was glaring at him, tapping her foot on the dead grass over the Pooles' final rest. Jack picked up the black canvas tote they'd brought along and crouched between the headstones. Out of a host of attributes, the one Pete used with greatest efficiency was her temper, and besides, she was right—they did have a job.

"Stupid bloody job, just like I said when you took it," Jack told her. Pete folded her arms.

"I spent near a decade of my life pushing paper around a desk at New Scotland Yard, so once you've dealt with expense reports and a DCI who thinks that equipment that works is a luxury, not a necessity, you can jabber on about stupid jobs."

Jack grimaced. "This is *my* talent, Pete, and I'm not a party trick. This is . . . well . . . frankly, luv, it's demeaning."

Pete pointed down at the grave. "Get to work, Winter. Before I lay you a smack in the head."

Jack heaved a sigh and unzipped the satchel, pulling out his spirit heart. The clockwork contraption, about the size of a melon, round, and made of brass, hung from a chain with a small chamber in the bottom hollowed out. Jack dug the plastic Baggie of galangal root out of the bottom of the satchel and breathed on a pinch of the stuff.

Just a touch of sorcery, just enough to wake up the

strands of magic that lived in the galangal. Jack rubbed the pinch between his fingers and tamped it into the chamber of the spirit heart. A stab of pressure hit him in the temple, and he rubbed his forehead before standing.

Pete reached out and touched him on the arm, the lightest of touches, on his leathers no less, but he still felt it, dancing down through his blood and nerves to his bones. Her power felt like goose flesh, like being touched by a girl you fancied for the first time, every time. "You all right, Jack?"

He gave her a smile. His head throbbed harder. "Close enough for horseshoes and hand grenades, luv. Let's have this over with."

Pete wasn't fooled by the lie, but she had the grace to step back and pretend that Jack was as skillful a liar as he claimed. Worry only showed in the space between her eyes, a small black line of a frown, as she got a small digital camcorder from the bag and readied it.

Jack supposed if he had any sense, he'd be worried, too. Using magic wasn't supposed to hurt, not him, not a mage of the *Fiach Dubh*. No one had ever accused Jack Winter of having sense, though. Of being a wanker, yes. A thief, a sinner, heartless scum, and a murderer, certainly. But sense, no. Jack thought that when someone *did* accuse him of sense, it would likely be time to hang up his spurs.

"All right, you dusty lot," he murmured, so low only the dead could hear. "Time to come give me a haunt."

Jack shut his eyes, holding the spirit heart directly out, arm straight as a divining rod. The clockwork pendulum swung gently, aimlessly. Jack inhaled and held the air. Panic chewed on the ends of his guts, scratched at his neck, and wormed into his brain. His body knew what he was about to do, and it was screaming.

It was times like this that Jack felt the longing for a fix like the grasp of a familiar lover—tight, hot, gathered behind his eyes, knotting him up, making him cold, telling him *I*

*have what you need. Take it and make yourself warm, make
yourself safe, taste the golden delights of the floating world.*

But Jack tightened his grip on the spirit heart, the cold
brass warming to the same degree as his palm, and the mur-
muring of the fix was drowned in a tide of other whispers,
crying and shouting, faint and fierce, buried and so old no
one knew they were buried any longer.

The dead came to Jack, and he let himself see.

In his hands, the spirit heart gave a *tick*.

Jack opened his eyes, the ghosts his second sight found
thick here as a crowd in Trafalgar Square. They stood, for
the most part, silent and staring at the living intruder on their
pale, witch-lit world. A few hissed at him, the black-eyed
revenants with their flesh hanging off their bones, the malice
of their lives following them in death like a shroud cloth.

Pete stepped closer to him. She couldn't see what he
saw, but she knew. She knew the chill of having the dead
always just out of view. "Should I say it?"

The spirit heart gave another tick, louder, stronger, and
Jack nodded. "Wake them up, luv."

"Mary and Stuart Poole," Pete raised her voice and
pitched it sharp. Jack flinched as a ghost drifted closer to
Pete, a girl with dark wet hair still tangled with the garbage
she'd drowned in. The salt-sour stink of the Thames at low
tide tickled his nostrils.

The girl ran her hand longingly across Pete's cheek.
Jack narrowed his eyes. "Oi. Not yours, missy. Shove off."

Pete shivered, and continued, "Mary and Stuart Poole,
we call you to this place. Come back to your bones. Answer
to us."

The ghost drifted away, her torn dress and lank hair
trailing behind her in a remembered river current. Jack felt
a pull at his arm, and the spirit heart began to tick faster
and faster, clockwork innards spinning like the earth was
revolving too fast.

"Mary and Stuart Poole," Pete said again. "Come back to your bones."

There was power in triplets. Jack had taught her that. Pete never forgot something when you told her once. She was sharp, the fine edge of a knife.

A tug on his arm warned Jack that his dwelling on Pete's skill at this, only her second spirit-raising, might have cost him his arse. The spirit heart was twirling now, like someone had spun a globe and walked away. The brass caught the low afternoon sun and threw off light, the whirring of the clockwork like a bird's heartbeat.

Jack pushed against the swirl of power generated by the beating clockwork, forced it into a shape. A focus like the heart, or salt, or stone, was important—raw magic pulled from something like a spirit could blow your insides out surely as a shotgun blast.

A halo, black, gathered around the spirit heart, touched it experimentally, the lightest of caresses, while the spirit heart shot blue sparks through the realm of the dead. Pete couldn't see them, but she stepped back all the same. "They coming?"

"If I have any say," Jack answered, and tugged at the curiosity, the suggestion of a mind and a body that floated from the graves and guided it to the spirit heart.

The heart stopped.